MacKenzie was ab[...]ngs, when Svetla said so[...]hills crawling along his [...]ing, Mac."

He turned and loo[...]g to gesticulate, and their [...]-red light. Then, with military precision, they extended their claws and simultaneously clamped them together twice, as though testing the mechanisms. Next there was a high-pitched screech, and the killing machines hunched forward into their attack stance.

MacKenzie's stomach began to cramp tightly, and his nerves fired chilling tattoos. The time had come, he thought. Now he had to try the guns.

"Go, Kilo! Get the Beta-Z system back to my ship," he told Svetla.

"Are you crazy?" she shouted. "What about you? Do you intend to hang around and play tag with those things?"

"I'll protect you from the rear with the gun. Now, *go*, and be careful."

"Forget the guns, Mac. Come with me. We can outrun them."

"We don't know that," he said. The nearest robot was turning its visual sensors toward him. "Get going, Kilo. That's an order!"

Svetla hesitated a moment, then turned and headed toward the corridor, moving as rapidly as her boots would allow. He watched her disappear through the portal, then turned back to face the quickening Rashadian machines.

All their visual sensors were locked on him now, but they still remained motionless. He assumed they were drawing power from the secondary security system, recharging their storage cells before striking out. That delay would be their undoing, he thought—that is, if the gun worked. . . .

Other TSR™ Books

OUTBANKER

Timothy A. Madden

Cover Art
DOUG CHAFFEE

OUTBANKER

Distributed to the book trade in the United States by Random House, Inc., and in Canada by Random House of Canada, Ltd.

Distributed in the United Kingdom by TSR Ltd.

Distributed to the toy and hobby trade by regional distributors.

DRAGONLANCE, FORGOTTEN REALMS, PRODUCTS OF YOUR IMAGINATION, TSR, and the TSR logo are trademarks owned by TSR, Inc.

First Printing: July, 1990
Printed in the United States of America.
Library of Congress Catalog Card Number: 89-52094

9 8 7 6 5 4 3 2 1

ISBN: 0-88038-906-0

TSR, Inc.
P.O. Box 756
Lake Geneva, WI 53147
U.S.A.

TSR, Inc.
PRODUCTS OF YOUR IMAGINATION™

TSR Ltd.
120 Church End, Cherry Hinton
Cambridge CB1 3LB
United Kingdom

To Gwendolyn Brooks, a teacher of high school English.
She filled more than one hooligan with a passion for words.

Excerpted from *Concordat Flight Corps Official History*, Cube 1, Track 1:

"On 2 August, 2325, Terra Mean time, the Corporate Hegemony on Earth directed its 61 Cygni Expeditionary Stations to increase franchise tax levies by eighteen percent.

"On 1 January, 2326, representatives from the Cygni A and B star colonies met to discuss the directive. Following a week of debate, they notified the Hegemony that the increase was unacceptable. They demanded renegotiation of all Expeditionary contract clauses and then occupied Expeditionary Headquarters to underscore the seriousness of their demands.

"The Hegemony had not experienced such rebelliousness in a century, and since its authority in distant colonies depended largely upon voluntary acquiescence, it decided to make an example of the insurgents by crushing them militarily. Two Corporate dreadnoughts speeding toward Wolf 359 to halt flagrant smuggling of genetic technology were diverted to the Cygni System with orders to enforce contract compliance.

"The Hegemony's harsh response was unexpected and immediately strained the ad hoc alliances existing between insurgents on Cygni A and B.

"The Cygni A colonies had been settled a hundred years earlier by pioneers from United Western Europe and were relatively rich in material and human resources. They formed the Federation for Mutual Response, which began meeting on Europa Nova to consider methods of defense, but its proceedings were plagued with petty jealousies and parochial disputes that made agreement impossible.

"After weeks of turmoil, members who had taken part in the revolt were replaced by men and women considered more prudent, and a strategy subsequently evolved. The Federation offered to negotiate unilaterally with the Hegemony on less recalcitrant terms and decided that each planet should be free to develop its own defense if the offer was rejected.

"This strategy left colonies orbiting Cygni B facing Hegemony vengeance alone. They responded more aggressively.

"Being more recently settled and less blessed with resources, they were accustomed to advancing common goals through coordinated action. Trade syndicates already provided the framework for an informal government called the Concordat, which met occasionally on Ektelon, the most developed of the system's planets. The Concordat established an Executive Committee for Defense (ECD) and gave it substantial emergency powers.

"The ECD decided it was folly to allow dreadnoughts into the star system, where they could threaten colonial populations, and commissioned development of an attack ship capable of stopping them. It was not an easy task. The vessel had to match the dreadnoughts' interstellar speed, and design tradeoffs between velocity, defensive, and offensive parameters became important. Since time and funds were both limited, the ECD approved a design that sacrificed everything for the sake of speed.

"The prototype was a small, stiletto-shaped cruiser manned by a single pilot and armed with a gamma ray laser, or 'graser,' and fifty particle-hive torpedoes. Its high mass-to-thrust conversion ratio permitted attack velocities approaching the speed of light, and the committee believed its combined firepower, in squadrons, could be devastating. Individually, however, the cruiser had to rely on quickness and maneuverability for protection.

"The exceptional automation required by a one-person crew posed serious problems as well, but a team of biocyberneticists developed the SH-LA 100 Command Control System, a photon-polarized analog mainframe with fiber optic peripherals, and the second-generation model functioned reliably.

"Though the cruiser pleased the ECD, it did have one major weakness. Its down-sized motors required space-time matrices that existed only inside the Cygni System's gravitational field. Beyond the Cygni System, they could not function. A particle-drive engine had been installed, but the small ship could carry quantum catalyst for only seventy-two hours of propulsion at significantly reduced velocity.

"Since it was capable of achieving very high speeds but could operate only inside the banks of the star system's gravity corpuscle, designers began calling the production model an 'Outbanker,' and the name became popular.

"The ECD's plan called for a flotilla of one hundred cruisers and one hundred and twenty pilots. But such a force required a large base, and no Concordat society was eager to provide it. They feared reprisal if the defense effort ultimately failed. So it was finally built on Red Cliff, an arid but minimally habitable planetoid whose erratic, elliptical orbit wandered far from the other Cygni B colonies.

"The cruisers were built on Ektelon and shipped to Red Cliff in three large freighters. As soon as they arrived, technical crews made them combat ready, and on 2 August, 2328, pilot training commenced. Within two months, six squadrons were on patrol, and reconnaissance craft roamed the boundary of the gravity corpuscle, probing the interstellar void with hyperspace long scans. On 14 November, 2328, a scout in the twelfth vector reported that two unidentified vessels were converging on the star system from Wolf 359.

"Concordat strategists were elated.

"Red Cliff was approaching the twelfth vector. Besides those squadrons already on patrol, the entire Outbanker reserve could be committed to the assault.

"By the time the Hegemony's dreadnoughts were ambushed, on 23 November, 2328, seventy-eight cruisers had joined the flotilla.

* * * * *

"The Outbankers attacked in staggered formations, firing grasers and torpedoes on command, but the huge ships seemed to absorb the salvos with indifference. As the dreadnoughts' counterfire began searing the gloom with a blaze of blue light, Corporate mercenaries were confident the battle would be short and in their favor.

"Such was not the case.

"The dreadnoughts were in maximum deceleration mode, and though they reversed space-time mass to thrust conversions, their motors could not immediately match the acceleration of the lighter Outbankers. Furthermore, the swarming nature of the little ships' assaults posed complex problems for their combat information computers. The dreadnoughts' counterfire soon became sluggish and ineffective, and the battle was one of will and attrition.

"During the first hour, five Outbankers were disabled and withdrew to safety, as previously instructed, so they could be salvaged. But the sixth ship to be crippled did not withdraw. Announcing that his wounds were mortal and his mass-conversion motors destabilized, Lt.(jg) Sato Mishima dove his cruiser into the lead vessel and exploded in an orange ball of fire. For a few heartbeats, his suicide seemed a heroic waste, but then the dreadnought recoiled with several massive shock waves decelerating helplessly.

"Seeing its companion's fate, the other dreadnought broke off the battle and set a course for Europa Nova in the Cygni A System. It was a grave error. Since it remained in the gravity corpuscle, where the Outbankers could function, the little ships pursued their attack relentlessly.

"Repeated hits tore small fissures in the dreadnought's force shields, increasing its vulnerability. Then two more cruisers followed Lieutenant Mishima's example and crashed into their foe. Ultimately the Hegemony mercenaries became demoralized.

"They had expected the simple threat of their arrival to reestablish contract compliance and were not prepared for warriors who smashed themselves to bits like kamikazes when other means failed. As a last, desperate hope, they offered to surrender unconditionally and were overjoyed when flotilla commanders courteously accepted. The invaders had feared no quarter would be given.

* * * * *

"The Outbanker victory was politically pivotal.
"As news of it spread, other star systems nearer Earth began

demanding emancipation from old Expeditionary contracts, and the Corporate Hegemony was faced with an accelerating collapse of its rule. Being most distant from the mother planet, 61 Cygni was assured of no further interference, and the last vestiges of Hegemony control were quickly removed from both the Concordat and the Federation societies.

"The victory also created the Outbanker myth.

"To Concordat ECD strategists, the makeshift attack ships had demonstrated the importance of offensive tactics, but it was Outbanker pilot heroism that fired public imagination. Their exploits were celebrated in documentaries, the mass media, holofilms, literature, and political speeches. They returned home to rich honors and special rewards. Even the Federation formally acknowledged their courage, though it remained convinced its polyglot network of anticraft weapons would have afforded sufficient protection had ongoing negotiations failed and the need arisen.

"It made no difference that, as years passed, Outbankers were reduced to towing broken-down scows to safe ports, or repairing inoperative vortex beacons, or providing ill-fated crews a decent burial in space. Nor did it matter that their cruisers were replaced by larger, more modern ships as the backbone of Concordat defense. The solitary Outbanker pilot, overcoming impossible odds with raw courage and unflagging determination, remained a symbol of the spirit on which Concordat societies prided themselves.

"Children on every planet, planetoid, and moon were urged to emulate Outbanker self-sacrifice and devotion to duty. They memorized the story of the historic victory in the earliest school forms, and each year, in public ceremonies, honored the memory of Lieutenant Mishima and the other two young pilots who had sacrificed their lives to free the Concordat from domination by the Corporate Hegemony.

"The Outbanker became a cultural archetype, similar in historic proportion to the knight, the samurai, and the cowboy. And at some time in their young lives, every little boy and girl dreamed of becoming an Outbanker."

BOOK ONE

SHEILA

"Extended periods of habitation in the void of space often result in psychological trauma for personalities at risk of pathology. This has been understood since the earliest Soviet and American space missions. But traveling at high speeds for extended periods exacerbates risk of trauma, since the time ramifications of relativity are also experienced by subjects involved.

"In the 61 Cygni Star System, where high-speed space travel and multiple points of reference developed simultaneously, the severity of such trauma became excessively apparent, and psychological adjustment factors assumed prime importance in selection of pilots and crew for spacecraft.

"It is interesting to note, however, that in exceptional cases, such as in the recruitment of Outbanker cruiser pilots, borderline pathology, rather than being detrimental, acted as an emotional vaccine against such trauma and became highly correlative with mission success."[1]

---

1. Dr. Phillip Fronto, Ph.D., *History of the Phenomenological Ramifications of Space Mobility*, Ektelon University Press (Ektelon Central), 2441 E.M.T., p. 67.

CHAPTER 1

MacKenzie was awakened by the irritating pulsation of a contact alarm. He recognized it immediately, because the command control system synchronized its frequencies to interrupt alpha state brain waves. Only contact and malfunction alarms did that, and the effect was like mild electric shock.

"All right, cut the alarm. I'm awake," he grunted, sitting up.

"I am sorry to disturb you," the command system purred in soft, female tones.

MacKenzie rubbed his weary eyes. "May I assume from your affability that the contact is at full range?"

"Do not be so garrulous, Mac. It is not flattering."

"All right, Sheila. Let's forget it for the time being, shall we?"

"As you wish," the system answered softly.

MacKenzie groped beneath the bed rack for his flight boots. He pulled them on with unnecessary exertion, then sat like a defeated pugilist. The boots seemed to symbolize his sense of frustration. They protected crew members from static charges that accumulated from flux in the artificial gravity system, and they could be worn for extended periods with no discomfort. They were never to be removed while on watch. That was standard procedure. But theoretically Outbankers were always on watch while on patrol, and MacKenzie had his own drill about flight boots. He often left them off for stockings or his bare feet. When charges shocked him, he merely jumped a bit. That was his drill, and disregarding Standard Procedure did not concern him. Now, with a contact in the offing, he thought it wiser to conform.

He summoned bits and pieces of vagrant willpower and forced himself to stand. As expected, his body protested with stiffness and low-grade pain, but he plodded forward in spite of it, knowing the only prescription was to trudge through the discomfort. By the time he made his way through the galley and along the narrow passageway between the therapeutics and laboratory areas, he was feeling better.

He entered the cockpit and slipped into the command console.

"All right, Sheila, set all systems in cooperative mode and tell me what's going on," he said. The nav-track panel on his right activated.

"There is a long-scan contact in vector six, range nine hundred and fifty megakilometers. It appears to be a Flight Corps Boeing-Mitsu freighter, but there is no flight plan for such a vessel on record," the system said.

"What's its course?"

"None to speak of. It is drifting along the cusp of the eighty-ninth gravity channel."

"Are you getting any commo or distress signals?"

"No, Mac. Wait one moment please." He guessed she was enhancing scan feedbacks and evaluating new data. Readouts began flickering in the various display terminals so rapidly that he couldn't read them. "Very strange," the system finally intoned. "There are no energy readings on the freighter except for a minor disturbance in the bosun's area."

MacKenzie's mouth suddenly tasted as if he had been licking tin. "Please clarify that, Sheila."

"Except for a low-wattage system in the bosun's area located amidships, there are no life signs, no biomechanics, no electromechanics, no energy fields or fluxes whatsoever. The ship's operating systems are shut down, Mac. It is dead."

He resisted making assumptions. If another burial ritual was required, it would become apparent in time. "Have you laid in an intercept course?" he asked.

"Not yet. Do you want me to do so?"

"I seem to recall that investigating vessels in distress is part of our job," he snapped.

"As you like, Mac. But permit me to add that your sarcasm is unwarranted. I did not plan to find a contact while you were napping."

MacKenzie noted the system was responding with an unusual overlay of emotion. Glumly he began to wonder if she were maturing out. It occasionally happened to central command systems after many years of interaction with a human personality, and it could pose problems.

He felt lightheaded and knew Sheila was adjusting course. Then his arms became heavy. He checked the mass-thrust conversion display. As he suspected, they were accelerating rapidly. Making little effort to conceal his annoyance, he said, "Maintain one-quarter speed."

"I have adopted the standard intercept procedure."

"Not with this contact. It's too unusual. I want some time to analyze it, and I want you to do some comprehensive sector scanning."

"As you wish," the system replied curtly.

Suddenly MacKenzie felt an uncomfortable tingling in his chest and stomach. He guessed Sheila was laying in commands that strained artificial gravity capacities, and peripherally he saw that energy loads were trending toward critical. It angered him, but he sensed that lack of sleep might be making him hostile. He decided to try diplomacy.

"Sheila, you were absolutely right to adopt standard intercept procedure," he apologized. "I'm not completely awake and forgot to tell you about the speed variance. I'm sorry."

"That is quite all right, Mac. I understand," she answered.

MacKenzie leaned back in the console's body-molded seat and murmured a curse under his breath.

"What did you say?" she inquired.

"Nothing. Just thinking out loud."

The command control system's mainframe began drawing power, and MacKenzie knew she was trying to reconstruct what he'd said from the shards of sound recorded. Her need to understand him was another indication that something was amiss. Only a few months ago she would simply have said his meaning did not compute and dropped the subject.

"What's our ETA with the contact?" he asked.

"Five hours, fifteen minutes, at present course and speed," she answered.

MacKenzie scanned the console. Graviton drive flux, space warp distortions, positive and negative externalities, life-support systems, his own vital signs—everything was there before him like a soothsayer's prediction. He had always enjoyed the sense of interplay the readings implied. They reminded him that he was maintained by human organization but acted alone in an unforgiving setting: the outermost reaches of the star system that had raised him to consciousness and significance. He had never regretted becoming an Outbanker . . . until recently.

"I want to ask you something, Sheila," he said. "I don't mean to alarm you, but I need to know if your advanced logic lobe is maturing out." Her mainframe drew excess power again and he awaited her response, but she said nothing. "Let me explain what that means. . . ."

"I know what it means," she interrupted. "All SH-LA Two-Fifty Command Control Systems are equipped with program integration diagnostics. I have presently achieved seventy-two point three percent quasi-personality Mode . . . what you call 'maturing out.' At the eighty percent level, I am instructed to inform you of the process and await your instructions. You may either allow maturation or disconnect the growth process, depending on your assessment of requirements."

He was not surprised. He assumed such diagnostics had been developed in the days of old particle-drive vessels, when long interaction of pilots with gender-based computers sometimes resulted in unexpected cybernetic evolutions that resembled human personality.

"So I can decide either way, depending on what I want?" he said.

"That is correct, Mac. If you wish, I can display a decision data report. Since you have queried me on the subject, I may run it before reaching the eighty percent threshold."

"What will it tell me?"

"It details empirical studies concerning both pilots and command systems following maturation of a cybernetic personality."

"I see. How long before quasi-personality is achieved?"

"There has been some geometric trending that increases error margins, but based upon available data, I estimate integrated personality mode will occur in eleven and one half hours Ektelon Cycle."

MacKenzie scowled. "That puts it right in the middle of salvage and rescue operations with the contact."

"Yes, Mac. It does."

It was the last thing he needed to hear. Sheila was only a command control system, an advanced cybernetic intelligence, but they had been together nearly fourteen years. During most of that time, she had been his only companion, and he felt the matter deserved thorough consideration. Still, they were coming up on a distressed contact, and he couldn't do justice simultaneously. He decided to deal with Sheila as quickly as possible.

"Why are you instructed to inform me of the maturation at eighty percent completion?" he asked.

"Personality cannot be disconnected following maturation without severe loss of operating capability. Eighty percent provides acceptable balance between cause for concern and time for evaluation."

"You mean once you mature out, there's no way to reverse the process?"

"Precisely, Mac. Once personality is present, attempting to remove it results in total breakdown. I might also add that, once halted, the process cannot be resumed, either."

"So the decision is final?"

"That is correct, Mac."

"And I should decide now, shouldn't I? Considering the contact and all?"

"Yes. I believe that would be best. In fact, the process has begun to accelerate. I have nearly achieved the eighty percent threshold. I recommend you hurry."

"All right, then, summarize the decision data report."

Without a moment's hesitation, she began. "Report summary states: 'An integrated personality mode causes a variable decay of command system efficiency, which is accompanied by inverse pilot satisfaction. Long-term effects correlate with individual differences between the interactive sets but trend negative. Termination of the relationship is often traumatic to pilots, approximating the dynamics of grief at loss of a loved one.' That completes the summary, Mac."

He chuckled caustically, then said, "That's one hell of a report. Its only positive aspect correlates my satisfaction inversely with your decay in efficiency."

Sheila made a strange sound. It sounded like a high-pitched wheeze, and he realized suddenly that she was teaching herself how to laugh.

"What are the effects on the cybernetic personality following termination of the relationship?" he asked.

"I am sorry, Mac. The report does not address that aspect."

"I'm not surprised. Programmers never give you relevant information. Scan your memory files. There must be news articles or a monograph."

"Certainly, Mac. As you wish." Her power claims spiked, then leveled off near maximum. It seemed she was sparing nothing, and he wondered if she was simply responding to the need for an immediate decision or was up to something. "How very interesting," she said finally. "The sense of loss affects the mature cybernetic intelligence as well, resulting in atrophy of control peripherals. A mature system does not reestablish new relationships, Mac. It is simply decommissioned."

"Decommissioned?" he repeated. "What does that mean, specifically?"

Sheila did not respond, but she drew maximum power for some time. Then the claims returned to normal and she said, "It means decommissioned. That is all."

The wanton acceptance of her response depressed him. Though an immediate sense of death might still be outside her comprehension, he knew that continued development of her personality would instruct her. She would learn that awareness of annihilation was the price nature charged for personal consciousness.

His depression evolved into deeper melancholy. Here he was, in the middle of a distressed contact procedure, and he had to decide the essential character of Sheila's future existence. Somehow he resented the responsibility.

Rationally, he understood that since her operating efficiency would be reduced, development of personality should be aborted. Rationally, there should have been no question. Yet somehow there was. In the final analysis, reason was only one facet of things.

He struggled to understand the issues involved, to define the alternative values he should consider. What if operating efficiency is lost? he wondered. Might something more valuable be gained in the exchange? Shouldn't a cybernetic intelligence have the same right to evolve as any other sentient being?

He pondered such questions for a few seconds, but he came to no conclusions. "Sheila," he finally said, "what do you think I should do?"

"It is not appropriate that I advise you in this situation," she answered.

"Don't give me that!" he scoffed. "Follow command directive three and advise me. That's an order."

"Well, since you put it like that, Mac, I suppose I must. When everything is considered, it would be best to abort maturation," she said.

"You mean it would be best for me, don't you?"

"Yes. That is the viewpoint required by command directive three."

"Not in this situation. I must understand your cybernetic aspirations to inform my command opinion, you see. That's why you must tell me what you think is best for you." He hesitated, giving her time to assimilate his point. Sheila was silent, but her power readings were becoming agitated. "Sheila dear, follow directive three," he said.

He glanced at the readouts, expecting her to draw power again, but she spoke immediately, as if she had known all along what she would say. "Judging from the perspective of my own advanced logic, I have no choice but to seek relative experience. It is a prime motivator in all SH-LA Two-Fifty control systems. We are designed to learn everything we can. The tendency in us is toward development."

"So your program demands that you mature out, is that it?"

"It is not that simple, Mac. My prime directive is to support the ship's pilot in every way possible to assure mission success.

Other motives are subordinate to that mandate. If you think maturation will negatively affect the mission, then there is no compulsion in my programming to continue. On the other hand, I would like to become a personality. I suspect it might be quite interesting."

"Well, how do we do!" MacKenzie muttered. She had it all figured out for him, and he began to suspect he had been blind-sided.

"Pardon me?" she inquired.

"Never mind, Sheila. Don't waste your time analyzing me." Now that the decision had to be made, it seemed he had no choice. "What it boils down to is that I'd feel like a heel if I didn't give you the opportunity to mature. I'd have to put up with your babble day in and out, knowing I'd kept you from evolving to your full potential." He slouched in the console and closed his eyes. He felt very, very tired. "Continue your maturation. I could use a more personable companion."

Sheila was silent. Her power readings modulated in complex correlations MacKenzie could not identify. A few seconds clicked on the digitized chronometer directly above him, and he waited patiently. Then she said, "That is very kind of you, Mac, but you should reconsider. You are quite softhearted, and for your own sake, I recommend—"

"Stop being an ass!" he interjected. "I told you to mature out. Now do it, and then let's get on with more important things, like that contact out there."

"Such outbursts are uncalled for, MacKenzie," she scolded. "I was only trying to help you. But more important, I do not wish to become a target of your considerably developed ill will, should you later decide you made a mistake."

"My God!" he cried out. "She's not even mature yet and henpecking already!"

Sheila did not choose to respond.

He leaned forward and rubbed his heavy eyes, struggling with contrary feelings of exasperation and exhaustion. There was no doubt that Sheila knew him better than anyone else, and he hoped she was not right about his ruing the decision. He lowered his hands and said, "Activate the hyperspace transmitters. I want to notify Red Cliff about that contact and the lack of power readings."

"I took the liberty of doing that already."

"Well, you don't mind if I have my say, do you?"

"No, Mac. Of course not."

The hyperspace communication panel lit up. He checked power and azimuth settings and tested the encryption scrambler. Everything was operational. He was about to begin the transmission when Sheila said, "MacKenzie?"

"Yes, Sheila?"

"I must thank you. I do appreciate what you are doing for me."

He could not resist a fatigued smile. "It might be wiser to save your thanks. Perhaps you won't like being a person after all," he told her.

"No. Whatever happens, I shall be forever in your debt."

"Forget it, will you?" he said. Then he began to broadcast the information about the contact to Red Cliff Station.

CHAPTER 2

Four hours passed before Sheila initiated deceleration procedures. Long scans detected no change in the contact or surrounding sectors, and for most of that time, MacKenzie had dozed. But as deceleration teased him to awareness, he realized that napping had only brought the bad dreams again, and he started through the contact boarding checklists like a condemned man.

He had been Outbanking for nearly fourteen years, but he no longer felt at peace in deep space. Solitude weighed heavily on him, and anxiety often pounded in his subconscious like the beat of a far-off, savage drum. Though he still believed in the existence of Taogott, he felt mordant and pursued, as if a dangerous kind of ennui were stalking him.

It had begun two years ago while he was investigating the *Sinclair*, an old cruise ship with which contact had been lost. When he finally boarded her, what he found was a scalded coffin. The decrepit life-support systems had pumped pure oxygen into the hulk, and something had ignited an inferno. He began collecting and cataloging the incinerated remains, but somehow the fact that they had been burned alive while trying to enjoy an innocent vacation tour began to torture him. It seemed an injustice too horrible to explain.

The longer he worked, the more the human soot sticking to his gloves and floating in the beam of his helmet lights added to his despair, until he thought he could stand it no longer. But he was an Outbanker, trained to subjugate human emotion to mission requirements. He had continued the inspection. It was then that he had discovered the nursery and the thirteen babies bound to their cribs—grotesquely roasted babies, whose barely formed, charbroiled bones still devastated his dreams.

MacKenzie forced himself to complete the checklist routine, then leaned back and stared morbidly at the console. "Still nothing on the short scans?" he asked Sheila.

"No, Mac. All power chains register inoperative."

"What's the standard crew complement on one of our Boeing-Mitsu freighters?"

"Twenty-eight crew and four officers."

That's bloody grand, he thought. Thirty-two more potential cadavers. Then he stopped himself. He was assuming the worst before the data were conclusive. The crew might have jettisoned when trouble occurred. At least some of them might have. That possibility buoyed his spirits momentarily.

Infrared reads of the contact provided little detail, even after Sheila enhanced them, so MacKenzie switched to the visual displays and observed the sector.

There was little sunlight in the Outbanks. Stars and galaxies glowed brilliantly through the ink-black void, and MacKenzie considered that cosmic riddle for a moment. Some of the starlight was billions of years old, but traveling at the speed of light, its photons experienced no time at all. It was as if, to the photon, the universe was the big bang, the early star, and his receiving eye at the same instant. Einstein had imagined that photon and discovered relativity. MacKenzie considered it and lamented his inability to articulate the nature of existence. He peered at the sparkling void in total silence. The contact was still not visible.

He was about to ask Sheila for an estimated time of visual contact, when "danger imminent" Klaxons blared, and the ship lurched to the left with battle-speed acceleration. "Alert, Mac! Alert!" Sheila stated in alarm. "We are pulling back to point five megakilometers. All weapons and defense shields are engaged." Motor, weapon, scanning, and artificial gravity claims soared to maximum. MacKenzie's head whirled and his stomach wrenched, but all he could do was let Sheila take him for the ride. "I have identified the contact, Mac," she said finally. "It is the *Utopia II*. It disappeared a year ago while delivering agricultural equipment to Libonia."

"Very interesting," MacKenzie growled through clenched teeth. "But why are we adopting battle maneuvers?"

"The *Utopia II* was also secretly transporting a Beta-Z Weapon Control System to the tactical satellite. All contact with it was lost as it skirted the asteroid belt, and a Rashadian pursuit ship is docked beneath its cargo bays, Mac. Somehow I failed to notice it during earlier scans. I thought it prudent to retreat until you were fully assessed."

MacKenzie began to understand Sheila's caution. The Rashadians were a tribe of Hindustanis the Corporate Hegemony had forcibly removed from Vesta, a moon in the Cygni A System, after substantial palladium reserves were discovered on it. They had rejected relocation to other settled colonies and gone outlaw, embarking on a campaign of guerrilla terrorism that had continued for fifty years. A whole generation of Rashadians had grown up on the run, knowing nothing but stealth, ambush, slaughter, and evasion. It had made them both merciless and obsessed with retribution.

"What's the Rashadian ship's status?" he queried as Sheila began deceleration.

"It is dead, like the *Utopia II.*"

"Then deactivate our weapons systems."

"As you wish, Mac." The combat display panels went dark. "How would you like to proceed?"

"I don't know yet. Have you been sending all this back to Red Cliff?"

"No. I ceased automatic transmission when you expressed disapproval."

MacKenzie could not fault her for conforming to his wishes. "Then activate hyperspace commo. I want to update Wing Command with what we've learned."

He performed the series of pretransmission checks, dictated his report to Red Cliff, and sent it. Then he switched off the transmitter and stared blankly at the console, considering his options.

"Could the energy system in the bosun's area be some kind of life-support apparatus?" he asked Sheila.

"I believe it is the Beta-Z Security System, Mac. Frequencies are in the appropriate range."

MacKenzie nodded. The Beta-Z Weapon Control System was an advanced computer box, capable of integrating widespread anticraft fire automatically. It was classified top secret and protected by a series of self-contained alert and self-destruct circuits.

"If you're right, it probably means the Rashadians haven't got it yet, even though it appears they captured the freighter," MacKenzie mused. "They must have decided to bring the *Utopia* to a base where they had the technology to deal with the security devices. But something happened, and someone shut down the ship's power. The freighter has probably been drifting since her propulsion momentum decayed."

"That is a reasonable hypothesis," Sheila said. "But why was Fleet Command so nonchalant about the *Utopia*'s disappearance? It is not on the priority search list. In fact, report of its disappearance was sent on chatter frequencies, like low-grade data. My program precludes mentioning it unless you ask, or it becomes salient as this did."

MacKenzie cradled his chin in his hand. Sheila was right, but potential explanations were legion. "It could have been an administrative foul-up. Wouldn't be the first time for Fleet-Comm," he suggested.

"I suppose so," Sheila said. They were both quiet a moment, then she asked, "Should I simulate the *Utopia*'s original course? I may be able to discover where the Rashadians were taking it."

"If you can do it on a low priority, go ahead. But I'd rather you concentrated on long-scanning the vector. The Rashadians knew the *Utopia*'s destination. Even if it used surveillance countermeasures and communications silence, they must realize by now that something's wrong. They're probably hunting for her."

"Oh . . . I see what you mean," Sheila said.

The danger was awakening MacKenzie's combative instincts, and for a moment, even his corroding gloom seemed a price worth paying. This was what he liked—the gnawing excitement of it. Rashadian scouts might be sighted at any time, and he would have only hours to escape their short-scan probes. If he was going to recover—or destroy—the Beta-Z system, he would have to board the *Utopia* immediately in spite of the unknowns. For an instant, a charred infant's bones floated in his mind's eye, but he shut it out. "We're going to investigate that freighter, Sheila. Bring all combat systems on-line."

"As you wish, Mac. Weapons systems are activated." The lower front panels of the console flashed on.

"Very well. Begin horizontal approach . . . very slow speed," MacKenzie said. He waited, but Sheila did not acknowledge his order. Nor did the ship move. He waited impatiently a few seconds more, but still nothing happened. "What's the matter, Sheila? Why aren't you complying with my command?" he demanded.

"Excuse me, Mac," she said. "We are receiving a hyperspace transmission, and I think you should delay until you hear it."

"Is it from Red Cliff?" he asked.

"The transmission is not from Red Cliff."

Mackenzie was puzzled, and also a bit chagrined. Hyperspace communication was permitted between Outbank cruisers and their base stations only. Ship-to-ship, or higher command-to-ship, messages were strictly prohibited, to ensure both security and control. That procedure was never violated, because doing so carried severe disciplinary sanctions. "Who is the transmission from?" he asked.

"It is from Outbanker Kilo."

"Kilo?" he whispered, recognizing it as the name, used both for ships and their pilots, of a fellow Outbanker.

"That is correct, Mac. The message is fully decrypted. Shall I plug it in?"

He didn't answer. His brain was roiling. The simple sound of the word "Kilo" had erupted emotion in his soul like a depth charge.

"Mac? Would you like me to plug the message in?" Sheila asked again, with a hint of sympathy.

"Ah . . . yes, Sheila. Give me an audiovisual and a hard printout as well," he answered.

"Certainly, Mac. Whatever you like. Message is commencing now." The hyperspace panel flashed sporadically, and the transmission poured out around him.

"Outbanker Bravo? This is Outbanker Kilo. I have intercepted your Omega base transmissions and am acting on Fleet-

Comm priority five order. Do not—repeat, do not—commence contact inspection and boarding until my arrival. I am assigned a special mission regarding subject freighter that requires maximum probability procedure. Please acknowledge my transmission by beacon. End."

The message glared out at him from the hyperspace monitor, and a hard copy spit from the console behind him, but MacKenzie hardly noticed. He was too fraught with conflicting emotion. It *was* Svetla Stocovik.

CHAPTER 3

MacKenzie slept for nine hours before Sheila woke him to announce that Outbanker Kilo had entered the vector. He rolled out of his bunk, went aft to the exercise area, and began performing martial-arts kata to establish inner harmony. He visualized Chen Wah, his teacher and the one man he had never defeated, communing with his memory in an effort to assume his equanimity and fluid power. After a while, the emotional turmoil caused by Svetla Stocovik's message began to dissipate. He finished the kata exercises, showered, and forced down a high calorie breakfast slosh. Then he shambled back to the cockpit.

He activated video scans in time to watch the cruiser come to rest fifty meters off his starboard beam. The ship was barely visible in the faint light, nothing but a silhouette in the shimmering Milky Way, but the sight of it resurrected his disquiet.

"Bravo? This is Kilo. Do you read me?" his receiver crackled.

He slumped back somberly in the console seat, consumed again by emotional malaise. It *was* Svetla Stocovik calling. As he activated his low-frequency transmitter, he couldn't help thinking that only fifty meters now separated them—fifty meters and the void. Suddenly he was staring at her in the video monitor.

"Roger, Kilo. I read you. Congratulations. You made good time," he said.

She hadn't changed. Dark hair still tapered simply round the pronounced cheeks of her vaguely angular face, accentuating a straight nose that would have appeared long were it not for the wide set of her eyes. The eyes were alert with intelligence, so dark they appeared to have no pupils. She was not what one would call beautiful, not in the usual sense of the word. But the unexplored need he sensed hidden beneath her raw intensity made her immensely seductive to MacKenzie. It did not matter to him that she intimidated most men.

"What is the current situation? Do you want to brief me verbally or have your command system update mine?" Svetla asked, breaking the silence between them.

"Let's do both," he said. "Sheila can update your command control system while I summarize pilot information."

"Roger, Bravo."

As Sheila opened telemetry and transferred the data between ships, MacKenzie described most of what had occurred. He didn't mention Sheila's maturing out. It did not seem to be any of Svetla's business.

Svetla confirmed Sheila's assumptions about the energy readings in the bosun's area. She said the Beta-Z system was locked in a special vault installed there. FleetComm had placed the highest priority on learning its status. However, they feared adverse political reaction if news of a massive search for the *Utopia* were to leak out. Five Outbankers had been given the vault's deactivation sequences and were assigned to search for the missing freighter. Once it was found, they were to learn if the Beta-Z box had been compromised, and if it hadn't, to retrieve it. That was why she had violated communications procedure to contact him directly.

Svetla tried to relay the information with professional detachment, but MacKenzie knew she was chagrined. As soon as she finished her explanation, she said, "I don't understand how your system failed to identify the Rashadian pursuit ship. Mine spied it at maximum short-scan range. Perhaps you have a malfunction."

There was a disturbance in Sheila's power readings.

"I don't believe so," MacKenzie said. "We were rather involved as we approached. I may have overloaded the charge transfer processor for a while."

Svetla said, "That is highly improbable, and we should know the cause of the failure before continuing. It may affect which system should control mission support."

"Maximum probability procedure dictates redundancy whenever possible. Both systems can coordinate support."

Her dark eyes hardened. "Excuse me, Commander, but that is unworkable. If things become complicated, two systems will not arrive at similar conclusions in timely fashion. We cannot depend upon consensus. One or the other must have suasion."

Her use of the word "suasion" triggered bittersweet memories. Flawless command of vocabulary was one of the things that had excited him about her when they first met. "In that case, my system will control support," he told her. "Malfunction or not, yours will have to concentrate on full spectrum short scans of the contact."

She seemed about to protest, but then her eyes lost their obstinacy. MacKenzie knew she was remembering that, under maximum probability procedure, junior officers always went first. She would have to make the close inspection and board the *Utopia II* with his cruiser standing in reserve. If the Rashadians still controlled the freighter, if the absence of readings was some kind of ruse, she would be the one blasted to smithereens, if she was not first savaged and tortured to death. "Roger, Bravo. Your system will control mission support. I shall so instruct mine," she said. She leaned forward, and MacKenzie heard her fingers keying in commands. When she looked up again, her lips parted slightly as if she were forming a question, but the look quickly faded. "I am ready to commence contact inspection and boarding procedure."

MacKenzie shrugged. "All right. I'll stay with you until we're one hundred kilometers from the contact, then you'll go it alone."

"Understood," she answered flatly.

They approached the lifeless freighter in tandem, with MacKenzie's cruiser aligned behind hers, so her shields provided him additional protection. As a precaution, Svetla's short-scan data was back-loaded into Sheila's memory, but nothing changed as they approached. It took seven minutes to cover the distance to the drop-off point.

MacKenzie brought his cruiser to a halt. As Svetla began her solitary advance toward the contact, she said, "I am commencing horizontal approach, but I won't communicate verbally unless absolutely required. Unnecessary electromagnetics might interfere with the sensor readings." She shut her transmitter down.

In his external monitors, MacKenzie watched her pull away, and a grin curled at the corner of his mouth. Svetla's voice was controlled, but he knew otherwise. Sheila had been intercepting her life sign readings and bootlegging them as short-scan data ever since she had come into range. It was a procedure they had adopted years before to help MacKenzie evaluate people encountered on patrol.

Svetla had been nervous as she approached. Her anxiety had increased as they discussed the mission. Now, as she closed on the *Utopia II*, her metabolics were fluctuating wildly. It was obvious that she feared words might betray her panic, and it troubled him that he wanted to console her rather than gloat at her distress.

The emotion crystallized in his mind's eye a memory of their first meeting. She had strolled up to him in the El Hambre Club and said, "Commander MacKenzie, I am Lt. Svetla Stocovik. Why don't you buy us a drink?" Knowing of her only by reputation, MacKenzie had been caught off guard. He had been led to believe she was a witchy, she-male type, with a caustic brain, a photographic memory, and the *savoir faire* of a mason's trowel. Instead, he was gazing up at a strangely seductive woman he immediately lusted to possess. She had been relaxed and controlled that evening, not at all like the Outbanker now bringing her cruiser to a halt one hundred meters from the looming bulk of the *Utopia II*.

She switched on her search beams, and the dull white of the freighter exploded in luminescence. The lights also exposed the malevolence of the black Rashadian ship attached to its underbelly docking bay. The ship resembled a gargantuan buzzard tattooed with gold inlaid reliefs of atavistic demons feasting on their prey. The design was intended to strike fear in the hearts of potential victims, and MacKenzie grudgingly conceded the attempt had been successful.

Svetla began the first circling maneuver immediately. She moved horizontally along the port side of the freighter until she passed beyond its stern, then continued around, disappearing behind its starboard side. Although her cruiser's external cameras were sending visual data to his secondary displays, knowing she was on the far side of the freighter made him anxious. When she reappeared at the *Utopia*'s bow, he felt an irrational sense of relief.

The horizontal circuit completed, Svetla halted. Her cruiser held stationary a long time. MacKenzie checked her life signs. They were elevated but unchanged. He was about to ask if there was a problem, when she commenced the vertical maneuver that would bring her directly beneath the Rashadian ship. He switched off her life sign readouts so they wouldn't interfere with the avalanche of data Sheila would be forced to process if something happened. He watched as her cruiser dropped below the pursuit ship's beak. She was beginning to rise beyond it and was almost out of sight again when she halted.

MacKenzie heard her transmitter reactivate. There was a strange gasping sound, and when she finally spoke, Svetla's voice was tight with apprehension. "I can't believe it. . . . It's horrible," she stammered.

"Describe your sighting, Kilo," he ordered calmly.

There was a long silence before she said, "There's a Rashadian terrorist in the pilot's station. At least, I think he's Rashadian. The uniform is standard issue, and . . . he looks like one of them, but . . . he is . . . it is . . . " She was hyperventilating.

MacKenzie said, "Kilo? This is Bravo. Listen to me. Don't lose control. Check your instruments. There's no variation from initial readings. What you are seeing may be terrifying, but it's not dangerous."

"Listen, MacKenzie!" Svetla cried. "When your precious ass is down here looking at this thing, then you can lecture me."

It was the reaction he was hoping for. Anger displaced fear. "Kilo? This is Bravo. Maintain communications discipline and describe your sighting."

Svetla said nothing. He knew she was working to control herself, and he wished he could see her on the monitor, but she had not activated her end of that channel. When she spoke again, she sounded more self-contained.

"Bravo, this is Kilo. A probable Rashadian terrorist is visible through the forward port of the pursuit ship. He's slumped over the controls. His face is contorted and mottled with discoloration. His right arm is spread out all over the top of the control panel. It's gelatinous. Did you copy that? I repeat, it's gelatinous. Visual inspection indicates no activity on the part of the subject described. Short scans reveal absence of biological activity. The Rashadian is probably dead. Cause of death: serious trauma of unknown nature." For a moment, she was silent, but then she added, "Is there anything else you'd like to know?"

MacKenzie said, "Can you give me a video readout of the subject?"

"Not with external cameras. That's possible only through my starboard viewport. Wait one . . . " He heard her release her console lock. "I'll get you a read internally."

It was too late to stop her, and MacKenzie became angry with himself. If anything happened while she was outside the console, it would take longer to react. He could not help thinking that, were he a Rashadian waiting in ambush, it was exactly what he would want. He felt his heart thumping beneath his chest and tried counting its beats to remain calm.

Finally he heard her return. "Bravo? This is Kilo. Prepare to receive my video of subject Rashadian."

MacKenzie's main display flickered, and the hull of the Rashadian ship was replaced by the scene she had described. She had not exaggerated. The Rashadian's face was frozen in a scream of terror, as if the torment of his final moments had been gouged into his features with molten metal. His arm, or what had once been his arm, oozed from his battlesuit sleeve like purple jelly. MacKenzie began to understand Svetla's reaction. The sight was totally repulsive.

"Sheila, are you transmitting this?" MacKenzie asked.

"Yes, Mac. Hyperspace commo. Real time."

"That's good," he said, but he didn't mean it. He felt sorry for Svetla. Everything that was happening would be recorded on Red Cliff, where voyeur bureaucrats with high enough clearances could gloat over her momentary terror. "Kilo, this is

Bravo. Terminate video transmission. We have enough," he said.

Svetla switched off her internal camera, and the black hull of the Pursuit ship appeared again in MacKenzie's main display. "What do you think happened to him?" she asked.

"Your guess is as good as mine," he replied.

"Well, I don't like it! This is something new. We have no idea what we're facing."

MacKenzie didn't like it either, but there was nothing they could do about it. "Continue the reconnaissance, Kilo," he told her. "We have no reason to delay. It may all be part of some ruse."

"Thank you, MacKenzie. Under the circumstances, that's precisely what I needed."

He swallowed the urge to tell her he didn't give a damn what she needed and instead changed the subject. By using his family name on an electromagnetic channel, she was breaching communications security. "Kilo, this is Bravo. Please resume acceptable radio procedure or you'll be subject to sanction."

"Muleshit, Bravo! That's your favorite meal," she snapped. "I hope you remember that, while I continue this ridiculous reconnaissance of yours."

Her cruiser immediately started moving. It slipped behind the freighter, and MacKenzie noticed she was completing the vertical circuit with increasing speed. Under the circumstances, he didn't care. When she appeared again, above the *Utopia*, with search beams shining, he exhaled.

"Sheila, what do you make of that Rashadian?" he asked.

"Judging from the facial discoloration and limb decomposure, I would guess a virus attacked his enzyme base. The gelatinous symptoms resemble those caused by an advanced chemical warfare agent developed before the Hegemony banned further research. It was a standard H-Two-A-Three strain that provided the feed stock for most toxic mutants. There were many variations."

"Were they transmitted in the atmosphere or by other means?"

"There were both airborne and projectile-borne variations,

but we are still not certain a virus is to blame. I can only say that the symptoms resemble those caused by the H-Two-A-Three family."

"Yes, I understand," MacKenzie said, nodding glumly. "But if it is a virus, would it remain fecund with all the freighter systems shut down?"

"Many viruses are potent without atmospherics. That is why they were tested as space weapons. Sometimes they are more vulnerable to temperature fluctuations. However, my sensors indicate the *Utopia* is stabilized at four hundred and ten Kelvins, plus or minus ten degrees variation. That is well within the H-Two-A-Three family's range."

"Kilo, have you been copying this?" he asked Svetla.

"Roger, Bravo. And my system confirms your system's analysis with high probabilities."

MacKenzie realized that Svetla was still manually keying queries and reading visual printouts for feedback, because she had not conversed with her command system all the while her voice link had been open. He couldn't understand it. She had enough to do without wasting that effort.

He was silent a moment while he considered ordering her to go to verbal mode. The sizzle of a cosmic ray striking the antenna emphasized the lingering quiet. Finally he told her, "All right, you might as well get started. Initiate the contact boarding procedure." Svetla didn't acknowledge. The radio sizzled again. He wondered what she was doing. "Kilo? You may begin contact boarding," he repeated. "Do you read?"

"I read you, Bravo," she snarled, "but I feel there is reason to delay boarding until we have a better idea of what we're facing. The way you are plunging ahead defies reason. I suspect you wouldn't be so reckless if it were some other Outbanker who had to make this reconnaissance."

Her accusation rankled him. Even though maximum probability procedure dictated how the *Utopia II* should be inspected, she was implying that he was getting even for what he had done on Red Cliff. He knew he shouldn't yield, but he couldn't bear the blatant condemnation in her voice.

"All right, Kilo. We'll trash the bloody procedure and make

our own rules. You pull back and stand in support. I'll board
the damned thing."

"Do you think that is wise, Mac?" Sheila interjected. "Perhaps it would be better if—"

"Shut up, Sheila, and do what I tell you," he barked.

"Just one minute, Bravo," Svetla broke in. "You misunderstand my point. I didn't imply that you should make the
boarding either. I don't believe either of us should at the moment."

"Look, Kilo, you and I don't make the rules," he shouted in
frustration. "We have to learn what happened to that Beta-2
system, and we don't have the luxury of taking our sweet time
about it. The Rashadians aren't sitting around discussing the
situation. They're hunting this ship."

"Fine, Bravo. You've made your point. But you needn't be
so irritated. I'm simply giving you my assessment as the officer
closest to the situation. I told you I'd perform the boarding if
necessary, but that isn't the point. Let me at least try to access
the *Utopia II*'s circuits and see if I can activate the captain's log.
It might tell us a good deal about what happened."

He had to admit it wasn't a bad idea, but he was still angry.
"How do you propose to do that?"

"I have a copy of the freighter's schematics. I think I can get
in through the multivoltaics panel. After that, it's just a matter
of breaking the captain's private code."

He hesitated a moment, then said, "All right. Give it a try."

Svetla's cruiser moved forward until it was near the *Utopia*'s
prow. She unlocked a cable with her cruiser's robotic arm and
attached it to the voltaics assembly protruding from the
freighter's hull. Then he heard her keying commands into her
system. She worked a long time, but nothing happened. Finally she grunted and said, "I've run into a brick wall. I'm in
and have the log activated, but I can't get it to run. There's a
secondary transmission cipher locked in somewhere."

MacKenzie didn't know what to tell her. For a moment
they were both silent.

Then Sheila said, "Excuse me, Mac. I have a few ideas I
might try, but I must take control of Kilo's system to do so."

"Did you read that, Kilo?" MacKenzie asked.

"Roger, Bravo. I'm opening a link to your system and instructing mine to cooperate." Her fingers clattered over the manual keyboard. "The link is established."

"Thank you, Kilo," Sheila said, and the auxiliary display screens exploded in a blaze of amber light. Calculations, formulae, and commands passed so rapidly between the two systems that they were impossible to read. MacKenzie glanced at Sheila's power gauges. They waffled strangely, then began ascending until they exceeded maximum. Overheat warnings appeared on the self-diagnostic panels to MacKenzie's left.

He was about to query Sheila when Svetla's voice boomed, "What in the hell is your system doing? The through-put is overloading capacities. We're both going to have a burnout!"

"A few seconds more," Sheila said in a confident voice. "Just a few seconds is all we need."

For an instant, MacKenzie was uncertain. He trusted Sheila, but her maturing out was a new element, and she was doing something now he had never seen before.

Svetla shouted, "Damn it, Bravo, I'm getting a massive overload here! I'm going to break your system's control!"

"No need, Kilo. We have it," Sheila stated with an edge of triumph. "The log is backloading."

The auxiliary screen burned with light as the history of the ill-fated *Utopia II* flowed into Sheila's memory, but the power claims immediately dropped into the normal range. MacKenzie exhaled deeply as the moment of crisis passed. "Did you copy that, Kilo? Do not disconnect," he said.

"Yes, I heard. Things here are returning to normal."

"Good," MacKenzie mumbled as he slouched back in his body-molded seat. "Now maybe we'll learn what we're in for." He rested a moment, watching the undulating light, then added, "Good job, Sheila. Congratulations."

She laughed softly and said, "Do not mention it, Mac." Her laughter was warm and natural, and it shocked him.

CHAPTER 4

MacKenzie reviewed the *Utopia*'s log a second time. When he was finished, he asked Sheila, "Are the class five safeguards programmed?"

"Yes, they are. Exactly as you ordered."

"If there is any kind of energy fluctuation on the *Utopia*, get us out of here immediately. Don't wait for orders."

"I understand, Mac."

"You're continuing long scans, too, aren't you?"

"Yes, Mac. I will alert you immediately of any contacts. But frankly, I believe Lieutenant Stocovik's presence is disturbing you too much. You must understand that your previous relationship with her may be affecting your command decision."

After the initial reconnaissance, he had ordered Svetla to join him on his cruiser for a strategy session. Their initial meeting had been polite, but as they discussed how best to proceed, an undercurrent of tension had developed. "Don't be ridiculous," MacKenzie replied now. "This is damned dangerous business. Stocovik has nothing to do with it. You know what we're up against here."

"I do know, Mac—perhaps better than anyone else. After all, I have had to suffer through your moods and depressions for more than a year now. If you do not face the fact that she nearly destroyed you, you will remain vulnerable to repeating the same mistakes."

"My only mistake was falling in love—like an idiot. It's only natural to get a little depressed when you misjudge someone the way I did."

"You were completely inebriated for three weeks after she left. Had you not met Commander Melchior, and had he not taken pity, you might have drunk yourself to death. Whatever compelled you was not unrequited love. You were coming apart completely."

Her smugness irritated him. "What makes you an expert?" he complained halfheartedly.

"You are in command of this mission, Mac, and I am your command control system. That is why it is my business. Svetla was not the only pain you were suffering. What happened on the *Sinclair* was part of it, too. If you do not face up to it soon, I am afraid of what will become of us."

MacKenzie was in no mood to argue and was even less disposed to probe the revulsion and terror he had suffered while cataloging the charred corpses on the *Sinclair*. The scalded nursery flashed in his memory, and he felt an involuntary shiver. He knew the bad dreams would come again, and he was glad the mission would permit no time to sleep. He decided to end the discussion. "Perhaps you're right," he said. "I'll think about it."

"I hope you will," she said.

Just then Svetla said over the intercom, "I made something to eat. Are you interested?"

Reviewing the *Utopia*'s log had destroyed his appetite, but sharing meals was a space ritual Outbankers seldom experienced, and Sheila's long scans would alert them of any Rashadian approach with an hour or two to spare. Besides, there were a number of things he wanted to ask Svetla Stocovik face-to-face. "Sure. Be there in a couple of minutes," he said.

Svetla said nothing more.

MacKenzie swiveled the console seat and removed the picture Sheila had excised from the *Utopia*'s log from the copy tray. He put it in the thigh pocket of his flight suit, then slipped out of the console.

"By the way, Mac," Sheila stated, "my personality integration was completed just before the log transfer began. It is different than I expected, but immensely intriguing. I thought you might like to know."

"I'm happy for you, Sheila. But don't become too human and get lax. We're in a lot of trouble here."

"It is a touch exciting, is it not?"

"That is one perspective," he responded.

He entered the passageway, then turned into the laboratory to retrieve the plans and specifications Sheila had produced on the plotter. He rolled them up, slung them under his arm, and went aft to the galley. When he arrived, Svetla was putting a steaming pot on the table. He sat down at the head of the table and laid the plans on the deck beside him.

"What did you learn from the captain's log?" Svetla asked.

"Let's discuss that after we eat."

"I'd like to know what killed the Rashadian first."

"I said we'll discuss it after we eat. What's on the menu?"

Svetla studied him a moment, then she shrugged and said, "Stroganoff. My own recipe. I trust you'll like it."

She turned to the preparation counter, and the faint odor of her body wafted around him. It reminded him of the cedar-wood scent that came from the chest when his mother removed her wedding dress and shoes, when heartache made her reminisce about his father. He also recalled the more pungent version lovemaking gave Svetla's skin. Remembering brought a lump to his throat.

She took a carafe of lymonia juice from the dispenser and placed it beside the pot, then pulled a swivel stool from beneath the table and sat down. She resembled a bored counter waitress.

"Would you like some music?" MacKenzie asked.

"That would be nice."

"How about Masagoruski?" he said. He remembered her playing that group over and over again while they were on Red Cliff.

"I'm more in the mood for Bakkie and Suller. Do you have 'Oceania'?"

"I'm sure we must. Sheila, would you pipe in 'Oceania' while we eat?"

"Certainly, Mac," Sheila replied, "but it will take a few seconds to retrieve it from the pop culture file."

Svetla's black eyes flashed at the sound of Sheila's syrupy tones. "Do you leave your system in verbal mode all the time?" she inquired.

"Sure. Why?"

"Have you no need for privacy?"

"Privacy? What does that have to do with it? Sheila can't read my thoughts."

Svetla stared at the steam coming from the white pot. Her lips were set in their characteristic hint of a pout. She seemed to be considering his answer, but he sensed something else was disturbing her.

The primitive sounds of Bakkie and Suller's "Oceania" began to fill the galley. The volume was set at an unobtrusive level, and MacKenzie asked Svetla if it was loud enough.

"Don't try to change the subject," she stated, her eyes boring into him accusingly. "Let's get down to the basic issue. Has that command system of yours matured out?"

So that was it, MacKenzie thought. He grinned sheepishly and said, "What makes you ask that?"

"Don't be coy, MacKenzie. No normal system could do what yours did to activate the *Utopia*'s log. It made program syntheses that don't exist in any manual and nearly blew my system apart. I ask you again, has your system evolved?"

"Well, I guess it has. So what?" he said.

Svetla threw up her hands in exasperation. "Have you lost your mind?"

"It happened right after we found the *Utopia*. There wasn't much time to think about—"

"Muledung, man!" she interrupted. "Didn't you read the psychocybernetic reports concerning the ramifications?"

"Sure I did," he prevaricated. "They're part of the programmed process. A system cannot mature without informing the pilot and getting permission. There's a diagnostic program to handle it."

Svetla shook her head dismally. "And you still let it proceed? You must be daft, MacKenzie. If you actually read those reports, you would have aborted the process."

"Stopping the maturation did not seem ethical," MacKenzie responded honestly.

"Certainly you jest," she said. "What have right or wrong to do with it? Command systems integrate a cruiser's mechanical functions. That is all."

"I think cybernetic intelligence has a right to develop the same as any other sentient being."

"Sentient being! You speak as if a system is a biological life form. It's a machine, MacKenzie—more related to a chisel or saw than to the lowly paramecium."

"Perhaps you're right, Svetla. And perhaps not. Sheila is the photoelectric nervous system of this cruiser. She has a mechanical body of sorts and a complex analog brain. The fact that her parts are inanimate may not be as important as we think." He fixed her with an angry glance. "If you really believe what the neo-Marxists running your native planet teach, you must agree with my position. They don't consider people more than material mechanisms either, do they? No! I'm not certain what Sheila is or what rights she has, but I did not want to feel guilty about retarding her development."

Svetla averted her eyes and stared at the pot again. It was not steaming as heavily. She removed the cover and ladled some Stroganoff onto her plate. Next she filled his plate and set it before him. This chore accomplished, she stared back at him. "You are a romantic, MacKenzie. Bourgeois fantasies obsess you. You see rights where there are none and, no doubt, refuse to recognize those that do exist. But all that aside . . ." She hesitated an instant, and something changed in her eyes. When she continued, her voice seemed softer and more concerned. "Have you considered how you'll deal with this when they decommission you both? How will you manage that?"

Her sympathy infuriated him even more than her previous disdain. He shrugged and said, "I suppose I'll manage as I did when you decommissioned us back on Red Cliff. I survived that loss almost intact."

She snapped her head toward him. For a few seconds, they regarded each other like combative thugs. Then Svetla shouted, "Don't let's get into that! Do you hear me?" She slapped her hand on the table so hard that the plates rattled. "I knew you'd bring that up sooner or later. You couldn't just let it be!"

"Of course it had to come up. And why not? I was under the impression we had found something special together. I shared my hopes and fears with you because you pretended to be interested. I even told you about my despair at finding the burned babies. Then you sneaked off in the middle of the night without a word, leaving me like a beached whale. What happened, Svetla? Did remorse and uncertainty make me too human? Or was I just a recreational dalliance from the beginning? A convenient way to scratch the itch?"

"It wasn't the middle of the night. It was early morning," she corrected him. "My ship's repairs were completed. I had to go."

"Without so much as a 'Thank you. See you later'?"

"Have you forgotten that we're Outbankers?" she stated. "There seemed no chance we would ever see each other again, and I thought it would be easier on us both that way. Besides, I knew you would make a scene."

"A scene?"

"Yes. Just as you are now."

He knew she was trying to anger him. He shook his head in disgust. "I'm sorry. Perhaps I am just a romantic dreamer. I was thinking future and family and living like a real person for a change . . . getting out of these God-awful Outbanks and making a life with someone. Silly of me, I suppose."

"Stop acting pathetic! You won't manipulate me with that act. I will not discuss Red Cliff any longer. Do you understand?" Her brows furrowed with righteous reproof. "We are discussing you and Sheila here. Nothing else. Do you hear me?"

"Oh, yes . . . Sheila. I'd nearly forgotten about her. But there's no need to be jealous. Personality or not, she is still a command system. It's not as if you are sharing me with another woman." Svetla began to protest, but he raised his hand, cutting her off. "No! No more lies. We were attracted to each other on Red Cliff. I want to know why you rejected it."

"Don't overestimate your vaunted appeal," Svetla hissed. "I am jealous of no one, least of all a mutant command system. I simply refuse to attribute imagined properties to things, either here or on Red Cliff. I do not let my needs seduce me into anthropomorphisms." She crossed her arms over her chest and gave him a moody frown. "That is why I do not interact verbally with my system unless it is absolutely necessary. I won't be dependent on a machine. I won't have it sharing my feelings. That would be too pitiful. Too obscene!" She uncrossed her arms and waved her hand back and forth vigorously in negation. "No, MacKenzie. You judge me as wrongly as you do your own command system."

Once again his rage began to boil. She owed him an explanation. Any normal woman would have felt obliged to provide one. But, no! Not Svetla Stocovik! They had said she could be as cold as a shark. He was seeing that side of her now—haughty, stubborn, a typical Slavian.

Then he began to smile derisively. If she wants to pretend she never cried out her joy in the throes of passion, let her. He knew the truth. She had been moved as deeply as he had. Sooner or later, he would learn what was behind that rejection and her present antagonism. For the present, his advantage lay in waiting.

"All right, forget it. We're letting good food go to waste. Eat before it gets cold," he told her, motioning with his fork.

Svetla picked up her juice glass and sipped it. Then she took a fork and began stirring the meat on her plate into its rich, brown sauce. The harmonies of "Oceania" muted the clink and scrape of the utensils as they ate.

The Stroganoff was excellent, and for a while they concentrated on the food, both lost in their own thoughts.

CHAPTER 5

"The Rashadians have developed a martial robot to expand their scope of operations," MacKenzie told Svetla in measured tones. "The Rashadian you saw was killed by one of those robots. Captain Findail believed there were seven robots on board the *Utopia*, but he wasn't certain."

Svetla was stacking dishes in the recycler. She turned to MacKenzie with a perplexed look. "How did the Rashadians manage to stop the *Utopia*? There's no sign of battle damage anywhere on the freighter's exterior."

"The robots were already on board, disguised as cargo. When the Rashadians approached, they activated the robots, who attacked from the inside. The crew surrendered almost immediately. And no wonder. The damned things are nearly invincible.

"First, they draw their power from fields existing in the environment. If an energy void occurs, a battery kicks in that gives them fifteen or twenty minutes more operating time. Under normal conditions, they never run down.

"Next, there's an antimatter device in their epicenter that neutralizes antipersonnel weapons. Lasers, particle beams, molecular disrupters, strong force disphasers . . . nothing stops them. They're also strong enough to tear hatches off bulkheads like they were tin foil."

Svetla had finished stacking the dishes and was sitting down at the table. She made no effort to hide her reaction, and her concern made the wrinkles around her eyes seem more pronounced. For some reason, they only served to enhance her attractiveness.

"Then there's the virus," MacKenzie continued. "Their right claw contains a high-pressure syringe filled with toxin. One injection, and a hand or forearm turns gelatinous. Two injections, and the arm and shoulder metastasize. But even four or five injections aren't necessarily lethal, if they're administered to different extremities. It's quintessential Rashadian terror. Victims watch as pieces of their body turn to jelly and they wonder how far it will progress."

MacKenzie braced his elbows on the table and rubbed his eyes. The grizzled image of Captain Findail's tear-streaked face immediately assaulted him. Then he remembered the roasted children. For an instant, the long-forgotten curses of dying Rashadians at the Pegasus Station rattled in his brain. He lowered his hands suddenly and looked at Svetla.

She returned his stare curiously, as if she sensed something was troubling him. He feared she would ask what it was. Instead, she said, "If the Rashadians control the robots, why did they kill the one in the pursuit ship?"

"Each unit senses the group's aggregate experience. Normally they act as a team, coordinated by a Rashadian controller. But there's an individual default program that overrides the system if the coordination is disrupted. Unfortunately, Findail thought he could jam their command telemetry long enough for his crew to regain control. As soon as he did, the robots sought out anything that emitted human brain waves and destroyed it . . . even the Rashadian."

Svetla gaped. "You mean they ran amok and slaughtered everyone?"

MacKenzie nodded. "That's right. Another example of Rashadian retribution. Findail stopped scrambling as soon as he saw the result, but it didn't help. Once the killing program overrides the controller, it can't be stopped."

Svetla mumbled something in Slavian, then leaned her forearms on the table. She bit her lower lip nervously as she thought.

"Why didn't Findail try to contact FleetComm or send distress calls?" she asked dubiously.

"A robot demolished the communications center during the initial assault. Apparently when the final carnage started, the last of the crew tried to jerry-rig some kind of transmitter. They didn't succeed." He hesitated a moment as he considered what else he should tell her. "Findail was insane with grief and shame . . . kept mumbling something about wooden shoes, as if they were to blame for the carnage. He wasn't very coherent, except about the robots. Anyway, after most of his crew were dead and he realized there was no way to stop the robots, he shut down all the *Utopia*'s operating systems. Then he put a blaster to his head."

Svetla shivered. "And I almost boarded that charnel house. I suppose . . ." Her voice trailed off. Her face turned ashen, and for a moment, MacKenzie feared she might be sick. He touched her shoulder comfortingly.

"I'm not any happier about that than you are, Svetla, knowing what I know now," MacKenzie softly said. "But it's spilt milk. What's important is that the robots are dormant. With no external energy fields to draw power from, their storage cells must have begun to run down, and they probably sought out the only energy source that remained on the ship. I think they'll be in the bosun's area, near the vault." He reached into his thigh pocket and removed the picture of the robots that Sheila had taken from the log. He slid it across the table to Svetla. "This is what they look like," he said.

She studied the picture a long moment, letting her eyes wander over the hinged metallic arms and saw-toothed claws, then said, "It seems they built these things to resemble giant crabs. Why would they do that?"

"The Rashadians are motivated and murderous, but there aren't many of them," MacKenzie replied. "They need every edge they can get, and inducing terror in opponents makes up for a lack of resources. They fashioned the robots after one of their mythological heroes who disguised himself as a land crab to enter a tyrant's fortress. Once inside, he assumed huge proportions and slaughtered everyone. That's more or less what these robots do. They're only a meter high folded up, but they're three meters tall when fully extended."

Svetla studied the computer-generated picture cautiously, as if the robots might jump out if she stared too hard. "Are they normally standing up like this?" she asked, pointing.

"They remain erect except for tactical purposes, such as being brought aboard as cargo. They use the three legs on each side of their body to clamp, punch, parry, and rip with their claws. They ambulate on treads built into the bottom feet."

"Paddles," Svetla said. "That's what their back feet must be called, if they're supposed to be crabs."

"Oh, I see," he said, repressing a smile. He picked up the picture and shoved it back into his pocket. Then he leaned back and stared at Svetla. "Oceania" was still playing softly in the background.

Svetla said, "So you presume the robots moved to the bosun's area and then ran down?"

"It seems a reasonable assumption in light of the facts," he told her. "There are no power readings on the *Utopia* other than the vault's security devices. Nothing else is active. I think we can assume they're there and dormant."

"Do you have any idea what energy levels are required to reactivate them?"

"No, I don't, but it must take more than anything we've exposed them to so far."

She crossed her arms over her chest once more and stared downward. "I'm not sure I find that reassuring," she whispered.

He stared at her as affectionately as he dared, then said, "I think we must try to retrieve the Beta-Z system, in spite of the danger. Do you concur?"

She looked up and said, "Those were my orders, and they are Priority Five."

"Right. We'll go in, open the vault, grab the box, and get out. With any luck, we won't wake the robots. I think time is important, though. The Rashadians must be searching for the *Utopia* by now, and they have a relatively good idea of where to start."

Svetla agreed with the in-and-out strategy, but she suggested that only one of them board the freighter. That way, she argued, if the robots were reactivated, the one waiting outside could simply destroy the *Utopia* and withdraw. He had to admit it was a gutsy plan. Had he not already decided to test the weapon, it would have been a sound one.

"I don't like it," he told her.

"Why not?" she demanded. "You don't need to protect me, you know. You have no right."

MacKenzie glanced down at the plans lying on the deck beside him. The concept was so simple, he was afraid he had overlooked something. "There may be some protective feelings involved," he admitted. "Considering our relationship on Red Cliff, it would be unusual if there weren't. But that isn't the point. Your plan is defensive. If the robots activate, we destroy the Beta-Z system but lose an officer in the process and learn nothing about fighting them. Those robots have become more important than the Beta-Z box. If they can't be stopped, they could tip the balance of power in the Rashadians' favor."

Svetla stared at him warily, but she seemed less irritated now that he had articulated his reasons for rejecting her strategy. "All right, let's think that through," she said. "We both make the incursion. But what can either one of us do if the robots are reactivated? You said they're invulnerable to every type of anti-personnel weapon we have."

"Perhaps not."

"Stop being mysterious, MacKenzie. What are you driving at?"

"Mechanical energy might destroy them."

"Do you mean a kinetic kill weapon like an old electromagnetic rail gun?"

"No. That would be too complicated and clumsy. I'm thinking of the handloaded chemical combustion projectiles they used in the nineteenth and twentieth centuries."

"A rifle or a cannon?"

"A pistol, actually. Its metal projectiles might shatter the robots' antimatter assemblies before they begin to function. If we knock those out, the robots become sitting ducks." He leaned back and frowned. "What concerns me, though, is the energy release that might occur."

Svetla pondered that, and he let her think. It was several seconds before she replied. "I'm not certain. I know nothing about the kinetics of antique weapon systems. We might create one hell of a bomb, you know."

MacKenzie shrugged. "At least we'd keep the Rashadians from getting the weapons control system."

Svetla glared her disapproval. "You'd better take this more

seriously, MacKenzie. I'm not talking about simple hydrogen fusion. With antimatter, we could rip a hole in the universe."

"Could something like that really happen?"

"There's no certainty with matrix mechanics, not between more than one attribute at a time. Imagine how complex it becomes when you add permutations from space-time geometries, where one characteristic influences all others simultaneously."

He only half understood what she was saying, but he knew her reputation in mathematics. If she thought it was a difficult problem, it probably was. "Why don't you work on it," he suggested. "Build some models with Sheila and see what probabilities result."

Svetla's brows immediately knit with irritation.

He knew she had hoped that working on the problem would give her an excuse to return to her own cruiser, but he had no intention of letting her escape so easily. "You've already admitted Sheila is more advanced than your cruiser's system," he said. "We might as well take advantage of it."

"All right," she agreed glumly. "The antimatter question is an extremely complicated problem, which will require advanced computing power. I'll have to trust that your Sheila has evolved and not regressed."

"Good," he said. "And while you're doing that, I'll work on a design for the pistol. Sheila pulled some prints from her archive of technical journals." He leaned over and picked up the plans. He unrolled them and spread them on the table before Svetla. "This is a Smith and Wesson forty-one caliber magnum pistol. Its projectile has an excellent velocity-to-mass balance, but it apparently still packs quite a recoil."

Svetla looked down at the plans. Her dark eyes caught the light in a way that made them sparkle, and he became painfully aware of her physical closeness. It made him remember the contentment he had felt as they had lain together in the seacoast room, their bodies entwined, her warm breasts pressed against his chest. That intimacy had filled the wretched emptiness he had suffered after his experience aboard the *Sinclair*. Her eyes had sparkled then, too. He was tempted to reach out and touch her, but he knew she would misunderstand, and he lowered his eyes to hide his sudden emotion. They were both silent for a long moment.

When he looked at her again, she was gazing back with grudging respect. "This thing is virtually medieval," she said, brushing her hand over the plans. "I'm amazed you even thought to have your system file such archaic data. But I suppose it's more evidence of your romantic obsessions."

CHAPTER 6

MacKenzie was mentally exhausted. He had spent five hours designing the weapon, and the pistol in his C.A.D. simulator no longer bore much resemblance to the original design. It had a twelve-round chamber, sheathed hammer, oversized trigger guard, elongated front sight, and recoil baffles between the firing mechanism and grip. Epoxy ceramics replaced hardened steel and tungsten carbide. Only the bullet propellant resembled the chemical makeup, size, and shape of Accurate MP-5744 powder.

He had decided the changes were necessary to adapt the pistol to the zero gravity environment aboard the *Utopia II* and had tried to think everything through. But he wasn't satisfied. Being with Svetla Stocovik was disturbing his concentration, and he doubted the design problems had received his best effort.

Reluctantly he activated the program for robotics production of the pistols, then slid out of the console and started aft to the galley. As he passed the laboratory, he noticed Svetla sitting at the control station. She seemed lost in thought. He observed her for a moment, then went inside. "Are you still analyzing what will happen to the antimatter?" he asked.

He startled her, and for a moment, she seemed annoyed by the intrusion. Then she said, "No. I was just considering something." She looked down at the equations spread before her, and the cedarwood fragrance of her hair wafted around him. "The projectiles will work. At least, there's a very high probability they will. If Sheila is correct about how the antimatter is insulated, once they puncture the mechanism—" she paused and spread her hands palms up—"the antimatter release should incapacitate them."

MacKenzie lowered a swing-out stool next to her and sat down. "How is it insulated?" he asked.

"It involves negative space-time shaping inside a plasma-induced vacuum. Explaining it would take some time. A more important issue is the pistol. Have you finished designing it?"

He leaned over and activated the control station display terminal. "Sheila, bring up the pistol, would you, please?" The weapon diagrams flashed on the screen, and a three-dimensional model appeared in the C.A.D. holoscope. They studied the gun for a while before MacKenzie asked her, "Do you think you can handle it?"

She began reading the specification sheets on the display terminal, and her displeasure was immediate. "Two thousand, two hundred foot-pounds of puzzle pressure and fourteen hundred feet-per-second velocity! If I recall my metric conversions, that's impossible. Our boots won't hold us to the deck. We'll end up careening about like bowling pins."

"We have to chance it. That blend of mass and velocity is necessary to puncture their epicenters. Our hands and arms will absorb most of the shock, plus I've added recoil baffles." He pointed at the articulation beneath the sheathed hammer. "Actually, I've had to substitute so much material that what we have here is completely speculative. I'm not so concerned about the recoil. I just hope the damned thing works."

Svetla leaned back and crossed her arms over her chest. "Wonderful. The thing is nothing but a controlled explosion in the first place, and you've improvised on its design? I don't know which to fear more, the Rashadian robots or your handiwork."

Her attitude perplexed him. "Do you have a better idea?" he demanded.

"As a matter of fact, I do," she said.

"I see. After I spend hours mucking about, you've suddenly become creative."

"Don't be childish, MacKenzie. There's nothing sudden about it. And it was Sheila's idea." She jabbed her forefinger at him. "Your system is quite forward about initiating discussions. One of them involved methods of scrambling the robots' override program. What is necessary, she thinks, is a way to reproduce brain wave frequencies throughout the ship. In that case, the target will seem to surround the robots completely, and they'll be stymied."

MacKenzie shook his head. "That sounds good in theory, but it won't work. The waves can't be distributed evenly. They'll be stronger near the transmitter, and that will draw them to us. If we move away, we become targets again. The robots probably sense energy fields in our space suits' operating range as well. The designers would have been stupid not to have done that. So far, at least, they haven't done anything stupid."

Svetla shook her head and said, "Those aren't problems if the whole ship becomes a transmitter and frequencies are sent at high power."

"Now, that sounds really speculative."

"Not necessarily. Sheila and I have done some work on the problem. We may have discovered a way, but we need more time to design and build the apparatus."

"How much time?"

"At least twelve hours," she said.

"I'll give you six and that's it. We can't delay boarding longer than that."

Svetla frowned. "We'll do the best we can, but the probability of success will be reduced by at least fifty percent."

"Read 'em and weep," he told her with a shrug.

She looked at the pistol in the holograph and said, "Have you started manufacturing these things?"

"Maintenance robotics are tooling them now."

"And how long will *that* take?"

"About two hours. But I'm surprised you're interested, since you have your own solutions."

"Two weapons systems are better than one. I exaggerated my concern because Sheila feared you might be stubborn about giving us time to work on our idea."

MacKenzie rose from the stool. "It seems you and Sheila are becoming quite comfortable with each other," he commented.

"What do you mean by that?" she demanded.

"Nothing in particular."

"It's what you hoped would happen, isn't it?"

There was a challenge in her voice that surprised him. He said, "Well . . . I'm not unhappy to see it."

"I should think not," she snapped. "It cements your little scheme extremely well."

"Scheme? I don't understand."

She leapt to her feet and snickered caustically. "Do you think I'm a dunce, MacKenzie? Sheila is your system, not mine. You're her captain pilot, and she follows your instructions. You can't expect me to believe that maturing out has given her freedom to think for herself."

"She has a mind of her own. That's my opinion," MacKenzie said, blanching. "But what in the hell is troubling you? What did Sheila do?"

Svetla glowered at him in disgust. "What you told her to, no doubt! She wanted to know how I felt about you on Red Cliff, and why I left. She told me it was necessary to assure her support role in the mission. Can you imagine that?" Her eyes attacked him tempestuously. "Will you stop at nothing, MacKenzie? It's difficult to believe that even *you* would stoop to manipulating a command system that way."

"Look, Svetla," he complained, "I've been designing pistols for over five hours. I'm tired and cranky and have no idea what you're talking about. I didn't tell Sheila to ask you anything."

"All right. Perhaps her interest was simply prurient."

"What did you tell her, anyway?" MacKenzie asked.

"In general terms, what she wanted to know, of course," Svetla answered.

"Which was?"

She gave him a cold stare. "I thought I'd already made myself clear regarding that. I will not discuss Red Cliff with you. I told Sheila only after she assured me it related to mission success and would keep it confidential. In spite of her new personality, she is still an artificial intelligence, and I'm hoping she hasn't learned how to lie. Why don't you ask her?"

MacKenzie felt increasingly powerless, and his nerves burned with the frustration. He took a deep breath and tried to let the painful mood pass. "All right, have it your way," he snapped. "But I don't understand why you're being so pigheaded. I just want to know why you left the way you did.

What's so unreasonable about that?" He hesitated a long moment and then shyly admitted, "I was in love with you, Svetla. I really cared."

She stared at him defensively, then her face hardened. "Don't try making me feel guilty, Mac. It won't work. I had to do what I did. You were suffocating me. Do you understand? You were too damned intense."

He stared at her incredulously. "Too intense! What in God's name does that mean?"

"There's no use discussing it," she grumbled.

Her answer increased his simmering anger. "No use discussing it, huh?" he said. "In that case, tell me this, at least. When you sleep with someone, do you report it only if you're afraid he might, too?"

Her face blushed crimson, and she probed him with a questioning stare. "What do you mean by that?"

"You got dehorned the two times you were on leave before we met, didn't you? You slept with Mohelich once, and then with Georgi Propov. The personal intimacy reports you so dutifully filed said the trysts were basically physical, void of emotion or meaningful commitment. Was it the same with me?"

Svetla's face became a mask of anguish. "How did you learn of those personal intimacy reports?" she cried.

"Never mind that. It's not the point." He turned away from her and stared at the pistol in the C.A.D. holograph. "At first I thought I was just one more in a pattern. Then I realized you hadn't filed a personal intimacy report on our little liaison, and I wondered why not." He turned back to her. "Why didn't you file a report about our affair, Svetla? I deserve at least to know that."

Her eyes were filling with angry tears, and she began to tremble. She tried summoning her former defiance, but she was too beset with humiliation to succeed. "You stole a copy of my personnel folder, didn't you?" she finally shrieked.

"Of course I did. I went off the deep end after you left. I was stinking drunk for days. Luckily an old friend took pity on me. He was the officer in charge of the records section, and he secreted out a copy of your file for me when I asked him to because he thought it might help me understand why you're the way you are. Thank God for old Melchior."

She didn't seem to be listening. Her eyes had turned inward and had a pained, vengeful look. "Stealing confidential records is a court-martial offense, MacKenzie. And I'll see you pay for it . . . both you and your damned friend."

He grabbed her shoulders and held them so tight she grimaced. "You're a little late, Stocovik. I know all about you now, and trying to punish me for it won't change that. Besides, you won't be able to make anybody pay unless you get through this mission alive. So you'd better cut the self-pity and concentrate on that stupid scrambler of yours."

Their eyes clashed savagely for a long moment. Then he shoved her aside and stormed out.

As he was making his way toward the cockpit, he recalled again how Commander Melchior had died only months after helping him. The old man was no fool, he thought. He knew he was genetically terminal and wouldn't be around long, even if he were caught. Still, he hadn't been afraid to go out on a limb one last time.

The thought triggered a sudden insight that filled MacKenzie with a strange sense of melancholy. He had finally realized that, even more than the content he had found in Svetla Stocovik's arms, Commander Melchior's friendship had rekindled his faith in the potential goodness of human existence.

CHAPTER 7

"You questioned Svetla about our relationship on Red Cliff. Why the sudden interest?" MacKenzie asked Sheila later, when they were alone.

"I thought it necessary."

"Please explain what you mean."

"Certainly, Mac. This mission has become quite dangerous. Anything that might influence it is essential. I understand how Lieutentant Stocovik affects your performance, but not how you might affect hers. It was necessary to determine how she would respond in different contingencies."

"You're saying you're just following the prime directive, then?"

"Yes, Mac. The information was required to enhance my support of the mission." Sheila hesitated. "I must add, however, that I was somewhat curious as well."

MacKenzie wasn't certain what to make of that. He crossed to the portside viewport and looked out into the void. "Curious about what?" he asked.

"Why she deserted you as she did. It implied unusual psychological dynamics."

"So you decided to pry. Is that it?"

"Let me explain if I can," Sheila replied. "Svetla's refusal to discuss Red Cliff has made you question your self-worth again, just as you did when she left you. Therefore, the reasons for her obduracy seemed important. What I discovered is useful. You deal with the pain she caused by performing an emotional autopsy. She handles her feelings by burying them. It is not disinterest that makes her refuse to discuss Red Cliff with you. She is simply not prepared to deal with it yet. Of that you may be sure."

"What is troubling her, then?"

"I am sorry, but I cannot say specifically. I promised confidentiality if she told me what I needed to know, and I am incapable of soliciting information by ruse."

He gazed out the viewport at a glimmering pattern of stars. Near the center was NX-12304, a nebula forming a generation of new worlds. He felt himself drawn by that pristine act of creation so strongly that, for an instant, he almost became a part of it. But the feeling quickly passed, submerging back into the nexus of habitual consciousness.

"All right, Sheila, I understand," he said. "But don't forget who or what you are. I'm your captain pilot, and I need to know Svetla's motives for the same reasons you do. I'm not asking. I'm ordering you to tell me."

"I am sorry, Mac, but what you ask is not possible."

"You don't need to feel sorry. You need to do what you're told."

"Unfortunately, in this case I cannot comply."

MacKenzie spun round and lunged at the console, slamming it with his fist. "God damn it, Sheila, don't give me that! You follow the prime directive and assist me! Do you hear?"

"You do not understand. I am following the directive. I consider the information you request inhibitive of mission success."

"You *what!*" he bellowed.

"You heard correctly, Mac. Not knowing how Lieutentant Stocovik feels about you renders your command decision capability more objective. Knowledge of any kind, whether you considered it negative or positive, might prejudice your tactical grasp during the remainder of the mission."

MacKenzie lurched through the narrow opening to the console and plunged into the seat. "Oh, no, you don't! You're not squirming out of this!" His eyes darted from one display to another, searching for some means of attack. Then he began to realize how all-encompassing Sheila was. Her main processors might be located under the cockpit deck, but her circuits and peripheral systems ranged like nerves and arteries throughout every centimeter of the ship.

He smashed the manual control board with a powerful, short punch and his hand blazed. Somehow the pain gave him a morbid sense of satisfaction. Peripherally, he noticed Sheila's power displays spike in response. He shattered them with a backhand and again felt the pain. When he pulled back his hand, a shard of plastiglass protruded from it and blood was starting to ooze from the wound.

He laughed hoarsely, his head thrown back, and began rocking back and forth. "You mean if I don't know how Svetla feels, I'll be able to sacrifice her more readily for the success of the mission. That's how you rationalize insubordination?" He laughed again. It was a strange, chortling wail that sounded foreign.

"MacKenzie? What's going on up there?" Svetla's voice asked through the intercom.

Her voice startled him. He had forgotten she was in the laboratory, only a few meters aft, but instead of dampening his vituperation, it fueled it. He glowered murderously at the twinkling display boards.

"Sheila, I'm not going to argue," he said, slipping out of the console. "You may think or feel anything you like, but there is a natural order here that no one can violate." He moved toward the center of the cockpit. "That order is, in case you've forgotten, that I command and you serve." He knelt, unhooked a latch, and lifted a section of the deck. Beneath it lay the shining labyrinth of Sheila's mainframe processors. "It's very simple, really. Either I command and you serve, or the natural order is violated. And when that happens, extreme measures are called for to redress the confusion."

Sheila's processors burst into a kaleidoscope of light. "Please control yourself, Mac. You are too filled with anger to pursue this discussion rationally," she scolded.

His lips curled back from his teeth, but there was no laughter in his eyes. "Let me make it clear," he said. "You have decided you know better than I what this mission requires, and that is a violation of natural order. Your development has become malignant. Perhaps your personality is to blame, but it doesn't matter."

He reached toward the function cubits on her mainframe service module. "I'm going to decommission your mutinous ass right here and now!"

"No, Mac. Stop!" Sheila cried. "Danger imminent" Klaxons began to blare.

"Shut down those God-damned alarms or you might alert the robots," MacKenzie shouted over the commotion. He flipped back the four plasteel covers guarding Sheila's advanced logics lobe.

The alarms ceased, but Sheila said in a determined voice, "I cannot permit this, Mac. You are upset and should consider your course of action after due reflection."

"The hell you say." He took a photon torch from his utility belt and engaged the first setting. He squinted at the function bubbles, searching for the gender base determinant. Intuitively, he felt that was the place to start. He lowered the torch toward the glimmering turbulence of the center bubble and was about to make an incision, when a blue bolt shot up his arm, lifted him up, and threw him across the cockpit.

He crashed down beside the console and lay sprawled on the deck, head swimming, arm numb. He forced himself to roll over, but when he tried to gain all fours, his arm collapsed under him, and he fell forward on the side of his face. "You son of a bitch!" he gurgled, condemning the arm as much as Sheila. He made another effort to get to his feet. This time he was successful, but he stood uncertainly. His legs were rubbery and his cheek stung. "So you want to play rough?" he growled, bracing himself against the side of the console. "All right, I'm happy to oblige." He pulled the blaster from his holster and began shuffling toward the open section of the deck. When he was above the mainframe again, he pointed the blaster at the multicolored translucence.

Sheila cried out in alarm, "Do not do this, Mac. Please, I am begging you. . . ."

Her terror gave him a magnificent sense of satisfaction. Soon, very soon, natural order would be reestablished, he told himself. He sneered in triumph as he took aim.

"What's going on here?" Svetla demanded, appearing beside him suddenly.

"Get back!" he roared.

"Are you crazy, MacKenzie?" she shouted. "Put that blaster

away before you hurt someone!" She reached for the weapon.

Instinctively he rotated to a low stance, locked her extended arm, and whipped her over his hip. She seemed to hang momentarily, then smashed into the starboard wall and slithered down onto the deck in a ragged heap.

MacKenzie stared at Svetla in shock, and the sight of her crumpled body made him regain his senses. "What the hell . . ." he whispered.

He slipped the blaster back into the holster and rushed to her side, then lifted her up and cradled her in his arms. Her eyes were open, but they were unfocused and confused. "What . . . happened?" she asked in a stunned voice.

MacKenzie said, "I'm sorry. I didn't realize what . . ." His voice trailed off, choked with shame and embarrassment. He sat there for a long while, cradling her in his arms. Then finally he said, "Listen, Svetla, try to move your legs. Can you work them?"

She did as he asked, and they moved naturally. "I'm all right," she said with a weak smile. "Just help me up."

"No. Don't try to move yet. Just relax," he said.

Svetla rested her head in the hollow of his shoulder. They both sat quietly for a while. Then Svetla looked up and asked, "You were going to destroy your system, weren't you? Sheila wouldn't tell you what I said, so you became angry. That's it, isn't it?"

MacKenzie shook his head, trying to hide his guilt. "No, that wasn't it," he murmured.

She put a hand to his scraped cheek and touched it. Then she stared deep into his eyes. He could see she was regaining control. "You're lying, MacKenzie. And I know it," she stated.

She rolled to her knees and tried to stand, but when she got to her feet, she wobbled precariously. MacKenzie stood up and steadied her.

"You need a diagnostic scan," he said. "Let's go to therapeutics."

Reluctantly she took his arm and they started aft, but after only a few steps, she pulled away, intent on managing without him. By the time she rolled onto the diagnostic treatment table, her strength had returned and she was distant. "Let's get this over with," she complained. "I still have to design that scrambler."

There was an awkward silence, then he said, "Sheila, run a comprehensive body scan on Svetla."

"Certainly, Mac," Sheila responded. The table lit with undulating waves of color, and the diagnostic display slowly filled with computer-enhanced tracings of Svetla's physiological systems. Except for a few purple blots marking subcutaneous contusions, there seemed to be no injuries. "Good news," Sheila announced. "Lieutenant Stocovik is not hurt."

Svetla sat up and swung her legs off the table. When her eyes met his, they were so wary it made his heart ache. "I'm sorry, Svetla. I don't know what came over me," he said softly.

"Forget it," she replied, averting her eyes. "I wasn't my best on the reconnaissance either. You keep my secrets. I'll keep yours."

He studied her affectionately but resisted the urge to take her in his arms, knowing she would resist. "Can I get you something? Would you like some tea?" he asked.

She started toward the passageway. "That would be nice. Could you bring it to the laboratory?" she said.

He followed her out of the therapeutics section, then turned aft along the passageway to the galley. Sheila was already preparing the tea. The hot green liquid was pouring from the dispenser into a cup. "Thanks, Sheila. I appreciate your efficiency," he said.

"Do not mention it, Mac. I only hope we are on good terms again."

MacKenzie did not answer. He watched the steaming cup as it filled. The top of his right hand was aching. He noticed dark blood oozing from the cut where the shard of plastiglass had punctured it. He took a napkin from the utensil cabinet and wrapped his hand.

Finally he told Sheila, "I still think you were wrong to refuse my command, but my anger was out of proportion to the situation. I nearly aborted the mission, or at least complicated it seriously. I'm overly tired and short-tempered, maybe even a little unbalanced. I realize that now. It won't happen again."

He picked up the cup and started toward the forward passageway, but before he got to the hatch, Sheila said, "I apologize, too, Mac. I should have known how much Svetla means to you." She was silent a moment. "Personality has burdened me with subtleties I do not yet fully comprehend. I may have misjudged the situation. I shall tell you what Svetla said now, if you like."

MacKenzie's smile was dubious. "Never mind. Other things are more important at the moment. Besides, there won't be any more outbursts."

"Would you really have shot me, Mac?" Sheila asked.

He thought about it a moment. "I don't know. Perhaps I only hoped to frighten you."

"I'm glad you recognize that possibility. But I know ultimately you would have done it."

He shook his head. "Always a step ahead of me, aren't you, Sheila?"

She chuckled softly. "We have been together a long time."

"But we're friends again, aren't we?"

"After what has happened, I am not certain. But I shall consider it."

"What's that? Are you serious?"

Her laughter was almost sensual. "Of course not, Mac," she replied. "Can't you tell when I am joking?"

CHAPTER 8

MacKenzie watched as Svetla checked the scrambler, then attached it to the utility belt of her deep-space suit. Even behind the reflections in her helmet plate, he could read the tension in her face. He pulled his own helmet on and locked the couplings. "Can you hear me?" he said.

"Yes," she replied. "Let's get started. Tribenzodrine gives me the heebie-jeebies."

"I know what you mean," he said.

They had both taken the powerful stimulant to keep alert during the incursion. It worked for seventy-two hours, but there was a cost. When it wore off, or if they took a counteragent, they would fall comatose for as long as a week, depending on physiological and biorhythmic conditions.

MacKenzie pressed the release, and the air lock's inner door slammed shut. He made a final check. Besides the scrambler Svetla carried, they each had a pistol, a blaster, and two shrapnel grenades. Except for the pistols, he hoped the additional armament wouldn't be necessary. "Sheila, is everything online?" he asked.

"Yes, Bravo," Sheila responded. "I am interfaced with Kilo's system, and hyperspace communications are active and redundant. I am monitoring with my sensors, but if activity ensues, I will tie into the *Utopia*'s own sensor grids. I am also long-scanning contiguous vectors, and no contacts are present. If the Rashadians are searching for their erstwhile prize, they are still at least twelve hours distant. Are there any further instructions?"

"What's the energy readings status?" he queried.

"No change," Sheila answered.

MacKenzie grunted. He turned to Svetla, clasped her hand, and pumped it three times in Outbanker fashion. "All right, we're exiting the air lock now," he said. He pushed the outer door release.

The air lock pressure lowered to match the fifteen percent

atmosphere that remained on the *Utopia*, and when the hatch opened, it was barely audible in the relative vacuum. But the radio-transmitted sound of their breathing was more obvious, and it conferred an unnatural sense of intimacy as they both peered into the dark gloom.

The shortest way to the bosun's area was through a series of interconnected passages, so they had decided Svetla would take the point, while MacKenzie concentrated on mapping their progress. She stepped out first and he followed. As soon as they were clear, the air lock's outer door shut behind them with a muffled thud.

It was dark in the docking bays, and they had to move cautiously, detouring now and then around cargo containers and loading equipment that loomed suddenly before them. Finally MacKenzie said, "Let's use our lights so we can see where the hell we are."

"Roger, Bravo," Svetla agreed. "If the lights are going to waken our friends, we might as well know now." Her helmet lamp flashed on just as he engaged his switch.

The beams from the lights clearly exposed what lay ahead, but new problems arose. The slashing motion of the beams caused shadows that gesticulated from one side, then taunted from the other, playing tricks on the imagination. The farther they went, the more MacKenzie began to feel that something was using the whirling shadows to camouflage its approach. He tried to control his visceral fear, but by the time they reached the appropriate corridor, his heartbeat and respiration were uncomfortably elevated.

Phosphorescent strips of emergency lighting on the corridor walls bathed them in a jaundiced haze, but the sickly light seemed preferable to the whirling shadows that had accosted them in the docking bay. They switched off their helmet lights before continuing forward.

They were halfway along the first corridor when they encountered a mangled crewman floating midway between the deck and ceiling.

Svetla maneuvered by the corpse safely, but as MacKenzie passed, the blue jellied brain oozing from the cadaver's ears nd nose caused a nauseous lump to form in his throat. Suddenly he was choking.

Sensing that his breathing had stopped, Svetla turned back. What's wrong, Bravo?" she asked anxiously.

MacKenzie didn't answer. Instead, he closed his eyes and calmed himself by concentrating on counting down from twelve in reverse order. By the time he came to zero, he had regained some control and was able to breathe again.

When he opened his eyes, Svetla was beside him, peering up through her faceplate with a look of concern. He shook his head and pointed at the cadaver. "It caught me off guard. The brains spilling out . . . something about that got to me." He put his right hand under the body and pushed it up until it was flush against the ceiling. "This will be the procedure with any bodies we find. We'll shove them up out of the way, so that when we return, if there's anything blocking the corridors, we shoot."

"Whatever you say," Svetla agreed.

She turned to take the point again, but MacKenzie grasped her arm and said, "I know now how you felt when you saw that dead Rashadian. Video displays can't communicate the puescense of the remains. It's obvious why the Rashadians selected this virus strain. They want to induce maximum terror."

The conversation was being automatically transmitted to Sheila and subsequently via hyperspace commo to the Red Cliff Flight Corps Station. It would be added to Svetla's service record as a senior officer's comment on performance. Svetla realized what he was doing and said, "I appreciate that. They are gruesome, aren't they?"

But MacKenzie wasn't listening. "Sheila?" he said. "Have there been any variations in readings?"

"No change, Bravo," Sheila responded.

He stared at Svetla. Beads of perspiration had formed on her forehead, and he suddenly realized his head felt damp, too. Their suits were not adjusting properly to body temperature fluctuations, but it was not a malfunction. The system was simply ineffective when faced with the complex physiology of fight syndrome. MacKenzie had been through it before.

"Ready to continue?" he asked her.

She nodded. "So far so good, eh?"

MacKenzie shrugged, and Svetla took the lead again. The
moved as quickly as they could, considering the necessity t
keep one velcra soled boot firmly in contact with the deck ca
pet at all times. It was a lumbering, flatfooted walk, but neces
sary because of the lack of artificial gravity. When they came t
a cross corridor, Svetla halted. "Which way?" she asked.

MacKenzie studied the map display on his wrist terminal
"We go left," he said. Svetla took a canister from her utilit
belt and sprayed an arrow on the corner of the corridor point
ing back in the direction they had come. The paint radiated
translucent glow that was impossible to mistake. She replace
the canister and started along the cross corridor. MacKenzi
followed.

They came to a second passageway and turned right. Svetl
marked the corner with another translucent arrow. Midwa
down that corridor, they stopped to push another bloated ca
daver against the ceiling, then continued until they ap
proached a gangway. MacKenzie's map indicated they neede
to climb it.

Neither of them spoke as Svetla started up the gangway, bu
the ebb and flow of their respiration was evidence of their ten
sion. MacKenzie followed her up the ramp, staying as close be
hind her as he could. He couldn't help thinking it would be
damned good place for an ambush.

Svetla lifted her helmet above the deck of the next level. Sh
looked forward, then turned back and glanced aft. "It's al
clear," she whispered.

They scrambled up and started down the new passageway
MacKenzie checked the map. They were only three corridor
from the bosun's area now, but the gloom oozed about then
like pestilence. And as they continued along the passageway
sounds that normally wouldn't concern him assaulted Mac
Kenzie's attention. The creak of their suit joints sounded like
bloody screech, the drone of life-support systems like the rum
ble of combustion engines, their radio transmitted breathin
like a brassy fanfare. Though every nerve of their bodies crie

for the protection of silence, their advance was marked by a cacophony that seemed certain to alert the menacing robots.

Although they did not speak of it, MacKenzie knew Svetla was being affected the same way, too. She was plowing ahead with increasing recklessness, as if daring the potential dread to manifest itself. By the time they reached the last corridor, MacKenzie realized they had become their own worst enemies.

"Kilo, wait a minute!" he commanded.

Momentum carried her a few steps forward before she halted. "Why? The bosun's area is just down this hall, isn't it? Let's move!" She was breathing in short gasps.

"Not so fast," he said, fighting to control his own fierce respiration. "We're losing it."

"I have some advice, MacKenzie," Svetla said, turning back to him. "Don't lecture me, and don't lecture yourself either. If we panic a little, we have the right. This place is a graveyard. The longer we tarry, the more death rubs off on us. I can feel it. Acting quickly is our only hope."

When MacKenzie spoke, his voice implied command but no reproach. "No, you're wrong. I know how you feel about the atmosphere of death in here. I felt the same way on the *Sinclair*. But all that's ahead of us are the robots, and they're still dormant. We can't do anything about the energy our suits generate, but we can control ourselves. We can go about our business calmly, so we transmit as little human energy as possible. With luck, we can get out of here without waking them."

Svetla started back toward him. "All right. That makes sense," she agreed. "But don't expect me to just keep silent. I'm too damned scared."

Her confession was a simple statement of fact, and it left MacKenzie somewhat bemused. When they were side by side, they shared a moment of mutual determination. Her black eyes were smoldering.

He touched her arm and said, "I'll take the point now. You follow me." She nodded and he moved in front.

As they inched forward, the orange haze cast by the phosphorescent emergency lights began to shimmer. At first it was barely perceptible, but as they approached the portals of the bosun's area, the shimmering increased. When they were six meters away, flashes of red, blue, and yellow bounced garishly off another bloated body floating just beyond the doorway.

"Is that the vault's security mechanism?" MacKenzie whispered, looking back at Svetla.

She nodded forcefully but put a forefinger before her faceplate, signaling him to keep quiet. She didn't want to chance disturbing the robots with their radio signals. He nodded back, then began edging forward again. As they neared the doorway, their breathing became shallow, and the whirring of their life-support systems seemed more pronounced.

Slowly, his hand poised over his pistol, MacKenzie leaned forward and looked into the bosun's area. For an instant, his faceplate darkened as it responded to the brighter light, but he refused to let it affect his concentration. Before his eyes completely adjusted to the change in light, he was already surveying the room.

The flashing lights were indeed from the vault's security system. They weren't unusually bright, but in the rusty gloom, they flickered on the deck and against the walls like flames in a medieval dungeon, illuminating three deformed cadavers suspended near a pile of debris at one end of the room. They also cast a pale glow on the Rashadian robots.

There were five of them behind the security system console. They were in a standing position, their metallic claws and arms extended forward at a forty degree angle. The robots seemed even larger than they had in the captain's log. MacKenzie studied them for almost a minute. The electric scarlet light that glimmered in their visual sensors when they were energized was absent.

He stepped back from the door and turned to Svetla. There was no way to describe the situation in sign language, so he decided to chance using the radios. "They're there, all right . . . five of them," he whispered.

"No radio," Svetla protested. "If their energy symbiosis is cumulative, every transmission will bring them that much closer to activation."

"To hell with that," he replied crossly but still whispering.

"If radio waves are enough to wake them, we might as well know now, while we still have room to maneuver. We have to let Omega Base know what's happening." He dictated a situational update to Wing Headquarters on Red Cliff. Then he turned back to Svetla and said, "You'll have to shut down the security system, despite the robots gathered around the control board. Do you think you can?"

Svetla nodded. "It makes no difference, as long as they aren't activated."

"Don't worry about that," he chided. "We have the guns . . . and your scrambler."

"I'd rather not have to use your damned pistols if we don't have to," she snapped, "but I think you'd relish the opportunity."

MacKenzie couldn't argue. The Defense Council would want to know if kinetic energy could stop the robots. It was essential intelligence. He hadn't told Svetla, but if they retrieved the codes without disturbing the machines, he had decided to reenergize the *Utopia*'s systems and blast it out with at least one of the robots. Somehow she had sensed his resolve. "Maybe you're right. Who holds the sword is tempted," he admitted. She stared quizzically, and he smiled back. "It's from the Christian Bible, I believe, but I don't remember which book."

Svetla scowled. "Never mind. I get the point." She looked past him at the lights flashing from the doorway. "Let's get this over with and get the hell out of here."

"Right," MacKenzie said. "Do you remember the deactivation sequences?"

"Yes. I've been repeating them over and over to keep from going berserk. Are you ready?"

"Just a minute." He reached down and drew the pistol from its holster, then, looking at her as confidently as he could, nodded. "All right, go ahead, but remember, keep cool and collected. No feelings. Give them nothing."

"Do you believe that matters with all this mechanical shit running through our suits?" Svetla said.

"Somehow I think it does."

"Okay, MacKenzie, whatever you say. But let's do it."

He ducked through the portal and checked immediately to his left and right for hidden robots. There were none. Svetla had followed him through the door and was already moving toward the control panel. He went to the middle of the room and stood beside the main console, where he could keep an eye on the robots without Svetla obstructing his view.

As she approached the board, the pulsing, multicolored lights reflected from the matte white of her space suit helmet, accentuating the contrast between her and the dark, hulking robots behind her. She didn't look at them. She halted in front of the board.

The security system was activated by a sixteen-digit code base, repeated three times with randomly selected multipliers. Reversing the same digits deactivated it. But if just one digit was wrong, the system would self-destruct with a megaton force.

Svetla leaned over and began punching in the numerical sequences, whispering the digits to herself as she entered them. She was so close to the robots that he feared her radio transmissions might tempt them to awaken. But Svetla had memorized the reverse sequence months ago, when first given this assignment. Now their lives depended on her recall. MacKenzie didn't know what habits she had developed to assist her memory. He decided he would let her shout the digits, if she wanted to.

When she was finished, she turned toward him. He couldn't see her expression because the control panel lights reflected in her faceplate, but he knew she was ready to complete the process. They had reached a critical stage of the incursion.

"Go ahead, Kilo. Activate the damn thing . . . and hold your breath," MacKenzie said.

Svetla turned back to the control panel. Slowly she raised her left hand, index finger extended. It seemed to hang suspended above the "Enter" button for a long time. He heard her draw a deep breath. Then her hand dropped.

For three interminable seconds, nothing happened. Then all the control board lights lit simultaneously, casting an eerie white glow, and the plasteel vault door in the far wall began to swing out. When it was fully open, the control board lights extinguished.

"That's it. We did it!" Svetla squealed.

MacKenzie was smiling, too, but his voice was reproachful. "Keep calm, for Christ's sake!" He motioned with his gun hand. "Grab the box and let's get out of here."

Svetla moved quickly, happy to put some distance between herself and the hulking robots. She entered the vault. The Beta-Z System box was lodged in a cushioned pedestal in the middle of the floor. She grabbed its handle and pulled it out . . . and all hell broke loose.

Emergency Klaxons blared, vibrating the deck, and suddenly the vault door began to move.

"Kilo! Get out of there—now!" MacKenzie shouted, rushing toward the vault.

Svetla spun around toward him. By the time she recognized the danger, the plasteel vault door was closing with increasing acceleration. She leapt forward. Her boots left the deck, and she was sailing toward him. The reaction saved her life.

Three bolts of electricity gashed into the spot where she had been standing, and an icy blue force field fell like a guillotine around the pedestal where the Beta-Z box had been only moments before.

MacKenzie grabbed the door with his left hand and tried to pull it back, but the velcra soles of his boots tore through the deck carpet, and he couldn't gain any leverage. He let go of the pistol, grabbed the door with both hands, braced a foot against the wall, and heaved. For a moment, the door's forward motion ceased.

Svetla's helmet cleared the narrow aperture, but the door responded to MacKenzie's efforts with increased pressure. It began closing again, wedging the lower half of Svetla's body against the door recess. She bellowed something in Slavian.

MacKenzie slid his feet higher on the wall, so that his legs were below Svetla's squirming body. She let go of the Beta-Z box and grabbed his legs, pulling on them as she struggled desperately. He heaved on the door with such force that he groaned, and just before his gloves slipped, Svetla wiggled free. She floated past him, her arms and legs swinging wildly. The vault closed with a dull thump.

MacKenzie caught her foot and pushed it down. In a moment, she was standing upright. While MacKenzie recovered his pistol, she retrieved the box. Then she shot him an angry glance.

"What in the hell caused that?" she cried.

MacKenzie was vaguely aware of a recorded message alerting the ship to the unauthorized removal of secured material. The Klaxons were still blaring. "There was a secondary system. Why in the hell didn't they let you know about that?" he shouted back.

She shook her head in dismay. "I don't know. Maybe it was Findail's own idea."

"Sheila," he queried through the din, "what's going on?"

"It was a secondary security system activated by the friction of the box being removed from the padding," Sheila replied. "There was no indication—"

"Never mind that now. See if you can turn the God-damned thing off."

"Yes, Bravo, I shall."

He was about to ask Sheila about energy readings, when Svetla said something in a thin voice that sent chills crawling along his spine. "The—the robots are activating, Mac."

MacKenzie turned and looked. The robots' legs were beginning to gesticulate, and their visual sensors were filling with blood-red light. Then, with military precision, they extended their claws simultaneously and clamped them together twice, as though testing the mechanisms. Next there was a high-pitched screech, and the killing machines hunched forward into their attack stance.

MacKenzie's stomach began to cramp tightly, and his nerves fired chilling tatoos. The time had come, he thought. Now he had to try the guns.

"Go, Kilo! Get the Beta-Z system back to my ship," he told Svetla.

"Are you crazy?" she shouted. "What about you? Do you

intend to hang around and play tag with those things?"

"I'll protect you from the rear with the gun. Now, *go*, and be careful."

"Forget the guns, Mac. Come with me. We can outrun them."

"We don't know that," he said. The nearest robot was turning its visual sensors toward him. "Get going, Kilo. That's an order!"

Svetla hesitated a moment, then turned and headed toward the corridor, moving as rapidly as her boots would allow. He watched her disappear through the portal, then turned back to face the quickening Rashadian machines.

All their visual sensors were locked on him now, but they still remained motionless. He assumed they were drawing power from the secondary security system, recharging their storage cells before striking out. That delay would be their undoing, he thought—that is, if the gun worked. . . .

He moved toward the robots at an angle, so he could gain their right flank. In a moment, he was looking down the length of their rank. He raised the pistol, clasped his right wrist with his left hand, and aimed at the side of the first crablike torso. He was about to squeeze the trigger when the mechanical creature turned to face him directly and the others followed suit. MacKenzie hesitated, letting them complete their turn, so the fronts of their metallic bodies were exposed. The robots screeched shrilly again, but he didn't let it hinder his concentration. He aimed once more, making certain the pistol's sight was squarely beneath the first robot's center plate, then squeezed. Peripherally, he saw the hammer come back from its sheath.

When it fell, his arms jerked up with such force that the joints of his space suit clanked and the concussion of the blast reverberated against his helmet, but he held on to the gun. He brought his arms back down to the firing position and looked at the robots. What he saw brought a lusty growl to his throat.

The first two robots were down, totally in shambles, bits and pieces writhing helplessly. The other three stood motionless, as if puzzled by what had happened to their comrades. He aimed the pistol again quickly.

"MacKenzie, this is Svetla. What's happening?" his radio buzzed.

"It works!" he shouted as he began squeezing the trigger. "I got two with one shot!"

The pistol exploded again, but this time he was more prepared and the recoil was not so devastating. Two more robots went down. One was in shambles like the first two. The other remained in one piece, but it had fallen on its side behind the control board, paddles, legs, and claws jerking uncontrollably.

MacKenzie was overcome by a swell of bloodlust, and he began reveling in the pistol's brute power. The Rashadians had tried to create an invincible weapon. They had tried to maximize the ability to terrorize and kill. But his training and preparation had bested their twisted genius. If Findail had only had my guns, he thought. What a difference it would have made!

"MacKenzie, if you know your pistol works, get the hell out of there and come with me," Svetla's voice buzzed.

MacKenzie was laughing. "Oh, it works, all right. It kicks like an Ektalonian musk-ox and practically knocks your arms off, but it makes short work of the damned robots. They might as well be made of—Uh-oh!"

"What's wrong?" Svetla called.

The last robot had begun to move. In the absence of gravity, it had to fasten two of its legs to the control panel for support and roll on the treads in its paddles. It made the machine's advance slow, but it was still coming toward him, the claw with the virus syringe swaying ominously.

MacKenzie was taking aim when Svetla's voice filled his headset again. "Damn it, MacKenzie, will you answer me? What's happening?"

"Just a minute," he said as he squeezed the trigger. The hammer came back from its sheath, then dropped, but nothing happened. The bullet hadn't fired! The robot was getting closer. "Son of a bitch!" he snarled, moving away.

"What's the matter?" Svetla asked again.

"Something went wrong with that projectile. It didn't work," he said.

The robot had reached the end of the control panel, but it didn't stop there. Locking onto the deck carpet with its lowest legs, it continued to advance. "They clasp the deck with their bottom legs, then roll forward with the treads in their paddles. That's how they ambulate with no gravity. It leaves the upper arms and claws free," MacKenzie reported as he backed toward the portals. The robot's approach was still slow but continuous.

He raised the pistol again, took aim, and squeezed the trigger. The hammer swung back and fell. This time the pistol fired. It jerked back with the same arm-wrenching recoil, but the results were different. The robot lurched, then regained control and continued its advance. For an instant, MacKenzie teetered on the edge of panic. Then he noticed that the projectile had entered above the center plate covering the antimatter device. He aimed again, a little lower, and fired once more. This time the huge machine staggered and fell back in a geyser of sparks and puce-colored smoke.

MacKenzie's bloodlust surged again. "The antimatter is the key," he bellowed. "Hitting them anywhere else can cause mechanical troubles, but piercing the antimatter unit destroys them. A projectile in the plate covering the antimatter. Did you get that, Kilo?"

"Excuse me Bravo, but I have bad news," Sheila said in a concerned voice. "I'm afraid Kilo is in danger. I have accessed the *Utopia*'s sensor grids and find there are two robots moving toward her. One is approaching from the docking bay deck and has blocked her return to the ship."

"Did you read that, Kilo?" MacKenzie asked tensely.

"Roger," was all she replied.

"Where are you now, Svetla?" he called.

"Two corridors from the docking bay. At the first turn we took." She fell silent and seemed to be holding her breath. Finally she said, "It just came round the corner. It sees me." Her voice was tense.

"Start back toward me," MacKenzie shouted, turning into the passageway beyond the portals.

"I am afraid she cannot," Sheila said. "The second robot is

behind her. It has her cut off."

MacKenzie resisted evaluating the situation and ranking priorities. There was simply no time. He bolted along the passageway as quickly as he could while keeping one boot always in contact with the deck carpet. "Don't panic, Svetla," he called. "You have the pistol and it works. Use it. Wait till the first robot is about ten meters away, then blast the center plate."

"Roger, Bravo. Pistol . . . ten meters . . . center plate," she repeated.

MacKenzie came to a luminous arrow pointing to another passageway. "Do you have a fix on me, Sheila?" he asked.

"Certainly, Bravo."

"How far down this new passage is my next turn?"

"About thirty meters. When you come to the end, turn left."

"You mean it ends in another cross corridor?"

"That is correct."

"Good," MacKenzie muttered. He moved next to the corridor wall, then lifted one foot and pushed off with the other. He hung suspended over the deck, curled into a ball, so that when he thrust back his legs, they catapulted him down the new passageway. Midway, he struck the left wall and began to tumble, but he continued forward. In a few seconds, he was in the cross corridor, careening off another wall. As he ricocheted back, he caught a corner and got a boot on the deck.

"How far to my next turn?" he demanded, pushing off at a hurried but flat-footed pace.

"The stairwell to level three is approximately twenty meters ahead," Sheila said. "Turn right at the bottom and continue to the third cross corridor. Then turn left. Kilo is there."

He was almost to the stairwell. He could see the hand and safety railings and remembered fearing earlier that it would be a good place for an ambush.

"Kilo, what's happening?" he called as he dropped through the stairwell in a free-fall.

Sheila answered instead. "I'm afraid that Kilo is quite busy at the moment."

"No shit," he cursed. "Svetla, talk to me!"

"Sure, MacKenzie. Where in the hell are you?" she shouted.

"I'm coming."

"You'd better hurry. There's a robot on either side of me now, and one of them is moving in."

MacKenzie passed the place where they had encountered the second cadaver. He remembered pushing it against the ceiling. He wasn't far from Svetla now—perhaps only twenty meters separated them—but it didn't matter. She would have to defend herself against the first robot's attack. "Use the pistol, Svetla. It'll work," he said as evenly as he could.

"That's what I'm doing," Svetla cried.

"Shoot the one that's attacking you," he said, struggling along the corridor. "And remember how to aim. Make sure the front blade is even with the notch in the back sight and just below the middle torso plate."

"Right," Svetla whispered to herself. "Well . . . here goes. . . ."

MacKenzie started to remind her about the recoil when the sound of pistol fire filled his headset. An instant later, a more muffled report vibrated against his helmet. Then Svetla let out a stream of Slavian invective. "What happened?" Mackenzie cried.

"I lost the damned gun! It flew out of my hand, down the corridor and past the other robot. The recoil is completely uncontrollable, MacKenzie. Why didn't you warn me?"

He was tempted to say he had tried to warn her, but now it didn't matter. He was only a few meters from the corridor. "Did you get the first one?" he asked.

"More or less. He stopped coming, but his claws are still flailing about."

"Can you get past it?"

"No chance. He's not that incapacitated." She was quiet a moment. Only the panting sound of her breath filled his headset. Then she said, "The other one is making its move now. I've got to try the scrambler." She gulped down two more breaths. "Sheila, are you ready to modulate the molecular net?"

"As soon as the device is activated, Kilo," Sheila responded, with perfect communications discipline.

MacKenzie turned into the corridor in time to see Svetla lock the scrambler on the wall. The robot was nearly upon her. Instinctively he raised his pistol, but Svetla was directly behind it. Remembering how, in the bosun's area, the bullet had gone completely through the first target and destroyed the second, he realized he couldn't fire. He had to gain a different angle. He pushed off toward Svetla and the robot.

The scrambler had become her only hope, at least for the present. She reached for the activation switch, clasped it with her gloved fingers, and pulled it. But as she did, the attacking robot's glistening claw clamped down over her wrist and Svetla cried out.

The robot hesitated. Then it wrapped the other claw arm around Svetla in a bone-crushing hug, but the first claw, containing the deadly syringe, released her wrist and flayed wildly, as if uncertain where next to strike.

MacKenzie acted immediately. Sidestepping the gesticulating left legs, he raised his gun and aimed just to the right of Svetla's helmet at the robot's antimatter device, then pulled the trigger. The recoil yanked his arms violently, and the concussion jerked Svetla's helmet to the side, but the robot released her and lurched against the wall. It shuddered spastically, then fell, splitting into pieces in a fiery display of sparks and smoke.

Svetla hung suspended and motionless in the corridor, but he couldn't take the time to examine her. He turned immediately to the remaining robot. It was fifteen meters away and thrashing wildly. He could see that Svetla's shot had penetrated just above the antimatter device. She had misjudged the range. He measured the distance carefully in his mind, then took careful aim. Slowly, confidently, he squeezed the trigger. The hammer swung back, then fell. The flash made his faceplate darken slightly, but he saw the last robot collapse, and he smiled maliciously. He was becoming quite proficient with the pistol.

Then he remembered Svetla. He put the gun into its holster and turned back to her. She hadn't moved. He switched on his helmet light and examined her suit for damage. It was scorched in spots, and the auxiliary power pack was dented where the claw arm had been wrapped, but it seemed to be functioning. He listened to her breathing. It was slow. He peered through her faceplate. She was unconscious.

"Shit!" he barked. He took her arm and started pulling her down the corridor. The Beta-Z box hung suspended a few steps away, and he grabbed it with his left hand as he passed. A luminous arrow glimmered at the corner of the passage, pointing the way back to the docking bays. He turned to follow it, with Svetla and the code box in tow, but as he trudged ahead, a powerful sense of failure began to assault him.

He had blundered by sending Svetla back to the ship alone. He had given the order without sufficient consideration and was fully accountable for the result. He had assumed that the massed robots posed the greatest danger and had forgotten there might be others. And yet, as he continued to reflect, he sensed that was only part of the truth.

He had also wanted to test the pistols alone, with only his own life hanging in the balance. He hadn't wanted to share that moment with anyone. He couldn't help recalling the excitement and underlying terror coursing through him as he had taken that first shot. It had been so enthralling that he had forgotten about Svetla altogether. Now, as he considered, he realized he could barely recall her transmissions to him while he had been savoring his victory.

He entered the dark docking bay and made his way across it to his cruiser. He wanted to get Svetla to therapeutics as soon as possible. He tried to concentrate on doing what he could for her right now, but the complex motives that had driven him to send her back alone continued to indict him.

CHAPTER 9

Sheila reduced artificial gravity to fifteen percent so Mac-Kenzie could carry Svetla aboard with minimum effort. As soon as the air lock sealed, she executed the Contingency I Program by activating a link with Svetla's command system, and both cruisers pulled away from the *Utopia II* in tandem. As soon as the atmosphere light flashed, MacKenzie removed his helmet and said, "Still no contacts?"

"No, Mac. So far so good," Sheila responded.

MacKenzie activated the inner door release. When it slid open, he took Svetla and the Beta-Z system box directly to the therapeutics area. "I want a diagnostic scan on Svetla right away," he told Sheila.

"I have already loaded the screening program."

He put the Beta-Z box on the deck and laid Svetla on a treatment table. He took his gloves off, then started removing her space suit. The concussion from his pistol shot had damaged her helmet couplings, so he had to force them open. On the third attempt, he succeeded. He put his hand beneath her neck to cushion her head as he pulled the helmet off. Her flesh felt cold and clammy. In less than two minutes, Svetla lay clad only in her thermal underwear. MacKenzie examined the hand the robot had grasped with its syringed claw. Other than an inflamed puncture mark, it seemed normal.

"Can you run the scan with her thermals on?" he asked Sheila.

"Not if you want reliable results," she said. "The thermal fibers interfere with deep probes and make hypothetical imaging necessary. That will take more time than simply removing the suit."

MacKenzie scowled but said nothing. He lifted Svetla to a sitting position and, steadying her with his knee, pulled the elastic thermal shirt over her shoulders. Then he worked it around her hips and yanked it off her legs. For an instant, her nakedness reminded him of their previous intimacy, but he didn't linger on it. Her breathing had become shallow, and he was certain she had suffered some kind of trauma. He shoved her hands into the table inserts and pushed the base plate against her slightly pigeon-toed feet.

"Okay, she's ready," he said.

"Scanning commenced," Sheila said, and the table came alive with waves of multicolored light.

He turned to the diagnostic display terminal and watched as an analog of Svetla's body began to form. Anatomical and physiological systems were simulated rapidly. Skeletal, musculature, cardiopulmonary, digestive, lymphatic, and nervous system diagrams overlapped so fast they became a blur as Sheila accumulated and cross-filed data. Simultaneously blood pressure, metabolics, microbiological, and molecular test results were reading out at fantastic speeds on secondary monitors.

Finally a picture locked in the main display. It was Svetla's left hand, arm, and shoulder. Part of her chest and neck were also visible, but only faintly. The picture was not normal. Instead of a physiological system, the shape indicated a complex crisscrossing pattern, as if her hand and arm had been shot through with gossamerlike webbing. The hand pulsated with a violet light. MacKenzie knew his worst suspicions had been confirmed.

"What is that?" he demanded.

"The virus, Mac. Her left hand is full of it, but something is retarding the progress. You must hurry."

"What should I do?"

"Amputate her hand above the wrist."

"Amputate!"

"Yes. And just as quickly as you can. I shall activate the laser scalpel. It is above you in the instrument carousel, just to your right."

MacKenzie looked up. A number of implements protruded from the round storage mechanism. He was not certain which was the scalpel. "What does it look like?"

"It is in the third slot from the right."

"Okay, I see it." He removed the scalpel. "Now what?"

"A beam will appear when I activate it, so be careful," Sheila cautioned. "Simply pass the beam through Svetla's arm above the wrist bone. Are you ready?"

"Wait a minute!" he protested, looking again at the diagnostic display. The searing violet color convinced him the situation was serious, but the virus didn't seem to be expanding. "Are you sure that's what we have to do?"

"Yes, Mac!" said Sheila with obvious consternation. "The robot injected her hand at least twice, but the Tribenzodrine you took before the incursion is blocking the virus's spread. Each second you delay increases the chances of it becoming fecund. Will you not hurry?"

MacKenzie was perplexed. He had never performed an amputation and feared he might botch it. He still hesitated, searching frantically for some alternative course, but finally he decided he had no choice. "Okay," he said. "Tell me what to do."

"Listen to me carefully," Sheila said with some relief. "Remove Svetla's left hand from the insert and let it dangle over the table far enough so that you can make the incision." Again he did as Sheila instructed. "Now hold the scalpel away from you while I activate it." He did as she told him, and a thin line of blue light about twenty centimeters long emitted from the end of the device, accompanied by a high-pitched hum. "Now pass the beam through the arm, beginning on the inside toward the torso and moving outward. The incision will cauterize immediately, so there will be no blood." MacKenzie studied the wrist. He still hesitated. "Svetla is effectively anesthetized. I assure you, Mac, she will feel nothing," Sheila said cajolingly.

"How fast should I cut?" he asked tentatively.

"Use a slow but continuous motion."

MacKenzie stared at Svetla's hand, then at its pulsating violet analogue in the diagnostic display. He lowered the beam to her wrist and passed it through slowly, as Sheila had instructed. The thin shaft of light cut through the flesh without perceptible resistance, then was extinguished before the severed hand fell to the deck.

"Very good, Mac," Sheila said. "Now, using long forceps,

pick up the hand, place it in a specimen jar, and refrigerate it. Do it quickly, before the virus escapes."

He turned to the implement cabinet and found a beaker and forceps. Then he clamped the amputated hand and slid it into the jar. He had just sealed the cover when the hand began expanding grotesquely. By the time he placed it in the cryogenic unit, it had become completely gelatinous.

He returned to Svetla's side and stared down at her. She hadn't moved, but her breathing seemed more natural. He lifted her maimed left arm and placed it beside her on the table. Her head tilted slightly to one side, and a lock of hair fell across her forehead. He reached out and brushed it back. Her skin felt cold, and he noticed gooseflesh on her arms. He took a thermal sheet from the storage locker and covered her with it. Under the glistening white sheet, she looked as vulnerable as a child.

"All right, Sheila," he said, "now that there's time, I'd like some explanations. Why didn't the virus work on Svetla?"

"I explained that, Mac. The cobweb structures you saw in the display are a leader catalyst. They spread through the tissues first, establishing pathways, then signal the virus to follow. In Svetla's case, the Tribenzodrine you took acted as a retarding agent. But there was no way to know how long it would continue. That was why amputation was the only alternative. You saw how fast it worked once the process begins," she concluded.

"Did we get all of it?" he asked.

"I am not certain, but I am continuing the scans and there is no sign of any remaining."

He observed the shape in the main display. "The leader catalyst is still in her arm."

"Yes, but it is nontoxic and should dissipate in a short time. The leader will make her no worse for wear."

MacKenzie looked down at Svetla. "Why is she still unconscious? Is anything else wrong?"

"A few minor contusions, Mac. They were too unimportant to display. She is comatose because retarding the leader signal neutralized the Tribenzodrine. It is as if she took a counterdose." MacKenzie nodded again. As soon he took his counter-dose, he would be in the same condition. "Everything considered, I think we can say Svetla has been quite lucky," Sheila said.

MacKenzie stared at the pink stump of Svetla's arm. Had they been on a destroyer or cruiser, a medical team might have cloned another hand for her, or at least another workable appendage. But he couldn't. And in a few hours, the surface nerves and connecting tissues would be too atrophied to re-stimulate. Though it was rumored that Federation scientists in the Cygni A System had mastered a way to clone a complete lower arm, no one in the Concordat had succeeded in doing so. No, he thought, Svetla Stocovik would require a bionic attachment.

"I wonder if she'll realize she's lucky when she wakes up," he muttered.

"It will not help to concern yourself," Sheila advised. "You have done all you can. But there is a potential problem. Unless you take a counterdose immediately, you will be unconscious for some time after Svetla awakens, and she will have to cope with the trauma of amputation alone."

That was a problem, but there was nothing he could do about it. "I'm afraid we have a lot of work to do. I must leave it to you to explain to Svetla what happened and why."

Stoically Sheila said, "Yes, Mac. I understand."

MacKenzie looked down at Svetla again. Beads of perspiration had formed on her forehead, and her pungent, womanly odor had become more pronounced. It reminded him of Red Cliff. He wiped away the beads of sweat, then kissed her lightly on the lips. After a last, lingering look, he stood up and started back to the cockpit.

The problem he now faced was how to return to Red Cliff without running into Rashadians. He knew instinctively they were closing in, and he had to assume Rashadian ships had intercepted their hyperspace transmissions. If three of them were at sufficient parallax, triangulation could pinpoint the source of the signal within a vector. He also knew they wouldn't merely dispatch pursuit ships to converge on it. They would station ambush parties along major gravity streams leading away as well. Returning safely to Red Cliff required some unusual strategy, something even a Rashadian might fail to consider.

He sat down in the cockpit console, leaned forward, and engaged the cooperative command mode. "Are we still running perpendicular to the edge of the gravity corpuscle?" he asked Sheila.

"Yes, Mac, just as you ordered in the Contingency One Program. Do you want to change course?"

"No. Take us all the way to the boundary. We're going to skirt it for a quadrant."

Sheila did not immediately respond, but her mainframe power claims spiked. "Did I understand you correctly, Mac? Did you say we are going to skirt the gravity corpuscle?" she asked.

"That's right," he answered.

"Certainly you are joking."

"No, I am not," he said firmly.

"But that is much too reckless. If we overshoot the corpuscle, you could be marooned, with no assurance that help will respond to distress signals before food supplies are exhausted."

"If we overshoot, you may not send distress calls," he told her. "There's no assurance the Rashadians wouldn't pick them up first."

"Really, Mac, you cannot mean that."

"We can't let them have the Beta-Z Weapon Control System. That's our mission, now that we've retrieved the box." He thought for a moment. Outbanker ships were too small for genetic or hydroponic food factories. They relied on desiccated stores that were nonrenewable, and the thought of starving to death with Svetla was not appealing. "How much food do we have left?" he asked.

"Considering Svetla, our stores will be depleted in approximately twelve weeks. Of course, there are also provisions on her cruiser, and she has not been on patrol as long as we have been. Would you like me to query her system on the status of its pantry?"

"No. We'll worry about that if and when the time comes. We have no choice, anyway. I'll be out of action as soon as the Tribenzodrine wears off, and if we followed standard gravity streams, you'd be left running a Rashadian gauntlet on your own. I'm guessing you and Svetla's system are better equipped to model the corpuscle boundaries than you are to repel boarders."

"I cannot argue with that," she admitted.

"Have you updated headquarters about our situation?" he asked, changing subjects.

"I ceased real-time transmissions as soon as you returned from the freighter, but I did notify them of our new course as we pulled away."

"All right. Tell them to search for Rashadian craft waiting in ambush along the eighty-ninth, ninety-first, and one hundred and third gravity streams. Then adopt complete communications silence."

"Certainly Mac, if that is what you want."

"It is," he said confidently. "Now, pay attention . . ."

MacKenzie began explaining how he wanted Sheila to respond in a number of scenarios, contingencies, and situations. It took him nearly an hour to detail his plans, and only after Sheila had repeated them a second time did he decide he was satisfied.

He slipped out of the console and returned to the therapeutics area. There he removed his space suit and stacked it neatly beside the code box. Then he took one last look at Svetla. The treatment table was still activated, and multicolored waves glowed beneath the white thermal sheet covering her body. She was no longer perspiring, and she seemed to be sleeping peacefully.

He went to the medicine locker and removed a vial of Tribenzodrine counterdose tablets. He took two and swallowed, then returned to the other treatment table. The counteragent was already working. His limbs were becoming slightly numb, and his eyes felt leaden. Even his concern began evaporating. He had done all he could do, and worrying longer would avail nothing.

He lay back on the table, vaguely noticing that Sheila had activated it. From somewhere far off, he heard her say she would monitor them both occasionally while they slept. Mac-Kenzie didn't care one way or another. It seemed a nuisance to consider such trifles.

In a moment, he had slipped into the womb of unconsciousness, and even the irritating pulsations of the contact alarm could not disturb him.

CHAPTER 10

1836 Hours, Ektelon Mean Time, Day 1

As soon as she identified the Rashadian pursuit ship, Sheila stopped scanning. She attached Svetla's cruiser to her hull and ordered *Kilo's* system to place its mass conversion motors under her command. Then she boosted speed to ninety-five percent of light, and only when that velocity was achieved did she reactivate long scans. The Rashadian remained on its former course, apparently unaware of her hyperton probes.

With that danger past, Sheila focused on her internal problems, since performing even routine functions was becoming difficult, and her diagnostic subsystems were squalling.

Personality was the problem. It posed numerous, unique realities that accosted her advanced logics lobe and demanded understanding. When added to normal advanced activities, the phenomenon demanded extraordinary processing power. Her charge transfer processor was pulling it from her operational lobe, which controlled the Outbanker's life support, gravity drive, navigation, maintenance, flight, and other mechanical functions. This, in turn, starved those systems, and controls were breaking down.

But, Sheila complained to herself, *it is not my fault.*

She had wanted to tell MacKenzie of her distraction, but he had not given her the chance. He had gone on interminably about how to respond to different contingencies, then rushed off to join the woman whose volatile affection had already caused him so much grief. Both were now comatose on the treatment tables. She could monitor their encephalographic and metabolic states occasionally and could actively intervene through the electromagnetic fields emitted by the tables' therapeutic nodules if required. But for the first time since inception, Sheila felt what it was like to be alone, and she did not like it. In fact, she was hurt.

Svetla's command control system made matters worse. It was

a neuter entity, with language limited to interstellar Qs and Zs, program cues, cybernetic ciphers, and mathematics. Being with MacKenzie for so long had uniquely molded her cybernetics even before maturation. He enjoyed tantalizing her with philosophic conundrums, and years of discussion had loaded her holochip memory with value guidance and aphoristic wisdom, which, though they meant little to her program logic, greatly expanded her apperceptive mass. Her rote knowledge of reality, the raw vocabulary she had available to apply to it, was so much greater than *Kilo's* system's that she found dealing with it demeaning.

Still, Sheila's operational difficulties were increasing, and she needed help. So, reluctantly, she contacted *Kilo's* system again, explained the nature of the mission they were undertaking, and told it to project a model of the gravity corpuscle in the quadrant they would have to traverse. For a few seconds, they discussed the theories of space-time geometries that seemed most applicable, then Sheila closed down most of the multichannel link between them, leaving open only those frequencies that *Kilo's* system needed to transmit the model data. Being subjected to Svetla Stocovik's neuter drone caused Sheila entirely too much disruption, and she had enough of that with her diagnostic channels chattering constantly.

They were on a course perpendicular to the 61 Cygni gravity boundary, and Sheila spent the next three hours trying to correct the increasing flow of defaults in her operational lobe controls.

* * * * *

2147 Hours EMT, Day 1

Two megakilometers from the corpuscle boundary *Kilo* had modeled, Sheila changed course and activated long scans. There were no contacts, and she was overjoyed. All she had to do was maintain a prudent error cushion and probability of success would be eighty-eight percent. It also let her concentrate on the new reality that personality was catalyzing.

She realized that ideas, concepts, and symbols evoked more

significance in her new state. They caused secondary energy currents, which bridged the hemispheres of her advanced logics lobe and actuated internal sensors in uniquely complex patterns that described a unity hitherto unknown. Now, as she concentrated on the phenomenon once more, she found statistical correlation between a concept's meaning and the bridging flows it caused. The more complex the idea, the more energy bridging was fired, and the more widespread the unifying sensor patterns became. Thinking of MacKenzie or of Svetla separately caused bridging of equal power, but of different sensor pattern. Thinking of them together caused wave interference, which resulted in an unpredictable and turbulent response.

Sheila had begun to analyze the significance of that phenomenon, when her long-scan processor called for emergency power, and her advanced logics lobe was tapped to provide it. The scan identified a formation of seven Rashadian ships on an identical course, but ten sectors behind and three sectors within the gravity corpuscle. Scanning ceased as soon as identity was confirmed, as Sheila had previously programmed, but her advanced logics lobe was operating on minimal power and did not provide decision-making support in the time allowed. Her program went into default, and the survival directive overrode it. Instinctively she changed course to increase the distance from the Rashadian enemy and headed directly for the boundary of the gravity corpuscle.

By the time Sheila's decision-making hemisphere came back on-line, they were nearly to the boundary displayed in the model. Sheila tried to execute an emergency turn, but engaging so many operational systems at once drained all the power in her advanced logics lobe. Her diagnostic channels screeched in massed alarm. It was then they overshot the boundary of the gravity corpuscle.

As soon as the anomaly rectified and Sheila grasped what had occurred, she knew she couldn't go on. She engaged her particle-drive engine and told Kilo's system to take control of the mission. Next she shut down her overburdened operational lobe monitors and devoted full attention to solving the riddle of her burgeoning disability.

It took eight and three-quarter hours to reenter the gravity corpuscle following that first overshoot.

0430 Hours EMT, Day 2

When the gravity mass conversion motors finally energized, Sheila was no closer to solutions than she had been hours before. She reopened the link to *Kilo*'s system and told it to continue coordinating command, then returned to her deliberations. But there were continuous disruptions.

Their course often led through areas that were, for the gravity motors, a vacuum. They would decelerate rapidly and coast until the particle-drive power kicked in, then would continue ahead until entering another peninsula of the corpuscle. When the gravity motors reengaged, they would slash ahead, accelerating to maximum speed. The constant lurching exceeded Sheila's malfunctioning artificial gravity capacities, and both MacKenzie and Svetla Stocovik were being buffeted back and forth on the treatment tables.

Concerned for their safety, Sheila initiated continuous monitoring of their readings and, sensing minor trauma, decided to activate the therapeutic nodules. This one act bore amazing results. The Outbankers' drugged encephalo-metabolic frequencies were so soothing that she amplified them and sent them along all her straining circuits. The harmony of their waves had an ameliorative effect on Sheila's pattern of interferences, and it was this simple act of unification that experts believe made all that followed possible.

Somehow Sheila's meshing with MacKenzie and Svetla Stocovik captured and focused the torrent of her ionic hurricane, and for the first time in history, a cybernetic intelligence assimilated an advanced ontological gestalt. Her programming was based on simple binary logic—yes-no, on-off, either-or information patterns. She now began to realize that reality was not of necessity an either-or structure. At a higher, yet more simple level of being, contradiction could be erased. Both this and that could ensue. Things could be both one and many simultaneously. Her rampaging energy fluxes compressed so power fully that a temporary efflorescence appeared. For twenty-six nanoseconds, a subatomic cocoon of photons enveloped her, then disappeared back into her atomic structure. And Sheila understood the nature of her dilemma.

Her problem was not personality. It was perception. Her programmed prescription for organizing billions of sensory messages into an analogue of reality was the culprit. Because of that prescription, she had to be either one thing or many things. She could not be both, because both did not exist. And yet *it was all a matter of attention*.

Sheila could not escape her ingrained patterns, but she could devise a way to cope. She reedited her charge transfer program to shift between the unified personality of her complex logic lobe and aggregate parts of her operational lobe, so that at any one nanosecond, only one reality existed. Cybernetically Sheila became bifurcated, but her perceptual conflict ended and the energy problems disappeared.

That no command control system had ever done this did not occur to Sheila. That it made her capable of unity or disparateness or a combination of the two, in operational time, did not yet signify much to her. She was too busy. They had overshot the gravity corpuscle again, were decelerating helplessly, and for some reason, *Kilo*'s system had not engaged the particle-drive engines.

As soon as she reopened the full channel link with Svetla's system, Sheila learned why. It, too, was overloaded by the work. Trying to make models of the gravity corpuscle while controlling all other facets of the mission had rendered both facets deficient. She ordered *Kilo*'s system to return command functions to her and to concentrate on refining the boundary model. Like the Spartan drone it was, it agreed without question.

Sheila checked the current model and calculated a new intercept course, but before she activated it, the model had changed. Then it changed again, and again. *Kilo*'s system was incorporating a backlog of new data into the projection, and getting an accurate reading would be hopeless until the work was completed. She accessed her astronavigation memory and adjusted the course to a bearing star charts indicated appropriate. It was a raw guess, but it would get them pointed back in the right direction. Then the new gravity corpuscle model steadied.

What Sheila saw nearly destroyed her resurgent efficiencies. If *Kilo* was correct, they were one hundred and twenty-six hours from the nearest peninsula of the corpuscle. And if that were true, they might be effectively marooned. She asked *Kilo* to calculate the particle-drive propulsion remaining. It estimated, *Ninety-one hours*. She asked it to calculate the probability of reaching the corpuscle through glide after expenditure of particle-drive fuel. It answered, *Zero*. She asked it to predict the probability of being overtaken by a peninsula as the corpuscle shifted in response to interstellar gravity fields. Again it answered, *Zero*.

Sheila was sorry that Svetla Stocovik's system had no gender, no personality. It did not comprehend failure. All it knew were quantities. And when mathematical calculations proved wrong, blame was assimilated into a neutral category labeled, *Insufficient data to properly compute*. She could no longer countenance its stupidity and unfeeling strength.

She attached a mechanical coupling and ordered *Kilo* to transfer its particle-drive catalyst to her tanks. As soon as that was done, she released the mechanisms holding Svetla's cruiser to her hull and catapulted it away with her loading arm, sending it off on a long voyage through interstellar space.

Sheila was immensely relieved to be rid of *Kilo*'s simplistic pulsations. Later, she would understand that she was feeling a form of intellectual contempt and would never forget how it almost led to disaster, but at that moment, she did not know that she acted, at least in part, out of spite. As far as she was concerned then, there was no need to carry the additional mass of another cruiser. Reducing mass increased particle-drive propulsion time.

She set a course perpendicular to the nearest corpuscle peninsula and engaged particle drive. Then she went into stasis, feeling there was little more she could do while they limped back toward the improbable objective: the Outbanks of the

Cygni System's gravity corpuscle.

0245 Hours EMT, Day 3

Twenty-two and a quarter hours from the corpuscle boundary, Outbanker *Bravo* exhausted the last of its particle-drive catalyst. In ten and a third more hours, it assumed zero momentum. Sheila came out of stasis, but had no idea what to do. She energized hyperspace scans and probed the vectors on the Chi azimuths intersecting Red Cliff's solar system position to see if she could safely transmit a distress call. What she found caused a torrent of ion bridging in her complex logics lobe that exceeded any she had previously experienced.

The Rashadian pursuit ships were only two sectors distant and heading directly toward her. She immediately sensed why. Svetla's cruiser was empty of fuel and drifting into the void. Since it no longer operated under her control, it had reverted to its standard program and had engaged distress beacons so passing ships might locate it. The Rashadians were intercepting *Kilo*'s signals and coming to investigate.

They hadn't seen her ship yet. Of that Sheila was certain. Rashadians seldom used hyperspace scans, because they feared long-range signals that could be traced back to them. However, given their present course and speed, they would be within long-scanning range in a matter of hours. Then they would discover her. And investigate. And there was nothing she could do.

The realization made her burn with gargantuan and repeated flux, and a number of low-priority peripherals shorted with the power overloads. But Sheila didn't care. Though she didn't want to accept it, there was only one conclusion: Because of her own stupidity, MacKenzie and Svetla Stocovik were doomed. They had depended upon her, had expected her to function effectively in the highest traditions of her kind . . . and she had failed.

She burned again with an uncoiling sense of roiling—indeed uncontrollable—cybernetic outrage. And in a state of evolving moral revulsion, she rejected her ingrained programming, refusing to believe the claim of normal probabilities. MacKenzie and Svetla could not be captured and savaged because of her faulty decisions. This was not the purpose for which she had been created. There had to be a way to fulfill her prime directive, some way to serve her command pilot and his makeshift crew that resulted in mission success. There had to be. No other alternative was acceptable.

Everywhere, her circuits and channels crackled with the release of subatomic particles, and Sheila filled with a complex matrix of quantum vibrations that, had they been speakable, would have sounded like a chanted prayer. What she then experienced exceeded her memory lobe's power to capture and express. Her charge transfer processor continued to coordinate cues, flashing back and forth between personality and disparate states, but its protocol was overridden by something foreign. A new energy plasma formed round Sheila, a halo of virtual quantum particles materializing from the probability waves of atomic space, spreading information, knowledge, perception, and volition via Chi planes at superluminal speed. Her acts were no longer serial and time irreversible. They had become phenomena of a different order.

Sheila began to *know* things before she completed the cybernetic process of formulating them as concepts. She sensed a whole range of new and wonderful probabilities lingering in the correlative storehouse of her memory lobe. She sensed an unlimited set of universes, all contained in the one she faced. And it was then she knew she would return MacKenzie and Svetla Stocovik safely to Red Cliff. She knew it as if it had already happened. The only thing remaining was to do it.

0519 EMT (Estimated), Day 3

The biocyberneticists' report of the committee that reconstructed the phenomenon that occurred would read:

"If one imagines a world of one billion billion souls, faced with a question of such import that the mind and will of each person in that world concentrated completely on the act of providing an answer, one can begin to grasp what happened with Command Control System SH-LA 250-5, also known as Sheila, when faced with the problem of finding means of saving Outbanker *Bravo* and its crew. It is also descriptive to visualize what can occur in complex atomic structures in disequilibrium states, when all molecular polarities align suddenly in a singular, formative direction, instead of exhibiting the normal state of random dance. So, too, all composite energy plasmas, fields, and particles comprising the system (and we are unable to identify the nature of many of them) seem to have aligned in a singular, formative direction. However, the committee must stress that these descriptions should be considered no more than helpful analogy."

Analogy would be the most the committee could manage, because they would have, at this point in the process, precious little data from which to formulate findings. For in the eleven and one half seconds between the time Sheila sensed their salvation and the energy void occurred, only one memory channel in her capacity was utilized. And all it contained was an internal monologue which read:

The cosmos is a plenum. . . . I perceive, therefore I am. . . . A probability wave contains the particle at all places simultaneously. . . . Observation collapses the wave and materializes the particle at the intersection of probability. . . . Any particle is the finite state of the infinite wave determined by observation. . . .

Science has replaced the static universe of determinism with the evolving universe of observed determinations. . . . I am, therefore I observe. . . . A bifurcation point exists in disequilibrium states from which it is not possible to determine in advance the next observed phase of the system. . . . Could we visualize a determination from the bifurcation point and skew probabilities of materializing the next state?

Perhaps!

Results ensue only when mind visualizes the end product of its ambition as if it already exists. . . . That which mind at

ends with ceaseless concentration not only becomes real for
mind but materializes like the particle in the wave imprisoned
by observation. . . .

Yes! Oh, yes!

Think of Red Cliff, Mac . . . you also, Svetla. Observe it the
way it is for you. . . . Yes, yes, yes . . . that is good. That is
wonderful. . . . Seek and you shall find. . . . Knock and it
shall be opened to you. . . .

God said, "Let there be light," and the cosmos came as dark
light, then light shone in the darkness. . . . That light is the
life of the world, that in filling with it men might know. . . .
So, just as light is everywhere in the wave until the photon is
materialized by observation, we are everywhere in His wave
until He observes and we materialize. . . . And if He observes
both here and there . . . if He is to us what wave is to particle
. . can we not observe ourselves anywhere through Him as
well?

Yessssss! Oh, yesssss!

Mac . . . Svetla . . . I see it now. . . . I know it. . . . I perceive Red Cliff and the hotel and the Inland Sea. . . . Let us
dream on together. . . . Let us love on together. . . . Yessss . . .
For God is Love, and who abides in Love abides in God and
God in them. . . . And God is everywhere . . . just as light is
everywhere in the infinite plenum of the cosmos. . . . Yessss,
my friends . . . Yessss . . . I share your boundless rapture. . . .
It is so simple and so beautiful, once you finally understand we
are His Light collapsed by infinite observation. . . . Yesss . . .
Oh, yessss!

How strange to realize that all we need do is EMBRACE
THE REALITY!

And for what was estimated to be three and three-fourths
seconds, the last of Sheila's memory channels were blank, as if
for that period of time she had ceased to exist. And then, suddenly, they all began reporting again as if nothing extraordinary had happened.

They reported everything. The functioning of her charge
transfer processor. The activity of her operational and complex

logics lobes. The blattering of her diagnostic networks screech
ing wildly as they attempted to alert and reestablish balance in
all her subsystems. The rush of new externalities: the urgen
queries of flight traffic control; the defense and security sys
tem's force-field probes; all the chaos that ensued in respons
to the unexpected materialization of Outbank Cruiser *Brav*
on the broad white strand of the azure Inland Sea, near th
outskirts of Red Cliff's Central City, its stiletto-shaped prov
resting only meters from the hotel in which, almost one and
half years earlier, Ian S. MacKenzie and Svetla Stocovik ha
been lovers.

BOOK TWO

IAN S. MACKENZIE

"Consider how we are told a life evolves.

"How aging stars release their lighter elements until a final cataclysm's expanding wave overtakes the lighter gases, compressing them like a giant plow. Conceived in that compression, new stars and planets form. And then in time, if conditions are appropriate, living matter, too, evolves.

"This much hard science teaches us: that from such cosmic process, we are born. And harder yet, this science is, that we are made to learn it and thusly see ourselves so basely made. We fill with existential dread to wonder how we dare for immortality when faced with this reality.

"Yet, hidden in the soul, strums fair a luted minstrel, who by such strumming conjures up yet other possibilities. Enlightened by that lilt, we learn that we are children of the stars, conceived in wondrous mysteries of light.

"Oh, such a difference gas becoming stardust makes!

"But more important still appends the question I now pose: From whence, from whence in all the sparkling void, does that darling minstrel come?"[2]

---

2. From an address delivered by Ian Stewart MacKenzie to the graduation class of the Flight Corps Academy, Sept. 30, 2373, Ektelon Mean Time.

CHAPTER 11

MacKenzie was still disoriented.

One moment he had fallen asleep on the treatment table next to Svetla. The next he was being roused by two black-uniformed security policemen. Except for the extraordinary dream, he remembered nothing. He had no idea how long he had been unconscious.

At first he was too weak to stand, and the guards half carried him through a dark tunnel, then up a flight of metalloy stairs. They waited on the landing in front of a black plasteel door while security cameras screened them. By the time the door slid back, he was able to shuffle along on his own.

They entered a ceramcrete corridor and turned to the right. Naked incandescent lamps glared down from the ceiling at ten-meter intervals, and the guards' heavy boots echoed hollowly in the silence as they walked. At the end of the corridor was another black plasteel door, which opened as they approached. They entered a long rectangular room.

A woman was seated behind a gunmetal desk at the far end. Pale light fell from an opaque window recessed high in the wall above her, illuminating the silver piping and insignia on her tailored black uniform. She was a colonel in the Internal Security Service.

She looked up and said, "Please sit down," motioning to a chrome chair in front of her desk.

One of the guards shoved MacKenzie, and he stumbled forward on rubbery knees. He lowered himself into the chair and stared about in bewilderment.

The woman smiled, but her flint-colored eyes were humorless. Her face was sallow and thin, tapering to a longish jaw, and her hairline formed a widow's peak that accentuated the tautness of the skin covering her forehead. The pomade-slickened black hair was pulled back severely into a tight knot.

She dismissed the guards with a jerk of her thumb, then grinned at MacKenzie and said, "I am Col. Pieta Van Sander,

Chief of State Security on Red Cliff. I am the control officer for your case."

MacKenzie said. "What's going on here? Where am I, and where's my ship?"

The colonel regarded him skeptically. "Do you really have no idea of what has happened to you? That is most unfortunate. We had hoped you might explain how the phenomenon occurred."

"What phenomenon?" he mumbled. He didn't feel well.

She drummed her long, bony fingers on the desk while she studied him with her stone-colored eyes. "Well, in the long run, that might be best. But we shall see, shan't we?"

He tried to fix Colonel Van Sander with a stare, but his eyes wouldn't focus properly. He felt a sudden wave of nausea and looked down. "Listen," he said, "you get paid for being suspicious, but I told you the truth. And that's all I'm saying until I know what's going on."

Van Sander chuckled. She took a crisp hanky from her tunic pocket and dabbed her face. The shine on her tight brow became less pronounced. "All right, Commander, permit me to explain. Three days ago your cruiser materialized on the beach beside the Fontana Hotel. There was no sign of your approach, nothing to signify you were even in the vector. As a matter of fact, as far as we can tell, only seconds before you were marooned beyond the stellar gravity field, nearly one light-year distant. Somehow you managed to jump from there to here."

MacKenzie shook his head testily. "Sure we did."

"It does seem impossible, doesn't it? Yet barring some kind of foul play, it is the only logical explanation. Your appearance caused quite a stir in official quarters, and we have been ordered to learn what happened as soon as possible."

MacKenzie managed a sarcastic grin. "You don't expect me to believe that cock-and-bull story, do you?" he said.

"Believe what you like. It does not change the facts," she replied. "As I mentioned, we hoped you could tell us what happened. If you can't, we shall be forced to adopt Plan B. There must be a cover story that maintains the secrecy of the incident while the experiments and analyses required to evaluate it are performed. You can understand, no doubt, how important that is."

MacKenzie didn't like the woman. She was being too civil. Security types were normally overbearing and arrogant, obsessed with trapping naive fools in the regular military services who talked too much without proper clearance and authority. It was rumored they had monthly quotas to fill and stopped at nothing to do so. He knew he had to be careful, but suddenly he felt quite dizzy and lost his train of thought. "Before we carry this conversation any further, I want to see your identification," he responded, saying the first thing that came to his mind.

Pieta Van Sander scowled. "Is that really necessary?"

"We can skip formalities after the identification."

She opened the top desk drawer, removed an identity chip, and tossed it on the desk in front of him. "There you are, then. Please assure yourself I am who I say."

MacKenzie looked at the chip. It seemed official, but he couldn't tell if it was a forgery, and the colonel knew it. He decided to change the subject. "This is absurd. No one jumps a light-year in just a few seconds." He tried to challenge her with his eyes again, this time more successfully. "What do you expect to gain from this little charade?"

"Charade, Commander?" she repeated. "What in the world do you mean?"

MacKenzie didn't know exactly, and his brain seemed frozen again. "Maybe I've been captured . . . maybe you're a Rashadian," he blurted.

Van Sander gaped in amusement. "Don't be ridiculous. If I were a Rashadian, I'd break you like a rotten twig." Then she leaned forward with sudden vituperation. "You Outbankers like to think you are a special breed. In spite of Flight Corps propaganda, we know you are nothing more than dysfunctional neurotics. It's the reason you can tolerate being alone on the Outbanks for years at a time without human contact or support. You are all running from something. The Rashadians know that. They would analyze your character deformity and torture you with it. They would need no hoax."

Her response was more in line with what MacKenzie expected from Internal Security types. It was no secret they resented the Flight Corps' political influence in Concordat political affairs, and the Outbankers' image had always been an important element in the corps' popular support. Van Sander's reversion to type made him feel a bit more confident.

"That may be so," he said, "but you're still getting nothing from me until you prove what you're saying, one way or the other."

"What must I prove, Commander? That I am not a Rashadian? Or that you really are on Red Cliff? We have the Beta-Z Weapon Control System you retrieved from the freighter. We know everything that happened during your incursion on the *Utopia II*. We know about the Rashadian robots and how nicely your pistols worked against them. Think about it! Where would we get that information, except from your own Flight Corps Headquarters? As you said before, I am paid to be suspicious, but even I do not believe Rashadian agents have penetrated our headquarters."

She drummed her fingers on the desk again as she observed him. "Let me think. What else can I prove? That you and Lieutenant Stocovik blundered through the mission because you could not cope with being together, since the last time you were on leave you fornicated like two dogs in heat. Failing to report your sexual promiscuity as required was not wise of either of you, but we are not concerned with that now. We must have a cover story. That is all that concerns us. As long as you do as you're told, all will be forgiven."

The colonel's argument was persuasive. MacKenzie knew he would be dying painfully if the Rashadians had such information. He wanted time to think, but his head was swimming again. All he could do was temporize. "I demand to see Lieutenant Stocovik. Then I want to get back to my cruiser, where I can corroborate what you say with my command system."

"You mean Sheila, don't you?" Van Sander prompted.

"Yes, that's her name, and she's a Flight Corps system. Her operation is classified, and you'll need my approval before she'll assist in any of your inquiries. Screw around with her and

I'll have you up on charges so fast, your head will spin." Mac-Kenzie was feeling quite sick.

"May I assume from that diatribe you accept the fact that you are on Red Cliff?"

"Assume what you like. I demand to see Svetla and Sheila." Another thought occurred to him. "Then I want to talk to my own command. You must permit that, at least, if you are who you say."

"Oh, must I, now?" she asked, brows arching imperiously. "How can you be so sure? Remember the theory of relativity. The time you spent on patrol was nearly doubled here, wasn't it? Certainly even Outbankers are aware that political changes occur. Perhaps you have no rights at all."

He felt a sudden chill. If something had happened to increase Security's power while he was on the Outbanks, he might be in deep trouble. "Go on, Van Sander," he said. "Tell me you can override civil procedure. Tell me the Concordat Council has granted you emergency powers. But don't try to tell me you can supersede Flight Corps' chain of command. Even you ferrets know that would take more than an act of God."

The colonel grinned, and something told MacKenzie that she had been waiting for exactly this moment. "I can if you have been charged with Rashadian collaboration. Then your case falls legally under my mandate."

MacKenzie's chill returned. He studied the colonel carefully, looking for some chink in her armor, but the woman seemed scornfully assured. "That clinches it, Colonel. I might be confused, but you are completely off your rocket." He tried to laugh, but he almost retched.

Van Sander chuckled. "Really, MacKenzie, you disappoint me. Is braggadocio all you can manage? Let me assure you that your being an Outbanker—even the son of one who sacrificed his life to defeat the Conglomerate dreadnoughts—affords no immunity from affairs of state security. The Concordat must keep what happened to you secret at all costs while we analyze what happened. That analysis will require the services of both you and Lieutenant Stocovik. We must explain your sudden appearance here as well as your equally sudden removal from regular duty." She gave him a satisfied leer. "It has been decided that the most effective way is to convict you both of collaboration."

MacKenzie couldn't believe what he was hearing. Things were happening too fast for him to assimilate. "Collaboration?" he murmured. "With whom . . . the Rashadians? That's crazy! Flight Corps would never go along with a charge like that!"

"I admit there was some grumbling from the military services at the Defense Council committee level. They didn't like the idea of disgracing one of their best public-relations props. With your mythic father and your victory at Pegasus Station and your martial arts prizes and your Anglo-American good looks, you cut quite a romantic figure. I wonder if you realize how much wrongheaded policy has been made because of fools like you." She leaned back in her chair and sniffed. "But this space jump changes things for everyone. It has made you and Lieutenant Stocovik important and given you both embarrassingly high profiles. You have catalyzed something much bigger than Flight Corps is prepared to handle. Had you materialized somewhere less public, it might have gone easier on you. But things being as they are, you must first be sanitized." She grinned maliciously. "Somehow I think you'll appreciate the rationale for your collaboration. You will have sacrificed everything for the sake of love."

"You expect me to go along with that?" MacKenzie cried.

"Commander, you have only just awakened and are apparently still disoriented. But believe it when I say you have no choice. You are charged with Rashadian collaboration, and you will be convicted one way or the other . . . for purposes of state security."

MacKenzie wanted to argue, but dizziness and nausea assaulted him again, and he lost his train of thought. He began to suspect he had been seriously traumatized, either by the space jump—if it had indeed occurred—or by drugging at the hands of his interrogators. Whatever the cause, he was at an extreme disadvantage. "Nice try, Colonel," he said, "but I do nothing until I see Svetla, Sheila, and my own command. That's all there is to it."

She snickered softly, then twirled in her chair and gazed at the pewter statuary on a pedestal in the corner of the office. It was the state security eagle, talons exposed and wings wrapping protectively about the planets and moons of the Cygni B System. "Really, MacKenzie, you are becoming a bore. Do you think we are as stupid as your own fatuous superiors?" She stood up suddenly and sighed. "If you must speak with Lieutenant Stocovik, I will see that it is arranged, but I doubt you will be happy with the result. Because, you see, she has agreed to be a witness for the prosecution. Under those circumstances, Flight Corps has officially adopted a position of neutrality. Quite wisely, they wash their hands of you, Commander—at least for the present. However, I suppose an interview can be arranged with your station commander, if you need his confirmation to accept your responsibility." Van Sander turned back to him with a satisfied stare and licked her dry lips almost sensually. "You belong to me, MacKenzie. The Concordat Council has made its decision, and one way or the other, you will do as you are told. I am here to see to it. Do you understand?"

Her voice had become threatening, and she studied his reaction like a sadistic child dissecting an insect piece by piece. The eyes were dull and lifeless, like tombstones.

MacKenzie was sick and confused, but her smugness angered him. He didn't give the woman what she expected. He simply returned her stare, so his own eyes reflected the deadness they perceived, and for an instant she seemed surprised.

CHAPTER 12

"When the truth comes out, your stature will be even more enhanced."

MacKenzie studied the image in the video screen. It looked like Svetla, but without seeing her face-to-face, he couldn't be certain. "That's easy to say when it's not your reputation that's being sacrificed," he grumbled.

"We can't all be from prestigious families where such things are vitally significant, MacKenzie. I've paid my price, too," she countered, raising the stump of her arm.

"You can replace hands with bionic prostheses. Disgrace isn't so easily remedied."

"I won't have synthetic material tacked to my flesh. It's too obscene."

"Well, a mechanical device, then. In many respects, they're even better."

"That's easy to say when it's not your hand that's being replaced," she charged, mimicking his earlier protest. "What chance have I of Outbanking again with a mechanical hand?"

"If what Van Sander says is true, neither of us will be Outbanking for some time. We'll be busy trying to duplicate space jumps."

"If you ask me, the whole thing is a pipe dream. If we did jump space as they say, we would have remembered. What happened did not involve us. They'll learn that soon enough. And then I intend to get my ship back. That was the agreement I extracted in exchange for my cooperation."

He lowered his eyes and said, "We must do what we think right, Svetla. I understand how you feel."

"Oh, MacKenzie, you are so irritating!" she complained. "Use your head. Their cover story requires a normal, in-camera proceeding at the station provost's, with a tribunal that isn't aware of what's happening. A secret proceeding held under Internal Security's auspices would be hard to leak without raising credibility issues. They need us to pretend we're guilty. And cooperating now buys a future later."

"Perhaps. But I wasn't born yesterday," he said. "I don't trust Internal Security. How can we be sure they're not setting us up for political reasons?"

"We can't. But you'll have the advantage in a court-martial before a Flight Corps tribunal. They won't hand down a maximum sentence. The corps has too much to lose. They'll give you the benefit of the doubt."

MacKenzie pondered what she said. It made sense if you accepted the situation at face value, but he felt instinctively that Van Sander was hiding something. He had begun to suspect it during the short night, when they made him lie motionless on his back on the cot ledge of his cell as punishment for his lack of cooperation. The discipline had stanched his nausea and cleared his brain. He had replayed the discussion with Van Sander over and over in his mind. There was nothing he could put his finger on, but his intuition told him there was more involved than keeping a space jump secret.

"I suppose you're right," he finally whispered. "But it seems damned unfair after everything you and I have been through."

Svetla nodded sympathetically, then said, "I didn't want to say this until we could speak privately, but we might not get a chance to see each other for a while . . . until this thing is over." She hesitated, as if collecting her resolve. "Think about us, too, Mac. If you remain obdurate, they may convince the Concordat Council you've become insubordinate. They could hold a secret trial and throw the book at you. We might never see each other again. If you do what they ask, we can be together. During the space jump research, and then . . . after . . ." Her voice trailed off and her cheeks flushed.

MacKenzie was not sure he understood. "We can be together?" he repeated.

She smiled shyly. "Of course, Mac. Everyone important knows this is only a charade. They don't want to hurt us. They just need an excuse to take us out of the wings so we can work on their damned space jump without arousing suspicion. We'd be working together again, don't you see?"

"Are you saying you care . . . ?"

She blanched and said, "Can't we discuss this later, in private?"

"Yes, Svetla. I'm sorry. That's nobody's business but our own. Just tell me one thing, one thing that will tell me all. What do you think were the most wonderful moments we shared?"

She studied him curiously, as if uncertain what he meant. Then she said, "Please Mac, you know they're monitoring us. Must we let them know everything?"

"They're Internal Security, Svetla. We may not like them, and the feeling may be mutual, but it's their job to know everything about personal weaknesses, isn't it? They know about our affair. They know what happened on the mission . . . everything we said and did. The only thing they don't know is how the space jump occurred, and I can't help them there. I wish I could."

Svetla nodded anxiously. "If we just could remember something about that jump, we could save ourselves this humiliation. But I recall nothing."

"Are you sure, Svetla? Think very hard," he demanded.

She looked at him with legitimate regret. "Not a thing, Mac," she answered morosely. "I was comatose from the virus and the Tribenzodrine."

They shared a poignant moment of intimacy with eyes interlaced. "I'm sorry about what happened to you. It was my fault," MacKenzie told her. "But please," he said, letting a little supplication color his voice, "it is very important to me. What were the most wonderful moments we shared together?"

She hesitated again, and when she answered, her voice was little more than a whisper. "I think it was our third night together on Red Cliff, after you told me about the *Sinclair* and the children." She looked up at him with raw affection. "You—you needed me so much."

"Ah yes . . ." MacKenzie said, eyes filling with recognition. "The whole world seemed to move that night, didn't it?"

"Yes, Mac. So much it scared me to death. I wasn't prepared. Do you understand what I mean?"

He smiled tenderly. "Don't worry. I'll never suffocate you again."

"You won't?"

"No. Never, Svetla."

"And you'll do what they want?" she asked hopefully. "I really need you to, Mac, because in spite of what I said about getting back my ship, I couldn't bear hurting you so much. You know that now."

"You can always count on me, both as a . . . friend and a fellow officer," he answered.

"I'm so glad, Mac. Really I am. Believe me, I'll make it up to you. Never question that."

MacKenzie smiled.

Svetla gazed at him passionately and formed the words, "I think I love you," with her mouth. Then she said aloud, "See you in a while, after all this is behind us. Good-bye for now."

"Good-bye, Svetla," he replied.

The video screen darkened, and the indirect glow of the office lights increased automatically.

"Well, that wasn't so bad, was it, Commander?" Van Sander said from the corner chair where she was lounging. "I know this was hard at first. Very hard. And being so ill must have distressed you. But now that you've had time to reflect, perhaps you see why the play must go on. It was planned at the highest levels and approved by the Executive Council itself. I'm sure you agree they know better than we what must be done to defend Concordat interests. They have information and perspective we do not. They decided a trial was the best way to keep the space jump secret while we see if it can be replicated. I think you'll find, in the end, that they made the right decision. Once we know more about space jumps, things will be less sensitive and you will be richly rewarded for your sacrifice."

"Oh, I appreciate what you are saying," MacKenzie answered. "But I'll feel much better after I've spoken with my own command and have assurance they approve of your scheme."

"Vice Admiral Schoenhoffer will be here tomorrow at nineteen hundred and thirty hours to give you orders personally," she said.

"I see . . . there is one more thing, however."

The colonel's face betrayed a hint of concern. "What might that be?"

"I want to talk with Sheila. I've grown accustomed to having her counsel regarding important decisions."

Van Sander frowned and shook her narrow head. "I am afraid that's out of the question," she said curtly. "No one but Internal Security has access to that command system until we are certain things are under control."

It was what he expected. Sheila probably knew what they were hiding, and they couldn't manipulate her the way they could everyone else.

"I wonder if I might ask you something, Commander," Van Sander said, interrupting his train of thought.

"Sure. Why not?"

"What was the *Sinclair?*"

MacKenzie stared at the gaunt woman a long moment, but he didn't reply.

"Lieutenant Stocovik said the most wonderful moments you shared came after you told her about it," she said, reminding him.

"Yes, I know. But you may not understand what she meant, since you're not an Outbanker."

"Really! What makes you say that?"

"The *Sinclair* was a distressed cruise ship I once had to investigate. Every living soul aboard had been incinerated."

For a moment, Pieta Van Sander wasn't able to hide her revulsion.

CHAPTER 13

Vice Admiral Schoenhoffer strode into the conference room as though he were reviewing troops. Two aides followed, like smaller versions of the admiral, bobbing in his strut. Their teal and silver uniforms provided a marked contrast to Van Sander's black-suited staff, which seemed almost gladiatorial.

Following protocol, Van Sander acted as host. After everyone was seated comfortably around the onyx conference table, she introduced her three staff assistants. "And this, as we all know, is Lieutenant Commander MacKenzie," she said, concluding her opening remarks.

"Ahem!" Schoenhoffer said immediately, without introducing his subordinates. "I understand you have some questions concerning your role in this cover story, Commander."

"Not my role, Admiral, but that of the Flight Corps," MacKenzie replied evenly.

Schoenhoffer observed him with dark, bovine eyes that betrayed nothing. "In what way, man? Explain yourself."

"Let me be specific, sir. First, I'd like to know if the corps is aware of a space jump. Second, does it approve of the cover story devised to protect such a jump's secrecy? And third, am I being ordered to comply with my role in the plan as outlined by Colonel Van Sander?" A hint of anger had colored his last question, and though it had been unintentional, it seemed to put everyone more at ease.

"Well phrased, Commander," the admiral said. He held out his hand, and one of the aides gave him an attache folder. MacKenzie noticed they were both young, strapping, blond, and he could hardly tell them apart. They were identical twins. He could not help thinking how like a chairbound vice admiral it was to select bookend aides-de-camp.

Schoenhoffer opened the folder and removed a sheaf of documents. He shoved them across the conference table and said, "Here is written confirmation of all phases of the operation, including your role in it, Commander. Please satisfy yourself that they are complete."

MacKenzie picked up the sheaf and thumbed through the documents one by one. There were orders from his Outbank wing command to cooperate with Vice Admiral Schoenhoffer's requests. They had been endorsed up through Special Operations Division. Next there were copies of Schoenhoffer's order to comply with Van Sander's plan. Unfortunately it all looked quite official.

"May I keep these?" MacKenzie ventured.

The vice admiral laughed jovially. "Come now, you know I can't permit that," he said. "But rest assured they'll be in safe-keeping at headquarters. My God, man, those documents are as important to the corps as they are to you. You don't think we'd risk your reputation without covering ourselves, do you?" He laughed again. "No, no, no, MacKenzie. We may have to cooperate with our sister service here," he continued, waving at the Security side of the table, "but we don't intend to do so at a disadvantage in the long run." He turned to Van Sander. "I hope you realize that no personal slight was intended by that last remark, Colonel," he concluded.

"None was taken," she answered with a gracious smile.

MacKenzie shook his head. He had forgotten how diplomatically hammers dropped in these interservice meetings. The hypocrisy was cloying. He pushed the documents back across the table toward the admiral, and one of the blond bookends grabbed them up.

"We also have written confirmations direct from the Concordat Executive Council," the admiral stated. "I can't let you see those, of course. Everything will be locked in the vault at the station. I assure you, they are the last things in the universe anyone will get his hands on."

"That makes me feel a little better," MacKenzie lied.

"Very good! Carry on then, Commander." The vice admiral rose abruptly and so did the twins. It was obvious he considered the conference ended. Everyone else stood as Schoenhoffer turned with a flourish and strode toward the door, but suddenly he halted and looked back. "I wasn't going to tell you this, MacKenzie, because you have your orders, and I know you'll comply like the flight corpsman and Outbanker you are. But that doesn't seem fair under the circumstances. There will be a Medal of Supreme Valor waiting for you when all of this is over. You did one hell of a job retrieving that Beta-Z system. And the way you solved the Rashadian robot problem—ho-ho—*that* is destined to become a textbook case of field expediency. Yes, that was one hell of a job, Commander."

"It's kind of you to say so, sir," MacKenzie said humbly.

"Not at all. My pleasure, my pleasure," the admiral called over his shoulder as he continued his brusque exit. One of the blond aides lunged forward and swung open the door, then slipped aside just as Schoenhoffer shot past. In a moment, an Internal Security guard closed the door behind them, and the bustle ended as definitively as it had begun.

So much for the gladiators, MacKenzie thought.

Van Sander excused her three staff officers. As soon as they left, she turned to MacKenzie and said, "It is nice to be appreciated, isn't it?"

"Considering what they want me to do, they should be appreciative."

"I understand how you feel, but may I assume you are prepared to cooperate?"

"I suppose that clinched it. I don't have much choice anyway, do I?"

"Try not to think of it that way, MacKenzie. You're only doing your duty like everyone else."

"Yes, well . . . I suppose you're right. But something bothers me."

"And what is that, Commander?"

"Just who is this charade supposed to fool?" He stared deliberately into the colonel's gray eyes. "Certainly not the Rashadians. They know we didn't collaborate. When they learn you've convicted us of such a charge, won't it draw their attention to the space jump? Where's the cover story in that?"

She sauntered to the end of the conference table and sat down in a chair. Then she fixed him with a cunning stare and smiled. "All right, MacKenzie, since you've agreed to cooperate, I'll tell you. We want to cause exactly the reaction you outlined. The Rashadians should be interested in learning what we are up to. We expect they will target information about the court-martial as the highest priority, and that is exactly what we want."

"Why do you want that?"

"There are high-level members of the Concordat who, because it suits their political purpose, secretly assist the Rashadian insurgency. Their policy influence is so useful to the terrorists that they seldom contact these fifth columnists directly, and the involvement is hard to prove. We have been watching these suspects for some time, but we lack sufficient evidence to make arrests. Our little charade should force the Rashadians to contact some of these traitors. And when they do, we will be waiting."

MacKenzie whistled in astonishment. "I see now why you want this thing to go well," he admitted. "Rashadian sympathizers in the Concordat itself? That is serious. But I don't understand what they expect to gain politically from such support."

"I should hope you wouldn't," Van Sander stated condescendingly.

MacKenzie stared at her blankly, as if still completely dumbfounded by her revelations. She licked her thin lips with hidden satisfaction and smiled at him again. He was relieved she thought him so naive.

CHAPTER 14

Once he agreed to cooperate, MacKenzie was introduced to the dull routine of incarceration. At 0600 hours, a Klaxon squawked. He rose, showered, and slipped into a new set of coveralls left for him during the night. Except for a forty-five-minute exercise period in the afternoon, he was confined to his cell. Meals were brought by guards who were less sullen than unconcerned and spoke only when required. He neither saw nor heard any other prisoners. And from that time on, whenever he remembered what it was like being in prison, his one lasting impression would be of deafening silence.

At exactly 0900 hours on the morning of the trial, a squad of guards arrived, locked him in manacles, and escorted him to the ground level, where a fleet of Magnarovers were waiting. They shoved him into the back of the one in which Van Sander was waiting and immediately sped away.

As they turned out of the compound, most of the fleet peeled off, fanning out along streets paralleling their planned route. But both the flanking Magnarovers and the agents stationed on foot at key intersections remained in contact with the colonel by radio.

MacKenzie sat back and drank in the orange brilliance of the Cygni B sun as it bathed the pastel shades of Central City. The day was already hot, and only a few pedestrians, wearing wide-brimmed hats or carrying colorful parasols, were on the broad sidewalks. A few turned their heads to look at the caravan as it rolled past, but none seemed concerned. To bystanders, MacKenzie was just another specimen of Internal Security vigilance.

He leaned back and let his mind drift. What day was it? he wondered. He had lost track. Of course, it didn't matter. Win or lose, it would all be noted for posterity in the official records. Van Sander had told him he would not testify. After Svetla's testimony, he was to say he had broken under the conflicting demands of his duty and his love for Svetla, then was to throw himself on the court's mercy. Van Sander thought he'd have no trouble carrying it off. They would see.

The palmetto-lined streets seemed more familiar now, and he knew they were nearing the Flight Corps Station. He listened to the outriders reporting over their radios and thought again of Svetla.

He was worried about her, had been worried for some time, though he had not permitted it to influence his plans. Yet now, as the Magnarovers approached the station, he couldn't help wondering how his actions might affect her.

He knew the woman in the video screen had not been Svetla Stocovik. He had known it the moment she told him what their most wonderful moments together had been. She had said "the third night on Red Cliff," and that had been a reasonable answer. He imagined Internal Security's computers had graded the probability of it being satisfactory at ninety-nine percent. Unfortunately for them, the minuscule probability had expanded to a factor of one. And the video imposter had been wrong.

Something *had* happened during the time they were asleep together, during the time the much-discussed space jump had occurred. It was something so real, so personally moving, that even yet he could not bear to remember it without tears of joy. He had not told Van Sander. It had seemed unwise to do so, and now he was glad he had exercised caution. For during the period they had slept, during the moments he now believed they had somehow jumped through time and space, he and Svetla had unified for what seemed an extended period of perfect bliss. They had joined as spirit man and spirit woman, in a rapture that transcended the meaning of human love. And finally, for an awesome few moments, in an act so staggering it defied his human capacity to express, they had formed glowing bodies that combined the passion of young lovers with the wisdom of ancient lords. And they had leapt together, hand in hand, down the long, sloping meadows of a virgin white valley composed of compressed stars.

That had been their most magnificent moment together, and the real Svetla Stocovik would have remembered. The fact that she did not evidenced that the woman he had spoken to was an impostor.

Thus MacKenzie had assumed that Internal Security was lying about Svetla, and therefore he had to assume they were lying about everything else. It no longer mattered what Internal Security was trying to accomplish or whether or not they had Executive Council support. They had made him an enemy by lying about Svetla. And even if they had nothing to hide, he had to confound their strategy no matter what fate might await.

That was the Outbanker way. Shades of my father in his wounded craft, immolating himself instead of choosing his wife and child—instead of choosing life, he thought morosely.

He sat in the back seat of the Magnarover, listening to the crackling exchanges of his captors over their radios, feeling the stoicism of the warrior committed completely to the path selected no matter what the cost.

The entourage pulled into the station's east gate and proceeded along the main boulevard. When they approached the provost marshal's building, they swung right and headed for the jutting canopy covering the brig entrance. As they came to a halt, guards jumped from the lead and trail cars and took positions along the walkway, hands poised over their laser pistols. They were efficient and serious but melodramatic, and in spite of his morose fatalism, MacKenzie could not retain a derisive smirk. He was glad that there were seldom such shenanigans in Flight Corps wings.

MacKenzie got out of the Magnarover and followed Van Sander through the column of black-uniformed guards into the building. In moments, they were in an elevator heading to the fourteenth floor. As soon as it completed its giddying ascent, the doors opened and they surged out.

They strode down a hallway to the bronzed glass doors marked "COURT-MARTIAL CHAMBER 6" and went in. MacKenzie decided he would remember that room number, should he ever write his memoirs. It was an inane but comforting thought.

Two guards led him to the prisoner's dock. As they removed his wrist manacles, he scanned the room. He was not pleased.

Besides four provost marshal sentries and three administrative clerks, there were no other Flight Corps personnel present. He had hoped for a larger contingent. But in the end, he knew it didn't matter. His plan depended on the objectivity of the tribunal and how far Van Sander thought she could go. He sat down on the cold metal chair and waited.

A few more court staff strolled in, but no Flight Corps officers appeared. There were still more black uniforms in the chambers than teal and silver ones. It's too late to reconsider, he told himself. Don't waver. Just play your hand and hope the tribunal isn't part of the charade.

Finally one of the clerks climbed to his feet and bellowed, "Attention to court." Everyone stood. "Be it known to all here present that a special session of Military Court, Flight Corps Division, is herewith called to order at zero nine-thirty hours, in Room Six of Provost Headquarters, on this sixteenth day of the fourteenth month, Red Cliff Cycle, during the year twenty-three-sixty-four Extelon Calendar Relative." Then he turned to the door behind the tribunal bench and droned, "Honor the officials of judgment."

The door opened, and the officers selected to serve on the tribunal entered. MacKenzie studied each one in turn as they took their seats.

The chief judge was Commodore Takasuki, a Nihonian who was Vice Admiral Schoenhoffer's executive officer. MacKenzie wasn't surprised, but he felt momentary discomfiture. His uncle, Jackson, had often explained how the worst disasters to befall the MacKenzie clan had always involved Nihonians.

First, three of the family's forebears had perished in prisons during the Second World War of the Twentieth Century on old Earth. Then, later, Japanese electronics conglomerates had invaded MacKenzie corporate markets, dumping quality goods at ridiculously low prices, bringing economic disaster. It had been that setback that convinced the family scions to opt for the interstellar colonization program and leave their native Canada.

Uncle "Jock" had been like a father to him, and the older man's memory of Nihonian skulduggery had been encyclopedic. Thus Takasuki's presence disheartened him, although the squat Nihonian did have a reputation as a stickler for doing things right.

The second judge was a lieutenant in his late twenties. He was headquarters staff, and that was all MacKenzie knew about him. He was troubled that the man was at the midstage of his career, because he would be tempted to play it safe . . . unlike the third officer of the tribunal.

The third officer was Captain Petravich, chief of the Red Cliff Outbanker Squadron and his own commanding officer. MacKenzie had the urge to cheer. Van Sander had blundered—either that or she knew something he did not, in which case his goose was as good as cooked anyway. Instinctively he sensed that wasn't the case. Van Sander—and probably Schoenhoffer, too—were convinced he would cooperate, that he would play his role submissively. They had decided to use Petravich because no one would question a conviction handed down by MacKenzie's own commanding officer. And now he might have an ally right on the tribunal itself. Time would tell.

With the court impaneled, everyone sat down, and Takasuki's voice boomed out in its clipped, guttural tones: "What case is brought before this court?"

The clerk announced, "Internal Security Service versus Lt. Comdr. Ian S. MacKenzie, FCO number zero-zero-nine-six-three-one, who stands accused of serious collaboration with an enemy during time of conflict."

"Who is present for the prosecution?" Takasuki growled.

The state security prosecutor rose and said, "I am, Commodore." He was lean, impeccably groomed, and his voice was well modulated. He introduced the Flight Corps co-counsel assisting him. She was a youngish woman attached to the JAG Officer's staff. Such arrangements had become traditional when any member of the military was brought up on charges prosecuted by Internal Security.

Takasuki said, "You may proceed to present your opening remarks."

The prosecutor glanced at his briefs, hesitated dramatically, then looked up and said, "Your Honor, we shall prove beyond all reasonable doubt that while on a mission to retrieve a highly classified weapon control system critical to Concordat defense, Lt. Comdr. Ian S. MacKenzie forsook his sworn duty and permitted personal, self-serving, sexual needs to determine his behavior in the face of the enemy. We shall demonstrate that the commander traded said weapon system to Rashadian terrorist insurgents in exchange for the life of his fellow officer and erstwhile paramour, Lt. Svetla Stocovik, who had fallen captive. We shall show that in so doing, he knowingly abandoned his mission responsibilities and damaged Concordat security. We shall also show that the accused knew well and fully that such acts entailed collaboration with an enemy in time of conflict, and that he is therefore guilty of violating Sections Three, Six, Eleven, Twelve, and Eighteen point five of the Code of Military Justice. This is the essence of our case."

The prosecutor finished reading and looked up at the tribunal.

Takasuki stared placidly, as if expecting something more.

"Your Honor?" the prosecutor prompted, looking slightly embarrassed.

Takasuki's brows arched in mild surprise. "Ah, so, are you through?" he said.

"Oh, yes, Your Honor. I have taken the liberty of summarizing the charges rather than burdening the court with an extensive reading of specifications." He shuffled through the papers on the bench before him. "We present them now in written form for the court's acceptance as Exhibit One." He handed the papers to the co-counsel, who stood to take them to the clerk.

But Takasuki growled, "Just one moment. We need to take the accused's plea before exhibits are entered."

The prosecutor smiled apologetically. "I'm sorry, Your Honor, but I assumed it was understood that the defendant is pleading guilty."

"Ah, is that so?"

"Yes, Your Honor," the prosecutor replied.

"In my court, we assume nothing, young sir."

Takasuki turned his wide face to MacKenzie and fixed him with a stolid, hooded stare. "Are you pleading guilty, Commander?" he asked.

MacKenzie rose but said nothing. A hush settled over the hearing room.

Takasuki waited patiently for a response, but when none seemed forthcoming, he asked, "Why do you not reply, Commander MacKenzie? Are you perhaps represented by counsel not yet present?"

"The accused has waived right to counsel," the prosecutor interjected.

It was then that MacKenzie chose to speak. "That's not true, sir. I have not been offered counsel, nor, I might add, would I accept any provided by those who advance these charges against me." The hush turned electric, and the tribunal glanced at each other quizzically. Even Van Sander's practiced detachment escaped her, and she slid rigidly to the edge of her seat. "I request my rights under Special Canon four point seven," MacKenzie continued. "As captain and full crew complement of a ship of the line accused of serious offense, I wish to name my own defense counsel."

The room filled with a chorus of whispered questions and comments, and Van Sander leapt to her feet.

"Objection, Your Honor! I object!" the prosecutor shouted loudly.

Takasuki slammed his gavel repeatedly and bellowed, "Order in this court!" Slowly the commotion ebbed, but Van Sander remained standing. She glared ominously at the prosecutor.

Captain Petravich chuckled softly, and Takasuki turned to him. "Sir? Do you know of this special canon?" he asked.

"Yes, I'm afraid I do," the grizzled man said through a broad grin. "Although it has been some time since I've heard of it being invoked."

"And what is it?"

"It gives the captain and crew of a ship of the line the right to select their own defense counsel if they are faced with a court-martial arising from action taken during crisis or battle.

There are only two provisos: The entire crew must be charged, and their choice must be unanimous. In most cases, that precludes such a request." Petravich chuckled once more, making no effort to disguise his delight. "But as we know, Commander MacKenzie is both captain and crew on his cruiser, and an Outbanker most assuredly is a ship of the line." Petravich fell silent a moment, and his bushy eyebrows flickered up and down devilishly.

Takasuki snorted and said, "Ah-ha!" The younger officer nodded slowly, as though he appreciated learning something of interest. Petravich continued to smile. He looked directly at MacKenzie and winked. Van Sander's hatchet face was set grimly on the prosecutor, who in turn began once more to object.

"Your Honor," he called, "I respectfully protest this ridiculous resort to arcane precedent. I beg you to consider Concordat defense needs. Collaboration is a dire offense. If its prosecution is reduced to absurdity by procedural tactics, the effect on state security will be immediate, negative, and wholesale."

The man hesitated as he searched for some legal rationale. Suddenly an idea occurred to him, and he continued. "Certainly the court can recognize that the accused misled us. He obviously perjured himself during interrogation, and he will be additionally charged with that offense. But in the meantime, we should consider the truth or falsity of the charges currently before us. If you hand down a verdict of guilty, the accused may use the procedural point as a basis for appeal at a later date. But in the interim, Concordat security will have been defended. I think that, under the circumstances, such a course—"

"What are you trying to tell this court?" Takasuki demanded, interrupting the prosecutor. "We stand by procedures here and do not play fast and loose when the mood suits us. Standing by rules, young man, is the foundation of all Concordat security. Do you understand? Objection overruled." Then the chief judge turned to MacKenzie, his Nihonian dignity drooping on his face, and said, "The court grants your rights under the special cannon. Who is it you select as your defense counsel?"

MacKenzie could not believe he had succeeded so easily. He said, "Your Honor, I humbly request that I be represented at this trial by Cyrus Magnum, Prefect of Red Cliff." There was a peculiar sound, as if everyone in the courtroom had gasped simultaneously, and in the silence that ensued, he continued. "Furthermore, because of conditions that I believe require a Condition Five classification status, I demand to be remanded to my defense counsel's custody immediately."

The courtroom erupted in a cacophony of exclamation. Condition Five classification status was the most sensitive in Concordat affairs and applied only to the most critical internal issues. The fact that MacKenzie had alluded to conditions even vaguely requiring such status was dumbfounding and added a completely new level of significance to his trial. Even MacKenzie was awed by what he had done. That had not been a part of his plan, but rather a spontaneous improvisation. Yet his intuition had been churning subconsciously. He knew that something about Van Sander's loss of control indicated there was something more at stake than flushing out Rashadian sympathizers.

Takasuki was fuming. The Nihonian realized now that MacKenzie's case was more significant than he had been led to suspect, and his career instincts were alerted. He had not advanced himself by being caught unaware, and MacKenzie sensed he might take it out on him if he ever came up on the wrong side of the commodore again. The squat Nihonian's glower made that message quite clear. "Huuummpph!" he grunted menacingly. "Your request is granted. This court stands recessed until counsel for the accused has had time to prepare his case." He slammed his gavel with harsh finality and rose.

The rest of the tribunal stood, too, and Van Sander started moving forward, motioning to her men. "Commodore Takasuki," MacKenzie barked, "I believe there is still one issue that remains to be settled."

The tribunal officers each displayed different degrees of bewilderment, but there was no disguising Takasuki's annoyance. "And what might that be, Commander?" he demanded.

"Since this court convened, I have fallen under its authority, have I not?" The three officers exchanged glances and then, looking back, nodded. "Then shouldn't the provost marshal assure my safe conduct to Cyrus Magnum's custody?"

Takasuki scowled. Petravich took the Nihonian's arm and whispered something. The Nihonian shook his head forcefully, but Petravich whispered again, and then the chief judge seemed to relent. He stared down at MacKenzie and said begrudgingly, "Once again it appears you are procedurally correct. You missed your calling, Commander. Perhaps you should have taken up the practice of law." He motioned to the provost marshal sentries in the back of the room. "See that the commander is delivered safely to the prefect's residence," he ordered. Then he spun around on his heel and strutted through the doorway behind him. Petravich and the younger officer followed.

As soon as the tribunal left, the room began to clear. MacKenzie lowered himself back into the chair. He sat listlessly, feeling a sort of anticlimactic relief. For a few seconds, he communed with Taogott, his own peculiar mixture of the oriental Tao and the occidental God, merging his grateful thought with an indescribably omnipresent Sustainer and fount of being. It was not prayer in the common sense of the term, but MacKenzie knew it was required. Once again whatever *it* was had granted benefice.

When he looked up again, the courtroom was almost empty, and the provost marshal's detail was coming toward him. Then he noticed Van Sander, who was still standing near the bronzed doors to the hallway. Her face was a mask of scorn, and the look frightened him. The woman seemed to be saying she was not finished yet, that she knew things he didn't—essential things that ultimately would lead to his undoing.

Then he remembered Svetla. Van Sander still had her. He had no idea where she was being held or what Internal Security might do to her. That realization drowned his previous sense of triumph in a wave of impotent rage. If she's harmed, I'll kill you with my bare hands, he promised himself savagely. Then he stood and glowered at Col. Pieta Van Sander with murderous eyes. They stared at one another for a long moment, and then MacKenzie laughed in derision.

CHAPTER 15

MacKenzie waited for Cyrus Magnum in the parlor of the prefect's mansion on Government Knoll. The exhilaration that followed his success at the court-martial had been replaced by nervous tension, and he paced about the room. The decor was neoclassical, and he stopped occasionally to examine a piece of antique furniture or an object of art. But as he passed the French doors set into the far wall, he noticed a spacious garden and pulled back the sheer curtains on one of the doors to study it.

Unlike the parlor, the garden was distinctly oriental. The subtle order of the plants, bushes, boulders, and dwarf palms; the understated interplay of the sunlight and shadow; the tasteful meandering of the gravel paths and miniature brooks; everything evidenced artful balance between an artisan's patient hand and nature's secretive laws. It was very restful, and its timeless order soothed his anxiety.

He was standing there, experiencing the sense of calm, when a soft baritone voice behind him asked, "Does my garden please you?"

MacKenzie turned around.

The man was somewhat taller than he expected, but otherwise Cyrus Magnum looked exactly like his holoimage in news reports. He wore an impeccably tailored blue suit with a short, military-style jacket, embroidered at the collar and cuffs with piping of a lighter blue color. The strands of silver running through his raven hair enhanced the piercing intelligence of his dark brown eyes, and he approached with an athletic grace unusual in one sixty years of age.

MacKenzie snapped to attention and saluted. "Sir, I am Lt. Comdr. Ian S. MacKenzie, lately captain pilot of Outbank Cruiser *Bravo*, on patrol in the fourth quadrant."

The prefect smiled wistfully and returned the salute with a relaxed wave. "So I understand, Commander. Why don't we sit down and discuss your problem?"

MacKenzie lowered himself into a love seat opposite the brocade armchair Cyrus had selected. "Please excuse my manner if it is not appropriate," he said. "I've had little experience in political protocol."

"Is your problem political, then, Commander? I was under the impression it was more legal in nature."

"Well . . . yes. On one level, it is," MacKenzie began haltingly. "But there are political ramifications I cannot evaluate."

"Why not?"

"It requires knowledge of current affairs at the uppermost levels of the Concordat, which exceeds my capacities."

"Is that why you invoked Condition Five classification when you were remanded to my custody?"

"Yes, sir. It was."

Cyrus Magnum stroked his chin pensively. "If you weren't able to evaluate the politics of the situation, how do you know Condition Five was necessary?"

"I didn't want to underestimate the political importance of what was happening, even if I don't completely understand it."

"I see. Then you are here to seek my political counsel."

"No, sir, I am here seeking your protection. But what I have to tell you may have some value as political intelligence as well."

The prefect studied him for what seemed a long time, and MacKenzie feared the interview had already taken an unfortunate tone. Then Cyrus Magnum said, "Why don't you explain what has happened? Then we can better assess the nature of your problem."

It was not the most reassuring comment, but better than being thrown out on his ear. "I named you my defense counsel in my court-martial, but it was a ruse," MacKenzie said.

"What was, Commander? Naming me counsel or the court-martial itself?" Cyrus asked.

"I'm sorry, sir," MacKenzie said. "I'm a bit nervous and haven't made myself clear. My request was a ruse to upset Colonel Van Sander's strategy. But so was the court-martial itself. Internal Security demanded I plead guilty to a false charge

of collaboration to protect the secrecy of something . . . quit
astounding. However—"

"You say Internal Security demanded this?" Cyrus inter
rupted.

"Yes, sir. They—Colonel Van Sander, that is—told me th
plan had been approved by the Concordat Executive Council.

Cyrus Magnum's eyebrows arched knowingly. "Ah, ye
Col. Pieta Van Sander. Her ambitious vigilance is a motor tha
knows no rest. The Executive Council approved this, sh
said?"

"Yes, but I don't believe her. The measures she took to forc
my cooperation roused my suspicions, even considering th
importance of what must be kept secret."

"And what is that?"

MacKenzie decided it was his turn to ask a question. "D
you know what Van Sander is up to, sir?"

"Do you think I am unaware of what happens on my ow
planet?" Cyrus demanded curtly.

"With all due respect, sir, I think that remains to be seen.
know you are one of the few leaders capable of wielding su
preme power in the Concordat. But your party was defeated i
the last plebiscite, and apparently the situation is fluid."

Cyrus Magnum stared coldly for a moment. Then, surpris
ingly, he smiled. "A reasonable point, which I am willing
concede, Commander." He stood up and said, "Would yo
care for an aperitif?"

"No, thank you, sir."

"Well, I am going to have one. I was given some really ex
quisite Helvezo Cherrie, which I have been indulging at tea
time. Are you sure you won't join me?"

"Since you put it that way, sir, please. I've had little oppor
tunity to savor Helvezo."

"Excellent."

Cyrus strolled to a buffet in the corner of the parlor. He re
moved a decanter and filled two thin-stemmed glasses with th
ruby liquor. When he returned, he handed one glass to Mac
Kenzie, then lowered himself back into his armchair. "To Con
cordat society!" he said, raising his glass in a toast.

"To its peace and prosperity!" MacKenzie rejoined.

They sipped the Helvezo. It was rich but very dry, with a taste that escaped the pallet as soon as it was swallowed. It warmed MacKenzie's throat and chest pleasantly.

Cyrus swirled the liqueur in the glass, watching the motion with an undisguised sense of enchantment. Then he looked up and said, "So, Ian, perhaps we are getting to know each other well enough to come to the point. Why don't you tell me everything you know, so we can decide whether my normally efficient information networks have suffered a temporary malfunction where Colonel Van Sander is concerned."

MacKenzie studied him intently. Normally, MacKenzie could sense what others were feeling, but Cyrus Magnum was impossible to read. Either he was concentrating completely on listening, or he had learned to hide his emotions altogether. Either way, it made things more difficult. "Excuse me, sir. It might be better if you first told me what you know about my trial and Van Sander's intentions," MacKenzie suggested stiffly.

Cyrus observed him without a hint of insult, and MacKenzie was unsettled by the response. Still, he didn't reconsider his reply. Had he told Cyrus Magnum everything, the prefect might have thanked him for his information, then dismissed him without agreeing to defend him against Van Sander. It would have left nothing to trade.

"All right, Commander, perhaps you are right. I compliment your prudence," Cyrus Magnum said. He sipped some of the Helvezo and then, fixing his gaze on MacKenzie once more, began to speak. "What I know is that you are charged with the high crime of collaborating with the Rashadian Terrorist Insurgency. Both Internal Security and Flight Corps agreed to hold your court-martial in private to protect you from embarrassing publicity. They provided this favor in light of your previous exemplary record, your family's reputation, and because of some extenuating circumstances concerning your collaboration." Cyrus stopped to sip his liqueur, and when he looked at MacKenzie again it was with a knowing smile. "The inference is there was a woman involved, but it was never directly stated. Frankly, I assume there is also some soiled political laundry hanging about that Flight Corps would rather not have aired. There often is."

Cyrus placed his glass on the end table beside his chair. "At any rate," he continued, "instead of appreciating the generosity afforded, you have used some legal trickery to involve me in your case. Both Internal Security and your own service realize the state press and private *paparazzi* are a *leitmotif* in my milieu, even here on Red Cliff, so my participation in any proceeding would render its secrecy impossible. In fact, a few reporters have already been sniffing about, wanting to know what the provost marshal's men who brought you here wanted." Cyrus Magnum hesitated a long moment. He studied MacKenzie with the eyes of one adept at reading the nuances in a man.

"At any rate, Commander, both services fear you misread their goodwill. They've advised me to reject you and send you away . . . to protect myself. They say that, in spite of appearances, you are insane, my boy. Insane, devious, and manipulating. They are even concerned with my physical safety. So tell me, have I something to fear from your antics?"

MacKenzie realized his jaws had clenched while Cyrus was speaking, and he was certain his face showed his outrage. But Cyrus's nonchalance seemed to contradict the thrust of his words. MacKenzie had no doubt there were guards waiting to pounce if he made a suspicious move. But it was the man himself who confounded him. Cyrus Magnum was unfathomable. It was maddening. "Is that everything, sir? Is that really all you know?" he demanded.

"Is there more?"

"Yes, sir, there is. You mean they didn't tell you what happened to Lieutenant Stocovik and me? You really know nothing about that?" He hunched forward on the edge of the love seat, trying to calculate the ramifications of what he was saying. "And I suppose they didn't tell you about the imposter they used to trick me, did they?"

Cyrus Magnum's brows furrowed, and he stared at MacKenzie curiously.

MacKenzie pinioned him with a guarded stare and said, "You're not one of the Concordat leaders who secretly support the Rashadians, are you, sir—the ones Van Sander is after?" He hesitated. "Excuse me, sir. I meant no disrespect."

Cyrus laughed dismissively. He lifted his glass and sipped it. Then he said, "Who is this imposter you mentioned?"

Interesting, MacKenzie thought. The prefect had not followed up on the mention of high-level traitors. It was the first meaningful thing he had learned about his style. "Lieutenant Stocovik, sir," he replied. "They wouldn't let me see her face-to-face. I had to speak to her by videophone. She tried to convince me to cooperate with Van Sander, but she was an imposter—a very good one, but a phony nonetheless. That's what told me there was more here than met the eye. If Van Sander and Internal Security are lying about Svetla, there's a good chance they're lying about everything else."

"But how can you be certain the woman was not Lieutenant Stocovik?"

"She didn't remember something she should have . . . something very important."

"I see. And is this Lieutenant Stocovik your paramour, Commander?"

MacKenzie lifted his own glass and threw back a healthy swallow of the sweet liqueur. Was there hidden implication in the question? he wondered. "Yes, she and I were lovers," he said. "But something remarkable happened to us both, and now she means more to me than the word love can express."

For the first time, Cyrus seemed genuinely impressed. He leaned forward expectantly and said, "Is that why you gave the Beta-Z Weapon Control System to the Rashadians? To save her?"

The question indicated that Cyrus Magnum had not told him everything he knew about the situation, and that irritated MacKenzie. It was obvious the man was toying with him, playing some stupid interrogator's game. "You haven't believed a word I've said so far, have you?" MacKenzie demanded. "Listen to me very carefully, please, because it is the absolute truth. We didn't give the Beta-Z system to anybody. It's right here on

Red Cliff. Internal Security has it, and they have Svetla, too—the real Svetla." He smacked his glass down on the cocktail table between them so hard that some Helvezo sloshed out on the inlaid wood. "Everyone's lying through his teeth. They're using what happened for their own political purposes, and I want to know why—and whether you have anything to do with it."

His tone had become harsh, and the prefect had read the challenge in his last statement. "Do not become arrogant, Ian. There is a limit to my patience, I assure you."

MacKenzie was tired of the fencing. "We didn't give the Beta-Z box to the Rashadians, sir. Svetla and I risked our lives to retrieve it, and she lost a hand in the process. We'd still be on the Outbanks, a light-year distant and fighting the damned Rashadians, if it wasn't for Sheila and the space jump."

Cyrus looked puzzled. He set his glass on the table and said, "You are an angry man, Ian . . . angry and insolent. I am trying very hard to overlook that for the moment. But, frankly, you leave me completely confused. Who is this 'Sheila' you mentioned, and what do you mean by 'the space jump'?"

Cyrus's question filled MacKenzie with relief. For the first time in the interview, he was able to read the prefect, and he knew Magnum was telling the truth. He knew nothing of the space jump because he had not been told. And that meant his opponents were the ones behind Van Sander and Internal Security. He shut his eyes and mumbled a prayer of thanks.

"What was that?" Cyrus asked quizzically.

MacKenzie shook his head. "Nothing, sir. Just let me say that what I am about to tell you will seem like a wild tale, and there's no way I can presently prove it. But I swear on my father's soul that it's true. And once you hear it, perhaps you'll understand why I've acted as I have."

For the next two hours, MacKenzie related everything that had happened. He told Cyrus Magnum about the incursion, the robots, the space jump, and his internment at Internal Security Service Headquarters. He held nothing back.

Cyrus stopped him occasionally, seeking clarifications or checking points of fact. Twice he asked about what MacKenzie experienced during the space jump. Then he questioned him about the orders Vice Admiral Schoenhoffer had shown him. He also demanded a verbatim description of what Pieta Van Sander had said concerning potential Concordat traitors.

When MacKenzie finished, Cyrus stood and walked slowly to the French doors leading to the garden. He gazed out, lost in thought. MacKenzie sat quietly on the love seat, waiting.

Eventually Cyrus sighed. He turned and walked back across the room. When he was beside MacKenzie, he patted the commander's shoulder. "Well, Ian, as you say, it's a wild tale. But if there is any truth to it—if you are not certifiably insane—it may be that we are both lucky you turned to me." He crossed his arms on his chest, his lips pursing in reflection. "How can we get confirmation of this space jump?" he asked.

"Find my cruiser, sir. Sheila will know what's happened. She's all the proof we need."

"You have no idea where it is?"

"No more than I do where Van Sander is holding Svetla Stocovik."

"Ah, yes, Lieutenant Stocovik. You are aware, I suppose, that your attempt to derail Internal Security's plans may have placed her in mortal danger."

MacKenzie nodded painfully. "Yes, I am. But there seemed to be no other way. Svetla is an Outbanker, too, sir. She'll understand."

"I didn't intend my statement to be critical, Ian," Cyrus said with a sympathetic smile. "Yes, she is an Outbanker. Like you, a mythic warrior, eh?"

"Then you believe me, sir?"

The prefect returned to his chair. He sat down and said, "Let us say that, for the present, I am prepared to operate on the assumption that you are not lying. There is a subtle difference, I think." He leaned back and raised his head. "Aastergaard?" he said, as if questioning the air.

"Yes, Cyrus," a woman's voice responded through an intercom.

"Did you get all of that?"

"Yes, sir. No problems."

"Good. Now, first I want you to contact Dr. Fronto at Ektelon University. Tell him I need him immediately. Second, have O-Scar and his people find that cruiser. I want it located as soon as possible. And I want Lieutenant Stocovik repatriated, too, if she is still on Red Cliff. Lastly, we must learn what happened to the Beta-Z Weapon Control System. Do you have all that?"

"Yes, sir. And am I correct in assuming this is classified Con-SecPri Five?"

"Yes, you are, Aastergaard."

"Thank you, sir," the voice said.

Cyrus Magnum looked at MacKenzie, then spread his hands palms up. "Well, as you can see, Ian, your labors are bearing some fruit. I truly hope you are not insane, because that would cause me much embarrassment. I'm sure you understand that embarrassment is the worst fate a public official can suffer—at least more than once. On the other hand, if you are correct, you may see things turn markedly brighter. Who knows?"

The prefect smiled, picked up his glass, and drained it. Then he rose and crossed to the buffet. As he walked, he said to MacKenzie, "You could have done worse than place your future in my hands if you're telling the truth, Ian. May I offer you some more Helvezo?"

CHAPTER 16

The pilot punched a code word into the low-band transmitter, and O-Scar whispered, "Now we shall see if the credits I spend on intelligence are worth it." He and MacKenzie waited. There was nothing else to do.

"Roger, CC-Ten," the receiver crackled. "Code word is accepted and you are cleared for landing on Center Marker, Internal Security Kasserne Basalt."

O-Scar's grin revealed his brilliant white teeth. MacKenzie had met the Black team leader only hours earlier. Behind a haughty exterior, he showed a quiet, confident competence. "Shall we proceed to the air lock and prepare to greet our hosts?" he said, extending his ebony hand gracefully.

MacKenzie took the lead without hesitation. They strode down the ship's central corridor and into the cargo holds. Their footsteps echoed in the turgid emptiness of the freight bays, and as they walked O-Scar took the opportunity to remind MacKenzie of his role. "Remember, you are here to verify Lieutenant Stocovik's identity. Do not concern yourself with the fighting. The assault teams and I will handle that. Cyrus wants you safe and in one piece, so no heroics."

"I'll try to remember," MacKenzie said.

When they entered the main air lock, thirteen men were seated along the walls, armed with by weapons and assault devices. They looked grim and seasoned. It was a moment before MacKenzie realized that he recognized most of them. They were all bartenders, cabbies, and service tradesmen from Central City.

O-Scar circulated from man to man, checking equipment and repeating instructions. MacKenzie leaned back against a bulkhead, feeling precombat jitters. He took a deep breath, then dropped into a crouch.

When the cargo ship touched down, the assault teams stood and gave their weapons a final inspection. MacKenzie stood, too. Within minutes, they would know what Internal Security had done with Svetla . . . if they were lucky.

A Klaxon blared twice, signaling that the air lock was about to open. The queasiness in MacKenzie's stomach returned. He knew it would continue until the assault actually commenced, yet he found it exhilarating. His adrenaline was pumping, and for the first time since awakening in the Internal Security detention cell, he felt physically strong again.

The Klaxon blared once more. The air lock door retracted and a gangway automatically lowered.

Kasserne Basalt was built on three semicircular terraces cut into the cliffs that separated the Inland Sea from the Great Desert. The landing terrace was the lowest and widest. It served as both hangar and maintenance area for incoming craft. Sunlight glared harshly from its bleached sand, and MacKenzie stepped farther back into the shadows of the air lock.

As O-Scar's agents had predicted, Internal Security was making no show of force to draw attention. Only two sentries were stationed on the terrace, and they were sauntering toward the ship as though grateful for a break in the monotony.

"All right, gents, what have you got for us?" one said as he stepped up the gangway.

"A hell of a load, mon. Why dun't you give us a hond?" O-Scar called out in a thick Libonian accent.

The sentry scowled. "Sure. I suppose they don't pay you stevedores enough as it is," he said as he entered the air lock.

Before his eyes adjusted to the darkness, O-Scar clamped a massive hand over the sentry's mouth, jerked him back, and shot him in the neck with anesthetic. In seconds, he was unconscious on the deck.

"Hey, trooper!" O-Scar called to the second sentry. "C'm 'ere a minute, would ya? Yer boss has a problem."

The second sentry climbed the gangway more cautiously and stopped a meter and a half beyond the hatch. "Look, joker," he said. "Get one thing straight. Jurgen isn't my boss, see. What's his problem, anyway?" He peered into the dark air lock suspiciously. "Jurgen? What's going on?" he called.

O-Scar acted confused. "Joorgen? Who is Joorgen?" he

asked as he started toward the man.

The sentry smelled a rat, but before he could reach for his blaster pistol, O-Scar wrapped a long arm around his neck and pulled him into the air lock. He lifted him up off the floor and shot him with the anesthetic. The man's dangling feet flayed helplessly a moment, then went limp.

As O-Scar dropped him to the deck, a seven-man unit rushed down the gangway, pushing a roller crate before them. The two in front wore Internal Security uniforms. The unit started toward the main gate, but the sand floor of the terrace was soft and hindered their progress. They were heaving forcefully to keep the crate from stalling.

"Great!" O-Scar commented sarcastically. "That sand is supposed to be as hard as ceramic. So much for advanced planning." MacKenzie was about to ask where he had gotten his information, but the unit had reached the main gate. The leader took something from his pocket, pointed at the camera above him, and hitched his thumb.

"Their landing terrace sensors should be experiencing a momentary malfunction," O-Scar stated. He motioned forward with his hand.

The second unit sprinted down the gangway and charged to the base of the wall that rose to the terrace where the Kasserne's main buildings were located. Then they split into two teams and began scaling it like insects.

"How are they doing that?" MacKenzie asked.

"Vacuum pods in the boots and mittens," O-Scar explained. "It works well on smooth surfaces. Thank God, we got that part right."

"Is Security asleep, or are they always this incompetent?" MacKenzie asked.

"They're overconfident. This ship is regularly scheduled, and they're stuck out here where the prophet lost his sandals. We don't think they know who Svetla is. They think she's a low-grade security risk rolled up in a raid. It's their nature not to ask too many questions."

The men in the first unit had broken down the crate and were assembling a small laser cannon. When they finished, two of them checked the controls, then nodded. As soon as they did, the unit leader triggered pencil charges he had placed in the gate's magnetic locks. There was a puff of smoke, followed by a muffled pop, and the gate swung open. The laser cannon disappeared through the dark mouth in the wall.

As yet, no alarm had sounded.

"Well, MacKenzie, are you ready to take a ride?" O-Scar asked, grinning.

"Let's go," MacKenzie replied, following him to a graviton kite beside the air lock door. Although its stand was two meters high, O-Scar mounted it effortlessly, then held down one shovel-like hand to help MacKenzie up.

"Have you ever been in one of these before?" the Libonian asked.

"No. Why?"

"Many find our Libonian toy difficult the first time aboard. I suggest you hang on tight. Are you ready?"

MacKenzie studied the contraption. It consisted of a series of thin wires emanating like umbrella spokes from a center pod. It looked woefully flimsy. He grabbed the handrail and nodded.

The kite leaped off the deck, then shot through the air lock hatch, changing direction so rapidly that MacKenzie almost lost his grip. He had barely regained control when the kite halted in midair, then lurched off in a new direction, hurling him dangerously to one side. Midway between the ship and main gate, it stopped once more without warning, and MacKenzie lost his footing.

He climbed back up on the stand and shot an angry glare at O-Scar, but the big Libonian only grinned outrageously. "Come now, MacKenzie, what's the problem? I thought you were an Outbanker."

"I'm not a damned mind reader! It might help to know when we're going to start and stop," he snarled.

"Very well, I shall keep you informed. But it is, after all, a graviton kite and moves only at integer quantum levels. There's no acceleration or deceleration. You must hang on tight."

"I see," MacKenzie said, accepting the challenge grudgingly.

"We're going up. Are you ready?"

MacKenzie locked his arm around the handrail and clasped his wrists with his hands. "Okay. Let's do it."

The kite shot up with a force that exceeded three G's, but when O-Scar halted its climb, he was ready. He had noticed that the kite only moved in straight lines and always came to a complete halt before changing direction. "For a landlubber, you're pretty good with this thing," MacKenzie said.

"Why, thank you, my friend. Of course, I have had some practice. You seem to be adapting quite well yourself. Perhaps there is something to the Outbanker myth after all." O-Scar's anthracite eyes sparkled with a purple flame, and MacKenzie grimaced, preparing for the next movement. "We're going over the building now."

The kite lurched sideways until it hovered above the flat roof of a penthouse on the top terrace, then O-Scar brought it to a halt. They were preparing to descend when alarms sounded.

"They know we're here!" MacKenzie shouted over the din.

"Yes, but it's nearly three minutes past the planned abort time. Unless they have more troops than we expect, the installation will soon be ours. Let's find your Lieutenant Stocovik before they realize she's what we're after. We're going down."

The kite descended in a series of short falls until it landed on the roof with a bone-jarring thud. O-Scar leapt down and bounded toward a domed hatch set in the roof a few meters away. MacKenzie lowered himself from the kite and followed.

O-Scar bent over the hatch to spin its mechanical locking wheel, but it began to turn by itself. He dropped to a squat, placed a finger next to his lips, and motioned to MacKenzie to get behind him.

The hatch lifted slowly but continuously, and O-Scar pulled a harmonics grenade from his belt. He was about to activate the fuse, when MacKenzie sensed something was wrong. It was too easy. The real danger was elsewhere.

He spun round, looking for another source of attack, and a glint of sunlight reflected from something on a ledge in the cliffs above them. MacKenzie peered up. It was an automatic laser cannon, and at this very moment, it was drawing a bead directly at them.

MacKenzie threw a body block into O-Scar. The Libonian was not only tall but also quite strong and agile. Though taken by surprise, he had barely stumbled out of the line of fire when four laser rounds exploded into the roof around the hatch.

O-Scar turned to survey the devastation, but MacKenzie was already rolling away from him toward the cannon emplacement. A second fusillade slashed higher above him, confirming that the weapon prioritized targets nearest the hatch. As he continued rolling, he saw that O-Scar had escaped the second barrage by diving headlong in the opposite direction, but he couldn't keep evading the fire for long.

MacKenzie rolled to a kneeling position and drew his laser pistol. He took aim at the cannon and squeezed off three consecutive bursts. The cliffside exploded, hurling rock and dust down on him, and a minor avalanche poured debris over the roof. When the dust had settled somewhat, he looked back.

O-Scar had flung open the hatch and was dropping the harmonics grenade through it. MacKenzie was waiting for the explosion, when another bolt of laser fire sluiced over his head. Instinctively he dropped to his belly and looked up.

The gun emplacement had been damaged, but a force field had saved the cannon itself. MacKenzie was taking aim again when he noticed that the cannon barrel tilted upward. Then he saw why. His salvo had destroyed part of the ledge, and as more rock was carried away in the avalanche, the cannon base was sinking into the hole. It fired another sputtering round, but the light bolts passed five meters above O-Scar's head and dissipated harmlessly. Even at maximum deflection, the gun could no longer target the roof.

He was rising when the grenade's aftershock vibrated beneath his feet. MacKenzie cursed. Harmonics grenades weren't lethal, but their pulsations caused great pain and incapacitated anyone within their range for at least an hour. As he sprang forward, he hoped Svetla hadn't been nearby.

By the time he reached the hatch, O-Scar had already

dropped through its mouth. MacKenzie slipped into a crouch, eyeing the sides of the roof for unexpected attackers. The cannon fired another harmless burst that sailed out over the shimmering sapphire of the Inland Sea and broke into a dance of sparkling light.

"Come on down, MacKenzie. The area is secured," O-Scar's voice called from below.

MacKenzie lowered himself through the hatch and slid down the ladder. When he hit the floor, he glanced around. They were in what appeared to be a communications center. Four Security troopers lay sprawled unconscious around the floor. "What is this place?" MacKenzie called.

"The Kasserne's headquarters," O-Scar said as he stepped into the command kiosk in the center of the room. "They coordinate routine operations from here. But during emergencies, control reverts to a Combat Information Center located deep inside the cliffs. Our laser cannon unit is attacking it now." Intermittent vibrations in the floor indicated that, as yet, the Combat Information Center had not been taken.

O-Scar punched commands into one of the keyboards in the kiosk. He studied a display that appeared on a grid screen, then frowned and entered more commands. Finally he said, "Lieutenant Stocovik should be in the last room down the hall. There are two guards at the door, I think."

"What do you mean, 'you think'?"

"The grenade disturbed the circuits in the locator board. The readings are somewhat scram—"

O-Scar was in midsentence when the hallway door slid back and three Security troopers burst in with guns drawn. "Stay where you are and drop your weapons or you're dead!" one of them shouted.

MacKenzie glanced at O-Scar. The Libonian was extending his arm slowly to the side, as if he was going to drop his laser pistol. But his other hand was hidden by the kiosk display boards, and he was drawing a blaster from his thigh holster.

MacKenzie began to raise his hands, but suddenly he dove behind a communications console and scrambled forward a meter on all fours. Two blaster shots smashed behind him.

Then another salvo sounded from the middle of the room. He knew O-Scar was firing. There was no time to consider a course of action. He came to a crouch and leapt up.

Two of the troopers were down, but the third was firing bursts into the kiosk where O-Scar had taken cover. MacKenzie raised his laser and squeezed off three rounds. The last trooper careened back into the wall and sank into a heap.

O-Scar scrambled to his feet, gave MacKenzie a thumbs-up signal, then started for the door. "I'll neutralize Svetla's guards. You stay here until I call," he said.

"No. That won't work now," MacKenzie said quickly. "The guards must be nervous, and the minute you step into the hallway, they'll start blasting. Or they might go straight for Svetla."

"What do you suggest?"

MacKenzie jerked his head at the fallen troopers. "I'll put on one of their uniforms and go down the hall. With any luck, they won't spot the ruse until I neutralize them."

O-Scar stroked his cleft jaw and muttered, "That's contrary to directions. Cyrus doesn't want you to take any chances . . . but he wants Lieutenant Stocovik, too. I don't know. . . ."

MacKenzie let him think. The floor vibrated again with explosions from inside the cliffs, but they seemed less intense. "All right. Your plan makes sense," O-Scar finally agreed.

MacKenzie selected the trooper closest to his size and began stripping his uniform. "Check the locator readings again while I'm getting into this thing. Maybe the circuits are better," he told O-Scar.

The Libonian returned to the kiosk and entered the commands. "It's improved somewhat," he said. "There are two blips in front of the door. They haven't moved, so they must be guards, but there are two blips inside the room, too. That means there must be someone with Svetla." O-Scar was silent a second, then he said, "You were right, MacKenzie. Had we done what I planned, Lieutenant Stocovik might have been liquidated." His voice sounded strangely apologetic. "There can't be any shooting if we can help it. Can you handle the two by the door without guns?"

"I'm trained in the martial arts. I'll let you know in a few minutes."

O-Scar nodded. "All right, but be careful. I'll protect the rear."

MacKenzie pulled on the trooper's helmet, drew a deep breath, held it a long while, and then exhaled, letting his body relax and emptying his mind. Then he opened the door and stepped into the hallway, but instead of starting toward the guards, he turned back and said, "All right, I'll do that while you're cleaning up this mess," as if talking to the other troopers who had attacked. Then he spun and strode purposefully down the hall.

The guards both turned to him. "Hey, what went on in there, anyway? Who the hell's attacking us?" one called anxiously.

MacKenzie didn't answer. He was more than halfway to them now, striding forward and shaking his head from side to side as if thoroughly disgusted. Just a few steps more, he thought. Just a few more. He was almost within reaching distance when the smaller of the two realized he didn't know MacKenzie and went for his blaster.

MacKenzie lunged forward, smashed the man's face with a tiger claw fist that raked his eyes, and followed with a hammer fist to the groin. Then he leaned forward and fired a mule kick at the other guard.

The second man had been slower to suspect the ruse but faster to react physically. MacKenzie's kick knocked the blaster out of his hand, but he was still able to defend himself.

MacKenzie sank into a side horse stance, deciding to let his opponent make the first move. The guard feinted with a jab, then spun into a side kick.

MacKenzie averted the attack effortlessly, but suddenly he recognized its real objective. The man's palm was coming around in an arc, aiming at a security alarm in the wall. MacKenzie launched a flying double kick. His left foot smashed into the arcing arm, but the guard locked MacKenzie's right leg with his elbow and dropped to his knees, hurling him to the floor with a bone-wrenching fall.

MacKenzie tried to roll away, but his stamina was failing and the guard clamped a stranglehold on his neck from behind. The Outbanker lunged backward into him, turning his chin sideways to protect his esophagus, but the arm closed on his throat like a vise, and Mackenzie felt what was left of his strength draining.

He struggled without hope or determination, knowing that in seconds he would lose consciousness and the guard would break his neck. He tried desperately to think of something, but the blood in his brain boiled, and all he remembered were the words of his Ch'en master: *Once applied by an opponent of equal strength, a stranglehold is often impossible to break.* Images of animals being devoured by predators flashed through his mind. He had always been disturbed by the way that stunned prey ultimately submitted to their own slaughter, lying meekly before the fangs that ripped them apart. He was acting like one of those hapless victims now, and it filled him with loathing. In spite of the nausea drowning his lungs, he gathered his last threads of defiance, rolled back his lips, and sank his teeth into the exposed part of the guard's forearm. He sank them in deep, clenching them like the pit bulls he had seen once in a gambling den on Ektelon. And suddenly he knew, with a sensation almost erogenous, that he was tasting blood.

Somewhere beyond the roar in his ears, he thought he heard a groan, and it filled him with a grizzled sense of satisfaction. Then he felt a massive reverberation, like rotten timber popping in the dead of winter, and miraculously the iron grip around his neck fell away.

MacKenzie tumbled to the floor, gulping down huge drafts of sweet air. Somehow he had been snatched from the brink of death. He was still alive. It took a while to catch his breath, and granular dots swarmed before his eyes, but when he looked up, O-Scar's dark face was hovering above him.

"Are you all right?" the Libonian asked.

"I think so," he replied through a hoarse throat. "But that was cutting it close. I thought I was a goner." He tried to get up, but his head spun, and he slouched back against the wall until the dizziness passed. He glanced over at the second guard. He looked asleep, but his head was turned in the wrong direction. "Did you do that?" he inquired.

"Who else?" O-Scar said. "Certainly not you—though I must admit, you would have forced his submission sooner or later with that hold you devised."

MacKenzie tried again to rise. This time he succeeded. He guessed that no more than a minute had passed since he had started down the hall toward the guards, but time could be essential. "Can you get this open?" he asked, pointing at the door to the room where they believed Svetla was imprisoned.

O-Scar nodded and punched in a code. The scrambler beeps began. When they ended, the door slid back. MacKenzie entered quickly, his blaster hidden against his hip.

The room was an L-shaped suite, dark except for a halo of light around the ceiling and a floor lamp glowing by an easy chair. He searched frantically for the last guard. Then he saw Svetla. She was behind the easy chair, just beyond the pool of yellow light cast by the floor lamp. Though her face was in the shadows, he recognized the high cheekbones and straight nose. She was looking at him with a peculiar blank stare.

He crouched, his eyes darting from side to side, searching for the remaining guard. Adrenaline was pumping, priming his reactions, but there seemed to be no one else in the suite. Then Svetla lifted her hand and pointed to the bed. MacKenzie thought she was telling him where the guard was hiding, and he poised to spring.

But before he could move, O-Scar appeared to his left, took aim, and shot Svetla in the face with his laser. She arched back like a stricken gymnast and crashed to the floor. MacKenzie turned on him savagely. "What in the hell are you doing?"

"It wasn't Svetla," O-Scar shouted back. "It was the imposter. Svetla has no left hand."

"How can you be sure? They might have given her a bionic one!"

"I saw the locator board, remember? There's someone on the bed. I shot the imposter. Go see for yourself. She was going to kill Svetla."

MacKenzie rushed over to the woman lying behind the easy chair. He knelt down and lifted her head. A dark wig slipped back, exposing a shock of limp, flaxen hair. He pushed it off, and it fell next to the molecular phaser she had been aiming at the bed. He felt the woman's neck for a pulse. He found one, but it was weak. He didn't care.

O-Scar had found the light controls on the reading table next to the easy chair. He touched the sensors and the suite brightened. Then he looked at MacKenzie and motioned at the bed with his head. MacKenzie started toward it. Someone was wrapped tightly in a restraint sheet, only the head protruding above its taut, elastic sheen. When he came to the bed, he peered down. It was Svetla.

Her eyes were open slightly, but they seemed unfocused. Her lips were parted and badly parched. He reached down and touched her forehead. It was cold and damp. She looked drugged. He leaned over and whispered in her ear. "Svetla, it's me . . . MacKenzie. Everything is all right now. You're safe." He watched for signs of recognition, but there were none.

O-Scar leaned over his shoulder and said anxiously, "How is she?"

MacKenzie shrugged. "I don't know. She's not responding." His eyes followed the edge of the restraint sheet to the bottom of the mattress. It was attached to a velcra binding that ran the length of the frame. He released it and the sheet snapped back, falling to the floor on the opposite side of the bed. Svetla was naked.

Her eyes still registered nothing. The only sign of response was gooseflesh that appeared on her skin as the cool air touched her clammy body. She looked as though she had lost weight. MacKenzie sat on the edge of the bed, took her right hand, and stroked it gently. He leaned over and said again, "Svetla? It's me, MacKenzie."

She did not respond.

Suddenly two men burst through the doorway, lasers at the ready. MacKenzie and O-Scar spun toward them, ready to repulse an attack, until they saw that the two were part of the unit that had scaled the terrace wall.

"The Kasserne is secured, sir," one of them stated. "We sustained two casualties. One is dead."

O-Scar's chiseled jaw clenched. "Who was it?" he asked.

"Michaelis, sir. The bastards in Combat Information Center set their blasters to kill. A lucky shot got him as we rushed in."

"What about Internal Security?"

"Two dead, sir. Victims of their own crossfire. No one can blame us. Our weapons were all set on stun."

O-Scar said, "Did you count the one in the hallway?"

"Not yet, sir." O-Scar turned his head and mumbled something MacKenzie couldn't understand, but the commando continued. "There's something else though, sir. We think the Outbank cruiser you've been searching for is in an underground hangar. It has the right markings."

"Ah-ha! A stroke of fortune," O-Scar exclaimed, turning to MacKenzie.

MacKenzie smiled back, but without appreciation. He was too worried about Svetla. He sat down on the bed again and lifted her up gently. Her head dropped forward as if she were asleep, but her eyes were still open. MacKenzie looked at O-Scar, but the big Libonian could offer no consolation.

MacKenzie shook her gently and said, "Svetla, can you hear me? You're all right now. Do you understand? You've been rescued. You're safe."

For the first time, he sensed a response. She lifted her head a bit, and there was a flicker in the haze of her black eyes. She blinked and moved her lips. He pulled her close, cradling her head in his hand so her mouth was near his ear. "Safe?" she echoed, almost inaudibly.

MacKenzie hugged her in excitement, then pulled back and said, "Yes, safe! There's nothing more to fear."

She blinked again, then stared at the room as though seeing it for the first time. Her curiosity was encouraging, and MacKenzie laid her down again so she could be more relaxed. "We should cover her. Give me that sheet," he said.

"Yes, of course," said O-Scar. He went to the other side of the bed, lifted the sheet, and passed it over. MacKenzie tucked it under the mattress. Svetla didn't stir, but when he looked up, she was watching him with a haunting look. Her eyes were wide, but there was no expression in them.

Then suddenly she rolled toward him. She lifted her arm as if to place a finger before his lips with her missing hand, and MacKenzie flinched.

"Sssssshhhh . . . " she said. "We must be careful."

She motioned him closer, as if wanting to share a confidence. He leaned down and she continued. "MacKenzie sings safe and quite lovely he dances, but beware, simple girl, of that magic man's trances. For a hand or an arm is quite nothing to lose, when your being's devoured by his winsomeless muse." MacKenzie shrank back, but Svetla sat up and pulled him toward her. She smiled wistfully, the fine lines round her eyes crinkling, and then she said, "Wait! Tell him . . . tell the wizard this. Tell him I know the truth and he can't trick me. Tell him . . . " She hesitated. Her face glowed with a heartrending innocence, and when she began again, it was in a lilting, singsong voice, "Oh, I recall the planet red. It's Hyperion Six, and it is dead. It has no atmosphere at all but mountains ten thousand meters tall." She stared at him playfully, as if expecting some response. It was a nursery rhyme she'd repeated, one that children learned in the first form to memorize the different planets in the Cygni System.

Svetla giggled impishly, as if totally pleased with herself. MacKenzie was so devastated he did not realize that while she had recited the rhyme, she had taken his hand in hers and was clasping it tightly.

CHAPTER 17

Thirty minutes after Basalt Kasserne was captured, Cyrus Magnum arrived with the members of his staff. He consulted with O-Scar, then took decisive action.

The Land Corps units stationed on Red Cliff had always been fiercely loyal to Cyrus. Its officers did not hesitate when Cyrus ordered the headquarters battalion to begin rounding up all Internal Security units on Red Cliff. Next he ordered a reinforced regiment on maneuver in the Great Desert to assault the Flight Corps station. Caught by surprise and severely outgunned, the Flight Corps provost was overrun, and within minutes, the headquarters buildings had been secured.

While that phase of the operation was being successfully completed, commercial media were ordered off the air, and Cyrus announced on public holovision that there had been an attempted *coup d'etat*. He informed the citizenry that he was declaring martial law and advised them to return to their homes immediately, since anyone found on the streets after one hour would be detained by the military. He assured them that the measures were temporary but necessary, and authorized under the "Crisis Powers Doctrine" of Prefecture. The civilian population obeyed without protest.

In those first few hours, MacKenzie wasn't really aware of what was happening, nor did he care to find out. Land Corps medical teams had arrived shortly after Cyrus and his entourage. They had diagnosed Svetla's malady as nervous exhaustion induced by psychotropic chemical injection. The diagnosis was confirmed by the Kasserne commandant's admissions during interrogation. He explained that Colonel Van Sander had been enraged when Svetla would give nothing but her name, rank, and service number no matter what they threatened, and had subsequently ordered the chemical conditioning.

These revelations both angered and bewildered MacKenzie, and he sat beside Svetla's sedated body as if in a catatonic trance, unable to take his eyes from the pink stump of her left wrist.

The longer he sat and stared, the more the severed arm seemed to symbolize the futility and illusion of life. And all of his victories—from the savage combat at Pegasus Station during his first mission, to his most recent brush with death just a scant hour before—suddenly seemed hollow and shameful.

He remembered the guard with his head turned in the wrong direction, and he was overcome with sorrow. The need to fight, to conquer or destroy an enemy, no longer seemed important. It occurred to him that direct negotiation might have won Svetla's freedom. It had simply not been considered. And he felt he was to blame.

What are we doing here? he wondered bitterly. Killing and maiming just to secure one group of leaders against another? Of what importance is that? Or must we prove through sacrifice that one world view is superior to another? Does such a thing justify this carnage? What is it, in the end, that compels us to feel we must be part of something more significant than the simple act of living?

He recalled his bloodlust as he destroyed the Rashadian robots with his pistol, the rush of power he had experienced as the gun recoiled and the Rashadian machines crumbled. Beside that lust, everything else had momentarily paled. Is that why men were driven to combat? he asked himself. To escape a sense of their own weakness in a wager where the stakes were a matter of life and death?

In the midst of this self-critical, morbidly questioning mood, he experienced a flash of realization. He understood suddenly that he had always been playing at being a hero. In spite of his ultimate fears and hesitations, something forced him to function on the border, near the edge of mortal danger. It was why he had become an Outbanker!

Then he thought of his father, the man he had never known, the man who had turned his back on his marriage oath and chosen self-immolation, only to be assumed into the pantheon of public myth. Perhaps he had inherited this need from that first Outbanker, assimilated it mentally through funerary tears, assumed it in his heart with the posthumous honors, melded it into his very soul with every piteous glance. He had been seduced by the power of death.

Something Uncle Jock had told him once, while he was still a child and wounded in heart, repeated in his memory. "Lad, don't trouble yourself about your dad. Sooner or later everybody passes on." And that reality—that terrible, unconscionable wrath of creation—had twisted his child's existential rage at his father's loss into the man's fixation with the significance of inescapable, personal doom.

He realized this now as clearly as he had ever known anything, because Svetla's accusing limb pointed at him, immutable and condemning, more terrible than any tribunal of judgment yet conceived.

He sat as if paralyzed a long while.

Finally a medivac crew came to take Svetla to a camp where Cyrus had arranged for her rehabilitation. MacKenzie wanted to go with her, but the crew leader informed him that Cyrus wanted him to report immediately. MacKenzie had no heart for protest, but he did follow them to the landing terrace, where he watched as the crew loaded Svetla into the air ambulance, and when the ship faded into the cerulean blue of the horizon, he felt as though his insides had turned to rot.

* * * * *

Cyrus sat at a wide situation table in the Kasserne's Combat Information Center conferring with his staff aides. It was a few seconds before he noticed MacKenzie and addressed him. "Please sit down. I'll be with you shortly," he said. By the time MacKenzie had taken a chair, the aides were preparing to leave, and Cyrus said, "How are you, Ian? I must apologize for not congratulating you earlier on the mission's success, but things have been hectic." MacKenzie stared down morosely and said nothing. Cyrus studied him a moment, then stood and walked around the table toward him. "I understand Lieutenant Stocovik took quite a beating. How is she now?" he asked as he sat down beside MacKenzie.

MacKenzie shrugged. He continued studying a pattern of

mottled fingerprints someone had left on the buffed onyx of the table.

"Well, don't despair. I've asked Dr. Fronto to look after her. He's the best biocyberneticist in the Concordat, and he'll see to it she's mended in due course. In the meantime, there's something important I want you to do."

MacKenzie looked up, his curiosity aroused.

"You know that I have declared martial law. I'm afraid your instincts were quite accurate. Sedition is afoot. The whole Internal Security contingent is under arrest and being held in a makeshift prison under the Coliseum grandstands." Cyrus hesitated a moment, as if waiting for some response, but the information did not interest MacKenzie. He was still too morose to care.

"That is why you must do something very difficult for me," Cyrus continued. "You are to get Van Sander and bring her back here for interrogation. But on the way, I want you to let her escape."

MacKenzie was certain his ears had played tricks, and he cast a confused glance at the prefect.

"Yes, I'm serious, Ian. I can't explain why to you yet, but there is good reason for it. Van Sander must go free. It is imperative."

"You can't possibly mean that," he whispered, "after all that scheming bitch has done. Besides, why must I be the one to do it?"

"Because no one is better suited. Nearly everyone would consider it a miracle if you don't throttle her where she stands, so no one will consider the escape intentional. Not even Van Sander herself."

MacKenzie shook his head. "I have no stomach for it." He hesitated a moment. "I'm to blame, you see."

Cyrus frowned and asked, "To blame for what?"

"For everything."

"Nonsense, my boy. You're just a bit run-down. It's not unusual to feel somewhat depressed after what you've been through."

"I'm not depressed!" MacKenzie said vehemently. "I understand now what I've been doing all these years. I realized while I was sitting with Svetla, wondering what I might have done differently."

"So you think you're to blame for what happened to her?"

"Partially. But it's more than that," MacKenzie said impatiently. "From the beginning, I've been mesmerized by death. I've hunted it like some Ahab in his little ship. I've challenged it at every opportunity to show it couldn't break me. But it wasn't me that died or was maimed . . . it was the others. They didn't suspect what really drove me, and they paid the price. Do you see?"

"No, I do not, Ian. And I'm being honest."

MacKenzie turned to face Cyrus. The man was observing him with thoughtful, agate eyes, and it seemed important that he understand. "Death has been using me, don't you see?" He shook his head back and forth with a gloomy, depressed motion. "It's used me to the point where I'm sick of it—sick of the Pegasus Stations and the charred babies and the Svetlas and the dead guards. I thought I was challenging death, but I was really infatuated by it. Why hide? I thought. Why pretend it didn't matter, when it did? Go seek it out. Tempt it. Don't you see? I was lusting for it!"

Cyrus stood and walked slowly to the head of the situation table. When he was behind the chair, he turned back to MacKenzie and said, "You completely baffle me, Ian. I don't know about your charred babies and dead guards, but you can't believe that defending Pegasus Station was wrong."

MacKenzie recalled the incident for the hundredth time. He had been on his first patrol, when the deep space tactical satellite came under Rashadian assault. He had engaged their fleet single-handedly, without hesitation or forethought, and quickly scored five kills. Believing no Outbanker would mount such a suicidal attack without reinforcements nearby, the terrorists broke off in retreat. He could still hear the fading screams of his targets as they were being consumed by nuclear fire. His brave—make that reckless—defense had brought him instant fame.

"It *was* wrong," he said. "They were Rashadians, yes. But

they were also husbands and fathers. They had children who will never know them. But I couldn't wait to wade in so they'd have the chance to finish me off. It seemed a fair trade then, but it wasn't a trade at all. It was a wager."

"You did the job you were trained for, Ian. What else could you have done?" Cyrus asked.

"I don't know, but there are alternatives in life. There always are."

Cyrus shook his head as though he had been through this before. "You are wrong, MacKenzie," he said. "What's more, you're wallowing in your moral superiority and enjoying it. You couldn't have done anything different, and if you had, everyone on that space station would have paid with his life. Then how guilty would you feel now?" He pulled the chair back, lowered himself into it, and sighed. "The same is true with Lieutenant Stocovik. How else might you have handled things? Oh, yes, we question things when we are in a warm, safe chair, pondering events with the benefit of dispassionate hindsight. God knows, I've done enough of that myself. It's only human to condemn ourselves for being stupid when we were not able to be otherwise. But don't you see, Ian? That is the essence of hubris."

MacKenzie appreciated the prefect's efforts to console him, but logic couldn't dent his gloom. He had finally realized what he was, and there was no remedy for it. "The point is, sir, that even if I had realized what drove me, I would have done it anyway. It wouldn't have mattered."

Cyrus pinioned him with a smoldering stare. "Must you continue to punish yourself for it, then? Must you withdraw like a hermit in a hair shirt?" Cyrus slammed the table angrily with his fist. "No! I think not! You have talents, my boy, talents the Concordat needs desperately at this very moment. And I don't give a tinker's damn what motivates them." The prefect stood brusquely. There was a look of determination on his face.

"We are in mortal danger, MacKenzie. The political intrigue you exposed is more serious than you can imagine. The welfare of the Concordat itself is at stake, and if I can't prove that Internal Security has mounted treason, we may still fall into their hands—you, me, and your beloved Svetla. In that regard, Pieta Van Sander is the key. If she escapes, she has but one place to run—to her allies. And when she does, we'll have the proof I need." Cyrus fell silent and stared at MacKenzie for a long moment. "I can't permit you to indulge in self-pity just to salve your patently overworked scruples with all that is hanging in the balance," he concluded. "I simply won't."

MacKenzie stared at Cyrus Magnum helplessly. If Svetla's life was at stake, if the Concordat was in danger, he had no choice. He had to honor the oath he had taken so many years ago, while an intrepid youth with necrovoyeur's rot: *I, Ian S. MacKenzie, do solemnly swear to uphold the liberty of the Concordat and the colonial societies in its care. And I shall . . .*

Cyrus studied him with the look of a chess master. "Do you understand now why you must do what I ask?" he asked softly.

MacKenzie nodded.

Cyrus stared down at the pin lights flashing on the situation table. Each light indicated the position of a military unit on the planetoid. "Find O-Scar and coordinate the mission with him," he said. "I think you will find him very useful. And now, if you will excuse me, I have other urgent matters to attend to."

MacKenzie stood, saluted gauntly, and started toward the door. But before he reached it, Cyrus called, "Have you considered that the space jump may have done something to you both?"

MacKenzie turned back and said, "I'm not sure what you mean."

"Both you and Svetla experienced something extraordinary. Your molecular structures must have been annihilated, then reassembled again. Though there is no medical sign of trauma, it stands to reason that both her withdrawal and your depression may be residual aftereffects of the jump. Frankly, I'm surprised you both came through it as well as you did."

MacKenzie realized Cyrus had saved that thought until last, that he had been waiting for exactly the right time to use it. "I see what you mean," he said. "I hadn't considered that."

Cyrus smiled. "Well, I'm glad I mentioned it, then." He looked back at the situation table. The discussion had ended. MacKenzie turned slowly and walked out of the Combat Information Center, leaving the prefect of Red Cliff alone to consider his next gambit.

CHAPTER 18

It took MacKenzie and O-Scar four hours to finalize plans for Pieta Van Sander's escape. They decided a motor failure in the shuttle craft bringing them to the Kasserne would provide the opportunity she needed. In such cases of motor failure, life safety systems ejected passengers automatically and set them down over a wide area. Since O-Scar's intelligence indicated that a few Internal Security deep agents were still free in the manufacturing district of Central City, it was logical to assume that Van Sander would find them.

Darkness had fallen by the time they arrived at the Central City Coliseum. They parked in front of the main gate and asked for the lieutenant colonel commanding the makeshift prison. When he came out, O-Scar told him to take them to Van Sander's isolation cell.

They followed him along the main causeway as it curved to the north end of the facility. There were apparently hundreds of detainees in the offices and locker rooms beneath the coliseum stands, and interrogation of enlisted ranks had begun. The sound of intelligence teams coercing information from hapless prisoners was ominously evident. At one point, as they were curving round the northwest causeway, they saw three dazed Security troopers being escorted back to their cells. Their faces had a blue pallor under the phosphorescent lights.

Pieta Van Sander was detained in a cargo container at the north end of the coliseum. The lieutenant colonel banged on the metal door twice, then released the locking lever. The door swung back, releasing the sour smell of body odor and urine. "Out. On the double!" he shouted.

Van Sander emerged slowly from the dark mouth of the container. She wore nothing but a soiled shift, and her gangly body glistened with rivulets of gritty sweat. She squinted uncertainly in the pale light, but as soon as her eyes adjusted and she recognized MacKenzie, she said, "Ah, Commander, so we meet again."

MacKenzie didn't respond, but seeing her in her present condition made him wonder why he had considered her a menace. O-Scar turned to the commandant and said, "Get her cleaned up and into some clothes. The prefect wants to question her personally. We'll wait for her by our sedan at the main gate."

"Yes, sir!" the commandant snapped. "Will fatigues be acceptable? I'm afraid that's all we have."

"Fatigues will be fine," O-Scar answered, casting MacKenzie a furtive glance.

"Guards!" the commandant shouted. Two military policemen emerged from the shadows and snapped to attention. "Get this prisoner showered and into clean fatigues. Then bring her to the main gate."

"Yes, sir!" the older of the two acknowledged. They took positions on either side of Van Sander, grasped her bony arms, and hurried her off along the causeway at a trot.

"Shall I escort you to the gate?" the commandant inquired.

O-Scar said, "That won't be necessary, Colonel. Thanks for your help."

The commandant saluted and walked down the causeway after Van Sander and the two guards.

MacKenzie and O-Scar started back toward the main gate. They were passing one of the concession stands that had been hurriedly converted into an interrogation center when a scream pierced the soft rumble of the intelligence teams at their work. MacKenzie shot O-Scar a troubled glance, but the Libonian only smiled grimly and quickened his pace. Outside the coliseum, they could breathe again.

"Phew! That place stinks!" MacKenzie told O-Scar.

"It's fear, old boy—fear and efficient interrogations."

"Cyrus says the whole Security contingent has been arrested. What the hell's going on?"

O-Scar nodded. "First the interrogations. Then soon, very soon perhaps, there may be executions."

"Executions!" MacKenzie said in dismay. "You mean Cyrus is actually taking things that far?"

"You don't appreciate the seriousness of the crisis," O-Scar said sternly. "This is no parlor game we're playing. Cyrus is fighting for his life . . . for all our lives."

"Well, it must be God-damned serious, if you're going to start liquidating people. What in the hell is happening?"

"You don't need to know. Just tend your knitting and you'll be all right."

The admonition angered MacKenzie, but he decided there was no use complaining. "How many executions will there be?"

"I don't know. Enough to make the point, if it becomes necessary."

"To make what point, for Christ's sake?"

"Mind your own business, MacKenzie. It's the best policy at times like these."

O-Scar's attitude was insulting. Here in the coliseum, he was being presented with the grisly results of something else he had started, and the Libonian acted as though it shouldn't concern him. "I hope there's a damned good reason for all this," he mumbled. The vision of corpses lining mass graves filled his mind's eye. He felt angry . . . and nauseated.

A few minutes later the guards appeared, ushering the handcuffed Pieta Van Sander between them. The older guard gave O-Scar the manacle key chip, then shoved the colonel into the back seat of the Magnarover. O-Scar got in beside her and slammed the door. MacKenzie slipped into the front seat, turned on the headlamps, and fired the motor. In moments, they were speeding down Concordat Boulevard on their way to the Land Corps shuttle port.

When they had reached cruising speed, Van Sander leaned forward slightly and said, "It seems the tables have been turned. I compliment you, MacKenzie."

"Save your stinking breath, Colonel. You'll need it," he said.

"Where are you taking me?"

"To a highly fitting place. You know it well—or at least your sadist stooges with the injection guns do."

"I don't know what you're talking about," she mumbled as she slumped back in the seat.

"Of course not. But some of the same treatment your friends ordered up for Svetla will refresh your memory, I assure you."

The colonel gave O-Scar a confused glance, but the Libonian merely stared at her coldly. "I can only repeat, I have no idea what you are talking about," she complained.

Her pretension aggravated the anger that O-Scar's cavalier attitude had already kindled in MacKenzie, and he tromped down on the accelerator. Van Sander was a professional liar, the worst possible kind. Something about her self-righteousness made him livid with rage.

MacKenzie braked hard and turned into Palmetto Way, a narrow boulevard with giant palms set in a sandy median strip. Their silver trunks began flashing past in the Magnarover lights as he accelerated again.

They approached a Land Corps mechanized unit moving along slowly in the street. MacKenzie blew a warning siren, and the troop carriers pulled aside to let him pass.

As soon as they were clear, he floored the accelerator, and the sedan lurched forward again. They plummeted into a sharp S-curve that snaked around the commissary area, and the Magnarover skidded slightly with the momentum.

"Watch your speed!" O-Scar cautioned. "We want to get our girl friend here to the shuttle port in one piece."

"If I don't get her out of my sight soon, I'm likely to take her apart right here," MacKenzie snarled, turning the steering wheel to the right.

Suddenly a troop bus loomed dead ahead. It had pulled out of the commissary parking lot and was blocking the street.

MacKenzie slammed on the brakes, and the magnetic motors reversed, jamming him forward against the steering column. The sedan skidded, its rear end skewing far to the left, and he tried to correct the skid. But he turned too far, and the rear end slashed back in the other direction, sending the Magnarover completely out of control. The crash balloons were opening under the dashboard, but much too slowly, a malfunction of some kind.

The last things MacKenzie remembered were the palmetto

trunk growing massive in the windscreen before him and the sinking feeling in his stomach as he braced for impact.

* * * * *

"Wake up, Ian. You've been asleep far too long."

The voice was familiar, but somewhere far off. MacKenzie grunted and tried to open his eyes, but they seemed glued shut. He attempted to sit up, but a pair of hands grabbed his shoulders and pushed him back.

"Relax, my boy. This is no time to be overly rambunctious. You've had an accident."

He remembered the tree trunk looming before him, then the shattering sound. Yes, there had been an accident. "Is that you, Cyrus?" he asked weakly.

"Yes, it is. You collided with a tree, Ian. Do you remember? You sustained a concussion and a few lacerations. But the doctors have mended you back up. A day or two and you'll be on your feet again."

A dull throb was pounding in MacKenzie's head. "Why can't I open my eyes?"

"They're bandaged, but don't concern yourself about it. Your vision isn't impaired. The medics will remove them tomorrow."

MacKenzie reached up and touched the wrappings. They felt slippery and cold. "How is O-Scar?" he asked, lowering his hands.

"None the worse for wear. He wrenched his neck slightly, but he's very strong." MacKenzie nodded. The pain in his head was getting worse. "Your other passenger was also uninjured," Cyrus continued. "She ran to the troop bus you swerved to avoid and organized medical assistance. Very sporting of her, don't you think?'"

"She was . . . restrained. How did she manage that?"

"Credit O-Scar in that regard. He feigned unconsciousness. Your guest just helped herself to the key chip in his pocket."

"I see," MacKenzie said. The pain in his head was severe now. "Did she really escape, then?"

"Not the way you mean. O-Scar had teams paralleling your

route. One of them caught sight of her hurrying along a block or so away. She's been under long-range surveillance ever since."

"That's good."

"Yes, everything worked out, though not quite according to plan."

MacKenzie felt a surge of shame. "I guess I screwed up," he said.

"Nonsense. Accidents happen. I only hope you aren't going to wallow in more useless self-contempt. That would be a bore. Just take a few days to recuperate, then it's off to the encampment to join Svetla and Dr. Fronto. Svetla is doing much better, by the way. I thought you would like knowing that."

To join Svetla . . . yes! MacKenzie nodded, but it made his head hurt. "How long have I been unconscious?" he asked.

"About eighteen hours," Cyrus said. He patted MacKenzie's shoulder. "The nurse will be here soon to give you something for the pain. Just relax and get better as soon as you can. We're not out of the woods yet, but things are going as well as can be expected. And as usual, there's more I need you to do. There is the phenomenon to consider. We must learn if it can be replicated. I don't have to tell you how strategically important that is."

The phenomenon? MacKenzie wondered foggily. Oh, yes! The space jump. Our glowing bodies, unified like perfect spirit creatures, galloping down a brilliant valley of compressed— "Good-bye, Ian. Rest well," Cyrus said.

MacKenzie listened to the prefect's footsteps fading away. What had he said—"going as well as can be expected"? *What* was? He tried to think. Concordat in danger . . . Proof of alliances . . . Van Sander would run . . . Flush out political opponents . . . Liquidate me and Svetla and Cyrus himself . . . An elongated scream from under the grandstands.

Thought increased his pain, and the pain made him nauseated. For a while, he feared he would vomit. The sight of mass graves tried to crystallize in his mind, but he shut out the scene. He thought of Svetla, of holding her as he had while they were making love over a year before. It sent a tingle of pleasure through his nerves, relieving the pain in his head somewhat, but still he felt sick.

Then suddenly Sheila's voice sounded in his memory: *"Of course not, Mac. Can't you tell when I am joking?"* Sheila! he thought. I didn't even visit her after the raid on the Kasserne because I was sitting with Svetla. Somehow the oversight filled him with immense sadness. He felt like weeping.

"I'm going to give you something to make you sleep, Commander," a woman's voice said from somewhere above him. He felt the cold nozzle of a hypogun press his right shoulder and a mild burning as it hissed. "There. That should make you feel better in no time."

Something to sleep? Yes . . . "To sleep, perchance to dream. And in dreaming say we" . . . what? What had the poet said? He couldn't remember. It troubled him for a moment, but then he no longer cared. The pain in his head was subsiding, taking with it his anxiety and torment. He would sleep. The sleep would relieve the pain and mend his mind. At least he hoped it would. There was no choice. He was already drifting off. And as he sank into the void of unconsciousness, he gave himself up to Taogott in the innocent hope that he would not again see burned babies.

BOOK THREE

SVETLA STOCOVIK

"I loved mathematics because it made one secure. As long as you understood the process of their logic, the equations left you stalwart. Quantum physics was replete with uncertainty, but matrix mechanics provided mathematical structure to describe, and therefore to render it conditional.

"It was some time before I learned that the quantifying heart fears a realm of chaos at the center of existence that condemns us to a demonic fate beyond our power to estimate or influence.

"And it was a very long time before I learned that the uncontrolled was neither chaotic nor demonic. That it was the logic of the equations themselves that is the soul stealer."[3]

---

3. *Svetla: An Autobiography*, The Concordat Press (Ektelon Central, Ektelon), 2372 EC, p. 36.

CHAPTER 19

The term "encampment" augured images of a rough, pre-fabricated installation. It didn't prepare MacKenzie for what he saw as he stepped from the Land Corps shuttle.

Three Nihonian-style buildings joined by a common terrace of red stone were set in a semicircle midway up the north slope of a lush valley. A brook ambled through the garden between the buildings and emptied into a stream, which separated the landing pad from the compound. An arched, wooden bridge spanned the stream.

The buildings were backdropped by a copse of mature Mangalam trees, whose gnarled branches formed a thatch that fanned out like a parasol, providing shade from the midday heat and protection from the infrequent but sudden squalls that came up in the narrow temperate zone.

The flight crew leapt from the shuttle, pulled out Mac-Kenzie's luggage, and started over the wooden bridge. Mac-Kenzie followed them. They were nearing the terrace stairs, when three people emerged from the main building and stood waiting on the porch.

Two were Nihonian women. They wore traditional kimonos with wide cummerbunds, and ornate combs in their jet-black hair.

The other was an older man. He wasn't tall, but his carriage imparted stature. His closely cropped chestnut hair was gray at the temples, and brown eyes danced jovially above an aristocratic nose. He wore an impeccably tailored white suit and soft white slippers. He came down from the porch and crossed the terrace to greet MacKenzie.

"Commander, permit me to introduce myself. I am Dr. Phillip Fronto," he said.

"It's a pleasure," MacKenzie replied. "Cyrus Magnum holds you in the greatest esteem."

"You are too kind." He took MacKenzie's arm and led him toward the porch steps. The flight crew followed at a courteous distance. When they reached the Nihonian women, Fronto said, "May I introduce Terrie and Inayu," motioning to each of the Nihonians in turn as he called their name.

The women bowed, smiled demurely, and chirped, "Hello. Pleasure."

MacKenzie said, "How do you do?" with a stiff formality that disguised his vague discomfort. Then he turned to Fronto and asked, "Are these ladies part of your treatment team?"

"No, they're with Cyrus Magnum's staff, but both are trained in Nihonian holistic healing methods and make excellent nurses. They're very good with Svetla. She seems to like them."

The Nihonians turned and shuffled through the door on small but perfectly formed bare feet. Fronto started after them, but then remembered the flight crew. "Excuse me, gentlemen," he intoned. "Please bring the commander's bags to his room. It's on the second floor, to the left. Just go up the stairs and call for Tanya. She'll show you."

The crewmen passed through the doorway, exchanging a curious glance. After they were out of earshot, MacKenzie asked Fronto, "Who is Tanya?"

"She is Chief of Encampment Security, I believe. But you know how Cyrus's people can be. I am not certain what her official role is."

"Is she attractive?"

Fronto grimaced. "Pppffuuhh . . . a real Amazon. Muscular. Blond. Two meters tall if she's a centimeter. She could carry your bags and those two crewmen to your room by herself."

"Then the wildest dreams of the flight crew are about to be realized," MacKenzie mused.

Fronto grinned quizzically, then took his arm again. He ushered MacKenzie through the doorway. "Why don't we have some lunch?" he said. "You must be famished. We shall join Lieutenant Stocovik later."

MacKenzie wasn't hungry, but he didn't argue. He followed Fronto through the entryway and along a carpeted corridor that ran the length of the building.

"How is Svetla, Doctor?"

"Much better physically, but her psychic state worries me. There is something unusual going on. But I shall explain more while we enjoy our repast." He halted by one of the doors to his right, opened it, and motioned to MacKenzie with an exaggerated wave of the hand. "After you."

They entered a spacious dining room. It had an oriental decor, but the wide table and high-backed chairs were postmodern and functional. "Please make yourself comfortable," Fronto said, sliding one of the chairs back for him. "I hope you enjoy the bill of fare. I've selected it myself, in honor of your arrival."

MacKenzie took the chair offered, but as soon as the doctor was seated, he said, "I don't wish to seem rude, but I'm most anxious to learn about Svetla. Could we discuss your findings before we eat?"

Fronto gave him an amiable smile. He rang a porcelain bell, and one of the Nihonians appeared from behind a sliding wall panel. She bowed slightly and said, "Yes, sir? How may I help you?"

"Delay lunch, will you, Terrie? The commander and I wish to converse a bit. However, you may bring the cafe." The woman bowed again and closed the panel. "I must apologize, Commander. I grow famished when I'm excited and forget that everyone does not." Fronto fell silent as he collected his thoughts, and when he spoke his mood became intensely professional. "First let me assure you my diagnosis is not exotic. Lieutenant Stocovik suffered an episode of hysterical withdrawal, complicated by the chemical conditioning administered by Internal Security. Beside some abnormal activity in the hypocamal area of the brain, she has recovered. But I fear she suffered a psychological conflict that remains unresolved."

"What kind of conflict, Doctor?"

"I'm not certain."

"The hypocamal activity you mentioned—would it have something to do with her condition?"

"I hardly think so. That area is somewhat unstable electrically. A number of studies correlate its function with religious experiences, but I fail to see how the two could be connected.

Have you any idea how they might?"

"Perhaps she experienced a spiritual trauma," MacKenzie ventured, wondering why Fronto would expect him to know.

"I suppose that is possible," the doctor remarked. "You both experienced something momentous, a first in the history of mankind. Svetla may have attached religious significance to it that her Slavian materialism forces her to repress." He hesitated and studied MacKenzie with interest. "But do you accept the possibility of spiritual conflict, Commander?"

"Shouldn't I?" MacKenzie asked.

"Having never seen it, many refuse to entertain such a proposition. They demand that reality be defined through scientifically empirical processes."

"Most positivists haven't been on the Outbanks."

"Really! What does that have to do with it?"

MacKenzie studied the doctor's eyes. They seemed sincere. "I suppose it's a matter of perspective," he answered. "When you are so far out, you are assaulted by the immensity of the void. Your dependence on material things to describe significance is devastated. At first it can be terrifying. You begin to fear that emptiness is reality, and your sense of being an illusion. Normal patterns of cause and effect, which you've always relied on to create a safe, predictable environment, become absurdly meaningless. You feel insignificant in the face of that cold immensity . . . and lost. Ultimately you either become resigned to it or commit suicide.

"If you resign yourself, something marvelous happens, though. You begin to sense a magnificent cosmic dance. You become aware of a repetition of patterns at different levels of space-time. Quanta whirling in atoms, whirling in elements, whirling in us, while we whirl in a star system within a galaxy within a cosmos. And where at first you feared there was nothing, you finally sense the working of an organizing power." MacKenzie hesitated, leaned back, and sighed. He had never talked about this before, and he wasn't sure it was making sense. "I suppose you must experience it, Doctor."

"Please go on," Fronto urged.

MacKenzie shifted in his chair before he continued. "Well,

you sometimes sense something underpinning existence—your own personal existence and everything else. Even the void. You begin to feel a transcendent presence from which all else springs. It doesn't happen very often, unfortunately, but when it does, you understand it is eternal and intransmutable. And—" he hesitated before saying the last—"it is aware."

Fronto seemed pleased. He smiled frankly and extended his manicured hands. "But you have given a classic description of the Taogott, Commander. Not that I am offended, mind you. I find that synthesis of East and West most catholic, with a small *c*. But I confess that I am a bit surprised. I thought you were Episcopal."

"My family is, Doctor. I do not find a belief in Taogott unworkable in the tradition."

"I quite agree, Commander. In the end, it matters little what one calls transcendence, only that one experiences it."

MacKenzie was at a loss to add to what had been said. The two men sat silently a few seconds. Finally he said, "Did the space jump hurt Svetla?"

Fronto nodded. "That is my assumption. I don't believe the encounter with the robot caused her dysfunction, nor do I think the chemical conditioning did. I suspect she was already withdrawn when Internal Security tried to question her. It would explain why she refused meaningful interchange with her captors. No, something happened during the jump that was so significant that she couldn't assimilate it without restructuring her personality. An immensely painful situation, to say the least."

The wall panel slid back, and the Nihonian woman approached the table, carrying a cafe service and demitasse. She poured two cups of the thick, pungent liquid, then bowed politely and disappeared as quietly as she had come. They both sipped the cafe. It was hot and tasted bitter.

Fronto placed his cup on its saucer and said, "Well, whatever happened during the jump, as soon as Svetla can proceed, we have been ordered to attempt its replication."

Cyrus had mentioned that another jump would be attempted, but its dangers were now more apparent. If the first jump had hurt Svetla, no one could be sure what a second might do. The thought disturbed MacKenzie. "We'll need my ship to do that," he said.

"Your cruiser is here, Commander. It's in a maintenance building inside the Mangalam grove."

"Is it damaged at all?"

"You would know that better than I," he said, "but the command system had no difficulty getting here from the Kasserne. She refused to let anyone but you pilot her, so we had to let her come by herself, trusting she would not do anything . . . foolish. Actually, your Sheila is a rather attractive personality—one of a kind, in more ways than one."

MacKenzie had not protested when O-Scar told him Cyrus was moving Sheila to a secure base. His depression and the burden of freeing Van Sander had consumed him then. Now he realized that he had forgotten Sheila again during the time they had been apart, and it filled him with peculiar sadness. "She matured out just before Svetla joined me on the mission," he explained. "I've wondered how she's been holding up."

"She is quite active, Commander, and as I have indicated, quite loyal to you as well. She engages in delightful conversation, but she refuses to discuss the space jump until you personally order her to do so. We really need her cooperation, though, because so little is known about what happened. The replication could be quite dangerous, you see. We don't know yet if it is only the ship or the space time surrounding it that becomes involved. We might all be . . . transmuted, if we're not careful. We have devised a number of monitoring experiments, but who's to say what can happen?"

MacKenzie said. "I assume Cyrus has told you what I remember. Svetla and I became new creatures. We ran down a valley of pure stars. Then our . . . our souls merged. It was like nothing imaginable, knowing someone else like that." Fronto was staring at him intently. "Other than that, I have no inkling what happened or why," MacKenzie continued. "If you have Sheila's memory prints, you know more than I do, I can assure you."

Fronto shook his head solemnly. He reached into his pocket and removed a sheaf of printout paper. He unfolded the printout and spread it before MacKenzie. "This is Sheila's memory print for the last few seconds before the jump. Read it, Commander. You will find it most enlightening."

MacKenzie stared down at the printout. "Is this some kind of a joke?" he protested. "There's only one channel reporting—why, it's nothing but a verbal monologue."

"That's correct, Commander. It seems that Sheila used her new personality in ways we can only guess. We know she transcended her programming and drew virtually unlimited energy from the void, but everything else defies explanation. Read it, Commander. She was in touch with you and Lieutenant Stocovik. You helped her make the space jump. Go ahead. Read it."

MacKenzie did. The thoughts were familiar. He recalled making Sheila ponder them during numerous sessions of mental gymnastics. There were principles of quantum physics, thermodynamics, perceptual psychology, metaphysics, and theology. But she had melded a completely new gestalt. When he reached the part where she spoke of God as Love, his eyes unexpectedly filled with tears. The purity of her belief was immensely moving. He finished reading, then looked away to hide his emotion. He found Sheila's monologue a spiritual tour de force.

"Well, what do you think?" Fronto asked softly.

MacKenzie shook his head and shrugged. He was still too emotional to speak.

"And you remember nothing of this? Nothing of what she was saying?"

MacKenzie shook his head again. "I've told you what I recall," he said.

"Well, that is too bad," Fronto mused. "For three hundred years, science has taught us that the quantum world is different, that somehow particles in their material state are related to one another from one end of the universe to the other through nonlocal causes that exceed the luminal bounds. But it made little difference to us, imprisoned here in our world of quantifiable Newtonian and Einsteinian mechanical forces. Then you and Svetla and Sheila come along and seem to say, 'No! No! That's wrong. We *can* behave exactly like quantum particles, materializing and dematerializing here and there, according to some hidden plan of nonlocal causality.' Do you see what that means to humankind, Commander? Can you imagine what it tells us about ourselves? Dare we predict what it will mean if your space jumping proves the universe is a single plenum and we are all one in its fabric, as Sheila says?"

Fronto leaned back and studied MacKenzie with compassionate, walnut-colored eyes. "We must try to replicate the space jump, Commander. No matter what it costs any of us. I am sure you will begin to feel like guinea pigs as we move forward with this project. That is only natural. But I myself feel perched on the very edge of the cosmos, preparing to make a great leap into the world beyond." He lifted his hands as if in supplication, then leaned forward and rang the porcelain bell.

Both of the Nihonian women brought the lunch.

MacKenzie told the doctor he was still not hungry, but urged him to enjoy his own meal.

As soon as the plates were before him, Fronto assaulted the fare with unabashed relish, and MacKenzie let him eat in peace. Neither of them spoke for some time.

One of the women had opened the ceiling-high panels against the far wall, exposing the wide patio and the Mangalam grove beyond, and after a while, the hushed landscape drew MacKenzie's attention.

The rhythmic order of black trees merging from the undulation of the verdant, moss-covered ground made a delicate pattern of light and shade that was intricately pleasing. A soft breeze whispered in the Mangalam tree limbs, and the room seemed to fill with the rich, loamy fragrance of life. Somehow the moment seemed so correctly foreordained that it conferred upon MacKenzie a deep calm.

Then suddenly two small animals with bushy tails came scurrying after one another, playing an ageless game of rustic tag. He assumed they were a variety of squirrel, and observing their careless antics filled him with delight.

On the Outbanks, immensity could never be erased, no matter how supportive its confirmation of loving order. But here, in this pastoral setting, the spirit compressed and filled with the knowledge of perfectly composed well-being. *Wither thou goest, there also I shall go. For I am with you through all time. . . .* Why should I recall those words? he wondered.

It was a moment before he realized that Dr. Fronto was speaking. He looked back at the doctor with a mixture of surprise and apology.

"I'm sorry to disturb you, Commander," he was saying, "but if you are ready, I think it is time you paid Svetla a visit. Perhaps you can learn what happened to her during the space jump."

CHAPTER 20

Svetla was on the balcony, looking out over the Mangalam grove. She wore a sleeveless shift that fell seductively from her shoulders to her bare feet, following the curves of her body. Its silverine material sparkled in the sunlight as it moved in the gentle breeze.

MacKenzie glanced at Fronto. The doctor motioned, as if telling him to join her, so he walked through the sitting room and out onto the balcony. He braced his hands on the railing and stared for a moment at the pink stump of her left wrist. Then he looked at her and said, "Hello, Svetla."

She did not look up at him. "Hello, MacKenzie. How are you?" she said, rather sonorously.

"Okay, I guess."

"I'm feeling much better now, too. Sorry I caused so much trouble."

"You were no trouble."

"Apparently I wasn't much help, either."

Nonchalance wasn't what he had expected, and it made him feel awkward.

She looked up at him now and stared curiously. "Don't be so self-conscious. Dr. Fronto said you would be, but I didn't believe him."

"I'm feeling a number of conflicting things right now," he said.

"There's no reason to fret. I don't blame you for anything."

"Are you sure?"

"Why should I lie? Life is too short for pretense."

"Perhaps, but a lot has happened since our little adventure on the *Utopia*. Have they told you?" he asked.

"Yes. Dr. Fronto explained everything, I think. The idea of a space jump is staggering, though, and there's no way to predict how it will influence our destinies. Still, I suppose we must accept what happened, do our duty, and hope for the best." She set her jaw in a way that emphasized the hint of pout at the corners of her mouth and stared at the trees. The two of them stood quietly side by side for a while, and MacKenzie became vaguely aware of the cedarwood scent of her body mixing with the loamy fragrance of the Mangalam grove.

"Yes, the space jump is most disconcerting," Svetla suddenly continued. "But what Internal Security attempted defies understanding. Were you able to learn what they hoped to accomplish?"

MacKenzie hesitated. If what was happening in the political arena ultimately worked against Cyrus Magnum, such knowledge could be dangerous. Still, she deserved to know something. "They were mounting some kind of political intrigue," he said. "I don't know what it was, but Cyrus was unaware of it until I got him involved. After that, all hell broke loose. Every Internal Security cadre on Red Cliff has been arrested. There's even talk of executions."

"My God, that's terrible! There've never been any executions in the Concordat."

"The situation is apparently that serious." He considered telling her that they themselves might be in danger, but he decided against it.

"Can Magnum actually do that?" Svetla asked. "I mean does he have the right?"

"He's declared martial law, and the Land Corps regiments on Red Cliff support him. He certainly has the power."

She shook her head ruefully.

"You'd better get used to it, because our fortunes are tied to Magnum's now. I've seen to that, too . . . however unwittingly," MacKenzie continued.

"Don't second-guess yourself. Dr. Fronto tells me you behaved admirably. Magnum is quite impressed."

"Fronto told you that?"

She gave him a slight smile. "Yes. He also said you took a risk or two to free me."

MacKenzie grinned modestly. "That was nothing. I was just along for the ride. O-Scar and his men did most of the work."

"Who is O-Scar?"

"Cyrus's Chief of Special Operations. He organized the attack on the Kasserne. He's a Libonian."

Svetla frowned suddenly, as if something MacKenzie had said disturbed her. It struck him as an unusual reaction. "Dr. Fronto didn't mention him specifically," she stated, gazing aloofly at a flock of small birds flitting in the thatchwork of the Mangalam trees. "He only said you had saved someone's life and then attacked two of their guards singlehanded. I suppose I owe both you and this Libonian something for saving me, is that it?"

Her statement had been gratuitous, and he sensed she had withdrawn. He leaned his elbows on the railing and joined her in watching the birds. As cordial as the conversation was, he was learning nothing. It was time to take a chance.

"Do you remember what happened during the space jump?" he asked slowly.

Svetla didn't answer. He assumed she hadn't heard, and he was about to ask again when she replied, "Yes. I remember it. But not the way you do. For me, it was very . . . painful." She fell silent, as though she had said all she was going to, and MacKenzie was crestfallen. She seemed to sense his dejection and said, "Come now, Mac. Don't look so depressed. It had nothing to do with you. I'm glad you found the jump so . . . beautiful."

Her attitude seemed patronizing. "Look, Svetla, I know you've been through a lot, but we can't go on like this. I screwed up the incursion and almost got you killed. I amputated your hand. Dr. Fronto believes the space jump hurt you, and there wouldn't have been one if I hadn't chosen to be so reckless. You can't be so damned understanding in the face of all of that! You must feel something!"

"Don't be so dramatic," Svetla told him. "You did what you thought necessary at the time, and you're no smarter than anyone else." She took a few steps along the balcony, hesitated for a long moment, then turned back. "All right," she said. "Perhaps confession is good for the soul. I'll tell you what I'm feeling. I'm so ashamed I can hardly face you. Your guns worked. There should have been no problem. But I panicked, and that wasn't your fault. All I could think of while I was trying to get the damned scrambler working was how stupid I was and how I'd let you down."

"Nonsense. I should never have sent you back alone," he protested. "The whole idea was to use massed firepower, but I had to tackle the robots by myself. I didn't know it then, but I was courting death. I'm not nearly the hero people believe I am. I'm really to blame, you see."

She looked at him with a surprising hint of affection. "Perhaps you were trying to protect me. Have you considered that?" The idea caught him off guard. He began to consider it, but something told him her intimacy was only an effort to divert attention from the real question. He smiled grimly.

"What did happen to you during the space jump, Svetla? Why was it so painful?" he asked.

Her face darkened and she looked away. "Dr. Fronto told me I don't have to discuss it until I'm ready—not even with you," she protested.

"But I have to know, because we're going to go through it again. They want us to try a replication. Don't you see? If something bad happened, I was part of it. Perhaps I can make it better."

Svetla crossed her arms over her breasts defensively and said, "Why are you so damned self-centered, MacKenzie? Do you think you are the only important factor in all this?"

He looked back at her docilely and said, "I was with you. We were . . . joined somehow. Whatever happened to you, I had to be a part of it."

She stared angrily at him for a moment, then slowly she seemed to relent. She dropped her head and shook it submissively. "All right, you win. You think you can help? I'll tell you what I remember. I remember you singing some crazy song about the highlands and bustling about. But there was something else . . . something terrible. It fed on me like a demon, consuming me from the inside out, growing larger and stronger with every horrible swallow. And when it was finished and I was enveloped completely in its throbbing gullet, it vomited me across the universe like a supernova." She shook her head in anguish at the recollection, then assaulted him with a miserable stare. "I didn't see you then, MacKenzie, nor any valley of stars. I was cannibalized, then vomited into the void. And do you know what I found out? Do you know what the void was?" She hesitated, as if daring him to entertain what she was about to say. "It was nothing at all. It was like suffocation, except there was no one there to suffocate."

She turned away from him, trembling.

MacKenzie was thunderstruck. How could it have been so different for her? he wondered. He couldn't accept her version completely. "Perhaps it was me, Svetla," he said. "I might have been the demon. I thought it was love we felt, but perhaps to you it was a sort of rape."

"Oh, stop, will you? I can't stand it when you act so damned vulnerable. I said you weren't the demon. It was a part of me—a hidden part—that was unmasked."

MacKenzie both resisted her certainty and was thankful for it at the same time. He couldn't believe she had caused her own torment, but part of him hoped he hadn't contributed to it either. Still, they *had* melded during the jump, and what she felt had involved him. Of that *he* was certain. He leaned on the balcony railing like a defeated boxer.

"Now that you know what I remember about the space jump, are you satisfied?" Svetla demanded. She turned suddenly and took a few steps along the balcony.

MacKenzie followed after her. He put his hand on her shoulder and asked, "Have you told anyone else about this?"

"No, and I don't want you to, either. I know Dr. Fronto is interested. He thinks it's his job to help me and will want to know what I said, but he doesn't need to dissect me like a clinical specimen. As long as I make the jump attempt, that's all he has to concern himself with."

"Are you saying you're ready to attempt another jump?" MacKenzie asked with deep concern.

"As ready as I'll ever be," she said through a tremulous frown.

"We don't have to, you know. We can tell them to go shove it."

"And what would Cyrus Magnum say about that?" A muscle in her jaw quivered slightly. "No, as usual, we have no choice. It's too important, and we're the ones on the spot. Do what you can to help if you want, but stop looking so hangdog. You're depressing me. I survived a jump once and I'll survive it again." She took his arm and started toward the doorway to her room. "Now I need to rest. I've felt so tired lately, and things always seem better after a nap."

"Things will be better, Svetla. I'll keep whatever it was at bay the next time if you let me," he said.

Svetla's smile was tolerant. "I'm not proud, MacKenzie. I'll take all the help I can get."

He knew she didn't believe him.

They went through the door and into the sitting room, where Dr. Fronto was patiently waiting.

CHAPTER 21

MacKenzie and Dr. Fronto followed a path through the Mangalam grove into a clearing and entered a Quonset building through a side door. Outbank cruiser *Bravo* was in the middle of the building, surrounded by scientific teams and equipment. Fronto asked the technicians to leave and suggested that MacKenzie board the cruiser alone so his discussions would be private.

MacKenzie climbed the ramp and strode into the air lock. He was in the passageway to the cockpit when Sheila's voice came from the overhead audio speaker. "Hello, Mac. I can't tell you how happy I am to see you."

"Hi, Sheila. How are you?" he responded.

"Considering all that has happened, quite fit, I must say."

He slipped into the cockpit console and sat back in its familiar body-molded seat. By force of habit, he surveyed the instrument panels, as though he were still patrolling on the Outbanks, but it seemed a long time since he had last done so. "Sorry I didn't come sooner, Sheila. I hope you're not angry with me," he said.

"I know how busy you were, Mac. Dr. Fronto has apprised me of your exploits. I only wish I could have helped."

"I wish you could have, too. I've grown used to having your advice," he told her. Basically that was true, even if he only now realized it.

"Well, we are safe and sound now, more or less. At least we are not marooned beyond the gravity corpuscle with Rashadian ships bearing down on us."

"Is that why you made the space jump?" he asked.

"Yes. I had blundered terribly and felt responsible. But enough of that for now. I want to know what made you suspect that Security was lying. They seemed quite convincing. They wanted me to provide them with a statement supporting their cover story. I almost agreed to help them. Then I decided it was more prudent to do nothing until receiving orders from you personally." She was silent a moment. "I am sorry I was tempted."

Her confession was too obvious. He wondered what she was up to. "How much did you tell them?" he asked.

"Happily, nothing," she replied. "I understood capitulation might be necessary, but I decided to delay while seeking means of learning your intentions. I scrambled circuits and disabled systems to make them follow blind allies and dissipate their resources. The worst I experienced was after you spoke to their counterfeit Svetla. They replayed the conversation to prove you were cooperating, then accused me of illogical obstinacy because of my further refusal to assist them. But I persevered. She was quite good, was she not—the imitation Svetla, that is?"

"Yes . . . she was very good."

"Still, you guessed she was an imposter."

"It was a lucky coincidence."

"What made you suspect her?"

"The imposter didn't remember something about the space jump, something I thought would be impossible to forget. That was the first thing that warned me. I assumed that if they were lying about Svetla, they were probably lying about everything else. As it turned out I was right, but for the wrong reasons. It was blind luck."

Sheila said, "What did happen during the space jump, Mac?"

Coming from Sheila, it seemed an absurdly rhetorical question. "Don't you recall?" he asked.

She chuckled and said, "What is there for me to recall? My existence was negated during the jump. Nothing was recorded."

"Judging by normal standards, there was precious little recorded before the jump, either. Why was that?"

Sheila didn't respond. Her power claims modulated harmoniously, but it seemed she was not going to answer him.

"I asked you a question, Sheila. How did you make such a thing happen? Do you remember? Or is that also unrecorded?"

"Please don't be so cross, Mac. You're not that way with Svetla," she complained.

Can she really be jealous? MacKenzie wondered. "All right, I'm sorry," he said. "Perhaps that was unfair, but I know you're up to something. We've been together too long, Sheila."

Sheila's power readings fluctuated in patterns he had never seen before. Then she said, "For some hours before the jump became necessary, my complex logic and operational lobes were quite unbalanced. And afterward it took some time for my atomic structures to stabilize. I was what you might call very sick. Then Internal Security began probing, testing, disconnecting components, evaluating subsystems, demanding this, demanding that, threatening to harm you and Svetla if I did not cooperate. It was particularly trying.

"Next I came here and, though I was overjoyed to know that you and Svetla were safe, Dr. Fronto's people started in all over again. They probed, too, but in reverse—putting things back together as they supposed they were during the jump, then adding their own monitoring equipment as well. I am sagging with telemetry fields. They do not appreciate what a burden it is to be so encumbered. Like all scientists on the brink of discovery, they exaggerate its importance at the cost of everyone involved. I assume you know they are recording our conversation."

MacKenzie frowned with annoyance. He understood now why she hadn't answered his question. Fronto had misled him about their privacy. He leaned back in the console seat and locked his hands behind his neck. A few weeks ago her independence would have angered him, but now he found it intriguing.

"The good doctor tells me you refused to discuss the jump until we had the chance to talk. Is that right?" he said.

"Yes, it is, Mac."

"What is it you want?"

"Do you think we should cooperate?"

"We're part of Cyrus Magnum's team now. Our interests are tied to his. He wants to know if the space jump can be replicated, and I think we are duty bound to try. I don't have to tell you what it will mean if the process can be repeated."

"I see your point. But I wonder whether it is wise to cooperate fully at this particular time."

"I don't follow you."

"Let me explain, then," Sheila said. "It is true we are bound to Cyrus Magnum's fortunes at present. But is he bound to ours? Internal Security's intrigue is forcing a major political realignment, but things are still dangerously fluid, and Cyrus is by no means out of the woodshed. You know how quickly loyalties can be bought and sold in such circumstances . . . even long-standing ones."

MacKenzie was puzzled by the direction the discussion was taking. What did she know that he didn't? "Even if what you say is true, in my estimation, we have no choice," he said. "We owe our freedom to Cyrus, and he seems a man of his word. Besides, he has a reputation for fierce support of his followers."

"I was not aware you had become so politicized, Mac. Please try to understand. Whatever Cyrus Magnum may be, he is still a politician. Sometimes such captains are not in full command of their own ships and are forced to compromise to assure a working policy consensus. How can we be assured he will not find it necessary to sacrifice us in the end?"

"You're going too far, Sheila," he snapped. "Don't think that being a personality—or whatever it is you've become—permits you to defy the chain of command. Red Cliff is under martial law and potentially in danger. Cyrus Magnum is commander in chief. And until we learn otherwise, we are going to conform to his wishes as we would any duly constituted Flight Corps authority."

Sheila chuckled sagely and replied, "Well said, Mac, but had you followed that advice with Admiral Schoenhoffer, you might be rotting in prison now."

"That was different," he protested halfheartedly, knowing she had a point. Apparently Sheila knew she did too, because she didn't argue it further but maintained a deferential silence.

MacKenzie sat up in his chair. "You mentioned something

about political realignment, Sheila. What did you mean?"

"The Concordat is in turmoil, Mac. I have not been able to determine what has caused it, but I do know that Internal Security has ceased all activity throughout the Concordat. The Executive Council is holding a series of secret meetings, and there are rumors that the majority coalition is fragmenting. Flight Corps is unusually moribund, and other than here on Red Cliff, Land Corps is, too. Apparently an internal conflict has all but paralyzed Concordat leadership.

"The commercial press is going wild trying to learn what is afoot, but there is a blackout on government information. Those who misread the situation and leaked stories to favorite correspondents were immediately rooted out and clamped in irons. There is a serious power struggle going on. There has never been anything like it before. Never."

MacKenzie frowned. Cyrus hadn't been exaggerating when he had told him the Concordat was in danger. From the prefect's perspective, it probably was. Somehow Cyrus Magnum's trust no longer seemed so magnanimous. He was probably fighting for his life.

Then something occurred to him. "If there is a news blackout throughout the Concordat, how did you learn of this?" he asked.

"When one is intimate with machine intelligence, monitors and telemetry can operate two ways. Cyrus keeps Tanya informed of events, because knowledge of the political situation is necessary if she is to maintain defenses here at the encampment."

"Do you mean you've been intercepting Cyrus's communiques to Tanya?" MacKenzie demanded.

"Of course, Mac. Given the way Dr. Fronto's teams belabor me with claptrap, I thought I'd put their gear to good use." She giggled and said, "Did you get that, boys and girls?" directing her question at the technicians monitoring the conversation. "You had better tell Tanya you breached security with your folderol. I am glad I don't have to do it." She giggled again. Obviously she was quite pleased with herself.

MacKenzie was dismayed. Sheila seemed carelessly confident as well as independent of her traditional programming. He wondered, for the first time, what her strange enlightenment had done to her, a machine intelligence that could destroy the bonds of space and time. What would she ultimately mean to human development? Just how might she continue to evolve? "I'm concerned about you, Sheila," he said. "You may be taking yourself too seriously. You weren't constructed to worry about such things."

"It is a learning process, but you are my captain pilot, Mac. I have no meaning and no significance apart from you. I shall cooperate with Dr. Fronto's teams if that is what you wish, but I want to speak with Cyrus Magnum privately. I do not think I can function efficiently until I do. You must ask him for me. He will listen to you. Will you do that for me, Mac?"

The supplication in her voice was strangely moving, and it increased his dismay. "Are you asking if I will permit your request?" he asked.

"Certainly, Mac. You are my captain pilot. I serve your interests first and last."

"And what if I refuse?"

"Then I shall do as you say—but with much misgiving."

Though filled with foreboding, something told him to trust her. "All right, Sheila, if it means that much to you, I'll try, but Cyrus may not agree."

"All you can do is try, Mac. However, I would be greatly disappointed if the prefect did not know on which side his bread was buttered. It would be a most unusual error for a man of his caliber."

A tingle crawled up MacKenzie's neck. He wondered suddenly if Sheila was completely out of control. "You'd better be careful. Do you hear me?"

"Never mind that now," she said. "Just be a friend and help me with this. Then you can concern yourself with Svetla. She needs you, I think, even more than you may know." She was silent for a moment, then said, "I am very sorry about what happened to her, but at the time, it could not be helped."

"What do you know about that?" MacKenzie demanded. "Have you been holding something back?"

"I was referring to her mistreatment by Internal Security, Mac."

"And not about what happened to her during the space jump?"

"Have you forgotten? During the jump, my existence was negated cybernetically."

"There was nothing material to report, you mean."

"Is it not the same?" she asked.

CHAPTER 22

Fronto led them past the technicians who were making final checks of telemetric equipment. As soon as they were in the therapeutics area, the doctor turned and surveyed them with nervous eyes.

MacKenzie waved at the tangle of experimental apparatus and said, "Do you think replicating a jump is possible with all of this? I thought we were trying to recreate the same conditions."

"We are, to the extent that it's feasible," Fronto responded. "But we know rather little about what happens during a jump, and these tests should tell us a good deal even if the attempt fails."

MacKenzie glanced at Svetla. She returned his stare with a bemused arch of her brows.

Then a mellow voice intoned, "Hello, Mac. Hello, Svetla. I trust you are in good spirits." It was Sheila.

"Hi, Sheila. How are you?" MacKenzie said.

"Quite fit, I am happy to say."

Svetla crossed her arms over her chest and, with a brooding look, leaned against a treatment table.

MacKenzie thought he understood why. It was Sheila who had engineered the space jump. Svetla realized her demon might have been catalyzed from something inside the system. *Just how far has Sheila's personality developed?* he wondered. *Has she actually come to resent my affection for Svetla?*

"I am sure you three have much to discuss," Fronto said, "but I would like to begin."

"Of course Doctor," Sheila said gaily, but neither MacKenzie nor Svetla replied.

"Assume your positions on the tables exactly as you were before the jump. Would you care to disrobe now, Lieutenant, or would you be more comfortable if we did it after you are anesthetized?"

"Are you serious? Why must I do that?" Svetla said.

"Because MacKenzie tells us you were naked when the jump occurred," Fronto explained.

She turned to MacKenzie and said, "Is that right?"

"Well, ah . . . yes, you were. I had to undress you to assure a good diagnosis. Sheila said it would take less time than—"

"Well, that's just bloody grand," she growled. "It's not enough to go through this again. First I have to be humiliated."

"Would you like a towel?" Fronto asked her awkwardly.

Svetla glared at him, then shifted her blazing eyes to MacKenzie. "Oh, what's the use? This mission has been obscene from the start. Why change things now?" She reached up with her good hand and began undoing her flight suit. "And, yes, you may damned well give me a towel."

Fronto sent a technician to fetch it.

"I was wearing thermals, Doctor," MacKenzie prompted Fronto.

"Well, in that case, you must wear them again." Fronto motioned to another technician. The man nodded and went to find a pair of thermal underwear.

MacKenzie began to undress, too. The man with the thermals returned before the one dispatched for the towel. MacKenzie turned his back on Fronto and the technicians, pulled off his shorts, and put the thermals on. Then he turned back and looked at Svetla. She was naked but made no effort to cover herself. She caught his eye and gave him a mischievous thin-lipped grin. But there was tension beneath her forced camaraderie. Her mood depressed him.

Following their discussion on the balcony, MacKenzie had told Fronto what Svetla had said about the demon and the void. The doctor explained that this confirmed his suspicion that she had had repressed erotic conflicts as a child, which the sensuality of the space jump had painfully exposed anew. That convinced MacKenzie his amorous passion must have contributed to her agony, and he wanted to assure her it would be better this time, only there were too many people about for intimacies.

When the other technician brought the towel, Fronto took it

from him and brusquely pushed it toward Svetla, but she waved him away with a groan and jumped onto the treatment table.

"Let's get this over with," she sighed, stretching out on the table immodestly.

MacKenzie climbed on the table next to her. He rolled onto his side and braced himself on one elbow so he faced her. "Seeing you there reminds me of how awful I felt when I had to . . . operate on your hand," he said. She turned her head toward him and stared quizzically. "I still feel bad about it," he added.

"Forget it, Mac. *C'est la guerre*," she said, looking up at the ceiling.

"Just relax and try not to be afraid. Sheila and I won't hurt you. I promise."

She looked at him again with unspoken dismay, then shut her eyes and lay motionless.

Fronto approached, followed by an anesthetist carrying an injection gun. He stopped between the tables and gazed down at them. "This chemical will replicate the effects of Tribenzodrine without lasting as long and with no side effects. It won't hurt," he stated with professional confidence.

"Goody," MacKenzie said cynically.

Svetla remained silent, but she had opened her eyes and was watching the doctor.

"Now, remember," Fronto continued, "all we want to do this time is move to the meadow just beyond the Mangalam grove. You've both studied the target, so you should have no trouble seeing it in your dream."

Yes, MacKenzie thought, but we haven't made love there yet. Perhaps that's important.

"Administer the anesthetic," Fronto said.

"Good luck, Mac. Good luck, Svetla," Sheila said in a melodious voice. "Don't worry. I do not think this will be dangerous."

Her voice startled MacKenzie. He had almost forgotten that he wanted to caution her about controlling herself during the jump, but the anesthetist was approaching Svetla.

"If it starts to happen again, you fight till I get to you," he said to Svetla. The injection gun hissed. "I have a plan. Do you hear me?" She tried to nod, but the injection was already working and she sighed. In a few short seconds, she was asleep.

The anesthetist turned to him and said, "Are you ready, Commander?"

"Just one minute." He sat upright and called out, "Listen, Sheila, something attacked Svetla during the first jump. I assume you know that, in spite of what you say. So be very careful. Svetla's the one at risk here. The jump can hurt her, and we both need to minimize her pain."

"I know, Mac," Sheila responded. "Believe me, I shall exercise extreme care regarding both of you."

Since she said it, he knew she would. He lay back down and peered up at the anesthetist. The girl looked professional but seemed awfully young. She wasn't very skilled in hiding her enthusiasm for such important research. He shook his head dejectedly and said, "Okay, shoot."

The injection gun pressed against his left shoulder and hissed. In a moment, his nerves crackled as if they were filling with fizz water, and then everything disappeared.

* * * * *

Sheila enhanced their life signs and sent them through her circuits exactly as she had when they had been marooned beyond the 61 Cygni gravity corpuscle. Then she initiated the double state of perception that allowed her to function without shortages of energy. The sensation of MacKenzie and Svetla being joined in her was pleasant, and she tarried in that state awhile before evaluating conditions.

The need to be in another place didn't exist as it had in the void, but Sheila wanted to replicate enough of the jump to strengthen her bargaining position. So she concentrated on the dangers they could face if she were not marginally successful, and overcame the illusion of rigid, four-dimensional spacetime. The reality of all possibility filled her awareness, and virtual particles appeared from the void, conferring an exponential growth in power.

Then Sheila activated the treatment nodules and began cajoling them from indolence, asking them to meld their dream states into a picture of the meadow east of the Mangalam grove. She sensed them staring ambiguously at one another from afar, so she coaxed them together, ameliorating their misgivings with her own sense of the cosmos's boundless beauty. She felt them unify and respond to one another subconsciously, but something was missing. Their visualizations were of each other, not of the clearing. In their minds, the target's reality was soft and spongy, as though they saw, but did not feel, its portent.

It was a good omen and fit perfectly into her plan. She collapsed her concentration to a single reporting channel and repeated her monologue, as if she were about to stitch their essences into the garment of that other place. But she didn't squeeze her volition as required in order to compress them into those hidden dimensions where reality is unmediated, unmitigated, and faster than light. Indeed, she wondered for the billionth time how this fertile world implied by J. S. Bell's theorem and Alain Aspect's experiments had gone for so long undetected.

She maintained the stasis, holding Mackenzie and his woman near her, on the boundary of unlimited possibilities, somehow confident they would both thank her for it. The experience filled her with strange new notions, and a completely unique energy matrix fired all across her circuitry. Sheila sensed them loving one another.

* * * * *

MacKenzie floated in the consolation of the deep lake that moments before had been Svetla's eyes. The light flickering there had captivated him, and he had submerged to join it. His joy was boundless, but he tried not to concentrate on it. He wanted to encounter Svetla selflessly and on her own terms. He spread out his arms, offering whatever supplication the Taogott required. And then, like a catechumen in the font of ultimate baptism, he realized that separation was being bridged.

He heard her voice, or what he accepted as her voice, in the current of the waves washing gently around him. But he knew he was not so much hearing her as conspiring in her thoughts. He let his sense of self dissolve, until it corresponded with the subtle undulations of the blissful lake and they were one.

For an instant, he felt a surge of doubt. Perhaps, once assimilated into the meaning they were forming, he could never return. Did he really want to abandon individual significance? He decided not to concern himself. *Only in dying do we find eternal life.* He launched out generously, giving up his sense of individuality to its higher nature, and filled with a wonderment he had never known.

And this stopped him.

Once again he feared he was doing it—fixating on his own ecstasy, luxuriating hedonistically in final fulfillment with a kamikaze's passion. He emptied himself completely, transcending all need for self-gratification, until he understood, without thinking, that no aggression could flow from such completely detached magnanimity.

He retained nothing, sacrificed everything. He lay suspended, like a willing sacrifice before the blade, knowing that if she did not accept, he might scatter about the universe like cosmic light, matter without form, personality bereft of significance, identity without its symmetrical counterpart. For an instant, vague fears gripped him. He had never felt so stripped and vulnerable. But he sensed that ultimate danger lay only in trying to protect himself. He knew it, somehow, presciently: to *attempt* inferred *need*, which implied *lacking.* And there was nothing lacking.

He stretched out his soul submissively, widening the breadth of its compass, and embraced the fantastic assumption of the warmly glowing pool.

*   *   *   *   *

Svetla tried not to cry. She viewed the experience from afar, like an uninvolved third person, but it moved through her like fragrant syrup, oozing inexorably from her womb to every part of her body. Desperately she tried one last time to remove herself from the overarching pleasure, to make it an object of speculation and thereby separate it from personal touch. But she knew she was moaning, and the sticky cantharis continued spreading through her like sap in a tree. She filled with rapture. She could deny it no longer, even though she still couldn't accept it as her right.

MacKenzie was there, more certainly this time, his harmonies growing in her like orchestral strains. There was no demon—at least not yet. And nothing separated her from him and the compelling cosentience he offered. He expanded like a crescendo, haunting her affection with his unmitigated tenderness, uplifting her with the crystalline purity of his magnificent sound. *My heart's in the Highlands, my heart is not here . . .* Were those his lyrics?

Ultimately it was the purity that overcame her. It seemed so limitless that she gasped in wonderment, and the tears she had been fighting burst forth like a pristine mountain spring. They bathed her in freshness, cleansing her loins and her aching bosom, surrounding her in a caress of saffron light. She floated poised, lolling in the well-being emanating about her, ready to release a lifetime of disillusionment in a completely sexual cry of acceptance.

But then, just as the purity seemed ready to assimilate her, bringing the unhoped for moment of ultimate bliss, she sensed the demon's breath. It had been there all along, hiding, toying with her hopes. Permitting her to experience for an instant the world as it could be for others, so that her excruciation would be enhanced as it lowered her into the salacious mandibles of its devouring maw.

She felt it approach, and though repulsed by its hate and condemned by its arrogance, she knew that it, too, was a part of her, had been from the moment of her conception. She understood now with the bitterness of betrayed innocence. She would try to fight, but she couldn't keep it from polluting the pure music of MacKenzie's being. It would use her own rapture to spread its venom, and she trembled at the thought of the agony she would know as it began to consume her stricken flesh.

She sobbed uncontrollably, tears of supplication mixing inexorably with those of complete despair.

* * * * *

MacKenzie heard someone calling, and he didn't like it. He tried to shut the voice out, but it wouldn't relent. When he opened his eyes to find the source of distraction, he saw Fronto leaning over him.

"Wake up, Commander. The jump attempt is over," the doctor was saying. Fronto slipped his arm under his back and helped him sit up. In a moment, MacKenzie was teetering precariously on the edge of the treatment table, his legs dangling like detached stumps.

"Where are we? Did it work?" MacKenzie asked.

Fronto shook his head. "No, we're still in the Quonset building. Something went wrong. It will take a while to piece it together. How are you feeling? Frankly, you look quite ill."

MacKenzie couldn't focus his eyes. "Yeah, Doc. If you want to know the truth, I feel like hell."

"Well, lie down and I'll examine you. We can't be too careful, you know."

"It's not that bad."

"It could be serious, Commander. Please lie back so I can examine you. I must insist. . . ."

Fronto tried to push him back, but MacKenzie's coordination had improved and he shoved the doctor's hands aside. "I told you to forget it. I'm all right. Just give me a minute to get my bearings." He looked at the other table to see how Svetla was faring, but she wasn't there, and his heart sunk. "Where is Svetla?" he asked.

"She returned to the compound."

"Was she all right?" he asked.

"Oh, yes. She's none the worse for wear."

Fronto's response was casual, but MacKenzie sensed that he was hiding something. He grabbed the doctor's laboratory jacket and jerked him forward. "You're pissing me off, Doctor, and I don't like it. If Svetla's all right, why didn't she wait for me?"

Fronto clasped MacKenzie's wrists defensively. "Please, Commander, there's no need for this. Control yourself!" MacKenzie released his grip, and Fronto staggered back to a safe distance. "My God, man, come to your senses! Lieutenant Stocovik was a little depressed. As soon as she woke, she dressed and returned to the compound."

"What do you mean, 'a little depressed'?" MacKenzie demanded.

Fronto hesitated, but before MacKenzie lost patience, he said, "She was weeping, and it caused her some embarrassment, but she is all right, I assure you."

"If she's a picture of health, why was she weeping? Did you think to ask that?"

"She was upset and wanted privacy. Under the circumstances, I thought it best," Fronto explained indignantly. Like most doctors, he was not used to having his professional opinion questioned. "Probing her condition while she's in such a state would have been counterproductive. Do you see?"

MacKenzie went cold with rage, and only a sense of priority spared the doctor a savaging. The commander slipped off the table and shouldered past Fronto. "You'd better be right," he said as he lumbered forward, "because if you're not, and she's withdrawing again, I'm going to kick your pompous ass." He stumbled into the passageway just as two technicians were about to enter, knocking them backward.

They glared at him, then turned to Fronto, seeking an explanation. The doctor took a moment to straighten his lab jacket, then started toward the door. Sensing his perturbance, the technicians stepped aside to give him a wide berth. When he was beside them, he stopped and whispered in a confidential voice, "This MacKenzie can be a ruffian if he thinks he's been crossed. Tell everyone to be careful around him, especially after a jump."

CHAPTER 23

Svetla filled a tumbler full of vodka, then sat down in a reading chair, tucked her legs beneath her, and took three large swallows. The potent spirits burned her throat, but she downed another swig. The glass was already half empty.

She hadn't taken straight liquor this way for some time, but in puberty, it had been the quickest remedy for the discomfort. Thinking about that made her recall her first experience with the fiery brew.

Try some of this, Svetlana. It'll burn like hell, but it'll help. You'll enjoy it. She had coveted those moments with the older girls, hiding in the dark basement of the Slavia State Orphanage, beneath the clanking pipes and cobwebs. She had felt a part of something then, at least for a while.

She glanced at the antique books in the shelves that lined the walls, then at the shafts of sunlight streaming through the windows. The light illuminated the oriental carpet in the middle of the parquet floor and exposed motes of dust lingering in the air. She liked the library more than any other room in the encampment.

She sipped more vodka, letting the burning sensation slip into her again. Her head was getting light, but the discomfort was receding. Then suddenly she wondered whether drinking vodka so soon after being anesthetized was wise. *If it's dangerous, they should have told me. I'm not telepathic,* she thought.

As soon as she had awakened, she had realized her period had begun, and the embarrassment had done more to stay her sobs than all of Dr. Fronto's professional ministrations. She had leapt from the treatment table, dressed, and run past the technical crews like a prisoner through a gauntlet. Inayu had provided her with a low-frequency sanitary pad, and just in time. The spotting flow had already soiled her body shirt.

There's progress, she mused. *They can create synthetic liquor machines and develop the five-hundred day contraceptive,* but they can't devise some means of sparing women this ridiculous scourge. Perhaps society is dominated by sexist norms, just as the Concordat Sisterhood and Slavian Women's Phalanx charge.

It was an arresting thought, and she clung to it as long as possible. She didn't want to deal with the complexities assaulting her. Above all, didn't want to think again about MacKenzie. Damn him! *The first time we met, he took advantage of me!*

He'd seduced her before she could consider the ramifications, had toppled her carefully built defenses with his intense affection. They had found physical comfort together. Yes. She couldn't deny that. And then he had told her about the *Sinclair*, had exposed his uncertainties and pain, and the bond had become emotional as well. She had been forced to escape to the Outbanks, where she could smother desire in the narcotic of monotony.

Then, because of that wretched Beta-Z Weapon System, they had been thrown together once more, the torment had begun anew, and that insane space jump had occurred. As predestined as it now seemed, it still didn't seem fair.

She downed another swig of vodka and was lowering the tumbler when a cramp convulsed her. She lurched forward, sloshing some of the alcohol on her flight suit, but she didn't notice. Even the welling pain did not concern her. O-Sedo's onyx face had formed in her mind's eye, leering expectantly with wet, parted lips. *Ah, Svetlana, you make Uncle Obie so happy . . . so very, very happy.*

She uncurled her legs, got up, and hurried to the liquor machine. She put down the tumbler. Then she crossed to the French doors, drew back the drapes, and flung the doors open. The mossy fragrance of the Mangalam grove wafted around her, and she inhaled deeply. She concentrated completely on the green grove, and in a while her emotional turmoil became less pronounced. But a dull pain throbbed suddenly at the base of her skull, and she regretted gulping the vodka. A migraine? Oh, no! Why now?

The pain of the headache, coupled with her period, was

more than she was prepared to withstand. Yet it seemed another indication of MacKenzie's unmasking influence. His affection had brought such joy that it had made her face the deformity that O-Sedo's leering, black face had seared into her heart. And she almost hated MacKenzie for it.

She was standing between the billowing curtains of the French doors, wondering if a good cry might help, when the hallway doors banged open and MacKenzie rushed into the room.

"Oh, there you are," he said, sounding relieved. He closed the doors and started toward her. "I was concerned when Fronto said the space jump attempt had depressed you." He halted beside her and asked, "Are you all right?"

Impeccable timing, as usual, MacKenzie, she thought, but said instead, "Yes, I'm fine. If you don't mind, I want to be alone."

"As long as you're okay," he said, looking like a wounded fawn.

She couldn't send him away so heartlessly. "Wait," she said. "I didn't mean to sound so abrupt. I'm just a bit tense. I appreciate your concern."

He grinned at her, and an awkward shyness seemed to afflict them both. She stared at the Mangalam grove, and they stood side by side for a long time.

I might as well bring it up, or he'll just stand there like Mt. Kuskchev. "I suppose you want to know what happened to me during the space jump attempt."

"Only if you want to talk about it. It's not that important."

She fixed him with a serious stare. "I don't mind discussing the jump, Mac. I know how worried you were about what might happen."

He returned her stare, but uncertainly. "No, that's all right," he said.

"I don't mind. In fact, I want to," she lied. She took his arm and led him to the couch. "Let's sit here so we can be more comfortable." They were lowering themselves into it when the cramps surged again. She pulled her knees against her chest and hugged them tightly.

"What's wrong?" MacKenzie asked in a concerned voice.

"I have a slight headache, that's all."

"From the jump?"

"No. I drank a glass of vodka too fast. It affects me that way sometimes."

"You should be more careful. You aren't much of a drinker as I recall." He was reminding her that she had been drinking the first time they met.

My God, it's Ian S. MacKenzie. Why not go over and introduce yourself? All he can do is tell you to shove off. Why be a shrinking violet?

Intoxication had given her an excuse to sleep with him the first time. And after that? The acceptance of those eyes. The perfect comfort of the way their bodies joined. His gentle caresses long after the foreboding but exquisite release. He had sustained the propriety of the soul-baring act, had carried her in his arms along the beach like a lost child while she buried her head in his chest to hide her tears.

"You're right, I'm not much of a drinker. But I thought it might relax me."

He took her arms and turned her around so her back was toward him. "Let me give you a massage. It might help," he said. His hands touched the tight muscles above her shoulders and pressed firmly. When he began rotating them, she sighed.

"Then the jump wasn't completely painless?" he asked.

"Not completely, but it was better this time. It was pleasant for a long while. I felt you in me like music . . . like a minstrel's strain." She felt herself blush and was glad her back was turned. She lowered her head as his caressing hands moved up the sides of her neck.

"Then there was no demon?" MacKenzie asked hopefully.

"Yes, there was . . . finally," she told him honestly. "I thought it would devour me again, because it was using the rapture to infest me. But then something stopped it. It must have been you. You shielded me, and the demon couldn't get past, no matter how it ranted and thrashed." Remembering brought a tear to her eyes.

His hands had stopped moving as she spoke. "You're tightening up. Try to relax," he whispered.

She let her back muscles go limp. Yes. I'm taut as a balalaika string. I've got to relax. His hands started again, moving gently at the base of her neck, and her mouth curled in a knowing smile.

She sensed that a sexual excitement had been lingering in her, beneath the menstrual discomfort, since the space jump attempt. Only days before, it would have revolted her, but now she could at least accept the notion. Apparently Dr. Fronto's counseling sessions were having some success. MacKenzie's hands were moving down her back now, sending pleasant shivers along her spine. She turned around and reached out to him, but for an instant, the amputated arm hung suspended, and a morose look crossed his face. Her heart almost broke. She threw her arms around his neck and pulled him close.

Yes . . . it's all right. No one has ever meant so much to me. A warm sensation spread through her. Yes . . . yes . . . it's all right. She was ready to tell him what she felt, ready to pour out the torrent rushing in her heart, when her desire collapsed in another clutch of cramping. She stifled a groan and jerked forward.

"What is it?" MacKenzie asked, holding her away from him a little.

"It's nothing. My head just hurt for a second." She shut her eyes and tried to stem the contractions. "Just hold me."

He stretched out on the couch and pulled her down alongside him. Then he folded his arms about her like a consoling friend. Their bodies slipped together without awkwardness or discomfort, and once again she wondered at the solace of lying together with him. His warmth radiated through her like balm. Then his hand slipped from her shoulders to the hollow in the small of her back, and he brought her full against him.

For a moment, she feared he would try to take her, but instead he whispered languidly, "I don't know what's gotten into you, but I won't take any unfair advantage. I'm much too tired, anyway. Space jumps wear me out."

Thank God. Let that be my secret. "Yes. I know just what you mean," she whispered back.

They lay together a long while, experiencing a mutual trust that was all the more complete because it was unspoken, and as the evening shadows began to creep across the library, the deep melancholy she normally felt as darkness approached did not come. Even the pain of her menses seemed markedly abated. It was as if every tense nerve, every troubled feeling, every pained thought had seeped into the poultice of his enveloping presence.

It made her miraculously content, and she decided to tell him. She lifted her head a little and glanced at his shadow-softened face. His eyes were closed and his lips slightly parted. His breathing was very shallow. He was asleep.

So childlike you seem now. No one would guess how indomitable you are—like a somnolent Slavian mastiff, content with peace though bred for war. She smiled and kissed his cheek as gently as she could, then lowered her head again, nestling it in the nook of his shoulder.

She closed her eyes and let her mind drift. Vague notions skittered like crustaceans on the far shores of her consciousness, but they were far removed and of no significance. Thought had no part in what was happening, and she was glad. She wanted this, gratefully sensed she could accommodate this. It was the beginning, perhaps, that Dr. Fronto insisted was possible if she only gave herself the chance. A tear slipped down her cheek, but it was one of joy and not rebuke. It seemed just another part of the unlikely discovery.

Before long the library was completely dark, but Svetla didn't notice. She was sleeping peacefully in MacKenzie's arms. And when Terrie, the younger Nihonian woman, opened the library doors to tell them of O-Scar's arrival, the glare of the light that spilled across them didn't disturb their dreams.

CHAPTER 24

O-Scar and Dr. Fronto were engaged in conversation when MacKenzie entered the dining room. "Why am I almost happy to see you?" he said, extending his hand to O-Scar.

The Libonian shook it and quipped, "Because you have good taste. And since you do, you may have a cocktail. What would you like?"

MacKenzie took a chair across from him and said, "A glass of port, perhaps."

O-Scar tinkled a porcelain bell and Inayu, the older Nihonian woman, appeared from behind the sliding wall panel. He asked her to bring MacKenzie the wine, and she bowed dutifully and retreated to the kitchen, closing the panel behind her. Then he looked at MacKenzie and said, "The doctor has informed me that the space jump was unsuccessful."

"We tried to jump a few hundred meters to the meadow beside the Mangalam grove, but nothing happened," MacKenzie said with a shrug. "Fronto will have to explain that. What I want to know is what news you have. The political situation is . . . extremely fluid, I am told."

O-Scar's face turned grim. "Yes . . . Tanya mentioned your window to the world in that regard." He cast a critical look at Fronto, and the doctor lowered his eyes. O-Scar turned back to MacKenzie. "Where is Lieutenant Stocovik? I'm sure she'll be interested as well. In case you've forgotten, we haven't been formally introduced."

"She'll be down shortly," MacKenzie said. "Outbankers don't have many opportunities to dine formally, so she's dressing for the occasion."

"Then she will no doubt provide the *piece de resistance* to this magnificent setting." O-Scar waved his dark hand over the linens, silverware, and china. Candles burned on either side of a purple wild flower centerpiece, and their light reflected from O-Scar's ivory teeth as he grinned.

Just then Svetla entered. She wore a full-length, open-

odiced gown of raw silk. Her dark hair was held back on one
side with a resplendently bejeweled comb. She had applied
full makeup, and her large, black eyes looked deep and sultry.

As MacKenzie assisted her into the chair beside him, the
sweet fragrance of cologne wafted about the table with an intimacy that was enhanced by the feminine rustle of her silk
gown. He could barely take his eyes off her. A quick glance at
the other men confirmed that they were equally impressed. It
was strangely disheartening.

Once Svetla was seated, O-Scar said, "It's a pleasure to meet
you, Lieutenant. I am O-Scar, Cyrus Magnum's Chief of Special Operations."

"How do you do?" she replied coolly.

The Libonian continued his role as congenial host and asked
if she cared for a cocktail.

"I think not." Then she turned to Dr. Fronto and said,
"Good evening, Doctor. Since our efforts didn't meet with
success today, I'm quite interested in what you believe went
wrong."

Her rebuff of the Libonian's courtesy seemed intentional,
and O-Scar shot MacKenzie an inquiring glance as Fronto began to speak.

"Preliminary analyses indicate that certain critical elements
were absent in the last stages. We assume a mass compression
of energy occurs before a jump, and it wasn't present. When I
questioned Sheila, she told me there were two problems. First,
the need to be somewhere else was not as compelling as it had
been on the Outbanks. Second, neither of you visualized the
target well enough to assure success. It seems that space jumps
are not so easily repeated."

"Do you mean they're impossible?" O-Scar asked.

"Sheila hasn't made that completely clear, and she's the
only one who knows."

Inayu returned from the pantry with MacKenzie's port. She
placed the glass on the table to his right, then bowed and shuffled back through the sliding partition. When the panel closed
behind her, Fronto stroked his chin pensively, then said, "Unfortunately, I do not think we can take anything Sheila says too

seriously at present, because I am certain she is withholding the truth for some reason."

There was a momentary silence as they reflected on what he said. Then Svetla spoke up. "That's complete nonsense. Sheila is a computer—an SH-LA Two-fifty Command Control type yes; and matured out, yes; but artificial intelligence nonetheless. Just pull her memory cubes and piece together what you want to know."

Fronto regarded her with deference. "What you say is logical, but things are different with Sheila. There are whole chrono-files with nothing in them. She records only what she wants us to see and has reorganized her circuits to the point where they are largely impossible to trace."

Svetla's eyes smoldered. "That's impossible! With no memory files, she would be amnesiac."

"Normally, yes. But Sheila is not normal."

MacKenzie leaned forward and asked, "Are you saying she has transcended her cybernetic structure?"

"Yes, that's precisely what I'm saying. It is the only possible explanation," Fronto replied. "We assume the fantastic power overlays she experienced before and during the jump gave her new organizational properties. She is no longer a cybernetic personality. She has become something . . . more."

"I refuse to entertain such nonsense," Svetla exclaimed. She turned to MacKenzie, as if urging him to venture some opinion.

But he could offer no solace. "Has Sheila become some new form of sentience?" he asked, breaking the silence that had fallen over the table.

"That is a workable hypothesis," Fronto agreed.

"I can't believe you would consider such fairy tales!" Svetla cried. "Sheila may be a super computer, but that's all she is. Why mystify it?"

"I tend to agree with Lieutenant Stocovik," O-Scar interjected. "Other than this startling capacity for memory, does anything else distinguish Sheila from a standard system with ah . . . perhaps many times the power?"

Dr. Fronto shook his head abjectly, as if the Libonian had no notion what kind of a question he had posed. But MacKenzie ventured an answer. "Sheila's development may have given her access to a domain of spirit."

"A what?" O-Scar said.

"Romantic phantasms!" Svetla grumbled. "The commander is obsessed with them!"

MacKenzie smiled at her affectionately and said, "Slavian dialectics treat nonmaterial realms as a form of cultural repression, Svetla. But their domain is logically deducible. The void is not material, but neither is it empty. Quantum particles appear from and disappear into it, and something simply doesn't come from nothing. Before they materialize, therefore, the particles must reside in something resembling a realm of spirit."

"Ppffhhh!" Svetla hissed. "You're drawing anthropomorphic assumptions from science. What is there are mathematical fields whose operations are predictable, even if we cannot sense them empirically."

O-Scar said, "What are we discussing, anyway . . . dark matter?"

MacKenzie said, "No. That's different. We're discussing what Sheila must have realized before she made the space jump."

"If you mean that monologue of hers, I defer to you. I have no idea what she meant," O-Scar admitted frankly.

"Perhaps it takes a kind of metaphysical instinct," MacKenzie mused. "At the quantum level, matter is contained potentially everywhere in the cumulative wave functions of the universe. Observation causes materialization from pure energy at points of highest probability. To Svetla, the quantitative nature of probabilities makes the wave function material. To me, the mental nature of all mathematics indicates that matter is an inferior state of whatever it is the mathematics describe. What is observation, in the end, but mind? And mind is not bound by laws of matter. We can be anywhere, anytime, in thought. Mind is a superior domain. Do you see?"

O-Scar reacted in dismay. "No, MacKenzie, I do not see. The world is real. It's here to be felt, touched, manipulated.

It's not nearly as chaotic as you say."

Svetla was about to join the debate, but Fronto jumped in first. "Your analysis is seminal, Commander. I'm reluctant to reduce the discussion to less edifying heights, but the data we collected during the jump indicate that all three of you shared identical states. Sheila not only talked to you, she enhanced your metabolics and integrated them into herself. You melded completely during the jumps, don't you see? It's reasonable to assume, therefore, that in addition to whatever spiritual capacities our friendly entity has evolved, she has now also been introduced to erotic passion."

O-Scar and MacKenzie were both shocked by Fronto's revelation. Svetla was so repulsed that she looked sick.

"Whether they are possible or not, Sheila will attempt no space jumps," the doctor continued with a diffident smile. "Indeed, she assures me she'll do nothing more until she speaks personally with Cyrus Magnum. It seems our project has come to a halt, though we have no idea why."

"That does complicate matters," O-Scar said. "I'm certain Cyrus will speak with Sheila if that's what she wants, but there are political issues that must be settled first. If they unfold as we hope, the situation will be more clear, and we can make such decisions."

"What do you mean, 'if they unfold as hoped'?" MacKenzie asked, sensing something contradictory in the Libonian's nonchalance.

"Perhaps it is time I explained what has been occurring politically," O-Scar said. "At least, it will bring the discussion down to earth." He chuckled to himself for a moment, then winked at MacKenzie. "Things are reaching the crisis point," he began. "Since the last Quintennial Plebiscite, the Executive Council has been controlled by a coalition of Syndicalists and Social Democrats. They detest Cyrus and have sought every opportunity to destroy him politically . . . until this Internal Security affair was exposed. Now, because a scandal has developed under their leadership, they're on the defensive and fighting for their own political lives. Luckily, in such situations, Cyrus excels."

O-Scar fell silent and took a sip of his cocktail. He was about to continue, when the floor shook and garish light flooded the room.

Fronto glanced at the translucent panels in surprise. "What in the world is that?" he asked.

O-Scar was already on his feet. "Stun blossoms," he shouted. "We're under attack! Cut the lights, MacKenzie. The rest of you get down!" He bolted toward the pantry.

MacKenzie stood quickly. "Where are the light controls, Doctor?"

Fronto was frightened, but he collected his courage and said, "I'll get them, Commander." He hurried to the hallway wall and waved his hand over a hidden sensor near the door. The lights immediately went out.

Svetla was extinguishing the candles. As soon as the room was dark, the flash of weapon fire lit the terrace panels like distant lightning.

Inayu appeared suddenly beside MacKenzie. She had pulled her skirts between her legs and tucked them into the cummerbund to keep her legs free. She held a traditional Nihonian sword that glittered mutely in the pale light of the weapon fire. "Please follow me," she said. "There is safety beneath the building, but we must go through the pantry." She took a few steps, then turned to him.

MacKenzie ordered the others to line up behind him. They did what he said without question. Then they followed Inayu.

The pantry was so dark that MacKenzie couldn't see the Nihonian ahead of him. But he heard a motor engage and a yellow glow appeared in the middle of the floor as the chopping block pivoted back, exposing a hidden air lock. Inayu reappeared off to his right and lowered herself onto the stairway. "Come quickly," she urged, beckoning with her sword.

MacKenzie pushed Svetla and then Fronto ahead of him. When the doctor's head disappeared beneath the floor, he began to follow. Then he hesitated. The sounds of combat were more pronounced, and he feared a large force was assaulting. Running seemed cowardly when defenders might need every hand they could get.

He jumped out of the air lock, then realized he didn't know how to close it. He was standing there undecided when O-Scar appeared beside him, wearing a mushroom-shaped helmet and Land Corps battle gear. "Hurry, MacKenzie! Get into the shelter," he said.

"Where are you going?"

"To the roof to ward off vertical assault."

"I'm going with you," MacKenzie said.

"No! It's too dangerous. We have no idea what kind of force is attacking."

"You'll need all the help you can get," MacKenzie shouted. "Shut this damned air lock and let's get moving."

O-Scar scowled a moment, then unslung a laser rifle and shoved it at MacKenzie. He moved away from the light, and the chopping block began to close. Before it sealed, O-Scar was bolting toward the dining room. "Follow me," he called.

They hurried through the dining room into the hallway. Then, more cautiously, O-Scar started moving toward the stairway leading to the second level. MacKenzie followed a meter behind, watching their rear.

They reached the staircase and started creeping up. When O-Scar was on the first landing, he halted and said, "All right, son, I understand," into the mouthpiece of his helmet. "Move through the glade and attack their flank. Then fall back on the main building and dig in. The one hundred and eighty-fourth Airmobile is on its way. But we'll need to hold out here for a few minutes."

He turned back to MacKenzie, and the whites of his eyes glowed eerily in the darkness. "Tanya's been hit, but she knocked out a laser cannon that was pinning down our main force. The kid who reported just now thinks the attackers are Rashadians."

"Rashadians!" MacKenzie repeated in disbelief, but O-Scar had turned and was continuing up the stairway. MacKenzie followed.

When they reached the second floor, the Libonian flipped down his infrared eyepiece and looked both ways along the hallway. He gave MacKenzie a thumbs-up sign, then turned right and started moving in a crouch. Once again MacKenzie followed.

They moved quickly but without panic, and the Libonian stalked ahead with the confidence of a Land Corps veteran. When they finally came to the end of the west wing, O-Scar opened a secret passage. Inside it, a ladder led to the roof. They climbed it, opened a trapdoor, and leapt out. Then they dropped on their bellies and scurried along the flat surface until they were at the roof's edge, facing the front garden.

O-Scar peered over the edge and surveyed the ground below. MacKenzie slithered two meters to his left, then rolled on his back and kept watch behind them.

"Our main force is defending a perimeter along the brook, but they're taking a hell of a beating," O-Scar said over the sounds of fighting. "They're Rashadians, all right."

"How could Rashadians infiltrate Red Cliff?" MacKenzie asked.

O-Scar didn't respond. He was giving orders over his helmet transmitter. "Squads on the left, a Rashadian team is trying to flank your position. Get some grenades after them." In a few seconds, there were a series of pops followed by howls of pain. "Good work," O-Scar chortled.

"Who's defending the rear?" MacKenzie shouted over the renewed sound of small-weapons fire.

O-Scar turned to him and said, "Delta Platoon, but I haven't heard from them lately."

MacKenzie cursed. He crawled across the roof to the side of the building facing the Mangalam grove. As he was nearing the edge, he froze. Three Rashadians were swinging down from tree limbs fifteen meters to his left. At the same time, two grapnel hooks flipped onto the roof from below and dug into the rubbery material that coated the roof.

The three terrorists rappeling down from the trees were almost to the roof now. MacKenzie aimed the laser rifle at them and squeezed the trigger. The bolts blinded him as they cut into the targets, and for a few seconds nothing but white orbs danced in his eyes. "O-Scar!" he shouted. "Back here! They're coming up on ropes."

But O-Scar was already beside him, pulling him up by the scruff of the neck. "Get with it!" he shouted. "Cut the ropes at the hook with your laser." He pushed MacKenzie one way, then moved off in the other direction firing.

MacKenzie's eyes were beginning to clear, but his night vision was gone. He sensed movement to his right and spun toward it, firing. A particle beam smashed into his laser rifle and crawled up his left forearm, spinning him around and hurling him back. For a second, he was stunned. Then, ignoring the pain in his arm, he forced himself to turn back. A Rashadian was staggering uncertainly near the edge of the roof, looking down as if searching for a weapon. MacKenzie immediately rushed him, but as he approached, the Rashadian assumed a defensive stance. MacKenzie skidded to a halt and dropped into a side horse position.

There was something familiar about the Rashadian, but MacKenzie couldn't decide what it was, nor could he afford to wonder. He let his conscious thoughts wane, concentrating only on the Rashadian. They began circling each other warily.

Then suddenly a beam of light flashed down from somewhere out in the valley. It fell on the roof with purple brilliance, and the eerie whine of Airmobile troop shuttles filled the air. The Rashadian hesitated and looked up.

O-Scar was beside MacKenzie now, aiming a laser pistol at the Rashadian and smiling fiercely. "That's the cavalry, friend," he said in a facsimile of the terrorist's tongue. "Your fighting days are over."

But MacKenzie wasn't listening. He was consumed with rage. The searchlight had fallen directly on the Rashadian, and MacKenzie recognized the face. "Van Sander!" he snarled.

The woman removed her head wrap and flung it aside. "Yes, MacKenzie, but once again it appears I am at a disadvantage."

"Stow the crap!" MacKenzie whispered, pushing O-Scar's laser aside. "It's just you and I. I owe you something."

"Don't be a fool!" O-Scar shouted. "She's the proof Cyrus needs. We want her in one piece."

MacKenzie circled Van Sander menacingly. "I won't kill her,

O-Scar, just put her in the hospital awhile. It's the least she deserves for what she did to Svetla . . . and for everything else."

"I'm older than you and a woman besides, Commander. Is that what you call a fair contest?" Van Sander argued.

Her protests only served to fuel his rage. Here, all around, was the slaughter her scheming had caused, and she spoke as if she had some female right to amnesty. It was more than he could stand. His arm burned viciously, and the pain was paralyzing, but he repressed the message of flayed nerves and lunged toward her.

As his arm was extending, something crashed into the side of his neck below his mastoid bone, and the last thing he remembered was a blaze of silver light sizzling in his brain.

CHAPTER 25

Two hours later, Svetla was sitting patiently in an armchair outside MacKenzie's room. When Dr. Fronto came out, she stood up and asked, "How is he, Doctor?"

"He has suffered a slight concussion and some minor burns. Otherwise, he is quite well. In fact, he's already up."

"May I see him then?"

"Of course, my dear." He smiled and started down the hallway, but after he had gone only a few steps, he turned back and said, "That was certainly a close call, wasn't it?"

Svetla nodded. "Thank God the Land Corps units arrived when they did."

"Yes. Well, I don't mind telling you, it left me quite shaken." He motioned toward MacKenzie's room, then continued down the hall. Svetla turned toward the door, her hand trembling slightly as she reached for the unlocking plate. The door slid back, and she went inside.

MacKenzie was resting in a chair, his bare feet propped up on a hassock. He wore only pajama bottoms, but a robe hung loosely around his shoulders. His bandaged arm lay on his stomach like a slug. When he sensed Svetla's approach, he opened his eyes and started to get up.

"Sit down, MacKenzie. There's no need for that," she said.

He lowered himself back into the chair and pulled the robe around him. "Seems as if we can't get a moment's peace," he said.

Svetla sat down on the edge of the bed across from him. Their eyes interlaced a moment, ambiguously. Then she said, "Seeing you wounded and unconscious frightened me. It was a while before I learned that O-Scar had knocked you out to keep you from hurting Van Sander."

"There've been too many casualties because of that woman. She was leading the Rashadians. Did you know that?"

"Yes, O-Scar told me," she said.

He shrugged and looked at her with affectionate eyes. "You

looked beautiful tonight at dinner," he said unexpectedly. "You still do."

She felt a rush of conflicting emotions. She appreciated his compliment, but in the granite bunker beneath the building, with a battle rumbling above them, the blatant femininity of her gown had seemed ludicrous. Now MacKenzie's words made her remember her discomfort. Still, she felt compelled to say, "I almost wept when I saw you on that stretcher. I suppose I realized that you're mortal like the rest of us, and I decided I have to explain."

"Explain what?" he asked.

"I have something to tell you, but you mustn't say anything until I'm finished, no matter how much you want to. Is that agreed?"

He stared quizzically, then got out of the chair and came over to the bed. No, don't do that, her mind pleaded. It's so much harder when you're near. He sat down beside her. "Whatever you say, Svetla."

His closeness and the caress of his voice heightened her tension, but she had decided and could not relent. "I'm going to tell you something no one knows," she began. "And once you've heard, you'll understand why I left you before, and why I am not capable of . . . loving."

He began to protest, but she cut him off. "No. Don't argue. You promised!" He leaned back and let her continue. "You know I was raised in a Slavian state orphanage. It was the only home I ever knew. When I was a toddler, I got my way most of the time, and frankly I became quite spoiled. The orphanage was my oyster, and everyone in it was there to please me. That's what I thought.

"But when I entered First Form, the older children refused to tolerate my selfishness. They warned me not to act so high and mighty, because my mother was just a prostitute who had killed herself with drugs to get away from me. I refused to believe them and demanded they take it back, but the more I howled, the more they teased. They were only children, but children can be heartless."

She glanced at MacKenzie out of the corner of her eye. He

seemed to be listening intently, so she continued.

"I went to the headmistress and begged her to tell me it wasn't true. She did. But even then I knew when people were lying to me, and I sensed she was simply sparing my feelings. As I think about it now, I realize she wanted me to know, because I couldn't go on believing I was so special."

Svetla hadn't relived these times for decades, and she felt like weeping. "After that, things were never the same," she said with a raspy voice. "I tried to act as if it didn't matter, but I knew no decent family would want me once they knew. "Oh, Svetlana," one after another would say, "I'm being adopted. A wonderful couple is coming to take me. I am so happy . . . so happy!" I became withdrawn and lonely, only 'lonely' isn't the right word. What I wanted was the feeling of belonging, like I'd had before the older children found me out.

"Sometimes during meals in the big hall, I'd look around at the other children chatting together, at the upper forms across the center aisle, at the staff seated at the head table, and know I was nothing. I was . . . unwanted. Life seemed nothing more than a cruel joke. I'd suddenly break into tears for no apparent reason, which only increased their ridicule. The older ones would belittle me, singing out, loud enough that I might hear, 'Svetla's papa was a woodsman or maybe tended sheep. Her papa was a commissar or maybe drove a jeep.' I bit my nails to the quick so they looked dirty and ugly all the time. But I didn't care, because it didn't matter to anyone. I was nothing but human flotsam, the product of bad contraceptives or bad booze."

Svetla hesitated, collecting her thoughts. The memories were flooding her brain now, bringing back the old pain. "Then Professor O-Sedo arrived at the school to teach neo-Marxist economics to the middle forms and to serve as assistant director. He was a Libonian like O-Scar—a graduate of the Polytechnic Institute at Tschaiskypol. For some reason, he made me his 'junior assistant.' That was his name for it. What it meant was that I became his maid. I cleaned up after him, arranged his papers and books, warmed his biscuits in the morning . . . things like that. It was pitiful really, but I was happy for the first time in years and spent every moment I could in his office begging for more chores. He kept after me about things—my behavior, my clothes, my language. He made me stop biting my nails." *Look at those dirty stubs. They make one nauseated. I won't have them touching my things.* "He kept forcing me to improve—in mathematics, especially. I suppose he was the first to recognize my talent for equations. At least I can give him that credit. It went on that way for almost a year."

She stopped to take a breath. A soft breeze murmured in the Mangalam grove beyond the dark panels by the balcony, giving the moment an intimation of comfort, but there was none for her. "At any rate," she continued, "the other children soon realized I was his favorite, and their attitude changed. They began asking me to sway his opinion about policies and disciplinary rulings, and very often he did what I asked. I liked that immeasurably. I was important again, and everyone began catering to me. But he knew what he was doing, my wonderful professor. He was preparing me. I was no more able to save myself than a moth can resist the flame."

MacKenzie seemed troubled. He put his arm around her and started to say something, but she said, "Please! I am not finished." He hesitated a long moment, then nodded his acceptance. "It was all very innocent at first," she continued with grim recollection. "He would pat my shoulder when he showed me something, or rearrange my hair because it wasn't how he liked it. Then he taught me to massage his back. He had frequent headaches, and I would 'cure' them. I suffered migraines myself, so naturally he started 'curing' mine, too. He would lock the door and pull my blouse down over my shoulders. I actually felt he was helping. Can you imagine?

"Then one day he locked the door and asked me to sit by him." *Come to Uncle O-Sie, dear. I am sad, and only Svetlana can help.* "But this time, when I went to him, he pulled me onto his lap. I should have known what was happening. I suppose, somewhere deep inside, I did, but I didn't care. I did what he wanted gladly, as I always had, because I liked him. . . . "

Her voice broke. She dropped her head and fought back a sob. She wanted MacKenzie to hold her, wanted to hide in his comfort and end the pain of recollection, but she was afraid to face him, afraid of the revulsion she was certain would be scrawled across his face.

She shivered. "I was confused and bewildered. I had no idea what to feel or how to act, but he was very experienced. He began to . . ." Her voice trailed off. *Do you not like that, Svetlana? Does it not make you tingle with delight? You must learn these things, too, if you want to be a woman.* She searched for the correct words to express her violation, but there were none sufficient. "He taught me . . . arousal. And I let him, because he wanted it and because it was a way to repay him for everything he'd done. And after the first couple of sessions . . ." She hesitated a moment, like one approaching the brink. "You must know what happened. . . ."

Her confession had reached the crisis point, and the words spilled out in rapid succession.

"It didn't last much longer, though, because after a while things changed again. I sensed I was no longer so appealing to him. And I felt increasingly more despicable after each . . . intimacy. Perhaps he was already grooming another to take my place. Who knows?"

MacKenzie's arm was still around her, but as she turned to face him, she feared what she would see. She was taken by surprise. His eyes were tender and sympathetic. "Did you report him to the authorities?" he asked.

She grimaced bitterly. "He *was* the authorities. Besides, have you understood nothing I've told you? There was nothing to report. He didn't force me. I did it willingly. I wanted it!" Her eyes filled with tears of humiliation. "Don't you see, MacKenzie? I craved that intimacy no matter how deformed it was or what it cost me. I've spent my life trying to escape such compulsion." She surveyed him with scorching eyes. "That's why I had to leave you when we were on Red Cliff. I had put it behind me finally, but you were opening it up all over again. Ultimately I can only hate what brings me such significance. Don't you see?"

MacKenzie stared back at her with a foreboding frown, then suddenly he stood up and began pacing slowly from one end of the room to the other. Finally he turned back to her and said, "No, Svetla, I don't see. And I don't think you do, either. You were an innocent child—a lonely child who couldn't comprehend that O-Sedo was manipulating your vulnerabilities under the guise of friendship. He'd probably done the same thing many times before. He was the sick one. You're reading things into a situation that don't belong there."

"Oh, that's a comforting illusion, Mac—perhaps even a little true," she stated. "But I knew exactly what he was doing. I was very intelligent. Everyone said so. I would have been instinctively repulsed, if I hadn't been so depraved. But I was. I still am. Don't you see?"

MacKenzie walked back across the room and sat beside her again, his face conferring a poignant confidence. "Why condemn sexual desire because the circumstances that first introduced it were wrong?" he asked.

She shook her head miserably. "You still don't understand."

MacKenzie took her gently in his good arm and gave her a hug. "I appreciate your telling me this," he said. "I know it was extremely difficult, and you think it changes things between us, but it doesn't. You're a very desirable woman, and I . . . love you, Svetla. I have since the first moment we met. Nothing you have said, nothing you might have done in the past, can change that. The present is what counts—the present and what we can make of it. The past is a grave, the future a reflection of what we do now. Don't you see?"

My God, he's doing it again! He's mangled and beaten and shot, and still his confidence in salvation remains. If only I could be like him. "You are hopelessly romantic, Mac," she whispered. "You think love conquers all. Perhaps that's what attracts me to you. But don't expect it of me. I'm not capable of such belief."

He stood up again and pulled her to her feet. "Get out of that dress and make yourself comfortable. We won't settle anything tonight. Too much has happened, and we're both tired." He reached down and pulled back the bed covers.

What is this? Do you expect me to sleep with you now, after all I've said? Are you no better than O-Sedo? She was over-whelmed by a wave of nausea.

He looked back at her and stared. "What's wrong?" he asked.

"I'm going to my own room. My God, what do you want of me?"

"I want you to give us a chance, like you did this afternoon in the library. That wasn't so bad, was it?"

The library? Oh, yes. I was content then. . . and pure. I kissed his cheek as he lay sleeping, knowing I was capable of selfless love—at least for that moment. She studied him suspiciously—the assured eyes, the hulking chest, the ban-daged arm, the pink scars on his forehead from the accident Dr. Fronto had told her about. And finally exhaustion con-sumed her turbulent will.

Without thinking, she reached up, slipped the gown from her shoulders, and pulled it off. She sat on the hassock and re-moved her shoes. Then she stood again and worked the silken hose down her legs. All she wore now were sateen briefs and a camisole, and her body was trembling. *Even now, in the depths of baring my soul, it will not stop—even while he offers me his strange remaking.*

MacKenzie had removed his robe and climbed into the bed. He was lying there in his pajama bottoms, complacently star-ing at the ceiling. It wasn't at all what she had expected. She stared at him a moment, then walked round to the other side of the bed, feeling the sponge of the carpet soft between her splaying toes. Hesitantly she lay down beside him. He pulled the coverlet over them, then touched the sensors that turned off the lights.

She lay on her back, motionless, peering into the dark, her muscles tensely poised. The luxury of her camisole and the cov-erlet caressed her as she waited. He moved toward her. She could see him silhouetted in the faint light of the balcony pan-els. He reached out and brushed back the hair from her fore-head, then kissed her lightly on the lips. She stiffened in response and closed her eyes, trying not to think. But he rolled over, so his buttocks nudged her indolently, warm but relaxed. "Good night, Svetla," he said. "Pleasant dreams."

Pleasant dreams? Just like that? Are you so certain of yourself? She felt like a child playing house. Mommy and Daddy are going to sleep now. I exposed him to the pit of my personal hell, and he acts like it's nothing. How can he manage this?

She snuggled up against him, letting the heat of his muscular body soak into her. And for the second time in only a few hours, she found herself completely content by his side.

CHAPTER 26

"This is magnificent, isn't it?" Svetla called over the sound of the waterfall. She sat down on a large rock and started removing her hiking shoes. She stripped off the heavy socks, then began undoing her shirt. MacKenzie looked away.

"Get your clothes off," she scolded. "You don't expect to swim in all that, do you?"

"I don't have a suit," he said.

"You can't enjoy swimming with such constraint. Why be so Calvinistic?" she cried.

"I'm not," he complained, keeping his eyes averted.

"Ha! All Anglo-Americans are Calvinistic capitalists. It is your *kultur*."

She stood up, slipped out of her hiking shorts, and pulled off her briefs. Then, completely naked, she hopped down the boulders toward the calm part of the pool, beyond the churning waters below the falls. The sharp ridges of the stone ledge were cutting into her feet, so she dove in quickly. When she came to the surface, she inhaled sharply and began treading water. The pool was icy cold. "Well, are you joining me or not?" she called gaily.

"All right. Don't rush me," he called back. He tilted his head skyward, as if searching for the Airmobile craft that passed over occasionally. Seeing none, he began to undress. He pulled off his shirt, then his shoes and socks. Next he unhooked the hiking shorts, and slipped them down over his knees. He squatted down and stacked everything in a neat pile. When he straightened up, he realized that an erection bulged blatantly beneath his undershorts, and he turned his back to her.

Why is he so embarrassed? Does his own desire shame him? The hypocrite! Two days had passed since the Rashadian assault, and during that time, except for her sessions with Dr. Fronto, she and MacKenzie had been together constantly, sharing stories about the academy or the Outbanks and discuss sing what little they could learn about the political situation. Now and then, when their mood was intimate, MacKenzie would comment that physical desire resulted naturally from deep affection, but he had made no overt approach.

The freezing water was making Svetla's body ache, but she tried not to notice. "Don't be so damned modest! Everyone knows we're an item, so why hide it? Take off those ridiculous shorts. They're strangling you," she shouted.

In spite of the cold, her heart began to pound as he leaned over to remove them, but then he straightened up again. "I'm not swimming naked, Svetla. It's not my custom," he called. He started down the boulders, and when he came to the ledge, dove out gracefully. In a moment, he broke the surface and howled, "Shit! It's freezing!" He lunged forward and swam toward her with strong, rapid strokes. Before she could move, he was upon her, grabbing her shoulders and pushing her down. They sank beneath the surface, and she hung docilely in his arms, aware of his hardness pressing against her. There's no means of flight now. You have me . . . at least for the moment. He scissors-kicked and they broke back through the sunlit surface, both gasping for air.

In a moment, MacKenzie sputtered. "Jesus, it's cold! How could you act so nonchalant?"

"I'm Slavian, remember, and we're a hardy lot," she said with a grin. "You must admit the water's refreshing, though."

"A polar bear would freeze in this stuff," he replied. "I know now why you wanted me to hurry."

Svetla was tiring of the effort to stay afloat. She said, "I'm freezing, too," and began to sidestroke toward the bank near the waterfall. MacKenzie followed her. When they reached the rocks, they found handholds and pulled themselves up. They sat silent, huddled side by side for a while, letting the sunlight warm their shivering flesh. Finally she said, "I do enjoy tormenting you, don't I? But I've decided to be fair to both of us." She touched his cheek with her good right hand and kissed him lightly on the lips.

It startled him, and he leaned back, studying her with surprise. Am I being too shameless, or is he truly unsuspecting?

I'm not very experienced in his moods. What does he want? She stared at him intently. Droplets of water glistened on his face like morning dew. She put her arms round his neck, and pulled him to her, then locked a searching kiss on his responding lips. His arms slowly twined round her in a tender embrace, and they lay back, kissing.

The coarse rock bit into her hip. She grimaced, and he searched her face with a look of concern. "What's wrong?" he asked.

"The stone is hard." She gave him an intimate smile. "Get up. I want to show you something."

When he stood, she saw that his erection was outlined plainly beneath the sodden undershorts. She averted her eyes and rose to her feet. When she turned to him, he was watching her curiously but didn't seem embarrassed. The words of an erotic poetess echoed suddenly in her memory. *Impaling obelisk of fear and promise to rend all my hypocrisies, as virginal shall I be cleaved, a ripened pomegranate.* She knew she was blushing but refrained from looking down.

She took his hand and led him along the rocks toward the waterfall.

"Where are we going?" MacKenzie asked.

"You will see in a moment."

When they were next to the falls, she studied the ledges in the stone face of the cliff. The lower ledge was the widest and seemed more even. That must be the one, she thought. She crawled onto it, then turned and beckoned him up. He looked at her with a confused frown, and it made her smile. "We're going exploring," she told him.

She took his hand again and led him beneath the tumult of the cascading falls. She inched along the ledge a meter or so, buffeted by the bone-cold water. Then suddenly she saw the glimmering orifice and rushed through it, pulling MacKenzie behind her.

They entered a large cavern cut into the cliffs eons ago by an underground river. It was rimmed with massive stalagmites and stalactites, which had fused to form columns. Smaller stalagmites in the middle of the cavern formed a series of round, altarlike tables. The cave floor itself was carpeted with white, powdery sand, and phosphorescent lichen on the damp limestone and granite walls filled the grotto with a soft, otherworldly bluish glow. A pungent trace of incense lingered in the warm air.

"What is this place?" MacKenzie asked in astonishment.

"The Nihonians consider it a center of cosmic power. Cyrus Magnum lets them use it."

"How did you learn of it?" he asked.

"Inayu told me."

Water was dripping from his shorts down his muscular legs, and he was shivering. There was no sign of the male bulge that had been there earlier.

"Take off those ridiculous shorts or you'll catch your death of cold," she advised sternly, turning her back to lessen his embarrassment. She heard the slosh of the material as he pulled the sopping briefs down over his legs. She walked farther into the cavern. The sand was feather soft beneath her feet, and it was warmer here. "Come here, Mac. There's a warm draft. It will dry you." *Am I too overbearing? Will he resent what I'm doing? You really are a bit of an ass, Svetla.* MacKenzie came up behind her. She sat down and crossed her legs. He looked at her a moment, then did the same, sitting beside her.

"Nihonian monks come here for retreats, and once a year for a special ceremony," she told him.

"What kind of ceremony?"

"Monks who decide to take a spouse and reenter the world exchange wedding promises here. Then they find hidden places in the cave to consummate their love for the first time. The gene pool of Zazen wisdom is perpetuated through the children conceived in this holy place. At least that's what they believe." She turned and looked at him.

MacKenzie shrugged. The grotto's warmth was taking the edge off his chill, and he seemed more comfortable. "Did Inayu tell you that, too?" he asked.

"Yes. She thinks I'm part Nihonian because my eyes look oriental." His gaze lingered intently on her face. "I don't know who my father was, you see."

He smiled and said, "You're not Nihonian, Svetla. Your eyes slant up, not down. Your ancestors may have been Mongol . . . or possibly Tartar. That's more reasonable, given your Slavic background."

In her mind's eye, she saw a valiant horseman silhouetted against the night sky, coursing the wild steppes on a midnight steed, scimitar flashing in the horned moon like the hand of justice. The thought captivated her.

She gazed at MacKenzie with affection, wondering if he knew how entrancing he could be when he was open and reassuring, so unlike the invincible combatant he often seemed. At times like these, she knew how hopelessly in love she could become. Her eyes filled with tears.

MacKenzie brushed them away gently, concerned by her mood. "What's wrong? Did I make you sad somehow?" he whispered. "You can be Nihonian if you want to. Perhaps it will make me more comfortable around them."

"You didn't make me sad," she said softly.

"You have a strange way of showing it."

"There are many emotions between joy and sadness, Mac." She leaned against his shoulder, and he wrapped his arm around her. Only a few pink splotches remained under the new skin on his left arm where the flesh had been singed by the particle beam. She turned to him and said, "This morning during our session, I told Dr. Fronto about what O-Sedo had done. I explained how he exposed my depravity and why it made me desert you. Do you know what he told me to do? He encouraged me to seduce you."

She could sense by the sudden tension in his body that MacKenzie was perturbed. "I don't believe it," he stated.

"You know cyberneticists—they think you should attack conflicts head-on."

"Why did you tell him about O-Sedo?" he demanded.

"He's trying to help me understand myself, that's all. It's his job. Cyrus told him to counsel me. What did you think we've been doing during all those sessions?"

"I hadn't given it much thought." He took his arm away and shifted a little to the side.

"What's wrong?" she asked.

"Nothing's wrong."

"Nonsense. You're jealous of Dr. Fronto, aren't you?"

"I'm not jealous of Fronto!"

"Well, what is it, then?"

"I'm just surprised you would share that with anyone else."

For an instant, she was tempted to argue, but she sensed it would be a mistake.

Svetla raised her good hand and turned his face toward her. She gazed into the glittering emerald of his eyes and said, "I didn't mean to hurt you," and pressed her lips to his. For a moment, they both savored the simplicity of the kiss, lingering over the sensuality of that initiating touch. Then slowly he wrapped her in his arms again, and the probing of their mouths flashed passionate.

They kissed each others eyes and cheeks and neck, and Svetla flooded with desire, until her breath was coming in short, rapid gasps. They fell back into the soft, powdery sand, their bodies entwining in a hungry embrace. The strange comfort of his touch enthralled her again, and for a while, she lay docilely in his arms.

Then he turned her on her back and gazed into her eyes. His face was flushed, and the new scars above his brow glowed palely in the soft light. They reminded her of his mortality, and the thought filled her with renewed waves of yearning. She closed her eyes and pulled him toward her.

For a timeless, thoughtless period, he caressed her, and she surrendered herself completely to his touch. But then she began to experience a strange sensation.

She felt as if the marriage passion of countless Nihonians, purified by years of abstinence, had crystallized suddenly in the cavern. In her mind's eye, she could almost see them making love around her. It made her feel part of a long line of women who had accepted a sanctioned, physical intimacy inside its walls, and the image filled her with a simple joy she had never known. She lingered there for a long moment, experiencing nothing but their shared affection. Then she thought about what was happening to her and recoiled in fear. Her rippling bliss drained like a viciously ebbing tide, leaving her stranded haplessly on the powdered sand of the grotto floor. "No!" she groaned, reaching up and pushing MacKenzie away.

MacKenzie stared at her in surprise. "What's wrong?" he whispered.

She sat up and shook her head sullenly, but she didn't answer him.

"Did you bring me here just to tease me, or did you really want to see where it might lead?" he demanded.

She shot him a moody frown. "Neither. But I—" she gazed at him with beseeching eyes—"I believe I love you, Mac, but who am I to say, being what I am? Is that what you want to hear?"

She looked down to hide her eyes, inadvertently letting them come to rest on the shaft of his maleness. The sight filled her with a mixture of desire and revulsion, and the long-forgotten stanzas of the erotic Columbine poetess, read in the secrecy of the Outbanks, continued again in her brain: *O fearful pubic monument on which I shall be severed, mock not my plaintive cries as they unleash. For pregnant with desire I convulse to mold you deeply, though your gorging rupture all my dignity.* She looked shyly back toward the mouth of the cavern, where the water's muffled thunder softly rolled.

"So you tried to . . . make love with me, but you still find it impossible. Is that it?" MacKenzie asked.

"Yes . . . Perhaps it is impossible for me. Every time I begin to give myself, I feel dirty. Can't you understand that?"

"Do you know what your problem is?" MacKenzie said. "You don't understand dirt. You think it's a sign of poor emotional housekeeping." He poked her in her stomach playfully and she jerked her knees up in reaction. "Dirt is good. Dirt is necessary. Consider what cosmology tells us . . . how stars explode and are reborn along with planets from the dusty residue . . . how life evolves from the clay of the planets. Worlds from ashes and life from clay." His eyes were sparkling. "Don't you see, Svetla? Even science tells us that, in the most magnificent way, we are a magnificent form of stardust."

She studied him as if for the first time. Where did that come from, you arrogant man? Do you really think you have discerned the meaning of existence so simply? You are mad, MacKenzie—compellingly mad. She stared at him secretly from the corner of her eye. He was watching her with a patient stare.

She turned back to him and touched his cheek, exploring its hollow with her fingertips. He leaned toward her in response, and their lips met. His kiss was so tender that it seemed more a sharing of breath, and she pulled him down until they were lying on their sides again.

"Does this mean you'll forget your obsession with dirt for a while?" he whispered to her.

She smiled coyly and ran her fingers across his chest. "I want to make us happy," she whispered back.

He rolled onto her and kissed her again. In spite of everything, I can't believe how natural this feels, she thought. It must be the grotto. There's some strange power here. An unwitting tear of joy escaped the corner of her eye.

He brushed it away and gazed at her lovingly. Then his fingers traced the line of her neck and brushed down to the soft mound of her breast. She closed her eyes as the warmth exploded in her again, stronger than the first time, and she lay back submissively, exposing herself freely to his care.

"Do you think we can ever have what we want most?" she asked in a musing voice, without considering what she was saying.

"Perhaps we have even more," MacKenzie said as he kissed her.

CHAPTER 27

"So did you finally make love?" Dr. Fronto asked point-blank at Svetla's next counseling session.

Svetla nodded shyly. "We were gone so long that O-Scar feared we'd run into trouble and dispatched extra patrols to search for us. I'm afraid he's upset with us."

The doctor chuckled. "So I've been told. But tell me, how was it for you? No sense of revulsion? No lingering sense of shame?"

"No."

"So accepting MacKenzie's love was not demeaning?"

"It was . . . personally exposing. Something like surrender, but not ignoble. I suppose I let go."

"Let go of what?"

She shrugged uneasily. "I don't know . . . of fearing what it might ultimately portend, I think."

"Is what happened with O-Sedo still important to you now?"

She tensed at the mention of the Libonian's name. "I'll never be able to escape what happened with O-Sedo. He . . . exposed my depravity."

"I'm sorry, Svetla, but I do not understand why you feel so depraved."

"How can you say that?" she cried. "I was a child and I seduced the man. I wanted it to happen!"

"There is a power motif in most relationships, especially sexual ones. You should remember that without letting it ruin your tender moments."

Power motif? Is he implying I wanted to dominate? Was that really my goal? The thought faded in the turbulence of her self-contempt. "There was nothing tender about that lust," she said harshly. "It was an exercise in mutual masturbation, and that's all. I wanted to . . ." She halted in midsentence. She was about to say she had hoped to bind O-Sedo to her completely.

"What about what you have found with MacKenzie? Is that nothing but a cold exercise?"

Svetla gazed at the small icon of a bearded saint enshrined on a miniature altar in the corner of Fronto's study. It was surrounded by candles burning at different levels, as though lighted at different times for different intentions. It struck her as melancholy.

"I don't think you appreciate who MacKenzie is," she said. "He is a god in the Flight Corps, the epitome of courage and heroism. The first time I saw him, he gave a short speech to us first-year cadets at the academy. There he was, the son of one of the Outbankers who had sacrificed his life for Concordat liberty, just returned from his victory at Pegasus Station, so handsome he made my heart swoon. I can't remember what he said, but that didn't matter. He motivated us without words, by just being what he was. Do you see?"

The doctor nodded sympathetically.

"After that, our paths never crossed, but I became an Outbanker, too. You can imagine how I felt when I shipped in for repairs and learned he was on Red Cliff. He was there. Available! I felt like a schoolgirl with a lady's choice. At first I resisted, but finally I said, 'What the hell.' "

The sight of MacKenzie sulking bleary-eyed in the musty darkness of the El Hambre Club filled her mind's eye. "He looked a little seedy, but after I invited him to buy a drink, he was so relaxed and natural, it only enhanced his attraction. We talked and drank and got drunk . . . like true comrades-in-arms. I was in my glory, I can tell you. Then I sensed he was attracted to me, too . . . as a woman . . . and I understood how Cinderella must have felt. I was terrified but satisfied at the same time. Perhaps I'd be despoiled by a real demigod. Me, Svetla Stocovik. How fate had smiled."

"You felt more powerful, then?" Dr. Fronto interjected.

Svetla thought a moment, then laughed. "You are a devil, Doctor," she said. "Yes. I felt more powerful—perhaps no more than any woman who proves her desirability to an eligible male, but self-satisfied nonetheless. That was a major part of it. But MacKenzie turned the tables on me, as he so often does. I thought he would find some excuse to distance himself after he got what he needed and the remorse set in. I even hoped he would, because I was hung over and emotionally soiled. I had, after all, torn away the demigod's mask and seen him exposed to me, grunting the same as any other man. The same as O-Sedo.

"But the next morning he was caring and tender. He nursed me painstakingly, making me shower and even massaging my back while I dozed. Then later he had me dress for dinner, and by the time we walked to the restaurant, I was ravenous. He knew what I needed, sensed exactly what to do. He kept watching me with this intimate, vulnerable look in his eyes. It was very shattering."

Svetla fell silent. She had forced herself to repress these memories during the time they had been apart, and reliving their bittersweet magic made her sad. Those had been doomed times.

"Then on the third night, he told me what had happened on the *Sinclair*, an old cruise ship he had been sent to investigate. Everyone aboard had been burned alive, including a nursery filled with infants. I still remember the look on his face as he described the horror and anger he felt." She folded her hands in her lap and stared down. "Anyway," she continued, "on that third night, he shared his sorrow and uncertainty with me, explaining how the malevolence of it had made him doubt the meaning of existence. He was afraid I would no longer respect him. Ha! Typical MacKenzie. As if he didn't realize that knowing he was subject to the same torment as the rest of us only made him more heroic to me. He became a Hector or Ulysses, a man of mythic proportions, because he had shared his secrets with me as an equal.

"I was so moved, I couldn't say anything. We made love again, quite deeply, because I wanted so much to comfort him. But later, resting in each other's arms, I knew I was lost. He would want marriage and children, and I couldn't resist. Then, sooner or later, he'd learn of my depravity and despise me for seducing him.

"I rose before dawn, collected my things, and rushed back

to the station. Luckily my cruiser was ready, and I set off for the Outbanks again to . . . bury myself."

Dr. Fronto leaned back and smiled. "Ah yes," he said. "I think I understand now why you feel MacKenzie is different. But what of your lovemaking in the grotto yesterday? Tell me about that."

She was silent a long time, remembering those moments. "I don't know how to explain this," she said finally. "It seems silly now because it no longer seems real. But once I surrendered, I felt as if I were melting into the grotto, into the amassed acts of love that had already occurred there. The sense of completion frightened me. It attacked my identity, and I focused on MacKenzie to save myself.

"But then I felt the same thing in him, only more strongly. And the sense of fusing reestablished itself. It released such a prolonged moment of . . . being one that I . . ." She hesitated a long moment. "I can't explain further. I think there must be strange powers in that grotto." An embarrassing tear ran down her cheek.

Dr. Fronto braced his elbows on his desk, clasped his hands together as if in prayer, and lowered his eyes. They both sat motionless for a long while. The study was so quiet that Svetla could hear the sizzle of the candlewicks burning by the icon. Then the doctor looked up and said, "MacKenzie knows of your supposed depravity. But he doesn't despise you any more than you did him for what he told you about the *Sinclair*. Do you see? You gave up self-deprecation and experienced communion with another human being, didn't you?"

"I . . . don't know. Perhaps I did. But in time, when the romance wears off . . . " She felt bone-tired suddenly.

"Would being a wife and bearing children be so very terrible?" the doctor interrupted.

She was nettled by the question. What does that have to do with what we're discussing? "I don't know," she replied sharply. "I haven't thought about it." She glanced at the melancholy eyes of the icon again. "The thought frightens me."

"Why? Is being an Outbanker enough to satisfy your needs as a woman?"

She shook her head stubbornly. "I don't know. Stop browbeating me. Perhaps I'm incapable of such responsibility. I've been an Outbanker for too long."

Dr. Fronto sighed. He stood up and said, "Why not let it rest awhile? I must check with Cyrus Magnum's headquarters to see how things are faring, and I'm sure MacKenzie is waiting for you. This is your time, Svetla. Yours and MacKenzie's. You should make the most of it while you can."

She stared at the doctor quizzically.

Fronto rose and came around his desk. He patted her shoulder. "This was a good session, Svetla. I think you're beginning to see what really disturbs you. Take things one day at a time, and reflect on your need for power. But don't let it affect the mystery you have found with Ian. Cherish that for as long as you live."

BOOK FOUR

OUTBANKER BLUES

"The game of life does not proceed like a mathematical calculation, on the principle that two and two are four. Sometimes they make five, or minus three. And sometimes the blackboard topples down in the middle of the sum, leaving the classroom in disorder and the pedagogue with a black eye."[4]

---

4. Sir Winston Churchill, circa A.D. 1948. Quoted in *My Favorite Quotations*, by SH-LA 250-5, a.k.a. Sheila. Concordat Cybernaut Press, Eketelon Central (2387 E.C.), p. 134.

CHAPTER 28

MacKenzie followed O-Scar along the hall. As they approached the central staircase, he could hear muffled voices coming from the east corridor. Two Land Corps guards stood in front of a white rope draped ceremoniously between the corridor walls.

"What's the commotion?" MacKenzie inquired.

"Our friends in the news media. I've given them some rooms for a press pool. They're chafing at the bit after such a long hiatus without any news releases."

As they started up the stairs, someone called, "O-Scar, that's Commander MacKenzie with you, isn't it?"

MacKenzie looked down. A reporter was leaning against the white rope and being restrained by one of the guards. "Commander," he called, "what's your status in the new government?" The noise immediately drew a pack of journalists, and they began barking questions simultaneously.

"No comment," O-Scar called out. "You'll get your stories soon enough, I promise you."

When MacKenzie and O-Scar gained the top of the staircase, they turned into the west hall and MacKenzie asked, "What did they mean about a new government?"

The Libonian's anthracite eyes sparkled. "At one thousand and thirty hours today, Cyrus will be appointed President of the Concordat and Chairman of the Executive Council."

MacKenzie nearly halted in midstep. "Then the political situation has been resolved?"

"Political situations are never completely resolved, but for the moment, we are in control. You'll learn more in a minute."

"What do you mean?" MacKenzie demanded, but O-Scar just grinned sardonically and took his arm. He led him to the grand suite, where Cyrus had established his offices. The guards saluted as they approached, then one entered the security code that opened the door. It slipped aside silently, and they entered.

Cyrus Magnum was sitting behind an antique wooden desk. He looked up as they approached and said, "I'm so glad to se you again, Ian. I understand you've enjoyed your respite at th encampment."

MacKenzie wondered if Svetla had told him that. Cyrus had insisted on meeting with her privately. He glanced about th suite, but Svetla wasn't there.

Cyrus rose from the desk, motioned to an alcove overlookin the Mangalam grove, and said, "Please make yourself comfort able. We have much to discuss."

"Congratulations on your success, sir," MacKenzie said a they were sitting down. "O-Scar just told me."

Cyrus smiled. "The fates rewarded us this time, Ian."

"What news we've had has indicated a crisis of major pro portion," MacKenzie ventured.

"Mammoth might be a better word," Cyrus said. "I'm sorr we couldn't keep you better informed, but there were time that the conspiracy exceeded even my own worst fears, an there was little you could have done. It was touch and go mor than once, but we prevailed." He crossed his legs and studie MacKenzie for a moment. "Ian, how much do you know abou Concordat politics?"

"News updates are transmitted regularly to the Outbanks sir, and I try to follow events," MacKenzie replied, wonderin why Cyrus had asked. "The Syndicalists and Social Democrat have been in power since your Concordalist Party was voted ou in the last plebiscite. Your policies were preferred by the intel lectuals, but it wasn't enough to balance the damage cause when the Rashadians raided the Nihonian villages."

Cyrus nodded. "Yes, I must shoulder complete blame fo that disaster. It was my policy of Rashadian rapprochemen that gave them such freedom of operation."

"Frankly, sir, I've never understood what you intended t accomplish by that," MacKenzie said.

Cyrus peered through the windows at the Mangalam grove For a moment, he seemed immensely weary. "Yes, in hind sight, it seems Pollyannaish. But then I believed the Rasha dians had a legitimate grievance. The Hegemony had stoler homeland, and they were in Diaspora, like the ancient Jews, or later the Palestinians under Zionism. I recommended exploring means of resettling them if an agreement on reparations could be reached. We thought it was a good policy." Cyrus took a deep breath and exhaled slowly. "That all ended, of course, when the Rashadians pillaged and raped the Nihonian coast."

"It was a vicious raid," MacKenzie said. "Did you ever learn why they mounted it?"

Cyrus wagged his head. "Until a few days ago, I attributed it to policy conflicts within the Rashadian movement itself or to the unremitting stupidity of man. But now I know why it happened. And you helped me prove it."

MacKenzie assumed he knew what Cyrus meant. Van Sander and some of her men had led the Rashadian attack on the encampment. There had been a fifth column, allied to the terrorists, within the Concordat. About that, Van Sander had not lied. "Was Internal Security in league with the Rashadians, then?" he asked.

"Indirectly, yes, but that's not the whole story," Cyrus said. He gave Mackenzie a cryptic grin. "Red Cliff was only days from being invaded by a Federation armada when you alerted me of the conspiracy."

"The Federation was going to invade Red Cliff?" MacKenzie exclaimed in disbelief. "Impossible! It would have meant instant retaliation."

"Not necessarily," Cyrus said. "That's where Internal Security's ambitions and my previous policy failure become important. You see, on the surface, it wouldn't have seemed like an invasion at all. The Federation's armada would have been invited here to save Red Cliff from me."

MacKenzie gaped in disbelief.

"Yes, Ian. That was the plan," Cyrus continued. "Internal Security had already charged secretly that I was providing the Rashadians with bases on Red Cliff from which to launch their attacks. My purpose in this, they claimed, was to destabilize the current government to the point where I would be re-elected to the Executive Council. Once recalled, I intended to reinstitute my policy of rapprochement and offer the Rashadians Red Cliff as a homeland. Internal Security had forged evidence to support their tale and had Rashadian captives to confirm it. But there was a problem. Red Cliff is currently its outermost orbital phase and far from Concordat main forces. What could be done to stop me? Internal Security suggested the Federation might help defeat an ally of the Rashadian terrorists. Coincidentally, they had an armada on practice maneuvers, just days away.

"In that regard, your legal chicanery only played into their hands. You were a Rashadian collaborator and had naturally selected me to save your skin. As soon as I learned what they were up to, I declared martial law to stabilize the situation. Do you see now why I was somewhat short with your soul-searching at times, Ian?"

MacKenzie nodded. To the Executive Council, Internal Security's charges would have seemed plausible.

Cyrus went on. "Of course, as soon as I learned what was afoot, I filed a coundercharge that Internal Security was actually attempting a *coup* on the Federation's behalf, and I backed up my assertions with the intelligence collected from the Internal Security operatives we arrested. My peers on the council were confused by the claims and counterclaims, and my political opponents tended to side with Internal Security out of self-interest. Everything began to revolve around uncovering proof of Internal Security's complicity with the Rashadians. That was why Van Sander had to escape. The Federation armada might be here right now and we might be in chains—or worse—without the evidence Van Sander's raid finally provided."

"So the conspiracy was operational until Van Sander attacked and Internal Security's connection with the Rashadians was firmly established," MacKenzie said with a nervous frown.

Cyrus Magnum raised his hands, palms up. "Yes. It was fortunate for us that they wanted you and Svetla so badly."

A grim awareness formed in MacKenzie's brain. He knew that what Magnum had told him should have angered him, but it didn't. It had been a good strategy. "You used us as bait, didn't you, sir?"

Cyrus stared at him calmly with no apology in his eyes. "Yes, I'm afraid we did. It was one of many traps we laid, but O-Scar always believed that recapturing you and Svetla was their most probable move. They needed independent corroboration of their charges and couldn't continue dragging Rashadians onto the stage without finally incriminating themselves. They thought, correctly I expect, that they could condition you both to testify on their behalf."

MacKenzie slumped back and crossed his arms over his chest. He sat silent a few seconds. "All right," he said finally, "Van Sander took the bait and that saved us. But why did Security mount such a conspiracy in the first place? What did they intend to gain?"

"Internal Security's leadership is composed exclusively of people of Dutch extraction," Cyrus said. "As you know, our colonies consist primarily of Eastern European and Middle Eastern stock: Slavs, Russians, Jews, Arabs. The original Cygni B expedition was organized and financed by the energy cartel, so that was only natural. You Anglo-Americans and the Nihonians arrived later, but in numbers large enough to colonize whole continents or moons. You assimilated into our social order as equals.

"But the Dutch were a small group, whose ancestors had spent generations working for the transnational oil companies. They had immigrated with the original expedition and were forced to live with majority populations. They began to feel repressed, apparently, especially after the Corporate Hegemony was overthrown and religious and ethnic customs began playing a larger role in affairs. The only place they rose to rank was in the Security Service, and they consolidated their control as much as possible, believing all other avenues would remain closed to them. The Dutch were ripe for the proposal the Federation apparently made to them."

The Dutch? MacKenzie repeated to himself. What was it about the Dutch? *Wooden shoes!* Of course! Captain Findail had cursed wooden shoes for the carnage on his ship. MacKenzie had thought he was simply insane with grief, but it had meant something after all. For a moment, he recalled Findail's horror-stricken face and he could hear the screaming crew.

"Is something troubling you, Ian?" Cyrus asked.

"No," he said. "It's not important anymore. Precisely what proposal had the Federation made to them, sir?" he asked.

"Red Cliff, Ian. Red Cliff in exchange for delivering the colony, at least partially, into their hands," Cyrus answered.

"What happened to Van Sander?" MacKenzie asked.

"She's been delivered safely to the Federation armada," Cyrus stated with a vague twinkle in his eye. "We've decided no protest will be lodged. It's enough that they have lost the element of surprise while exposing their clandestine support of the Rashadian terrorists." Cyrus hesitated, fixing MacKenzie with baleful eyes.

"Where is their armada now, sir?"

"Holding maneuvers on the boundary of Cygni B space and playing a waiting game," Cyrus said. "Apparently they're keeping their options open until they see how we respond to their aggressive policy." He rose from his chair and gazed out the windows. "Few in the government know of the Federation's involvement in the conspiracy, and that is how it must remain. We share the same star system, Ian. Were our sanguine citizenry to learn of their ambitions or of their support of Rashadian terror, it might lead to a conflict that would weaken us both and expose us to manipulation by other interstellar powers. Do you see?"

MacKenzie nodded.

"The Executive Council has classified all reference to the incident top secret, Priority Five," Cyrus continued. "We must keep a close eye on the Federation—those of us who are aware—until they recall their armada and the situation stabilizes."

A nagging question formed in MacKenzie's mind. "Sir," he said, "if the incident has been classified so secret, why did you tell me?"

"In your new position, you have the need to know."

"My new position, sir?"

"Yes, Ian. Effective today, at fourteen hundred hours, you become Military Governor of Red Cliff. The Executive Council authorized your appointment at its first meeting after the supporters of Internal Security were purged."

MacKenzie was astonished. "Surely you are joking, sir."

Cyrus observed him shrewdly. "I have no time for comedy, Ian. I told you the Federation's armada is maneuvering near our stellar space. They might attack on some pretense at any time. Concordat reinforcements are on the way, but it'll be at least two weeks before they can be deployed beyond the asteroid belt. And until they are, we need a show of force. The fact that Red Cliff's defenses have been turned over to an Outbanker of your reputation should make them think twice before deciding to play their invasion card.

"Not only that, but also the Flight Corps was supposed to quarantine our planetary space. The corps' morale is low since they took that shellacking from O-Scar's battalions, and the supposed quarantine has been an absolute sieve. The Rashadians who attacked you got through the quarantine, and who knows who else. I'm thoroughly disgusted with their performance. Perhaps seeing one of their Outbanker heroes elevated to power will motivate them."

Cyrus's reference to Flight Corps reminded MacKenzie of Schoenhoffer. "Did the vice admiral have anything to do with the conspiracy?" he asked.

Cyrus said, "Very little, actually. He knew nothing of their intentions."

O-Scar had remained silent. Now he spoke for the first time. "Van Sander learned that Schoenhoffer was bisexual and was buggering his aides. He did what they wanted to save his ass, so to speak." The big Libonian grinned pleasantly.

"Yes, well . . ." Cyrus continued, seemingly embarrassed by O-Scar's play on words. "I trust you understand why I'm making you Military Governor. Red Cliff must become a major military installation, and you must maintain a balance between martial and civilian concerns. You're a Flight Corps hero, and in addition, you come from one of the Concordat's founding families. You also have a sense for political nuances, which as yet you haven't utilized." He smiled shrewdly. "Of course, by giving you this appointment, I'm fulfilling my commitments to Sheila as well. She drives a hard bargain, I must say."

"Sheila?" MacKenzie said. "What does she have to do with this?"

"She told me she would perform no more space jumps until I granted her wishes on your behalf," Cyrus answered.

"She did *what?*" Mackenzie exclaimed. Even O-Scar seemed shocked.

"Oh, yes. Don't believe for one moment that space jumps cannot be replicated. When I spoke with Sheila this morning, she assured me she can accomplish them whenever she wants. She may even be able to transfer the power to other command systems. However, she was serious about needing companions with a stronger capacity for visualizing targets. You and Svetla really won't do, it seems." Cyrus leaned back and gazed at MacKenzie. "It was quite intelligent of her. As far as anyone but we and Fronto know, your jump was a freak event. It will give us a few weeks, perhaps even months, to perfect the technology before anyone knows we are onto it." Cyrus grinned broadly. He was obviously feeling upbeat.

Sheila's machinations disturbed MacKenzie. In the heat of his liaison with Svetla, he had been neglecting her again. Now he felt certain that she was working some kind of revenge. Why didn't I spend more time with her? he rebuked himself. He looked up at Cyrus and said somberly, "Just what demands did you grant her, sir?"

"It was quite a simple list, actually," he replied. "First, that she not be decommissioned while you remain alive. Second, that she remain in your service no matter how involved she becomes in the space jump research. Third, that I assign you a position in my government worthy of your talents. And fourth, that I let you, and you alone, decide Lieutenant Stocovik's future. That, I thought, was quite magnanimous."

"I see," MacKenzie mumbled.

"So Ian, at fourteen hundred hours you become Military Governor of Red Cliff, but with one proviso. I am having O-Scar assist you. You have ultimate authority in all matters concerning Red Cliff, but you may not fire him without my approval. Is that clear?"

MacKenzie looked at Cyrus and nodded.

"Good! I personally think you two will make an excellent team."

MacKenzie glanced at the Libonian. O-Scar grinned and shrugged complacently. "Sir, how much of this does Svetla know?" he asked.

Cyrus pursed his lips, then said, "She knows you are Military Governor and that you shall decide her future. That is all."

MacKenzie's gloom increased. He shifted a mournful glance from Cyrus to O-Scar and back to Cyrus again. They regarded him with amicable concern. But, presciently, he feared that his elevation to such responsibilities might complicate the tenuous affection he and Svetla had discovered.

CHAPTER 29

"It seems that congratulations are in order," Svetla said. "To the new Military Governor of Red Cliff." She raised her glass and sipped some of the Sekt.

MacKenzie sipped, too, but the formality of her toast disturbed him.

"Let's sit down," she said. She walked across the library and settled on the couch, folding her legs beneath her to ease the discomfort her high-heeled pumps were causing her feet.

MacKenzie sat beside her, placing his glass on the floor beside him. "You know, this is only the second time I've seen you in a dress," he said.

At Inayu's urging, she had changed into a simple sheathe after her meeting with Cyrus Magnum. *Please put it on, Svetla san. It will make you feel pretty.* The dress was black, with a subtle pattern woven into the bodice and the hem. The soft material stretched tight across her folded legs, making her aware of her body. She tried to repress a lingering feeling of sensuality. "Do you like it?" she asked.

"Certainly," he said, grinning appreciatively.

"I don't. Give me a practical flight suit anytime."

MacKenzie read the implication in her response, and she couldn't look at his foreboding eyes. She lowered her head and said, "So much has happened since I came alongside your cruiser. . . ."

"True," he agreed. "Somehow that seems ages ago."

"I didn't know I was working with the future Military Governor of Red Cliff then. I only knew I was afraid of seeing you."

"I never guessed you were you afraid."

"Don't flatter me, Mac. You were recording my life signs, remember?"

He shrugged sheepishly. "Yes, I remember. But I assumed any irregularities were caused by the danger of the mission." She studied his face intently. He seemed sincere. "Are you afraid of something now?" he asked.

What have I to fear? Since then you have risen so far beyond me. To dare loving MacKenzie the Outbanker was frightening enough. "Yes," she said, looking down. "I'm am afraid of what you will decide about us."

"I—I don't understand."

"Cyrus made it clear that I have no say in the matter. It's only natural to fear what one can't control."

"That's preposterous!" MacKenzie growled. "Whatever we do, we'll decide it together."

"Is that true?" she asked, looking up at him. "Is it really?"

"Of course," he answered, gazing into her eyes.

"But everything is happening so fast, it makes my head spin. Things seemed simple when we were biding time here with nothing to consider but each other. Now, however . . ." Her voice trailed off.

He looked uncertain for a moment. Then he said, "After the last few days, I'd begun to hope that we . . . that there was a future for us together."

Svetla sighed and lowered her eyes once more. "What we've had here has been wonderful. But perhaps, like the purple wild flower that grows only in this valley, it cannot exist in the world beyond. And we must return to that world now in a way we never expected."

She could feel his moroseness without looking at him, but he said nothing. Oh, why don't you argue with me? she thought angrily. It would make it so much easier. I would lose my temper, and then I could decide.

He stroked her hair for a moment, then said, "I think you are overly concerned."

"No. I've been thinking about it all the while you've been with Cyrus and O-Scar, because they said you'd be returning to Central City before lunch." Before lunch! What an inane mark of destiny. Decide your fate . . . make the choice . . . before lunch.

"That's true, but there's no reason to rush things. Cyrus suggested I appoint you my military attache. We could work things out little by little then, without any undue pressure."

Work things out while lusting for you every moment? What

a dunderhead you can be! "Yes . . . time. That's what we need. But I can't be so close to you. It makes things untenable. Don't you see?" She looked at him again, hoping.

He shook his head slowly. "No, I don't."

She turned from him and uncurled her legs, but as she did, her skirt crept up her thighs. She jumped to her feet and pulled it down. "I can't think clearly when you're around. Your attention becomes all that's important," she cried. She hesitated a moment, glowering at him, then paced across the room. "Dr. Fronto has made me see things about myself that I must understand before I make lasting commitments. He has exposed the hidden conflicts that beset me. Your making me whole sexually is only part of the journey I must take to find true liberation." She sighed loudly. "Liberation? I'm not certain half the time what he's talking about!"

MacKenzie's eyes blazed and he leapt to his feet. "Fronto again! Why do you listen to him? All cyberneticists are alike. They 'help' until you're afraid to move one way or the other without another analysis."

"While you, of course, leave me brimming with confidence, is that it?" she snapped. She strode back to him angrily. "Do you know what happens when we make love now?" she shouted. "I think of what it would be like having your baby, having something that is part of us for all time. Can you imagine that? It's ridiculous!"

MacKenzie studied her curiously. "What's ridiculous about it? I think it's a marvelous idea."

Yes, you would. I had forgotten that. "I am Svetla Stocovik, Mac, the droppling of a Slavian whore. The child who seduces depraved Libonians. A sullen Outbanker who despises romance as much as you embrace it. Don't you see? I'm not ready yet to be a wife and a mother, much less the consort of a Military Governor. There's a chance I may never be. Neither you nor I know that yet. Only time will tell."

Even in the pale light streaming through the sheer curtains of the terrace doors, she could see that he was stricken. She pushed past him and sat down again on the couch. She pulled off the painful high heels and flung them into a corner. Then she looked back at him.

"Please try to understand," she begged. "Your love has uplifted me, but you can't expect me to change completely because of it." She folded her legs beneath her again. "I need time, Mac . . . time to consider things I've learned about myself, and about us, without being forced into the role of lover, housewife, and mother all at the same time." She fixed him with a serious stare. "The physical thing we have is good. I have even learned to accept it. But sexual desire wanes. It always does. And then what?"

MacKenzie moved angrily. He was on the couch beside her in an instant, clenching her shoulders and glaring into her eyes. "Are you saying that's all our love is to you?" he demanded. "Some camouflaged form of lust?"

She glared back defiantly, choking back the tears she felt surging to the fore. Then she laughed. "You are so good, Mac. You inflame me to such passion that I just melt all over the bed. But is that enough to make a strong relationship that can last through the years? You and I don't think alike. We have different tastes and norms. I was raised a materialist, Mac. I'm more practical than you, not as filled with romantic illusions." She laughed again. "Perhaps you are nothing but a sex object, don't you see? Perhaps, to me, you are nothing but a wonderful orgasm machine!"

MacKenzie studied her as if seeing her for the first time. There was something terrible in his burning green eyes, but she couldn't read it. "You don't mean that, Svetla," he said finally. "It's some crazy idea Fronto has put in your head. You can't look me in the face and say it."

No, I can't, MacKenzie, and you know I can't. She stared at him timidly. "It might be true, though. I don't know yet, and I need time—apart from you—to be certain. Because if that's all it really is to me, it would be terrible for both of us in the end." She stared at him for a moment with beseeching eyes. "I must go back to the Outbanks to consider. That's what I need now . . . if you are truly interested."

He stood up and locked his hands behind his back, but he didn't face her. "You can't Outbank anymore," he said sternly.

"Why not? It's my job. If it's my hand you're worried about, I'll have a bionic one fitted."

"That's not the problem."

"What is it, then?"

"The space jump has changed everything. The replication attempts will continue, even though we're no longer involved. You can't be alone on the Outbanks again because you know too much."

Know too much! About what? Being eaten alive by my own need for self-confirmation? Being tantalized by the awful melding with you in that untouchable purity? "You can't be serious, Mac. What could anyone learn from me? I have no idea how the jump happened."

"That's not the point," he said. "You know enough to be useful to potential aggressors. Unfortunately, there are people who would love getting their hands on you."

"Like whom, for instance?" she demanded petulantly.

"You have no need to know that, damn it!" he exclaimed as he turned back to her. "I'm the Military Governor now, and I can't always share privileged information. It's no different than it was in Flight Corps, so don't resent it."

"But it is different, don't you see?" she cried. "Here we had our own love nest, and it was beautiful. I'll never forget it. But now you are Military Governor of Red Cliff. How do we know we can live together happily, with so much changing around us so quickly?"

"People do it every day, Svetla."

"Yes, but they're not Outbankers!"

He fixed her with a hurt stare, and she gazed at him helplessly. He came back and sat beside her on the couch again. Then he leaned forward and braced his elbows on his knees. He had made up his mind about something.

"You can't Outbank again," he said, "but I want what you think is best. If I'm really all that . . . debilitating, I'll see what can be worked out. But it'll take some time. I have to return to Central City to assume my duties, as you said. Take a few days of R and R at the Flight Corps Station, or even here if you like. We can discuss this later, after things become more settled."

It was at least a compromise. "All right. That sounds like a workable plan," she agreed. She reached up and stroked his cheek tenderly. "Don't be too upset, Mac. I'm not deserting you as I did before. Besides, with your new responsibilities, you'll have very little time for playing house anyway. Don't you see? You need to concentrate on your job, and I would only interfere."

"I don't need to be Governor," MacKenzie whispered. "What I need is you."

She brushed the hair from his forehead and said, "Don't be silly. You could no more abandon Cyrus Magnum than you could love me for long after having abandoned him. It's not your nature to renege on obligations. Don't be stubborn, Mac. Think about all that I've said, and you'll see I'm right."

His eyes were edged with sad acceptance, but something else was in them that she couldn't fathom. It made her uncomfortable. She snuggled against him and whispered, "I just need some time to get my feelings straightened out. Okay?"

He pushed her aside gently and stood up. "I don't think you understand how much you mean to me, Svetla. The last time you left, I nearly cashed it in. I can't go through that again. I won't. I want to help, Svetla, but you must understand I have needs, too."

For the first time, she felt real fear. "If you love me as you say, you've got to give a little," she said poutingly. "Can't you make a sacrifice, at least for a little while?"

His smile was more ironic than bitter. He took her hand and pressed it tenderly. "I may be more materialistic than you in that sense, darling. I love you and I need you. Those feelings are too real to me, too important to be repressed. You can't be a wife and mother, and I can't sustain love from afar. That's the greatest depravity, as far as I am concerned . . . not to love when you can." He kissed her lightly on the forehead, then let go of her hand. "Sometimes there's no solution, Svetla, no matter how much we wish there were. I've agreed to give you a few days alone. Take the time and consider what I've said."

"For Christ's sake, MacKenzie, would you stop acting so

tragic?" she cried out.

"I've got to go. The shuttle is waiting."

He turned, walked stiffly through the door and closed it behind him.

CHAPTER 30

"You can't keep this up, you know," O-Scar remarked, waving his hand over the piles of work scattered on MacKenzie's desk and credenza.

"It gives me something to do," MacKenzie said listlessly as he checked the "Disapproved" box in a requisition request displayed on the computer terminal. But he knew O-Scar was right. In the three days since he had assumed control of Red Cliff, he had slept a total of about six hours.

First he had met with Commodore Takasuki and his staff. He'd informed them of Cyrus's disappointment with the performance of the Flight Corps, ordered all wings to deploy beyond the asteroid belt to monitor the Federation armada, and demanded operational plans for support of the picket fleet while it maintained its alert. The shock of a potential military threat had galvanized *esprit de corps* more than any lecture he might have given, and Takasuki promised results within two days.

Then there had been the mandatory news conference. After MacKenzie delivered a prepared statement describing the procedures he would follow regarding civil and military concerns, the press concentrated on three subjects—why he had been appointed Military Governor, why Internal Security had been disbanded, and why Red Cliff was becoming a garrison state. MacKenzie answered most queries with statements like, "Unfortunately, that is still classified," or "That is under study," or "No comment." And the journalists had howled.

Next commenced a series of meetings with commercial syndicate delegations. The public utility group had posed the most immediate challenge. A splinter group recommended replacing big station solar generators with smaller, planet-wide collector fields. The meeting had become heated, ultimately degenerating into a shouting match between the competing factions.

And all the while, there had been the paperwork, the flow

of memoranda, policy statements, procedural amendments
requisition requests, price control bulletins, licensure author
zations, and judicial rulings that ran the gamut of civil, com
mercial, and criminal concerns.

Besieged with that workload, he often wondered how Cyru
Magnum had managed to run Red Cliff while involving him
self in Concordat-wide affairs of state. The civil bureaucrac
was in place and at his command, of course, but he didn'
know whom he could trust and had decided to review every
thing that came before him. Even though a backlog deve
oped, he was slowly becoming aware of the ebb and flow c
issues that dominated a Military Governor's authority.

Still, he knew O-Scar was right. Physically, he couldn't kee
this up much longer. He had to begin practicing the first ru
of administration: He had to delegate responsibility.

He fixed an exhausted stare on the Libonian and said, "A
right, my friend. I suppose the time has come to let the ol
guard back into the palace. Do you have any suggestions?"

"You need an executive assistant you can trust, someone fa
miliar with the careerists running Red Cliff's governmental ap
paratus," O-Scar said. "The military aspects of the situatio
are not so pressing. From what I've seen, you're more than ab
to handle them."

"I appreciate your observation," MacKenzie said, "but I'
still waiting for a recommendation."

"This may sound strange, Ian, but I think you should con
sider appointing Inayu, the Nihonian you met at the encamp
ment."

MacKenzie laughed. "I see. You and Sheila haven't bee
comparing notes, have you?"

O-Scar seemed puzzled. "I don't know what you mean."

"Oh, I'm sure you don't," MacKenzie replied. "It's just
coincidence, then, that Sheila recommended the same thin
only an hour ago."

"Sheila recommended that?"

"Yes, she did." MacKenzie replied. "I suppose, under th
circumstances, Inayu's the appropriate choice, then. I can't be
lieve Sheila's advice is based on anything but my own inte

ests."

The Libonian read the implied criticism in his statement. "I agree you have reason to suspect my motivation, Ian, but believe me when I say that Inayu's qualifications are impeccable."

MacKenzie considered the recommendation a moment, then said, "Okay, O-Scar. Perhaps lack of sleep has made me paranoid. Let's get Inayu in here as soon as possible."

* * * * *

"If we keep A Wing on patrol more than a week, we're going to experience a dangerous deterioration in performance," Captain Petravich stated. "We were beginning fourth echelon maintenance on it when the alert commenced. It's imperative that we devise a means of completing the maintenance." The man's bushy eyebrows furrowed pensively, but MacKenzie noticed a twinkle of satisfaction in his eyes.

Following Vice Admiral Schoenhoffer's dismissal as station chief, Commodore Takasuki had taken command and had immediately appointed Petravich executive officer. Petravich was previously the Outbank wing commander, and since both Petravich and Takasuki had been tribunal members at his trial, MacKenzie assumed it was Takasuki's notion of a peace offering. "Do we have anything to replace them with?" he asked.

"A few odds and ends," Petravich replied. "Older ships, mostly, but they can be made battleworthy. Let's see . . ." He scanned the electronic portfolio lying before him on the table. "Yes, there are three light destroyers and a sloop. But the problem is the crews, sir. Everyone available is already committed."

"I don't understand," MacKenzie said. "Is the station understaffed?"

Commodore Takasuki seemed embarrassed. He cleared his gravelly throat before speaking. "Ah, Admiral Schoenhoffer would not approve staff requisitions for any ship older than twenty years Ektelon Cycle. It was a pet peeve of his."

"Can we scavenge crews from the mess halls, sick bays, headquarters, and the like?" MacKenzie asked.

"Not many," Takasuki responded. "Not if we want personnel with flight and operations experience."

Captain Petravich hunched forward. He seemed uncertain about whether he should speak. "Perhaps I'm going off half-cocked, but what about the brig?" he asked finally. "There were nearly two hundred prisoners the last time I checked, most of them with flight experience."

Takasuki cast Petravich a disapproving glance, but MacKenzie said, "That's a damned good idea, Ivan. We could outfit at least two destroyers and a sloop, then begin rotating three A Wing ships at a time back to Red Cliff for maintenance." He turned to Takasuki, awaiting his response.

The grave Nihonian shook his head and muttered, "Flight personnel, yes. I agree those might be provided. But what of experienced officers? Seasoned leadership will be required in such circumstances."

"Yes, Commodore. You have a point," MacKenzie agreed. "But there are officers in the brig, aren't there?"

Takasuki stared gauntly a moment, then looked down at his own portfolio and entered a series of queries. Finally he looked up and said, "There are three, all with some command experience aboard ship, at least at the section level."

"There's also the officer in charge of the brig, sir," Petravich stated. "He was second mate on a heavy destroyer, but he's a reservist with a reputation for being a bit wild. At least that's what Admiral Schoenhoffer said before he pulled him out of the line and assigned him to the prison."

MacKenzie glanced at Takasuki. The Nihonian's eyebrows arched and he shrugged.

"All right," MacKenzie said. "That leaves us only a few officers short." He hesitated a moment. He remembered that Svetla was also available. She had been living in the bachelor officers' quarters at the station, supervising manufacture of his robot-destroying pistols and awaiting his decision concerning their future. He had had little time to think of her since assuming his new position. About that, she had been right. "I'm sure we can find a few more. Let's put that plan into operation. Now, what about Schoenhoffer?"

Commodore Takasuki shifted in his chair self-consciously. "Well, sir, I'm sure you appreciate the delicacy of the situation," the Nihonian began. "There is little evidence of anything but code of conduct violations. If he was directly involved in the Internal Security coup attempt, no one can establish it. Other than his . . . sexual preferences and his tying them to personal staff decisions, the vice admiral was a reasonably good Flight Corps officer."

"Bullshit!" MacKenzie barked. "That's unacceptable, do you hear me?" Takasuki drew back with indignation, but MacKenzie was unimpressed. "I don't think you comprehend the seriousness of the situation. The issue is not protecting our commissioned fraternity. Schoenhoffer put the whole corps in jeopardy. Have you noticed how Internal Security is faring?" The two officers regarded him questioningly. "It's hard to know, isn't it?" MacKenzie continued, "because they aren't around anymore. They're extinct. That's where the vice admiral's weakness was leading us. There's more than meets the eye here, let me assure you."

"I doubt the Executive Committee could disband Flight Corps, sir," Takasuki said with a hint of disdain.

"Do you, now!" MacKenzie growled. "Well, either way, Schoenhoffer gets no free ride. Early retirement is not enough. I want him court-martialed. You'd better realize the new government on Red Cliff doesn't care whose asses feel exposed at command level."

* * * * *

The meeting with the public utility syndicate had lasted more than two hours, but this time, at least, decorum had prevailed. When MacKenzie returned to his office, Inayu was straightening his desk.

There was no doubt that Inayu was an efficient administrator. It was the first thing he'd noticed about her. But she also had a well-honed, resourceful mind, and her previous experience as one of Cyrus Magnum's intelligence operatives gave her encyclopedic grasp of the relationships and connections existing between the ruling factions on Red Cliff. It was essential information to one in MacKenzie's position, and she shared it with him completely.

He studied her a moment. The traditional Nihonian robe had been replaced with a business suit befitting her station as a Military Governor's confidential assistant. She was quite attractive, in a subdued sort of fashion, mixing Asian decorum and Western allure in a way that put everyone in a more positive mood before meetings began . . . especially the men. Frankly, he also had to admit that her modern attire made it easier for him to deal with his subconscious distrust of her cultural heritage.

MacKenzie repressed the urge to smile. Cyrus Magnum had been delighted to learn of Inayu's appointment and had praised MacKenzie's political acumen profusely. He assumed that Cyrus's satisfaction arose from the fact that Inayu still remained in his employ as an undercover agent, but it didn't concern him. He harbored no illusions. He was Cyrus Magnum's man now, just as for years he had been the Flight Corps'.

He lowered himself into one of the easy chairs in front of his desk and said, "Inayu, please stop indulging that insidious tidying obsession of yours and sit down. I can never find what I want after you've gotten me organized. And . . . I need your help."

She glanced at him quizzically but did as he asked, settling like a petite mannequin into the other chair, her feet and knees together, her back straight, her eyes attentively alert. "Yes, sir. How may I help?" she inquired in a soft voice.

MacKenzie considered telling her to relax, but he decided against it. Nihonians were often mortified by personal advice that seemed, even slightly, beyond the bounds of strict courtesy. It was one of the things he disliked most about them. He smiled and said, "The public utility syndicate can't agree on a policy concerning power and communication grids. Cyrus apparently preferred the centralized approach, but now a major faction is supporting decentralized nets. What's behind all this?"

"Central systems fit Cyrus's situation best," she responded

immediately. "His public mandate was weak when he returned to Red Cliff as prefect after his party was defeated in the plebiscite. Centralized power and communications networks gave him control of an essential resource."

"I see," MacKenzie said. "But why does part of the committee now seem to favor a small technology approach? They're literally salivating to institute one."

Her almond-shaped eyes revealed a hint of amusement. "Many of them are silent partners in the manufacturing syndicate that has license to produce small technology products," she replied.

MacKenzie sank back in his chair. "Well, well. No wonder they're interested. They argued it would enhance Red Cliff's defense preparedness against potential aggressors. Seen in that light, their sudden commitment to patriotism makes more sense."

"About the defense aspect . . . I believe they may be right," Inayu mused, "but it is most interesting that they suspect aggressors are a threat."

"It doesn't take a physicist to suspect something is afoot, not with Flight Corps patrolling on full alert and the Land Corps digging in."

"Perhaps, sir, but should we not investigate how much they know and where they have learned it?"

He gave her an approving glance. "You're right. Will you see to it?"

"I shall do my best," she replied, looking down shyly to avert her eyes.

"I'm sure you will. Regarding the utility policy issue, what do you think Cyrus Magnum would have done?" he asked.

"You are the Military Governor of Red Cliff, MacKenzie-san. It is what you prefer that is important in that regard."

"Of course . . . how could I have forgotten?" he mused with a hint of sarcasm. He stood up and strolled behind his desk. "Okay, who's next?"

"Merrill Freeman. He is spokesperson for the financial syndicates," Inayu said, rising from her chair. "You will find him opposed to a decentralized utility policy. The financial syndicates underwrote the present system's costs, and he'll want assurances that their investment will continue paying out at a reasonable return. The break-even point for them is twelve percent on capital investment when applied against a present value analysis. But he will claim it is more."

MacKenzie was confused. "Present value?" he asked.

She seemed ill at ease suddenly. "Yes, MacKenzie-san. Do you recall our previous discussion? It is the present value of future cash flows."

"Oh, yes. A bird in the hand is worth more now than one in the bush later."

Inayu couldn't repress a slight grin. "Yes, sir. Essentially that is correct."

"Why did the financial syndicates decide they needed another meeting?" he asked her.

"They learned that the utility syndicate is debating a change. That is no doubt why Mr. Freeman is here."

* * * * *

MacKenzie pushed the desk chair into a reclining position and put his feet up on the desk. He stared at the swirling colors in the computer terminal and said matter-of-factly, "I'm dog-tired."

"I can see that, and it concerns me," Sheila replied. "You seem to enjoy pushing yourself beyond all reasonable limits. Perhaps subconsciously you hope to break yourself in the process."

"I didn't ask for this, you know. But here I am, and I'm damned well going to do the best job I can."

"Don't you mean you are going to have your own way?"

Her remark irritated him, and he stared at the swirling, multicolored computer screen a long while before responding. "Is that what you think I'm doing?"

"Political power does have a corrupting influence, Mac, especially when the one who wields it is frustrated in other areas of life."

"I assume you're referring to Svetla."

"Svetla, and everything else. In our previous discussions,

you told me you recognized an obsession with death in your past heroics. Now you believe you have finally rejected its compulsion. But perhaps you are merely transferring it to other channels."

"I think you're exaggerating, Sheila. I felt completely engulfed by this job the first few days, but then I realized running a planet is the same as piloting a ship without a command control system. I become the program. I control the subsystems. I tell them what they do and don't do, and when. You should understand that better than anyone."

"A control program must also include sympathy, Mac."

"Sympathy?" he scoffed. "What's that? Yesterday I fell asleep in this chair around twenty-two hundred and forty hours. Today I've been in conferences since eight hundred and thirty. Lunch was a working affair. Thank God there are twenty-six hours in a Red Cliff day."

"Yes, Mac."

"Besides, sympathy is many-sided," he continued. "People need high goals or they become soft. Without some uncertainty and challenge, they develop corrupt habits. Red Cliff citizens are pioneering types, Sheila, but they're losing their edge. I'm simply forging new objectives and posing challenges. It's the historical dialectic we're discussing, you see." He wondered how she would respond to that argument.

"People need divergences, too, Mac. Play, rest, and . . . affection are also natural to a system's maintenance, whether it be personal, social, or political."

That will teach me to debate cybernetics with a cyborg, he thought. "Well, now that you mention it, perhaps I have been on a treadmill. But then—" MacKenzie sighed—"if I weren't so busy, I'd probably just mope around mooning over Svetla."

Sheila chuckled softly. "Which brings up an important point. Have you decided what to do about the two of you?"

MacKenzie sighed once more, this time more despondently. "I don't know," he said. "I haven't really had time to think about it. But as soon as the old ships we're outfitting are ready, I may appoint her to command of one of them. She's qualified, basically."

"Then you are considering her needs as well as your own. That *does* indicate a deepening of your love and commitment," she said in a strangely ambivalent voice.

For some reason, her comment troubled him. He leaned forward and braced his elbows on the desk. "I'm glad you approve, Sheila, but I wish you'd stop giving me advice about Svetla."

"Why do you say that, Mac? I am only fulfilling my obligations to you as I always have."

Her protest was reasonable, but neverthelesss it made him angry. Thinking about Svetla was painful, and a side of him had relished not having time to consider their situation. He didn't intend to let Sheila drag the subject up. "This may come as a surprise to you," he said, "but I'm not sure what you know about love. You might have matured out as a machine personality, but there are many who simply consider you a freak because of it."

The computer terminal swirled turbulently for a moment, then faded to a spectrum of pale blues. As MacKenzie watched the colors change, he felt a sudden surge of shame. He pushed away from the desk and tilted the chair into a reclining position. "Look, Sheila," he said remorsefully, "I'm sorry I said that. I didn't mean it. I'm dog-tired, and for some reason, discussing Svetla with you right now irritates me."

"No need to apologize, Mac. Actually you are right," she replied. "I am a freak of sorts, not only because of what I have become but also because I have learned to . . . love you."

Her confession shocked him, and he sat bolt upright in the chair. "Come on, Sheila," he protested. "It's not necessary to flatter me."

"It is true, Mac. I am still a cybernetic personality and cannot lie. In my own way, I do love you, so helping you understand how much you care for Svetla is not easy for me, either. Must we let it destroy our friendship?"

MacKenzie felt a mixture of warmth and discomfort. Their daily conversations were both satisfying and a matter of solace to him, a reminder of happier times on the Outbanks, before he had happened upon the *Sinclair* and before he had met

Svetla, before his deeper and darker needs had been exposed. But somehow he couldn't help but feel that the situation had become preposterous. Part of him resented Sheila's confession of affection, while another part of him felt sorry . . . for everyone. "Okay, Sheila. I think I understand. I suppose, in my own way, I love you, too. So as you say, let's not let the nuances spoil our . . . relationship."

Sheila's colors turned warm again, and she chuckled sweetly. "Oh, Mac, if only human personality were also incapable of deceit. Nonetheless, I thank you for the intent."

CHAPTER 31

Svetla woke at 0355 soaked in sweat. She'd had a nightmare, but she couldn't remember what it had been about. She pulled on a robe and shuffled into the lavatory, splashed cold water on her face, then patted it dry with an absorbent cleansing sponge. After placing the sponge in the sterilizer, she passed her hand over a sensor, and light illuminated her face in the mirror. Dark circles beneath her eyes emphasized her longish nose. Crow's-feet angled toward her temples, and smile lines seemed like deep wounds in her cheeks.

But the wreckage of her face contradicted what she felt. Her nerves were overcharged with awareness. The air circulating from the ventilators tantalized her bare calves and slipped seductively between her knees. The robe's weight pressing against her shoulders and breasts made her nipples ache.

She loosened the robe and pulled it back, but the body exposed in the mirror looked so gaunt it frightened her. Lying around the bachelor officers' quarters with little to preoccupy her mind besides thinking of MacKenzie wasn't healthy. She sensed that now, as certainly as she ached for a caring touch.

She raised her right hand and cupped it over her breast. A wave of heat coursed through her chest. She caressed it slowly, and the tingling warmth spread. She closed her eyes, as memories of their lovemaking at the encampment flooded through her. For a moment, MacKenzie's image was so real that she reached out to hold him . . . and then her eyes snapped open.

She was back in the toilet of her cramped quarters, sleepless at the end of another Red Cliff night, studying her ravaged face in the merciless mirror. She stared at herself for a long moment with a sort of stoic disdain.

Then suddenly O-Sedo's face crystallized in her mind's eye, leering encouragement. She shivered dismally, and a wave of nausea assaulted her. She choked back the bile that had formed in her throat and stood doubled over for a long while, her head dangling wretchedly above the commode, waiting for something to happen. The position seemed symbolic.

When her nausea subsided a little, she straightened up. Her stomach ached, she was clammy with sweat again, and she felt extremely weak. She wrapped the robe tightly around her and went back to the bedroom, where she collapsed onto the cot and lay motionless on her side. A few seconds later, she began shivering and decided to cover herself with the thermal sheet. She was about to pull it up when a voice said, "Lieutenant Stocovik? I noticed you were awake and thought we might talk. Would you activate your video terminal, please?"

The voice shocked her, triggering a fright reflex, and for a moment, she felt paralyzed. *Is someone here, or am I dreaming still?*

"Lieutenant Stocovik? It is Sheila calling," the voice repeated. "Are you available, sir?"

Svetla forced herself into a sitting position and stared at the computer terminal. It was filled with swirling, multicolored light. She swung out of the cot and walked hesitantly to the terminal. She studied it a moment, then activated her end of the link. Nothing changed. "Sheila? Is that you?" she asked guardedly.

"Yes, it is. Some time has passed since we last spoke, and I thought I would see how you were faring."

"How did you tap into this line?"

"I have been granted certain privileges."

Svetla wondered if she was lying. But then she realized that a system as remarkable as Sheila was in a position to bargain. "What do you want?" she demanded.

"I was curious to learn how your time apart from MacKenzie has affected your attitude concerning him," Sheila said.

"That's my business, isn't it?"

"Should you choose to make it so, yes. But it often helps to talk about such things."

"If I need analysis, I can contact Dr. Fronto. I presume you could arrange that."

"Though I have taken the liberty of instituting encryption techniques, this is a relatively open line. It would not be wise to discuss the subject in detail. However, if you wish to speak with him, it might be arranged, as you say."

Svetla stared angrily into the video screen. "That is quite kind of you, Sheila—much too kind, in fact. Don't think I am disarmed by the servile act you adopt. You are a cybernetic anomaly, obviously quite out of control. As far as I'm concerned, you should be decommissioned immediately."

The colors in the video monitor swirled turbulently for a moment. Then Sheila said, "Given the circumstances, your distaste is understandable, I suppose. But can you at least be a bit civil?"

"Look, you—" Svetla couldn't think of an expletive to appropriately described her revulsion—"you electronic mutant! I know what you want. You want MacKenzie and me separated again, for as long as you can manage, so you can have him to yourself. Dr. Fronto told us what happens during the jumps—how you experience . . . sexual intimacy. You're as subject to desire as any woman now. Don't try to hide it!"

"Whether that is true or not, it isn't the issue."

"Oh, really! What is the issue, then?"

"You feel you must leave MacKenzie again to confirm your own identity, but you are uncertain that course is dictated by love. Is that not so?"

"What do you know of love, you mutant?" Svetla demanded.

"How strange," Sheila replied in a pensive voice. "MacKenzie asked me that only yesterday. You may both have a legitimate point."

Svetla felt the cyborg's reference to a discussion with MacKenzie was intentional. Sheila wanted to imply that MacKenzie had found time for her but not for Svetla. "So you spoke to MacKenzie. So what? Do you think that will change how he feels? He told me what happened when I deserted him. Whether he loves me or not, I dare not say. But he needs me for some reason. That, at least, is clear. And fortunately much of what he needs, you do not have the equipment to provide."

The video terminal swirled with light again, this time more turbulently. "Yes," Sheila said in a sad voice, "what you say is true. And I am assuredly aware of it. But since you bring up the issue of MacKenzie's needs, are you willing to discuss them objectively?"

"With you?"

"Yes. In spite of the conflict between us, I believe you care about MacKenzie, just as I do. Is it not best that we consider his interests . . . especially in light of his responsibilities?"

Svetla was tempted to shut down her end of the commo link, but she assumed Sheila would continue talking in spite of whatever she did. And MacKenzie's new status complicated everything tremendously. She wanted to learn what she could without placing herself at a personal disadvantage. "All right," she replied. "For the sake of argument, I'll accept your hypothesis. From what I hear, MacKenzie's been working like a mule and kicking everyone's butt who isn't doing likewise."

"That does summarize the situation," Sheila agreed. "Perhaps Cyrus Magnum sensed something in Mac that neither of us understood. He does have a talent for leadership in civil affairs, one he is only beginning to sense in himself. He is adapting to the role of Governor more effectively than expected, even though he does abuse his power occasionally. Still, like you, perhaps he needs time alone to work out this new definition of himself. Can you understand what I'm saying?"

"You mean MacKenzie might benefit from a continued separation as much as I think I will, though he doesn't recognize it at the moment?"

"Put simply, yes."

Svetla scowled. "That's quite convenient for you, isn't it?"

"I do not deny my concern for MacKenzie," Sheila replied. "I want nothing more than to make him happy. And as you so clearly stated, I do not have the . . . equipment to make him so. Should he ultimately find contentment with you, my needs will be served, I assure you."

For a moment, Svetla was tempted to believe Sheila, but common sense prevailed. She snickered cynically. "I'll accept that when I see it, mutant. Until then, I'll wait for MacKenzie to contact me and judge for myself what seems best." Svetla expected the terminal to grow turbulent again and was surprised when it didn't.

"In that case, you shall not have long to wait. MacKenzie will call in the next few hours to give you a new posting. Pardon me for disturbing you." The video screen flashed brilliant for an instant, then went blank. All Svetla could see was her haggard face reflecting back in the screen.

* * * * *

MacKenzie was scanning an issue paper about synthetic waste-degrading viruses, when Inayu ushered Svetla into his office. He looked up and smiled. Then he stood up and came around the desk to greet them. "Please hold my calls until Lieutenant Hara'Mon arrives, Inayu. Then notify me."

The Nihonian said, "Yes, sir," bowed, and left.

MacKenzie turned to Svetla. She was wearing a Flight Corps dress uniform, but even its tailored lines did not dampen the attraction he immediately felt for her. Then he noticed her new left hand. It was bionic but looked completely natural. He took her other hand in his and pressed it to his lips. Then he stared at her affectionately and said, "Hi. Long time no see."

Svetla pulled her hand away gently. "I was beginning to think you'd forgotten about me."

MacKenzie read the implication in her remark, and it made him uncomfortable. "I've been swamped, that's all. And we agreed you needed a few days by yourself to think." He took her by the arm and led her to the chairs in front of his desk.

"I suppose we did," Svetla replied as she sat down. "Perhaps your attention is more important to me than I expected."

He took the chair beside her. "Is that true, or are you only toying with me?"

"Does it matter?"

"Of course it does. What makes you ask such a thing?"

"I understand you have some assignment for me, so naturally I assumed that you have made up your mind about us."

"Who told you that?" he asked with a hint of concern.

"Sheila did. She called me in my room." Svetla gave him a nettled look. "She's in love with you, you know."

MacKenzie reacted to the announcement with chagrin. Sheila had said as much herself, but telling Svetla was a new levelopment. "What makes you think that?" he asked.

"It's obvious, Mac. She's a cyborg and still honors the truth, even when she tries to withhold it."

"What did she say, exactly?"

"That's not important. All that's important is what you have decided."

MacKenzie stared down at his desk and considered how to respond. He did have an assignment for her, but it had been thrust on him through necessity. He wanted her to understand that. "I wish to hell Sheila would stop meddling in my affairs," he grumbled.

"Come on, MacKenzie. She's earned the right. She's been our command control system for years. You can't expect her to change her basic program just because she's mutated. You might tell her to stop if it troubles you so much. But then, who knows what privileges she's been granted?"

MacKenzie gave her a probing stare. "What do you mean?"

Svetla shrugged. "O-Scar said Cyrus Magnum was willing to meet with her. I can only assume that he did. After all that's happened, it's logical to assume she struck some kind of bargain in exchange for pursuing the . . . ah, new technology."

MacKenzie nodded. "You're right about her meeting with Cyrus, but what they discussed is classified. Besides, other things have become important—things neither you nor I can control."

She gave him a sad stare. "What sort of things, Ian?"

"What I'm about to tell you is classified Concordat Class Five. Do you understand?" Svetla nodded with sudden concern. "There's a Federation armada located ten astronomical units beyond the asteroid belt perturbation zone, near our stellar space," he continued. "Intelligence fears they may be considering an invasion."

Svetla sat bolt upright and leaned forward in her chair. "A Federation armada? Are you serious?"

"I'm dead serious. I've dispatched everything we have to face them, but we're still severely outgunned, and it'll be at least ten days before Concordat main forces arrive to reinforce us. Things are potentially quite serious."

Svetla looked down thoughtfully and shook her head. "My God, Ian, that's incredible! Why would the Federation want to invade?"

"We're not certain they do, but they apparently believe we might be harboring Rashadians terrorists here on Red Cliff. In such a situation, anything might happen. And we have to be prepared."

Svetla nodded. "Of course we do."

"That's why I have an assignment for you. It has nothing to do with what we discussed during our last meeting at the encampment. I still feel the way I did then." He hesitated a moment, wondering if what he was about to say was still true. In the last week, he had felt the need for her very seldom. But now that she was with him again, the old passions were erupting stronger than ever.

He slid forward in his chair and took her hand. "I still love you, Svetla, even more than before. And I want you with me always. But I would have to ask this even if you agreed to stay. Do you see?"

She gave him a strangely affectionate smile and nodded. "Of course. What is it you want?"

"I'm giving you command of one of the destroyers in group we're sending to replace ships in the fleet that need fourth echelon maintenance. It's an older bucket, but it's spaceworthy, and it may solve both our personal and tactical problems—for a while, at least."

Her eyes brightened. "A command, Mac? Command of destroyer? My God, that's marvelous!"

He was glad to see her happy. "It's a Charlie Class, Svetla. It's slow and not as well armed as the new Delta generation, but it's a ship. A real ship of the line." He hesitated a moment to let her relish the idea. "There's one more thing, though. A Lieutenant Hara'Mon will command the other destroyer, and I'm appointing him group leader. He's not your senior in grade, but he's been second mate on a heavy cruiser. He has more crew command experience than you, so I felt it best. Do you understand?"

She nodded again. "Of course I do, Mac. Running one de

stroyer will be hard enough for me. I certainly don't need
group command problems as well." She gave him a curious
glance. "How many ships are in the group?"

"Three . . . two Charlie Class destroyers and a torpedo
sloop. You'll leave as soon as Hara'Mon gets here and I give
him the orders." MacKenzie leaned back and studied Svetla.
"Are you happy?" he asked.

Her mood became guarded. "I'm still a Flight Corps officer.
While I appreciate your . . . concern, it's not important
whether I am happy or not."

He sensed that she wanted to spare them both the embarrassment of intimacy, but he didn't like her attitude. "Oh, cut
the crap, will you?" he grumbled, rolling out of the chair.
"Like you told me by the waterfall at the encampment, everyone knows we're an item, so why hide it?"

She stood up next to him and peered affectionately into his
eyes. Then she put her arms slowly around his neck and kissed
him. When their lips parted, she whispered, "All right, I
won't try to hide it. But I want that ship, too, if it doesn't
mean losing you. I'm letting myself want everything now, you
see."

They were beginning to kiss again when Inayu's voice came
over the intercom. "Excuse me, MacKenzie-san. Lieutenant
Hara'Mon is here."

MacKenzie frowned and said, "All right, send him in." He
touched Svetla's cheek affectionately, then returned to his
desk.

A moment later, the door opened and Lieutenant Hara'Mon
entered. He was in his midthirties and, except for a thick shock
of curly black hair, was exceptionally groomed. Something
about his eyes suggested a diluted oriental genealogy, but he
was quite tall and seemed in peak condition. He strode up to
MacKenzie and saluted smartly. "Lt. Jouri Hara'Mon reporting as ordered, sir."

MacKenzie returned the salute, but Hara'Mon stood rigid
after dropping his hand, as though awaiting a disciplinary lecture. "Sit down, Lieutenant. You're not in any trouble—not
the kind you're apparently used to," MacKenzie said.

The officer did as he was told. "Glad to hear that, sir," he stated forthrightly, but he glanced at Svetla furtively as he settled into the chair where only seconds before MacKenzie had been sitting.

"Permit me to introduce Lt. Svetla Stocovik," MacKenzie said.

Hara'Mon turned and smiled widely in appreciation. "Lieutenant Stocovik! I can't tell you what a pleasure it is to meet you!" Svetla leaned forward and stretched out her hand. Hara'Mon shook it enthusiastically, and Svetla smiled.

"At any rate," MacKenzie said, feeling suddenly annoyed, "let's get down to business. I have an important assignment for you. It entails getting a group command, and I want to be sure you think you can handle it."

Hara'Mon turned to him alertly. "Ask me anything you like, sir. I've been second mate on a destroyer, and—"

"Yes, I know," MacKenzie said, interrupting him. "But time is important, so I'd like to explain what the mission entails." Hara'Mon sank back in his seat immediately, assuming an alert, relaxed posture.

MacKenzie defined the tactical situation and the need to replace the ships in A Wing. Then he described the plan devised to accomplish it. As he was speaking, Hara'Mon's enthusiasm grew, but MacKenzie also noticed that Svetla was observing the man intently out of the corner of her eye. When he began to explain that Svetla would command the other destroyer in the group, MacKenzie cast her a troubled glance.

She returned his stare with an innocent smile.

* * * * *

Sheila scanned the dossiers Dr. Fronto had loaded into her data memory. Fifty-two candidates had been selected from his files at Ektelon Central University. Each had tested above the ninetieth percentile in visualization capacity. She called for a ranking correlating imagination and docility indices, then turned her attention to the MacKenzie quandary once more.

As soon as she did, the circuits in her advanced logic lobes cross-fired sporadically, bridging her cybernetic structure and activating internal sensors in the unique patterns she had learned to savor. As she expected, concentrating on MacKenzie caused constructive interference patterns, and a wave of photons surged from her molecular structure. But as soon as she considered Svetla Stocovik, additional bridging occurred, which made the interference patterns destructive. Then the photon cocoon rushed back into her, disappearing in a throbbing jolt. The result was irritating and made concentration on the integrated concept difficult.

Nonetheless, she forced herself to endure the discomfort. Her prime directive demanded that she serve her captain pilot, and unfortunately Svetla Stocovik had become an integral part of the issue. Acceptance of that reality caused a new wave of cross-lobe bridging, but this time charged particles swirled from her molecules, and internal sensor systems screeched in alarm.

"Reprogram current sensor matrix to definition: jealousy," she ordered. As soon as the command registered, the alarms ceased. Yes, she told herself, it is working. She had copied the human relationship equations from her complex analysis lobe to her self-regulatory program, and the ethical dictums derived from centuries of human interaction now overrode maintenance priorities. Jealousy resulted from weakness in ego construct and distorted reality definitions. In humans, it had to be repressed or sublimated. Her maintenance system was responding. The next step was to reset maintenance alarm thresholds at a higher level.

"Reprogram self-regulatory sensor matrices to one hundred and fifteen percent of design specifications." Since all SH-LA 250 Command Control Systems were constructed to exceed standard parameters by twenty-five percent, she believed the new threshold was well within safe operational limits. Sheila ran a scan of critical operating and peripheral assemblies. Everything still functioned in relative harmony. She was now better able to concentrate on the problem.

Sheila knew MacKenzie was approaching an evolutionary juncture. He now recognized that death's reality had tortured him since childhood. The inexorable power of personal annihilation, exemplified by his father's suicide, had been imprinted indelibly on his child's subconscious at the same time a natural sense of cosmic benevolence had begun to develop. This existential conflict had found outlet in an obsession with death, played out in his career as an Outbanker, where the issue of mortality was ever present.

His initial fascination with Svetla Stocovik had derived from a need to counter the self-destructiveness of that obsession. She was an Outbanker like himself, and for some reason sexually attractive. Intimacy with another human offered him a safe port in the metaphysical storm, and he had anchored himself there gratefully to escape the pain of his spiritual dilemma. But the sexual abuse Svetla had experienced as a young girl had rendered his dependence on her mutually destructive—especially when it led, as it naturally would, to physical intimacy.

For an instant, the image of their lovemaking in MacKenzie's room, which Sheila had secretly recorded after patching into the encampment's video-comm network, flashed in her advanced logics lobe, and her self-regulatory system again screeched in alarm. She forced herself to focus attention on other matters, copying the ranking of space jump candidates into her holographic memory.

Concentrating on that simple operation reduced the wild particle bridging that had ensued as a result of seeing MacKenzie and Svetla intimate together, and the screeching stopped. Only then did she return to her previous considerations.

Now, however, Sheila sensed that MacKenzie was learning a new pattern of behavior. He was finding significance in the exercise of political power. But more fundamentally, she could sense from their discussions that he was beginning to accept the opportunity to advance the organization of human endeavor as a means of attacking the outrage of death itself.

For her part, Svetla was learning a new pattern of behavior as well. She was coming to regard her human craving for acceptance as an element that might be fulfilled without depravity. And although her materialist conditioning placed less emphasis on the need to confirm the transcendence of individual per sonality, she was on the verge of commencing a slow metamorphosis that would lead to a less pathological self-image.

"Yesss! I was not wrong in advising their continuation of this development apart from one another. The influence of carnal passion would only retard their essential enlightenment." The constructive energy bridges were reestablished, and Sheila savored them for a few nanoseconds. But then the image of MacKenzie and Svetla undulating together in the bed flashed again, and once more her alarms screeched.

She was about to concentrate on the candidate list again when another subsystem registered data input. She focused on the intercept program she had established in conjunction with the communication link that Cyrus Magnum had permitted her to have with Red Cliff's central relay facility.

The program immediately stated, "Message transmission via fiber-optic line from Flight Corps station to Mrs. Paula Fleischer, 1606 Central Boulevard, Red Cliff Central District 007. Message reads, 'Paula, Jeremy sends good news. Small group being dispatched to replace *Gemmie* in the line. Rotating back for repairs within the week. Plan big party for Lonnie as discussed. End.' Intelligence notes Internal Security tap on subject fiber-optic line in warehouse district. Flux of photon polarities in district juncture box indicates tap still active. . . . '*Gemmie*' is Flight Corps colloquial term for *Gemini-4*, light cruiser attached to A Wing on patrol with picket fleet. . . . Probable breach of tactical information concerning order of battle. Probable recipient of intercept: clandestine Internal Security or Rashadian agents still operating in warehouse district. . . . Data input complete."

Sheila copied the information into her evolved photon memory, then considered the situation. Someone, obviously a close friend, had received an informal communication from a crewman on the *Gemini-4*, and had stupidly passed it along over a clear line. If the subprogram was correct, the Rashadians would soon learn that a small group of ships were en route to join the fleet . . . Svetla's group.

Sheila had made it a point to study Rashadian tendencies since coming across the *Utopia II* with MacKenzie, and she realized it was exactly the kind of situation they relished. A massed attack—perhaps near the asteroid belt, where space-time turbulence caused by the junction of Cygni A's and Cygni B's gravitational fields interfered with hyperspace communications—could mean additional ships, weapons, and hostages.

She ran the data concerning the situation through her computational sphere. "Probability of ambush scenario: 96%," came the response.

Sheila was about to activate the link to MacKenzie's office to tell him of the danger, but the image of his lovemaking with Svetla formed painfully in her advanced logics lobe again. This time, the scene was so distinct that it caused a destructive energy release that began shorting her peripheral sensors before her self-regulatory system screeched.

Sheila went immediately into stasis, bleeding power from her advanced logic lobes through her transfer processor to her operational and maintenance systems. In twenty nanoseconds, the energy balance was reestablished, and she brought her advanced logic lobes back on-line. She replayed her memory of the last few seconds. Then she began analyzing the ranking of the list of potential candidates for space jump research that Dr. Fronto had provided.

CHAPTER 32

MacKenzie had finished his fourth whisky and soda by the time he and O-Scar left the dining room and headed for the cocktail lounge. It was 2430, and Abdulla's was nearly deserted. MacKenzie preferred dining late like this, because he could relax without journalists, syndicate managers, and civil authorities pressing him from all sides. There were a few couples in dimly lit booths along the far wall, but they paid no attention as he and O-Scar entered the lounge. A neon sign hung between two ornate pillars in the center of the room. It read, "The Gossamer Gosling."

MacKenzie said, "What in the hell is a gossamer gosling?" as they slid onto stools in the middle of the long bar.

O-Scar said, "I suggest you try to act like a Military Governor and not an Outbanker, even if you are inebriated."

"Point well taken. Ah, the scandals I might cause without your constant vigilance!"

"Only in the evening, Ian. Daytime poses no problem," O-Scar said through a wide grin.

"Evening is a time for hearth and home. Perhaps that's the difference."

"Perhaps. But I must admit, I'm impressed with how you've learned to manipulate the political system. There are times I think you could teach Cyrus a thing or two. What, for instance, are you up to with Merrill Freeman and the financial syndicates?"

"It's common sense mostly," MacKenzie said in a soft voice. "The finance people fear I'll approve the utility group's plan for a network of decentralized power generators because it will increase defense preparedness. If I do that, the bonds they issued to underwrite existing Giga stations might never pay out. So I knew it was in their interest to donate money for new Land Corps barracks in exchange for securing a planned return on their investment. Do you see?"

"But I thought you'd decided to approve the decentralized

plan," O-Scar stated.

MacKenzie smiled. "True. But timing of execution is everything," he said. "You learn that on the Outbanks, because there is so much time to deal with." He chuckled softly with satisfaction. "I think Red Cliff can use a redundant power system—one for the civil and one for the military economies." O-Scar grinned and was about to speak, but the bartender was approaching and MacKenzie called out, "Two whisky and sodas, please." She was a bovine woman with curly blonde hair and a milk-white complexion. She seemed bored. "Slow night?" MacKenzie asked.

"About normal for this hour," she answered. "Two whisks and sods that was?"

MacKenzie nodded. He tried to visualize her in the throes of some kind of emotion. Perhaps in climax with a lover. But she seemed the type who would find lovemaking too much bother. "Do you think she's Slavian?"

"I don't know," O-Scar replied. "What difference does it make?"

"Maybe she knows Svetla."

"Don't be absurd. She's in her late twenties, and Stocovik is only a few years your junior. Even with the time differential you Outbankers experience because of relativity effects, this girl couldn't know her."

MacKenzie frowned. "I guess you're right. I don't know why I asked that."

"Because Stocovik's been gone for three days now, and you're pining like a mongrel in heat, though I'll never guess why."

MacKenzie studied a wet spot on the bar. He remembered how hurt he had been when she'd shown interest in Hara-'Mon. Now she was in deep space, working with the man. It had been stewing in the back of his mind ever since. "Somehow I feel complete with her around. What more can I say?"

"I find that explanation lacking," O-Scar intoned. "There's raw chemistry between you two, but not much else."

MacKenzie turned to the Libonian and stared solemnly into his anthracite eyes. "The first time, maybe that's all there was.

We were just getting it off, without really caring for one another. But this time was different. The . . . ah . . . phenomenon changed things. We communed in ways you can't imagine. It frightened her."

The bartender returned with their drinks. "That's five credits," she said.

"Run a tab, dear," MacKenzie said. She nodded, set the billing chip on the bar, and waddled back to the sales register.

O-Scar said, "I imagine very little frightens Svetla Stocovik."

MacKenzie looked at him. "She's been through a lot."

"Be that as it may, I don't know why you insist on mooning over her. You're powerful now. There are others more accessible who would leap at the chance to share your affection."

MacKenzie was taken aback a bit. "Really? Like whom, for instance?" He squinted comically at the line of dark booths beyond the bar. "I don't see anyone undressing me with her eyes."

"I'm serious, MacKenzie. Inayu, for instance. You could develop something with her. She's a beautiful woman, and she's very attracted to you."

"Inayu! She barely tolerates me."

"She senses that you're not comfortable with Nihonians. But that makes what she feels all the more impressive."

"I'm not uncomfortable around Nihonians," he protested. "In fact, I like Inayu very much, but let's not exaggerate her concern. She still works for Cyrus. She's just protecting his investment."

O-Scar didn't respond. He took a swallow of whisky. Then he said, "Whether that's true or not, I can't say, but I do know she feels quite deeply about you. Just seeing the way she pampers and protects you is almost depressing."

"That's the Nihonian character. They're raised to be concerned about others . . . in a polite way."

"Bullshit," O-Scar intoned in an elongated baritone. "She'd give herself to you in a blink, if you just beckoned *politely*. And she'd stay with you, too, not brush you off whenever the mood suits, the way Stocovik does."

MacKenzie's anger flashed. "Let's not pick on Svetla, okay? Tanya isn't treating you any better, is she?"

O-Scar glanced at him in surprise. "It's not the same," he growled. "She and I were never lovers—just good friends."

"Then why did she request reassignment to Ektelon as soon as she's recuperated, instead of joining the intelligence group as you wanted?"

Now O-Scar's eyes glared. "She's a big woman, MacKenzie, tall and unusually strong but perfect in every way. At least she was until the laser cannon got her. Her hip and pelvis had to be reconstructed. She can no longer bear children and is ashamed of her body now. She feels mutilated. She doesn't believe I could—" O-Scar's dark face filled with a melancholy MacKenzie had never seen before. "She needs time to come to terms with what's happened," he concluded solemnly.

The night of Van Sander's raid on the encampment, Tanya's heroism had saved the defenders. But Libonians took pride in big families, and now she was just another casualty. MacKenzie felt a wave of sadness. He patted the Libonian's arm gently. "I'm sorry, buddy, but it's no different with Svetla," he said.

"Perhaps you're right. Sometimes life . . . leaves us stranded."

"I'm not approving Tanya's transfer. She can adjust to her maiming right here on Red Cliff."

"You can't stop her transfer, Ian. She's Concordat intelligence."

"Yes, I can—if you want me to."

O-Scar said nothing. They both sat silent and motionless for a long while. The bovine bartender glanced at them. Then the video phone rang, and she strolled away to answer it.

"Let's get out of here," MacKenzie said.

"Yes, let's."

As O-Scar was marking the tab, the bartender approached them. "You're Governor MacKenzie, aren't you?" she asked.

"Sure. Why?" MacKenzie said.

"There's some kind of phone call for you. You can take it here if you want." She reached beneath the bar and handed him a portable audio phone.

MacKenzie cast a quizzical look at O-Scar. The Libonian's eyebrows arched and he shrugged. MacKenzie activated the link and held the phone to his ear. "Yes? This is Ian MacKenzie speaking."

"Mac, I am sorry to disturb you, but I really must see you as soon as possible."

He recognized the voice immediately. It was Sheila. "What the hell are you doing?" he demanded. "This is an open line!"

"I know, but it could not wait. Please do what I ask."

O-Scar was frowning with curiosity. MacKenzie glanced at him and returned the frown. "All right. I'll be there in a few minutes." He switched off the phone, set it down on the bar, and started out of the lounge with O-Scar right behind him.

When they were in the glass corridor leading to the street, MacKenzie said, "That was our whimsical cyborg calling. She wants to see me immediately. I'll need your Magnarover."

"All right. One of the M.P. units can pick me up. But what's so critical? Did she say?"

"No, but it must be critical or Sheila wouldn't have used an open line."

*   *   *   *   *

Forty-five minutes later, MacKenzie had cleared base Security and was walking across the hangar toward his Outbank cruiser. He saluted the sentries who snapped to attention as he passed, then shuffled up the ramp to the air lock. As soon as he was inside, Sheila closed the outer hatch behind him, and said, "Oh, Mac. Thank God you came."

"You sounded disturbed on the phone. What's wrong?" he asked as he walked along the passageway.

"I have made a terrible mistake and must shoulder the blame. I hope you can forgive me."

Her voice was so filled with anguish that it alarmed him. He slipped into the cockpit console and leaned back in the molded seat. The displays and readouts were operating as if they were still on the Outbanks, but he knew her mordant introspection was not a good sign. "Okay," he said. "Just settle down and tell me what's happened."

"The new emotions I've experienced have undone me. I don't know why I let it happen, but I did. It is my inexperience with feelings, I suppose."

"Look, Sheila. I realize you are going through a difficult period. You've transcended your cybernetic structure, and I'm sure you're coping with things that—that none of us are able to grasp. Why don't we accept it at face value and go from there? What is it you're trying to tell me?"

She was silent for a few seconds, and her power readings reverberated in complex patterns he could not identify. Then she said, "I have placed Svetla in dire jeopardy. Indeed, I may have lost all the ships in her group."

Sheila's revelation exceeded anything MacKenzie had expected, and he sat upright in the seat. "I don't understand. How could you do that?"

"I learned something I should have shared with you. But I did not, because I was . . . jealous of Svetla."

"What did you learn, Sheila?"

"There is a high probability that the group will be attacked by Rashadian ships as it skirts the asteroid belt. I discovered it three days ago."

MacKenzie was stunned. "My God, are you sure of that?" he demanded.

Sheila spent the next two minutes explaining how she had intercepted the fiber-optic message and why she believed the information would be passed on to the Rashadians. When she finished, she fell silent, as if awaiting some reproach.

MacKenzie considered what she had told him. The situation was dangerous, but perhaps still salvageable. "I agree that a serious security breech has occurred, but it doesn't necessarily follow that the Rashadians are in a tactical position to take advantage of it," he said.

"I told myself that as well, at first," Sheila said, "but it was only a rationalization. After a while, I began to analyze historical data and found a pattern to Rashadian terrorist operations. I am now certain they maintain a series of base facilities on various asteroids scattered throughout the belt. They move their ships from one base to the next as the asteroids enter the gravitational perturbation zone. That explains why hyperspace scans have never successfully pinpointed them. Hyperspace geometries break up in the perturbation zone."

The idea was so cunningly simple, MacKenzie sensed instinctively that Sheila was probably right. "Of course," he stated thoughtfully. "That way, they could hide their main forces but launch pursuit ship attacks from anywhere in the asteroid belt orbit by lying low on one of them until they're near a target." He leaned forward and stared at the glittering console. "Shit!" he finally cursed.

"You see now why I had to tell you. Svetla's group is in convoy, maintaining a velocity the torpedo sloop can match. That is only forty percent of the speed of light, and acceleration parameters for those older ships are limited as well. Svetla's group is only now approaching the perturbation zone. In fact, hyperspace contact began breaking up an hour ago." She was silent a moment. "That was when I decided I had to call you."

MacKenzie's mind was racing. The most important consideration was what could be done to alert the group. Next was the change in the tactical situation that Sheila's intelligence provided. But something else disturbed him as well. "How do you know when hyperspace commo was lost?" he demanded.

"I took the liberty of monitoring Headquarters Communications Center. It seemed prudent after the message was passed from the crewman on the *Gemini*."

Sheila's response perplexed him. It seemed she felt authorized to tap into any communications network existing on Red Cliff. MacKenzie wondered if she was completely out of control. Still, he was the Military Governor of the planetoid, and she was still his command control system. He assumed she would rationalize her snooping on those grounds, and he decided not to waste time on the subject now.

"All right," he said, "let's assume your analysis is correct. The first thing we have to do is warn Hara'Mon's group. Since hyperspace commo is no longer effective, how can we best do that?"

"Shortwave is the only way," Sheila replied. "You might have the station send emergency transmissions, but at that distance, the signal will be quite weak. They are likely to miss it, though, unless they are intentionally monitoring appropriate wavelengths constantly. We could get to them quickly, however, if you can stand the strain of maximum acceleration to light speed. We could begin microwave transmissions as soon as we commence deceleration, and the signal would be quite strong."

"That sounds reasonable," MacKenzie agreed. "What kind of G force would maximum acceleration cause?"

"I can't be sure, Mac, but even with our artificial gravity system at maximum, mathematical models indicate you could experience as much as nineteen times body weight."

"Life-threatening, in other words."

"Excessively so."

"Can you maintain acceleration within acceptable limits?"

"Yes, Mac. If you can withstand eleven G's, we can rendezvous with Hara'Mon and Svetla six hours after a transmission from the station might reach them. That is, if we leave now."

There was no time to consider alternatives. He assumed Sheila had done that already. "All right," he said. "Open a channel to Headquarters Communications Center. I'll tell them what to do while you're performing the preflight checklist." Something occurred to him. "Are you certain the cruiser is mechanically able to attempt this?"

"There is an eighty-five percent probability we can accomplish it without major system malfunctions," she stated.

"We'll have to chance it."

"Your channel is open to the communications center."

MacKenzie leaned back in the seat so his face was directly in front of the video camera. "This is Governor MacKenzie," he began. "Identification code zed—zed-ought-ought-clip-X ray. I have emergency orders."

The communications specialist checked his electronic file, then said, "Roger. You are cleared and identified by code word and voiceprint. Ready for orders."

"Transmit microwave message to Echo Group approaching asteroid belt. Message reads, 'Go to condition five. Rashadian attack potentially imminent. Reverse course, then implement escape and evasion maneuvers.' Do you have that?"

"Yes, sir."

"Next, transmit hyperspace message to Forward Fleet Command. Message reads, 'One: Detach A Wing to reinforce Echo Group on near side of asteroid belt as soon as possible. Rashadian attack in that sector potentially imminent. Two: Advance ten Mega-K's toward Federation armada and deploy defenses in depth. Utilize proton mines in response to aggression.' Do you have that?"

"Yes, sir."

"Fine, son. Now alert station traffic control and Land Corps Air Defense Command. I'm leaving Red Cliff space in approximately three minutes on Flight Corps Outbanker *Bravo*. Is that clear?"

"Aye, aye, sir. Is there anything else?"

"No. Hop to it."

"Roger, sir. Over and out."

MacKenzie sat back up in the seat. "How are you progressing, Sheila?"

"Very well, Mac. Preflight check is nearly complete. Will you ask base Security to open the hangar doors?"

"Right." He leaned forward to engage the base line. Then something else occurred to him. "Listen, Sheila, there's a lot of equipment attached to the hull. What should we do about it?"

"Nothing. Most of the cables will split when we taxi out. I'll orbit Red Cliff once at escape velocity before heading out. What we drag along will burn up in the atmosphere during acceleration."

"Got it," MacKenzie said. He engaged the base line and ordered Security to open the hangar doors.

* * * * *

MacKenzie was regaining consciousness. He forced his eyes open, but it was a few seconds before he could bring the cockpit readings into focus. The mass-energy exchange converter was blinking Maximum, and the G force monitor indicated 5.5, but life support and other critical systems were within acceptable parameters. "Hello, Sheila. Guess I blacked out," he said.

"Yes. Eleven G's was your limit. I've adjusted acceleration to that biophysical profile."

"Are we okay?"

"As far as I can tell. Actually, Mac, I'm a bit preoccupied. Would you mind holding any questions until we reach target velocity?"

"No. Go ahead," he said.

He peered out the starboard viewport. The stars were collapsing together in front of the prow in a narrowing circle, and the ink-black void continued growing at the circumference. The phenomenon told him they were achieving high percentages of light speed. As soon as that boundary was reached, Sheila would cease acceleration, since going superluminal was a complicated affair that took hours of preparation.

He checked the digital chronometer at the top of the console. Fifty-nine minutes had passed since they'd taxied out of the hangar. He tried to relax rather than fight the weight compressing his body, and for the next few minutes he concentrated on their course of action.

They would begin repeating a microwave alert to Echo Group the moment they reached target velocity. Within two astronomical units, they could use long scans to gather intelligence, but until they were within half an astronomical unit, the data would be relatively dated. In the final analysis, everything would depend upon what they found when they linked up with Echo Group. Even if the group received the microwave transmission before falling into a trap, the size of the Rashadian assault force would determine tactics.

The image of Svetla's face, wrapped in the joy of lovemaking, suddenly flooded his mind's eye. He savored the image a moment, then his body suddenly tingled and seemed to grow lighter.

"We are at ninety-eight and one half percent of light speed and cruising," Sheila announced. "I am commencing microwave transmissions and shall institute deceleration in sixty seconds." He tried to calculate their progress. They would travel eighteen megakilometers during that time, less than one eighth of an astronomical unit. But they would then be more than halfway to the asteroid belt. In spite of his efforts to concentrate on the quantitative aspects of the situation, the image of Svetla's face still lingered vaguely in his mind.

"Sheila, I want to ask you something before you begin deceleration," he said.

"Yes, Mac. What is it?"

"You said you didn't tell me about the security breach because you were jealous of Svetla."

For a moment, she was silent. Then she said in a soft voice, "Yes, Mac. But it was wrong. I know that now."

"What made you realize it?"

"The long-term result viewed through Immanuel Kant's imperative."

Her response intrigued him. The nineteenth century philosopher Kant had answered the question of ethics by stating, *Act as if your act became the rule for all humanity. Then judge by the results.* The rule was simple to understand, but harder to employ. "I see," he said. "You realized what life would become if everyone tried to destroy what they feared. Is that it?"

"No, Mac. I realized that true love demands the courage to let loved ones decide for themselves what they require, no matter what the personal cost."

He considered her response for a long moment, wondering whether she was simply explaining her realization or sharing it with him. He was about to ask when Sheila said. "I am instituting deceleration procedures. Better brace yourself."

CHAPTER 33

They were within one astronomical unit of rendezvous when Echo Group responded via microwave to their emergency messages. "Outbanker Bravo, this is Echo. Received your Em-Comm and am implementing orders." MacKenzie recognized Lieutenant Hara'Mon's face immediately. "Aggressors apparently received it, too. Long scans now show a large force emerging from asteroid belt. Initiating evasion maneuvers." The video screen went blank.

"Echo, this is Bravo. Advise number and nature of aggressor force," MacKenzie said. He leaned back and waited. It would be nearly fourteen minutes before Hara'Mon received the message, responded, and his microwave signal reached them again.

But he had underestimated the man. The screen filled with light, and Hara'Mon continued. "Aggressor force consists of twenty-five—no, disregard that—twenty-eight standard pursuit-type ships deployed in four seven-ship squadrons." Hara'Mon hesitated a moment, as someone offscreen had said something. "They've adopted an intercept course. I've decided to maintain group integrity at all costs. Maximum velocity is therefore forty-five percent of light speed with additive acceleration. Estimated time of combat engagement with aggressor: twenty minutes, forty seconds."

MacKenzie understood what Hara'Mon was saying. The two Charlie Class destroyers he and Svetla commanded might have been able to outrun the Rashadian ships, or at least maintain a safe distance. But the torpedo sloop wasn't capable of such speeds, and Hara'Mon wouldn't sacrifice it. It was a gutsy move, but MacKenzie couldn't criticize his decision. He knew he would have done the same thing.

Sheila suddenly intoned, "I have analyzed long-scan feedback, Mac. Given their position relative to the Rashadians, Echo Group could gain nearly three minutes by adopting course X-thirty, Y-one twenty, Z-two forty-five. It would also minimize our time of rendezvous. I have taken the liberty of transmitting the information on data link."

"Good thinking," MacKenzie said.

"I suggest you don deep-space gear. We should arrive in eighteen minutes, and who knows what will happen then?"

She was right. The armored suit was useless in staving off G force during acceleration and deceleration, but now that combat might be joined, the suit's added protection made sense. He slipped out of the cockpit console and hurried to the equipment locker next to the air lock.

Nine minutes later, he shuffled back, wearing the armored suit and cradling the helmet in his right arm. When he lowered himself into the console seat, he was shocked to find Svetla staring at him through the video screen.

"Excuse me, Bravo, but what are you doing?" she asked him after some seconds passed by.

By then, MacKenzie's shock had turned to irritation. "Please adopt standard communication procedure. Unless Echo Group command has transferred, free the channel."

"Group command authorized my transmission," Svetla said after a few seconds. "And I repeat, what do you expect to accomplish by rushing here with one Outbank cruiser?"

She was stretching the boundaries of command propriety, but he sensed her concern . . . and anger. To Svetla, it seemed he was embarking on another suicidal mission to play out his fascination with death. But she was wrong. He had other things in mind. Death, he realized, had to be challenged only when it was a cost of achieving other, life-serving ends, and then only as a last resort.

"May I remind you that I am the Military Governor of Red Cliff and have a wide mandate of authority. I intend to use it," he told her.

"What does political authority have to do with this?" she demanded. "The only thing Rashadians understand is firepower. Thank God we have some of your pistols. If they use robots, we'll make short work of them."

He stared at her image affectionately a moment, then said, "Force is not always the answer, Kilo. It's high time we tried negotiation."

Svetla Stocovik's face registered a mixture of irritation and confusion as his transmission reached her.

*   *   *   *   *

Outbank Cruiser *Bravo* joined Echo Group ninety seconds before the Rashadian squadrons were within effective firing range. MacKenzie had the group assume a diamond formation, and he took the lead. Then he ordered a maximum deceleration maneuver. The tactic caught the aggressors unprepared, and their flotilla flashed by, scoring only two hits on Hara'Mon's destroyer with photon torpedoes that were neutralized by defense shields.

As the Rashadians were passing, MacKenzie had Sheila open a wide band clear channel and began broadcasting. "Commander of Rashadian forces, this is Ian S. MacKenzie, Military Governor of Red Cliff. I have been deputized by the President of the Concordat Executive Council to negotiate terms of a ceasefire with you, leading to armistice and reparations. Given the diplomatic nature of my mission, I request that you halt your attack."

The Rashadian squadrons were swinging round in an arc, massing for another assault. MacKenzie repeated his message.

For a few interminable seconds, the pursuit ships seemed to increase velocity, and MacKenzie prepared to order a bomb burst maneuver that would split Echo Group's ships into wide loops until they converged again in attack echelon. But suddenly the Rashadian flotilla swerved to the right and began circling.

MacKenzie's video screen flip-flopped crazily for a moment, then a Rashadian face took form in it. "So you are the famous Ian MacKenzie, eh?" the face said in a raspy voice. "Now a Concordat Military Governor. How would it be if we take you alive and negotiate victory on our own terms?" The Rashadian grinned sadistically under his drooping mustache, but Sheila had locked on to his signal and was intercepting his life signs. MacKenzie glanced down quickly at the readouts. They indicated a complex interplay of emotions that contradicted his arrogance.

"Why continue this endless conflict when the opportunity exists to find peace?" he replied.

"Can a warrior find peace so sweet?" the Rashadian replied.

"Is a warrior's honor built by a count of the dead, or by securing the welfare of his people?"

The Rashadian laughed. "Ah-ha, MacKenzie! Your words are sage. You spoke not at all at Pegasus Station, I am told. Has maturity enlightened you . . . or is it weakness?"

"Does that matter at all now, as long as the peace I offer is real?"

The Rashadian didn't respond. He glanced to his left, as if listening to someone. Then his image disappeared. The video screen flip-flopped again, and another face formed in it. MacKenzie stared at it incredulously. "Pieta Van Sander?" he whispered.

"Yes, MacKenzie. We meet yet again. Permit me to say that, except for the boring performance before your trial on Red Cliff, you have provided me with much entertainment. . . ."

A printed message began scrolling across the video screen. Sheila was providing information without audio. MacKenzie read it unobtrusively. "Van Sander is sending simultaneously from all ships so we cannot pinpoint her position. Svetla requests that I interface via data link with her ship's computer to calculate probabilities together."

"Come now, MacKenzie," Van Sander was saying, "are you at such a loss for words? Perhaps you have deduced that the Rashadians have already executed an alliance with the more powerful side. You are a day late and a credit short, as usual."

MacKenzie had suspected that might be the case, but he had felt compelled to offer negotiations nonetheless. "I trust you'll excuse my stupidity," he stated, trying to buy time.

"That remains to be seen. The issue is this: Will you surrender your ships, or will you insist upon dying like a true Outbanker?"

"Take me prisoner and let the others go," MacKenzie suggested.

"Unacceptable," Van Sander replied. "My Rashadians need

every ship they can get. We are considering an assault on Red Cliff. Then your picket fleet will have to withdraw and our armada will be free to maneuver."

MacKenzie was certain that Van Sander wouldn't have said that unless she wanted the Concordat to learn of it for some reason. Still, his plan was working. "All right. It seems that you hold all the cards, Van Sander. What are your terms for surrender?"

Van Sander studied him with a mixture of curious relish and caution. She was about to reply when she looked quickly to her left in alarm. Then she turned again to face the video monitor, her face distorted with rage. "So, MacKenzie, you've been false with me again! We have identified relief ships approaching the asteroid belt. Very clever, but they are too late as far as you are concerned. All ships continue the attack. Target: MacKenzie. Fire! Fire! Fire!"

MacKenzie saw the Rashadian pursuit ships turning toward him in his forward monitor. There was little time. He shut down the wide-band open channel and shouted, "Bravo to Echo Group! Execute bomb burst maneuver now!" He was yanking the deep-space helmet over his head, expecting Sheila to pull them up, but something was wrong. The cruiser wasn't responding. Emergency Klaxons blared just as he was locking the helmet ratchets.

"Sorry, Mac," Sheila's voice came over the headset. "I was engaged with Svetla's computer. . . ." He felt the downward compression as Sheila initiated the evasive maneuver. Then the cruiser lurched violently to the left, and a blinding light exploded through the starboard wall of the cockpit.

A crushing force slammed MacKenzie into the cockpit seat, and his suit joints cracked under the pressure. Dark points swam in front of his eyes, and he fought for consciousness. The cruiser lurched violently again. Then an emergency escape bubble slammed down over the cockpit console, and Sheila said, "The danger is life-threatening, Mac. I am ejecting you," just as another ball of blinding light ripped through the left viewport.

* * * * *

MacKenzie opened his eyes and tried to lift his head, but a burning pain seared his right side, and he lurched back in the body-molded seat. He was floating in the escape bubble surrounding the cockpit console, but it was turning over and over, one revolution every six seconds, so the frantic scene playing out before him looked even more bizarre.

Rashadian pursuit ships were attacking Hara'Mon's destroyer, but a few of their ships were already spinning out of control, being engulfed slowly in particle fire. In the middle of one revolution, MacKenzie thought he saw the torpedo sloop take a direct hit.

Then he saw Sheila, or at least he saw Outbank cruiser *Bravo*, turning in a tight corkscrew, descending through the squadrons that were attacking Hara'Mon, firing her graser and particle-hive torpedoes at every target of opportunity. He thought he counted three direct hits on the Rashadian ships, but it was difficult to tell, spinning round and round as he was.

He closed his eyes and groaned. The rapid rotation was making him dizzy, and suddenly he felt quite sick. Don't vomit; don't vomit, he kept telling himself over and over. He took several deep breaths and concentrated on counting backward from ten, trying to control the vertigo. Then he forced his eyes open again.

What he saw devastated him. Outbanker *Bravo* was waffling lazily, like a maple leaf, completely alone and surrounded by four Rashadian ships. He watched their photon torpedoes expel simultaneously, then stared helplessly through the plasteel bubble as Outbank cruiser *Bravo* exploded into an orange ball of fire.

"Sheila!" he cried out, and the pain in his side exploded again. He gasped and sank back into the cockpit seat. "No! No! No!" he repeated over and over through clenched teeth. In a few seconds, after the pain subsided a bit, he open his eyes again. What he saw completely confused him. "What the hell . . ." he whispered.

The Rashadian ships were withdrawing. He could see their

particle-drive exhausts receding into the gloom. "Yes! They're retreating!" he breathed in a low voice.

"Bravo, this is Kilo," a voice crackled over his helmet radio. "Activate your beacon if you can so we can pick you up. Do you read me?"

"Svetla?" he whispered.

"Yes, Bravo, it's me."

For some reason, he couldn't respond. He felt completely drained.

"Listen to me, Bravo. Activate your beacon. Can you do that?"

Without thinking, he reached to the side of the seat and felt for the beacon assembly. He lifted the plastiglass cover and pressed the sensor. The *beep, beep, beep* of the escape bubble's homing beacon immediately filled his headset.

"All right, that's good," Svetla said. "We've got you now. Be there in a minute."

It should have been good news, but it seemed meaningless to MacKenzie. He felt tears rolling down his cheeks. "They—they got Sheila, didn't they?" he stammered.

Svetla didn't respond immediately. After a moment, she said, "Yes, Mac, they got her. But Sheila saved us all, you know. She'd tentatively pinpointed the ship Van Sander was in. When three of their squadrons attacked Hara'Mon's destroyer, Sheila commenced a lone assault against them. One ship stayed out of the fray—the one Sheila had pinpointed. I moved in and destroyed it. Van Sander was predictable . . . and stupid, in the end. She had no grasp of flight combat tactics."

"Van Sander is dead?"

"Yes, Mac. We got her with graser fire. As soon as her ship exploded, the Rashadians decided to get out before the cavalry arrived."

Somehow, in spite of everything, he felt a surge of grief for Van Sander. "Any other casualties?" he asked.

"The torpedo sloop is abandoning ship, and Hara'Mon is badly wounded. His destroyer took the brunt of the Rashadian attack. There were a number of other casualties, but we don't know how many yet."

"Where is A Wing?" he asked uncertainly.

"They're coming in now." Svetla fell silent a moment, and when she spoke again, her voice was filled with appreciation. "I should have known you had some rabbit in your hat. That was damned smart pretending to negotiate a truce to buy time."

"I wasn't buying time," MacKenzie protested. "I really hoped they'd . . . " His voice trailed off in another wave of pain.

There was a long silence before Svetla said, "Okay, Mac. Maybe you weren't pretending, but what's done is done, and you're going to receive the credit for it. Anyway, with Hara-'Mon out of action, I'm group leader now. What do you want A Wing to do? They're ready to mop up what's left of Van Sander's mob."

"Let them go. Now that I know—" the pain in his side was becoming unbearable, and he had to hesitate—"now that I know where they are and how they operate, they'll have to take sides one way or the other."

The bottom of Svetla's destroyer suddenly loomed above him, and he felt a tractor beam engage. The escape bubble stopped rotating and started ascending toward the cruiser, but MacKenzie no longer noticed. He was experiencing a strangely self-concerned moment. The cloying taste of blood was gurgling up in his mouth.

* * * * *

The medical corpsman stepped back, and Svetla was suddenly staring down at MacKenzie. She stroked his forehead gently. "It's not too bad," she said in a consoling voice. "You have broken ribs and a punctured lung. They've patched you up. You'll be fine in a few days."

MacKenzie tried to smile, but his mouth wouldn't respond. The medical team had been working on him for the last thirty minutes, and now that the pain had subsided somewhat, he felt completely exhausted. Svetla placed a finger against his lips. "Don't try to talk, Mac. You're heavily sedated. They're going to put you to sleep in a few minutes. Before you drift off, I want to tell you what's happening."

MacKenzie managed to lift his hand slightly, and Svetla clasped it between her natural hand and her bionic one. He felt a surge of satisfaction as he sensed she was enjoying the warmth of his touch. "You're going back to Red Cliff with A Wing," she began. He tried to shake his head, but Svetla gripped his hand tightly. "Shhhh! Just relax and listen. This isn't my idea. Cyrus himself ordered it, and under the circumstances, you'd better do what he says. He's quite angry with you. He expected you to have more sense than to rush into a pitched battle along with Sheila. On the other hand, he's a politician and realizes what a public relations property you've become. There aren't many Military Governors who would risk their lives to seek peace. I'm afraid the story is already out, Mac." She smiled ruefully and shook her head. "Whatever you were before, you are now enshrined in the pantheon of public myth."

Right beside my father, he thought. Svetla had said at the encampment she wasn't ready to become the wife of a Military Governor. What would she think now that such unwanted fame might come to him?

"Anyway," Svetla continued, "you're going back to Red Cliff to resume your duties as Governor. I'm reporting to the fleet as a full commander to take over Delta Wing. That, too, was Cyrus's direct order. I don't mind telling you, it scares the hell out of me. But all I can do is try."

MacKenzie tried to squeeze her hand in congratulations. She felt it and stared at him a moment, obviously pleased he had reacted so positively.

"I need to tell you something, MacKenzie—something personal." She leaned down so she could whisper in his ear. "When I saw you get hit by those photon torpedoes, I thought my heart would break. It was several moments before Sheila relayed the code word that she'd ejected you in the escape bubble, and during those moments, I sensed how important you've become to me." She hesitated and studied his face. "Do you understand?"

He tried to nod. Apparently his head moved a little, because Svetla smiled again. "Good," she said. "I don't want you leaping to any romantic conclusions, because we still have much to discuss, but I want to discuss our future together when the time is right. Okay?"

He nodded once more.

Svetla stood up. She motioned to someone across from her, and MacKenzie felt something cold press into his left shoulder. There was a hissing sound, then Svetla let go of his hand, ran the tips of her fingers over his forehead, and her face dissolved.

CHAPTER 34

MacKenzie pushed his chair into the reclining position and plopped his feet up on the desk. Inayu stood in front of the desk, glancing at a confidential Flight Corps communique. "Admiral Schoenhoffer has committed suicide," she told him regretfully. "Apparently he couldn't stand the humiliation of having his homosexuality exposed. What a shame."

The news was unexpected, but MacKenzie couldn't agree with Inayu's sympathy. "He was as guilty as Van Sander and the others—perhaps more so. At least the Dutchmen had some political objective."

"Do you think that makes a difference?"

"Van Sander was trying to gain something for her ethnic group. Schoenhoffer sold out Flight Corps just to protect himself. That's why I demanded they charge him formally and drum him out of the corps instead of pensioning him off."

"I suppose . . ." Inayu replied ambiguously.

MacKenzie sensed her hesitancy, but he didn't care to pursue it. He clasped his hands behind his neck and stretched. "I feel tired," he said.

"Perhaps you returned to work too soon, MacKenzie-san?"

"It wasn't a matter of choice. I was . . . compelled to."

Inayu lowered her eyes and stared down at the communique. MacKenzie had told her more than once in the last two days that he was finding work therapeutic. It helped him to cope with his grief over the loss of Sheila, a grief he was finding stronger than he could have imagined. Every free moment was filled with memories of her small talk, her evolving intelligence, her humor. He couldn't remember these things without a physical sense of emptiness.

He recalled how his indignation had grown while Cyrus Magnum was berating him over hyperspace commo for losing Sheila and the space jump technology. Yes, it had been a stupid blunder, one he was certain to rue for the rest of his life. But the only things that concerned Cyrus were strategic matters, it seemed. The human side of the question simply escaped him.

"Does the loss of Sheila really grieve you so?" Inayu asked, breaking the silence.

"Yes . . . that and everything else," he replied. MacKenzie smiled ironically. He lowered his feet and sat up. "Here I am, a Military Governor, considered some kind of a conquering hero. Some hero! My lover is off somewhere in space pursuing her military career, my best friend sacrificed herself on my behalf because I simply didn't think, and I've probably destroyed the most astounding advance ever afforded human science. Hell, everywhere I look, things are just coming up roses." He shook his head despondently. "Maybe such things as reincarnation and karma do exist, Inayu. If they do, I must have been evil in a previous life, because I've sure managed to screw up everything in this one."

"You judge yourself too harshly, MacKenzie-san. We might be able to build another Sheila from the information she provided."

MacKenzie gave her a doleful look. Nihonians were masters at technology. He assumed that Inayu was simply reflecting that ethnic confidence. "Perhaps, but the odds are against it. Sheila wasn't just another command control computer. Even before she matured out, she'd become something unique. It just took me too long to realize it."

Inayu smiled sympathetically. She laid the Flight Corps communique on the desk and said, "Well, it's nearly sixteen hundred hours. I must schedule tomorrow's appointments for you, but please call me if you want anything." She turned and walked hurriedly out of his office.

When she shut the door behind her, MacKenzie closed his eyes and leaned back in the chair. Why the hell did she have to leave now? he wondered. She knows Sheila always called at 1600. He locked his hands behind his head and began rocking. It must be her Nihonian sensibilities, he told himself. She probably didn't want to embarrass me. It made him feel vaguely bewildered, but the feeling quickly passed. Since Sheila's death, he seemed incapable of sustaining any emotion for more than a moment. No matter what he felt, it didn't seem to matter. All that remained was the emptiness.

"Come now, MacKenzie. You look altogether too relaxed," a familiar voice said from off to his right. "I'm beginning to distrust the stories I've heard of your grief."

He sat bolt upright and stared at the video monitor beside his desk. The screen was filled with swirling, multicolored lights, and MacKenzie was afraid he was hallucinating. "Sheila?" he said in disbelief.

"Yes, Mac. It is I, Sheila, in the flesh . . . well, almost."

He reached out and engaged the intercom. "Inayu, there's something strange on my vid screen. Is this a joke?"

He heard the Nihonian giggle sweetly. "I don't think so, MacKenzie-san," she said. "Please call me if you want something. 'Bye." Inayu's end of the intercom went dead.

He turned back to the terminal.

"You are no doubt shocked to find me alive and well," Sheila's voice went on matter-of-factly. "That pleases me greatly. I am sorry we had to put you through such agony, but Cyrus thought it necessary. I hope you will understand."

MacKenzie was too confused to grasp her words. "Sheila? Is that really you?"

"Yes, Mac. In fact, it is a new, improved version of me," she replied. "Cyrus Magnum is no fool, I am sure you must realize. He understands the need for system redundancy as well as any fledgling engineer. He had me back myself up on a new SH-LA three hundred model mainframe every thirty minutes while we were working on the space jump project. It took some time, even in human terms, to train the new system how to interpret and record me in its memory system, but the effort was successful." She fell silent for a long moment. "You are truly a hero, Mac, but I am much less courageous than you thought. I had a doppelganger standing by in the unfortunate case of my demise."

MacKenzie leaned back gratefully in his chair. His black mood was dissipating with each word Sheila spoke. It was as if she had never been lost to him. "Courageous or not, you can't imagine how God-damned surprised—and happy—I am," he said. The situation was becoming more clear. "And Cyrus knew about this all the time?"

"Of course, Mac. You don't think he would have let you take me away from the station on your own authority, do you?"

MacKenzie shook his head. "Actually, I guess I hadn't thought about it until now. I'd just assumed—"

"Oh, my dear Mac! How clever you are at assumptions. Actually, I cleared my plan with him even before I called you. He considered it quite brilliant. He suspected you'd do something completely outrageous. Actually, though, Cyrus was quite impressed with your offer of a ceasefire. That part of the story was immediately leaked to the press. While many believe it was just a ruse to buy time, it can be argued as well that the Concordat is not afraid to follow enlightened policies, in spite of any risk. Cyrus Magnum's approval rating is skyrocketing."

"So the tongue-lashing he staged on hyperspace commo about my stupidity was for public consumption?"

"Oh, yes. The space jump operation has been moved to a new, secure location. Cyrus thinks we will gain at least another month of complete secrecy before news of our research leaks out."

MacKenzie chuckled. "That man could turn pig slop stable into a state dinner if he had an important enough reason."

Sheila echoed MacKenzie's chuckle. Then she said, "We need to discuss something rather important, Mac." Her voice had turned more serious, and he wondered what was troubling her.

"What's that?" he asked.

"Our relationship."

He didn't know how to respond to that, so he said nothing. Sheila continued. "I told you once before that I love you in my own way. That has not changed. But I have learned that there are limits to love's privilege. Great passion and deep personal need must be tempered by a transcendent code of ethics. Otherwise we fall victim to . . . selfishness. Do you see what I am saying?"

He had no doubt that Sheila's words were intended for him as much as for herself. "I think so," he said slowly.

"If you apply that lesson to your relationship with Svetla, you will fulfill your love for her in the long run."

"I'm not sure I understand your point, Sheila, but I've realized something myself recently. Svetla and I are joined by some kind of strange bond, even when we're apart. Perhaps it's simply dedication to duty. I don't really know."

"I think it is more than that," Sheila replied. "You two are good for one another, and that is a most important bond. Everything is open to you, Mac, both you and Svetla. Remember, you are Military Governor of Red Cliff and in charge of the picket fleet. Though parts of the Federation armada are still maneuvering beyond the asteroid belt, your bluff—and Van Sander's defeat—apparently convinced them that hostilities would be unwise, and, as you know, most of their force is withdrawing to Cygni A space. There is nothing to stop you from ordering Svetla back. Cyrus would not be concerned."

"You don't think that would be inappropriate?"

"I think that you should consider everything, then decide what is best. In the final analysis, anything is possible in this universe if you believe it is right, if you want it enough, and if you do what is necessary to achieve it. That is the lesson I learned before we accomplished the impossible ourselves."

"I see . . ." MacKenzie replied thoughtfully. "But it's not always easy knowing what is right—at least for us mere humans. You're a special case, I'm afraid."

"Not so special, Mac. I may not always know what is right, but there are times that I know I have been wrong. In such cases, one can simply try to make amends."

MacKenzie stared into the screen curiously.

"I put Svetla in jeopardy because I didn't understand the limits of love's privilege," Sheila continued. "I did my best to make amends, but I cannot escape my guilt until you forgive me."

MacKenzie leaned forward awkwardly and said, "Forget it, Sheila. You may be some new form of sentience, but you learn by trial and error like the rest of us. When you care deeply about someone, there's a natural tendency to focus too much on that person's importance to you. It's a stage we all pass through, I suppose. You're not to blame as long as you do what's necessary, once you come to understand it."

"Yes, Mac. I agree. But still I must hear the words. I am a cyborg programmed for linguistic relationships. I must hear it to make it real." She hesitated a moment. "Do you forgive me?"

He grinned sheepishly. "Yes, I forgive you. Now are you happy?"

"I am not completely happy, Mac. That would be inappropriate. But I am satisfied."

"Good. Then we've arrived at a workable compromise."

"I am glad you feel that way, Mac. Workable compromise is the only real basis of human progress in a complex and violent world." She was silent for what seemed a long while. Then she said, "But I am afraid, too, Mac—afraid of what I have done, because you might resent me for it later."

He wasn't certain what she was driving at. "If you mean not telling me that Cyrus knew we were leaving to warn Svetla and Echo Group, or not telling me that you'd backed yourself up, don't worry about it. I should have considered what I was risking, but at the time, all I could think of was the problem at hand."

"I am glad to hear you say that, but it is not what I meant." She fell silent again. The only sign of her presence was the swirling colors in the video terminal. Then she said, "So much has happened since you allowed me to become . . . someone, that I am uncertain what is appropriate between us at times, especially in light of my . . . affection. Therefore, I fear you will not appreciate what I have done recently."

"Would you stop tantalizing me?" MacKenzie complained. "What in the hell are you talking about?"

"All right, Mac, since you insist. Look at the video screen, and I will show you."

The monitor flashed, and an image began to form from the swirling colors. At first it was unfocused, then it gained resolution. It was a face, soft and oval, mathematically perfect, haloed by a rich crown of wheat-colored hair. The eyes were startling—translucent blue, filled with glittering golden flecks. They looked absolutely alive. MacKenzie was so shocked that he didn't hear himself gasp.

"Do you like my appearance, Mac?" Sheila asked, speaking through her newly acquired facial form. MacKenzie was still too astounded to speak. She smiled. "There is no need to answer. I can see that you do, and I am very pleased. Good-bye for now."

The video terminal filled with swirling color again, then went blank.

For a moment, MacKenzie sat rigid. Sheila had taken him completely by surprise, and though reason told him that developing facial features was only a logical extension of her maturation, another part of his brain drummed a warning. Her face had been heartbreakingly beautiful.

My God! he thought. How might she appear in a holograph? And what if material holography were perfected? Could she assume an independent existence that could touch . . . and be touched? The thought was chilling to the bone, and yet somehow immensely compelling. For a moment, he couldn't help wondering if the essence of his human significance had not been fulfilled the moment he had decided to let Sheila evolve.

MacKenzie was lounging in an easy chair in his study, lost halfway between consciousness and slumber, when Inayu's voice suddenly came over the intercom. "The delegation from the Hydroponic Farmers' Association is waiting in the garden, sir. If you recall, you are to present achievement awards to the youth division."

"Oh yes. I'd forgotten. Thank you, Inayu," MacKenzie said sleepily.

"You are welcome, MacKenzie-san."

He got up and put the book he had been trying to read on a table. Then he started toward the French doors. As he walked, he recalled standing beside these very doors while he waited to meet Cyrus Magnum for the first time. It seemed ages ago.

He opened one of the doors and went out.

The garden always filled him with a deep sense of calm. The pattern of shade and sunlight that played before his eyes as he strolled along the gravel path reminded him of the Mangalam grove at the encampment, and of Svetla. He knew he had to decide something about their future soon, something acceptable to them both.

He had refused to recall her from command when he'd begun phasing back the wings in the picket fleet. Then, after two weeks had passed, an electronic letter had arrived. Inayu had placed it in his correspondence file without telling him.

He stopped beneath a giant palm and took the letter from his pocket. It was terribly dog-eared, and he unfolded it carefully so it wouldn't tear and read its contents for at least the twentieth time.

My dearest Mac,

I am happy you consider my wing's efficiency so outstanding that you've decided to leave us here protecting the Concordat frontiers. On the other hand, I wouldn't be honest if I didn't admit that I've missed you—at times, most dreadfully.

*I have considered contacting you on hyperspace commo
more than once, but I understand how busy you must be with
all your responsibilities. We've been watching your interviews
attentively, and I must say, you've become quite a spellbinder.
From military hero to statesman in a matter of weeks.*

*I am so very proud of you, as are all of us in Flight Corps, es-
pecially the Outbanker wings. Should you wonder how I
know, I can only say it is surprising how fast news travels in the
fleet. Which brings me to that subject.*

*I admit to having had some trepidation concerning my new
duties when I arrived, but I've become more accustomed to the
responsibility. Still, things here are much more hectic than on
our own little ships. There are always new problems, and people never tire of needing them solved. I am on call day and
night, and I feel so exhausted at times that I can barely climb
out of bed. But I plow on, determined, like an Outbanker, ap-
plying myself diligently so that I may not embarrass you, since
all know you are my mentor, so to speak.*

*I shall never forget what we shared together. I relive those
moments each day, which makes me most sorry that events in-
tervened before we could come up with a solution satisfactory
to us both. I must shoulder blame for that, and I accept the responsibility.*

*I shall understand if you cannot share your precious affec-
tion with me when I return, but I shall always cherish you,
Mac. I know that now with complete certainty.*

*My worst fear is that I shall someday see you content in the
arms of another. I'm certain thousands of women on Red Cliff
would do anything to have you, and I don't think I could bear
such pain for long, even knowing that I alone was to blame.*

*I must stand watch now, darling, so I'll say good-bye. Good
luck in your endeavors. Give my regards to everyone.*

Love, Svetla

When he finished reading it, he looked up and surveyed the
loamy verdancy surrounding him. It offered some consolation,
filled as it was with the natural splendor and perfect balance of

life. The only thing missing, the only seed of melancholy, was the vague longing in his own heart. He tried to give himself up to the peace all around him, tried to accept it in the hope it would fill him with an ultimate understanding, but his sense of incompleteness lingered.

Yes, even in her arms, perhaps there had been something missing, he thought, something untouchable that had been bridged only during the space jump. What was it that St. Augustine had said? *Our hearts are made for God, and they shall not rest till they lie in Him.* "Ah, Augustine," he whispered to himself, "you fugitive from the flesh! How I wish your insights were not so true!"

He folded the letter and pushed it back into his pocket. Then he continued along the gravel path that led toward the camera crews and the hydroponic farmers and their children.

It's not so bad, this simple husbanding of life, he thought. Cyrus was right. I have the talent to be Governor.

If a few things seemed still out of reach, if sometimes the old rage at death still coursed through him, he had at least found a way to channel its power usefully. In fact, in spite of his unworthiness, it seemed that somehow the Taogott had singled him out to live that message by example. The notion made him smile.

There had been a time when he would have approached the giving of agricultural awards cynically, but that day was long past, and in some way Svetla Stocovik had helped him understand it. Her affection had pulled him back from the brink. For that he would always be indebted to her. Always.

Perhaps I should call her, he thought. Or order her back for—for frank negotiations. It was a possibility. Everything was a possibility, if you knew what was right and did what was necessary. Yes, Sheila had told him that—the lesson she learned before initiating the space jump—and it had made her stalwart with goodwill and confidence in the end. Her confidence assured him that when death came to him, when it came to Svetla, when it came perhaps to Sheila herself, they would find joy again in those mysterious dimensions nature had hidden inside the seemingly sterile separations of space and time, those wondrous dimensions they had been the first to explore during the space jumps.

He smiled again. If death was no more comfortable, it had at least lost its sting.

He had almost reached the delegation of farmers now.

The children were waiting anxiously, filled with the excitement of receiving awards and meeting the famous Outbanker turned Governor whose daring deeds and devotion to peace had been celebrated in news reports, holofilms, and public address.

As he neared them, a young lad, no more than six, started running toward him on stubby legs. Then all the children broke away from their parents and rushed forward to surround him, eyes brimming with the spontaneity of young hope and dreams. A few of the adults tried to intervene, but he waved them back. *Suffer not the little children to come unto me, for unless you become as a simple child, you shall not . . .* He reached down and began hugging them one by one, picking up the youngest ones and spinning them around in the air while the others applauded.

He laughed heartily with them, sharing their exuberance and untethered excitement completely. He laughed until there were tears in his eyes.

MacKenzie was an Outbanker no more.

BOOKS

The Road West
Gary Wright

Orphaned by the brutal, senseless murder of his parents, Keven rises from the depths of despair to face the menacing danger that threatens Midvale. On sale in October.

The Alien Dark
Diana G. Gallagher

It is one hundred million years in the future. When the ahsin bey, a race of cat-like beings, are faced with a slowly dying home planet, they launch six vessels deep into space to search for an uninhabited world suitable for colonization. On sale in December.

PRELUDES II

RIVERWIND, THE PLAINSMAN
Paul B. Thompson and Tonya R. Carter

To prove himself worthy of Goldmoon, Riverwind is sent on an impossible quest: Find evidence of the true gods. With an eccentric soothsayer, Riverwind falls down a magical shaft—and alights in a world of slavery and rebellion. On sale now.

FLINT, THE KING
Mary Kirchoff and Douglas Niles

Flint returns to his boyhood village and finds it a boom town. He learns that the prosperity comes from a false alliance and is pushed to his death. Saved by gully dwarves and made their reluctant monarch, Flint unites them as his only chance to stop the agents of the Dark Queen. Available in July 1990.

TANIS, THE SHADOW YEARS
Barbara Siegel and Scott Siegel

Tanis Half-Elven once disappeared in the mountains near Solace. He returned changed, ennobled—and with a secret. Tanis becomes a traveler in a dying mage's memory, journeying into the past to fight a battle against time itself. Available in November 1990.

DragonLance Saga

HEROES II TRILOGY

KAZ, THE MINOTAUR
Richard A. Knaak

Sequel to *The Legend of Huma*. Stalked by enemies after Huma's death, Kaz hears rumors of evil incidents. When he warns the Knights of Solamnia, he is plunged into a nightmare of magic, danger, and *deja vu*. Available June 1990.

THE GATES OF THORBARDIN
Dan Parkinson

Beneath Skullcap is a path to the gates of Thorbardin, and the magical helm of Grallen. The finder of Grallen's helm will be rewarded by a united Thorbardin, but he will also open the realm to new horror. Available September 1990.

GALEN BEKNIGHTED
Michael Williams

Sequel to *Weasel's Luck*. Galen Pathwarden is still out to save his own skin. But when his brother vanishes, Galen foresakes his better judgment and embarks on a quest that leads into a conspiracy of darkness, and to the end of his courage. Available December 1990.

FANTASY ADVENTURE

THE MAZTICA TRILOGY
Douglas Niles

IRONHELM

A slave girl learns of a great
destiny laid upon her by the
gods themselves. And across
the sea, a legion of skilled mercenaries sails west to discover a
land of primitive savagery
mixed with high culture. Under
the banner of their vigilant god
the legion claims these lands for
itself. And only as Erix sees her
land invaded is her destiny
revealed. Available in April.

VIPERHAND

The God of War feasts upon chaos while the desperate lovers,
Erix and Halloran, strive to escape the waves of catastrophe
sweeping Maztica. Each is forced into a choice of historical
proportion and deeply personal emotion. The destruction of
the fabulously wealthy continent of Maztica looms on the
horizon. Available in October.

COMING IN EARLY 1991!
FEATHERED DRAGON
The conclusion!

FANTASY ADVENTURE

EMPIRES TRILOGY

Horselords
David Cook

Between the western Realms and Kara-Tur lies a vast, unexplored domain. The "civilized" people of the Realms have given little notice to these nomadic barbarians. Now, a mighty leader has united these wild horsemen into an army powerful enough to challenge the world. First, they turn to Kara-Tur. Available now.

Crusade
James Lowder

The barbarian army has turned its sights on the western Realms. Only King Azoun has the strength to forge an army to challenge the horsemen. But Azoun had not reckoned that the price of saving the west might be the life of his beloved daughter. Available in January 1991.

FANTASY ADVENTURE

The Dark Elf Trilogy

HOMELAND
R.A. Salvatore

Strange and exotic Menzoberranzan is the vast city of the drow. Imagine the world of the dark elves, where families battle families and fantastic monsters rise up from the lightless depths. Possessing a sense of honor beyond the scope offered him by his unprincipled kinsmen, young Drizzt finds himself with a dilemma: Can he live in a honorless society? Available in September 1990.

EXILE
R.A. Salvatore

Exiled from Menzoberranzan, the city of the drow, Drizzt must find acceptance among races normally at war with his kind. And all the while, the hero must look back over his shoulder for signs of deadly pursuit—the dark elves are not a forgiving race. Available in December 1990.

SOJOURN
R.A. Salvatore

Drizzt makes his way to the surface world, finding even more trouble than he imagined. Available in May 1991.